COLD SPECTRUM

ALSO BY CRAIG SCHAEFER

The Daniel Faust Series

The Long Way Down
Redemption Song
The Living End
A Plain-Dealing Villain
The Killing Floor Blues
The Castle Doctrine

The Revanche Cycle

Winter's Reach
The Instruments of Control
Terms of Surrender
Queen of the Night

The Harmony Black Series

Harmony Black
Red Knight Falling
Glass Predator

COLD SPECTRUM
CRAIG SCHAEFER

47NORTH

Text copyright © 2017 by Craig Schaefer

Published by 47North, Seattle

www.apub.com

Amazon, the Amazon logo, and 47North are trademarks of Amazon.com, Inc., or its affiliates.

ISBN-13: 9781542047210
ISBN-10: 1542047218

Cover design by David Drummond

Printed in the United States of America

COLD SPECTRUM

PROLOGUE

In another life, Senator Alton Roth might have been a Shakespearean actor. Big, broad-shouldered, and vibrant, he had a voice that boomed to the farthest seats of the packed auditorium. From her perch backstage, watching the rally on a bank of monitors, Nadine mouthed the words along with him. She'd written them, but they sounded better on Roth's lips. *A tale told by an idiot,* she thought, *full of sound and fury, et cetera.*

"Amazing," said the voice from the doorway. "Your lips move—the puppet speaks. I don't even see the strings."

They hadn't met, but she knew the man on sight, from his two-hundred-dollar haircut to his lime-green high-top sneakers. "Bobby Diehl," she said.

"Nadine . . . Ashton? Is that the name you're using this week?" He flashed a hundred-watt smile, easing past her bodyguards and sauntering into the control room like he owned the place. "It's true, what they told me. You really do bear an uncanny resemblance to Taylor—"

"Choose your next words very carefully."

"Admittedly not a fan of country music, but her shift to pop was a welcome and, I think, entirely warranted career evolution. Anyway,

I heard about the little trap you set for me, out in Chicago. Figured I should drop by and introduce myself before you did it again."

"Don't take it personally," Nadine said, glancing back to the screens. "You were just a means to an end."

Bobby held up two fingers. "A pair of ends. Harmony Black and Jessie Temple. Except the way I heard it, they left the Bast Club in bullet-riddled ruins and skipped along on their merry way."

Nadine's eyes darkened. She shot a glare at her men.

"Clear the room. *Now.*"

The control-room door swung shut. Now it was just her, Bobby, and the sound of applause washing in over the tinny speakers as Senator Roth raised his arms in triumph.

"We have mutual interests," Bobby told her, "and a mutual problem."

"Vigilant Lock."

He pointed finger guns at her. "Bingo. Of course, it's a bigger problem for you than it is for me. After all, as far as the public knows, the good senator—and myself—were nearly killed by a lunatic who planted a hundred pounds of plastic explosive under a casino. But you and me, we know the rest of the story. And so do our enemies. If they don't already know that Roth is backed and bought by the courts of hell, they will soon enough. And given that a handful of public officials are secretly members of an organization dedicated to undermining demonic activity, that's gonna make Roth's impending run for the White House . . . a tad rocky."

Nadine's bubblegum-pink lips curled in a condescending smile. "You don't know the rest of the story. Trust me—Vigilant Lock is less of a problem than you might believe. I'm working an angle or two."

"Aren't we all? I think I know the name of your angle: Operation Cold Spectrum."

"Do you know more than a name?"

"I know it's something very big, very bad, and something the powers that be want to keep dead and buried," Bobby replied, "along with the men and women who carried it out. Only problem is, they just won't stay dead. We've witnessed a miraculous resurrection. Two survivors, on the run, ready and able to spill all the nasty little beans. Retrieval teams are already hunting for them—and so are Temple and Black. Follow that trail and you could win *all* the prizes."

Nadine rounded on him. She curled her arms, squinting as she looked him in the eye. "How do you know this?"

Bobby offered her a cocky smile. "It's called RedEye. An NSA surveillance project. Real-time coverage of nationwide cellular-phone traffic, with full analytics and keyword scanning. It's Echelon on steroids. Very secret. Very scandalous. I helped invent it. Anyway, I don't have access to the system as it stands—I cashed in and handed it over to the Agency before I realized how much *fun* I could have with the damn thing—but I've got a tap on the director's phone."

Nadine took a step toward him. She tilted her head, lips slightly parted. "Can you . . . *get* access to it?"

"Would you like that? Mmm, that'd make Senator Roth's presidential campaign a little smoother, wouldn't it? Imagine being able to crack the cell phones of every primary contender. Every rival campaign worker. Every journalist. See, I can't get at RedEye on my own, and the egghead behind the project littered the system with biometrics and kill switches to guarantee he's the only one who can operate it. Job security. But a little birdie tells me you can be *very* convincing. I propose an alliance."

"It's true," Nadine said. "But nobody gives something for nothing, and you're no friend to the courts of hell. What do you get out of this deal?"

Bobby pointed to the bank of monitors. "Isn't it obvious? I want to play with your toy. Diehl Innovations could win big under the Roth administration. I've even got a puppet of my own for a first-draft cabinet pick. In the short term, though, it's a matter of self-preservation.

Temple and Black are hounding my heels, same as yours. Plus . . . I'm trying to join a very exclusive social club. The eradication of Vigilant Lock is my membership fee."

"The Network." Nadine turned her back on him. Musing as she studied the screens. "So the rumor is true—you are a servant of the Kings. I should kill you where you stand. My court has a standing bounty on Network operatives."

"C'mon, Nadine. Just because my friends don't like your friends doesn't mean *we* can't be friends. Who's going to tell? Hey, have you seen *Hamilton*?"

"I'm not fond of musicals."

"Oh," Bobby said, "you couldn't get tickets. No, no, I understand. See, my favorite part is when Jefferson and Madison have dinner with Alexander Hamilton—not a lot of love between these guys, right? But they meet behind closed doors, and presto, they hammer out the Compromise of 1790. The beauty is, it all happened off the record. What was said? What was promised? Lost to history. All we have are the results."

He moved close behind her. Standing at her shoulder, both of them watching the flickering screens.

"My friends could be your friends, too," Bobby murmured. "And no one needs to know. So let's hook up. We destroy Vigilant, get your pet idiot into the White House, and carve up whatever's left of the nation when we're done having a good time. I know you've got bigger ambitions than this, Nadine. Or should I start calling you . . . *Princess* Nadine?"

She glanced back over her shoulder. One pert eyebrow raised, the curve of a half smile on her lips.

"I like your tone." Nadine turned. She jabbed a sharp bubblegum-pink fingernail at Bobby's chest. "One thing. Harmony Black and Jessie Temple. I want them. Alive."

"And my friends want them dead. That's nonnegotiable."

Nadine tilted her head at him, curious. "Were you under the impression I was going to invite them to tea?"

"I suppose," Bobby said, "there might be some wiggle room. Here, I brought you a present."

He handed Nadine a phone, slender with a case the color of shimmering rose gold. She turned it in her hand, looking it over.

"The DiehlPhone Four. I thought these weren't out until next month."

"Advantage of owning the company. This is more than just a sneak preview: it's fitted with a special exclusion chip. That surveillance system I mentioned, RedEye? Can't see or hear any information that passes through it. At least, assuming they haven't changed my original source code too much. I've been using the chip myself, and the FBI hasn't come kicking my door in—and believe me, they would if they were listening in on my conversations. Let me know how many you need—I'll get all your people kitted out with these. Good data security is so important these days."

"I'll take a dozen," she said, "for starters. Now, about those two Cold Spectrum survivors—" Her new phone pinged.

Bobby grinned and pointed at the screen. "And there you go," he told her. "Happy hunting."

# # #

Linder's stretch limousine was the safest place in the world. A rolling office, off the grid and freely mobile, with tinted windows and concealed armor that could take a direct hit from a fifty-caliber rifle. Run-flat tires, an NSA-grade countersurveillance suite, and electrified door handles. He liked to stay buttoned down, doing his business on the move. The limo was quiet and anonymous, just like he was.

Tonight he'd been forced to shed his steel cocoon. It sat at the edge of an airstrip, cast in bands of stark electric light and hungry dark, as a cold night wind rustled down from the overcast sky. He stood on the tarmac with his hands in his trench-coat pockets, staring into the belly of a C-130 cargo plane as the backloading ramp slowly rumbled down.

"This is a mistake," he said. He didn't spare a glance for the tall, thin man at his side. His companion had a receding hairline and a nose like a raptor's beak.

"The mistake," the other man said, "was trusting you to manage Vigilant Lock's operations. We've had an attempted bombing in Las Vegas, an assassination attempt against a sitting senator, you *lost* a captive servant of the King of Wolves—"

"Ben, I told you, I have a team on it—"

A sharp glance. The twitch of his hooked nose.

"That's Director Crohn to you. We aren't *friends*, Linder. You're nothing but the hired help. And as for the team in question, I understand Temple and Black are refusing to come in for debriefing?"

"We're trading voice mails. It's a complicated situation."

The landing ramp touched down. Men gathered in the plane's belly, unclipping webbed harnesses, rising from steel seats and standing to attention. They moved like soldiers but dressed like backwoods hunters, with long, scraggly beards and tinted Oakleys. Silent, their every move pregnant with the promise of impending and sudden violence.

"Panic Cell," Crohn said. He strode up the ramp with Linder at his heels. "Report."

One of the men flipped a lazy salute. "Present, accounted for, and ready for mayhem. You point, we shoot. Any questions?"

"None. We have three targets. Primary: two fugitives on the run, their locations recently uncovered by NSA signals traffic. Wanted dead, not alive."

"And the third, sir?"

Crohn gave a sidelong glance at Linder.

"One of our own's gone rogue. As of this moment, I'm declaring Jessie Temple and her entire team as new additions to the Hostile Entities registry. Capture them if you can; kill them if you have to. One way or another, I want them brought to heel. I will be leading this mission personally."

Linder started to say, "Agents Temple and Black—"

Crohn cut him off with a wave of his hand.

"Aren't the problem. Their support team is. We eliminate April Cassidy, they'll be rudderless. We take out the Finn boy, the teenager, they'll be deaf and blind."

"I think you're letting your personal feelings interfere," Linder told him.

Crohn turned, slowly, his eyes narrowed to venomous slits.

"I taught Dr. Cassidy everything she knows. She's the *second*-best profiler the Bureau ever built, and she's gotten sharper with age. The wolf and the witch are nothing but weapons. Blunt instruments. We take out Cassidy—the rest of the team falls like a house of cards. To that end, I've requisitioned a little help." Crohn looked to the men. "Bring her up."

From deeper in the plane, a cell door clanged. Leaden footsteps echoed off the metal flooring, the crowd parting.

Linder's gut clenched.

"No," he breathed. "You can't be serious. No. Absolutely not. I was in favor of bringing in Panic Cell in case we needed them, but this . . . Director Crohn, I'm registering my formal objection, and the rest of the Vigilant directorate is going to hear from me. This is insane."

The new arrival gave him a smug smile and a flip of her hair, a flowing lion's mane dyed in streaks of rainbow color.

"Mikki Ziegler," Crohn said, "aka Mikki McGuire, aka Mikki Howl. Welcome to Vigilant Lock. Your freedom—and your continued survival—is fully dependent upon the success of this mission."

Mikki held up her shackled wrists and snickered.

"Aw, I feel like part of the team already. Now, how about one of you little bitches uncuffs me? I just can't wait to go and burn a few people alive. You know, for Uncle Sam and the American way. I'm feeling so very patriotic all of a sudden."

ONE

Late October had come to Oregon, with a bitter winter waiting in the wings. **KEEP PORTLAND WEIRD** screamed the yellow writing on the wall as we cruised down Burnside in a rented Ford. Not helpful advice. If we did our jobs right, things would be a lot less weird by the time we left town.

"I don't like Halloween," I said.

Jessie Temple looked over at me from the passenger seat, her frizzy black hair pulled into a bun, and tugged down her dark glasses. She stared at me over the rims, flashing her uncannily turquoise eyes.

"Seriously, Harmony?" she said. "I figured that was some kind of big, you know, witchy thing."

"It's amateur night. You know how on Saint Patrick's Day, all the people who can't hold down a can of beer go out and become champion drinkers?"

"Been there, done that, got the T-shirt and the monster hangover."

"Halloween is the same deal," I said. "The one night of the year that communing with the powers of darkness and trying to conjure demons sounds like a fun party game."

"I've clearly been going to the wrong parties."

"It's the one night when our job isn't 'fight the forces of hell' so much as 'save idiots from themselves.'"

Jessie leaned back, rubbing her shoulders against the seat, getting comfortable while I drove.

"Isn't that a good thing, though?" she said. "I could use a few more nights like that. Hey, Halloween's still a few days away. We might get lucky."

We'd spent the last week pinballing from New York to Nevada and back again on the trail of a conspiracy, our little cell of operatives more or less officially going rogue. Seemed like a routine job at first: Vigilant Lock's covert mandate was to hunt and eliminate occult threats to the United States, and the band of robbers who'd murdered four people at a midtown Manhattan bank—robbers infected with the power of the King of Wolves, just like my partner, Jessie—certainly fit the bill.

"Not sure how much of our current situation could be described as lucky," I said.

"We took out my mom's pack. Three Wolf King worshippers dead, and one on permanent ice—that's not a bad day at the office. Plus, you know, uncovering that whole secret assassination-program thing."

"Which circles back to Douglas Bredford."

Everything circled back to Douglas Bredford.

On our first mission as a team, we'd found Bredford drinking himself to death in a backwoods Michigan tap house. He might have died when someone put a bomb in his trailer, but he'd still been with us every step of the way since, leaving clues and backup plans that unfurled in our path. A trail of string guiding us through a maze of razor wire.

Bredford had worked in black ops for the government, same as we had, years ago as part of a program called Cold Spectrum. We didn't know what the program was, or what he did, only that his time in the shadows had left him a broken and bitter drunk. A man on the run, after forces in DC—possibly including Linder, our own boss—decided that he and his team had to be eliminated. We'd coerced Burton, the director of RedEye, into becoming an asset for us, and he'd recounted the story of the night he found Bredford lurking in his kitchen with a gun.

"Let me tell you about the good fight, Burton," Bredford had said. "Let me tell you who I am. I'm the soldier who fired the last shot, at the last battle, for the future of humanity. The war is over. Humanity lost."

"We unearthed RedEye," Jessie said, "an NSA program that can spy on anyone's phone, anytime? Taking that out counts as another win for the good guys."

"We . . . didn't take it out. RedEye is still active. And spying on people. Right this minute."

Jessie gave me the side-eye. "Yeah, because we're kinda using it right now. I'm counting this as an inevitable *future* victory. As soon as we track down the names on our list, we're flying back to New York and putting it out of commission for good. Priorities, you know?"

Burton Webb, RedEye's inventor, had managed to hide two of Bredford's teammates inside the labyrinthine surveillance system. Protecting them from being hunted and killed. And now he'd given us their names. Removing their cloak of invisibility came with a price tag, though: if we could find them, so could anybody else with high-level NSA access. Including the people who very much wanted to close the books on Cold Spectrum permanently.

I tapped my earpiece. "April? Kevin? Everybody in place?"

The dry, older voice of April Cassidy, tinged with an Irish brogue, echoed in my ear. "We're on overwatch. I'm just running some last-minute background checks, but the trail is clear now that we know what to look for. After Cold Spectrum, Houston Coe reinvented him-self as Houston Dalenta. He was a professional gambler before his recruitment, and it looks like he's gone back to his old habits: traveling between Atlantic City and Las Vegas and a hundred small-town casinos in between, and holing up in Portland when he's flush on cash. One companion, Luis Perez—not sure if he's a roommate or a lover. They're discreet. No visible ties to the government or the occult underground."

"How about our second survivor?" I asked.

"She's gone off the grid entirely. If she's still alive, she's deep underground—metaphorically, literally, or both. Give me time—I'm working on it."

"And I'm putting the finishing touches on a little surprise," Kevin said, sounding pleased with himself. "A new piece of field gear to help you two out."

"Does it shoot people?" Jessie asked.

"No," he said. "I think that's what your gun is for."

"I have *a* gun. I want *two* guns."

The GPS pinged. My stomach tightened as I pulled a left, tires rumbling into a parking lot outside a three-story apartment building in faded red brick. Jessie usually greeted stress with a wink and a joke. I swallowed mine, bottling it up for an explosion that never came.

I swung into a spot and killed the ignition. And paused, just for a second, looking up at rows of windows shrouded behind black iron-work grates. Up on the third floor, a lace curtain ruffled. Someone peeking down at us. Jessie touched the back of my hand.

"Harmony," she said, "you good to go?"

"Ready for anything. Ready to finally get some answers, anyway."

"How do you want to play it?"

"Nice and easy," I said, pushing open the car door and stepping out. "This guy's been living in hiding for a decade, waiting for a bullet. We've got to be careful not to spook him."

"I don't know, you are pretty spooky sometimes."

I checked my reflection in the car window. Black suit, white blouse, necktie the color of sea foam. A cold gust of wind washed over me, mussing my hair, and I pushed the unruly bangs back into place. Good to go. Jessie's olive jacket tugged back as she got out, flashing her shoulder holster and the badge clipped to her belt.

The halls were clean, lived-in, middle-class, with a wall of polished mailbox cubbyholes and a community-announcement corkboard by the front door. I paused, glancing over the tacked-up ads. Dog walking, babysitting, a new yoga center down the street. Not exactly a hotbed of intrigue. We got onto the shoe box–size elevator and hit the button for the third floor.

"Linder left another voice mail, trying to get us to come in for a debriefing." Jessie watched the doors rumble shut.

"He knows we know something. He just doesn't know *what* we know."

"Way I figure it," she said, "in about five minutes, we're gonna know everything. Then we've just gotta decide what to do about it."

Around a bend in the corridor was apartment 308. One of the neighbors was baking an apple pie; the sweet aroma drifted out, filling the narrow hallway. Jessie and I stood side by side. We shared a glance, she nodded, and I knocked.

The man who opened the door was in his late forties, dressed in a turtleneck and shabby jeans, eyes wide behind tortoiseshell glasses. The apartment behind him was lived-in messy, with a scattering of magazines on the coffee table and a half-finished landscape on an artist's easel by the window.

"Can I help you?" he asked, with a look reserved for door-to-door salespeople. I showed him my credentials.

"Special Agent Black and Special Agent Temple, FBI. Are you Houston Dalenta?"

His head ducked like a turtle trying to squirm back into its shell, and his eyes went everywhere but on me.

"N-no," he stammered, "I'm Luis. Houston isn't . . . he's not home."

"Do you know where we can find him?"

Luis swallowed hard. I'd interrogated murderers who looked less guilty. "He's out. Shopping."

"Then you won't mind if we wait for him," Jessie said.

She smoothly stepped around him and into the apartment. Projecting her quiet authority and taking over the room. I followed her in and shut the door behind me, standing like a wall between Luis and the only way out.

"He . . . he might be a while," Luis told her. "I mean, you shouldn't waste your time. Just give me your card or something, and I'll call you as soon as—"

"Luis," I said, my voice firm enough to shut him up, "we're not here to arrest anyone, and whatever you're trying to hide, trust me: we probably don't care. We have reason to believe that your roommate is in serious danger, and we need to bring him into protective custody. Please, help us to help him."

His gaze dropped to the off-white carpet. He bit his bottom lip hard enough to turn it white.

"I'm not supposed to get the cops involved. They'll kill him if I do."

"We're already involved," I said, "and we're not going anywhere. So your best course of action is to level with us. Where is he, Luis?"

Luis paced the floor, shaking his head. He flailed a hand in strangled desperation.

"Houston is . . . he makes his money playing cards, okay? And he . . . he's got a system. The kind of system where he never loses."

"He cheats," Jessie muttered.

"I didn't say that. I did not say that. Honestly, I don't know how he does it. He just . . . when he needs cash, he goes to a casino, and he gets it. Simple. Except he got caught. The Diamondback, this place in Atlantic City. I *told* him the place is mobbed up, that he was pushing his luck."

"They caught him?" I asked.

Luis's head bobbed. "He got a message to me. He said they didn't hurt him—much—but he couldn't leave. I don't know what they're doing to him in there. Only that he's safe so long as I don't call the police and I keep my mouth shut."

Back when I'd been working a case in Vegas, before joining Jessie and her team, I'd heard rumors about the Strip. That every casino had somebody on the payroll who knew about the occult underground and kept a sharp eye out for anyone trying to augment their luck with magic. It'd make sense for Atlantic City to work the same way. And considering he'd spent time working for a covert government program, I highly doubted Houston Dalenta was any kind of mundane cheater.

What could the Jersey Mob do with a captive magician? All kinds of ideas came to mind, none of them pretty. Whatever the situation, Houston wasn't coming home on his own. Not without our help.

A chorus of slamming doors jarred me from my thoughts. I moved to the window and pulled the curtain back, looking down at the street below. Three black sedans had pulled up to the curb at once. Doors swinging open, men in dark suits and glasses boiling out like ants from a kicked hive. And a woman in scarlet, pointing and barking orders, her hair done in a perfect blonde bob. I recognized her in an instant. My heart kicked against my rib cage.

Nadine.

TWO

"We have to leave. Now." I nodded at Luis. "We've gotta get him out of here."

Jessie stood beside me at the window. "Damn right. Looks like somebody followed the same trail we did. You up for a rematch?"

Nadine was what we called an incarnate: a demon powerful enough to create her own body out of raw willpower instead of hijacking a human skin. Enough willpower to punch through walls if she felt like it, plus an arsenal of twisted magic. And we had recent history together.

We'd faced off in a nightclub in downtown Chicago. A hostage situation, engineered to draw us into the line of fire. We had embarrassed Nadine's kid, an infernal bounty hunter, and it turned out Nadine had a thing for carrying a grudge. Nobody in Vigilant Lock's history had ever been able to kill an incarnate, but Jessie and I came damn close— until Nadine got her claws into me and taught me what a succubus is capable of.

I still woke up in the middle of the night. Aching. Thirsty, no matter how much water I drank. Feeling like I had ants all over my skin. I didn't tell Jessie that. It was getting worse. I didn't tell her that, either.

"With nothing but our sidearms?" I asked Jessie. "And the Bast Club was a free-fire zone—this building is full of civilians, and these walls don't look too thick. We start shooting, innocent people are going to get hurt."

"*Shooting?*" Luis's eyes grew wider behind his glasses. "Wait, what's going on? Who's shooting?"

Another car arrived on the scene. A cherry-red Cadillac Escalade with tinted windows screeched up to the curb, almost hitting one of Nadine's gunmen. He jumped clear at the last second, arms flailing.

"Wait a second." I crouched low, staying to one side, and opened the window a few inches so I could hear what was going on. A gust of crisp wind blew across my cheeks and fluttered the magazines on the coffee table.

A pair of suits hustled out of the front seats, the wind catching the tail of one man's jacket and baring a chrome pistol in a holster. He opened the back door of the SUV like a chauffeur and stood at attention as the passenger gracefully stepped out.

"Don't look now," Jessie murmured, "but I think Portland just got weirder."

The woman was tall, slender, draped in a tailored trench coat of snow-white leather. Her hair, scarlet, braided, and worn in a French twist. And Nadine looked all kinds of unhappy.

"No," she snapped, marching toward her. "No, no, *no*! You can't be here. Leave."

The new arrival responded with faint amusement, her voice a low Scottish burr. I leaned closer to the open window, straining to hear.

"I think you have that backward, Nadine. Oregon is part of the Court of Jade Tears. My prince's territory. You're here without permission. Very naughty of you."

Nadine stuck her finger in the woman's face. "The *pit* with you, Caitlin! Unlike *you*, you filthy-handed commoner, I'm a noblewoman. I have the rights of travel and hospitality."

The name struck a chord. Fontaine, another bounty hunter, had given us a heads-up: for reasons unknown, two demonic courts had put a temporary no-kill order on our heads. Whatever they were scheming about, Fontaine reasoned, it was something they thought only Jessie and I—their sworn enemies—could get done.

"You're useful," he'd told me, "just don't know what you're useful *for*. Caitlin and Royce are formidable on their own; on the rare occasion when they team up, well . . . something big is in the wings."

"You do possess those rights," Caitlin said agreeably, "for now. Your little friends here, though—they don't. So you should make them get back in their cars and drive east, all the way home. Immediately."

Nadine lifted her chin, trying to get eye to eye with the taller woman. Bristling.

"And if I don't?"

Caitlin opened her coat and flung it back like a gunslinger from an old Western. I expected to see a six-shooter on her hip. Instead, she bared a coiled bullwhip with a long brass handle.

"If you don't," Caitlin replied, "then I'm within *my* rights to dispense discipline as I deem appropriate."

Nadine took a step back. Her hand fluttered behind her. A few of her men caught the hint, running, skirting the side of the apartment building. Others made for the cars, looking more afraid of Caitlin than they were of their own boss. I wasn't entirely convinced they were leaving, though.

"Your prince will hear about this," Nadine snapped.

Caitlin smiled and nodded. "Yes. He will. From me."

The second Nadine turned her back, Caitlin raised her head and looked directly at me. Spotting me up in the third-floor window, her gaze drawn to mine like a laser. She mouthed a single word, one I couldn't miss: *Go.*

"That is some damn fine advice," Jessie said, on the move and headed for the door. "Luis, this place have a back way out?"

"There's . . . there's a second stairwell, yeah. Can someone tell me what's going on? Please?"

I drew my Glock 23, holding the matte-black pistol in a tight two-handed grip, following Jessie.

"Stay behind us," I told him, "stay quiet, and keep your head down. Things are about to get a little scary, but we'll get you out safe, I promise."

"*About* to get scary?" he said.

"Shh."

The hallway was clear. We hustled fast, making our way around another bend, headed for a back stairwell near a battered trash-chute door. We took the stairs single file, Jessie on point, rounding the tight bends with our ears perked. Just as we reached the second-floor landing, the door burst open and a blur hit me from the right, throwing my back against the railing. He had eyes like broken and runny egg yolks, and he bared rotting, yellowed teeth as he grappled my wrists, fighting for my gun. He wasn't alone. His buddy jumped Jessie, the two of them rolling, Luis jumping out of the way as they landed hard on the concrete steps.

My attacker—a cambion, his human veins pulsing with demon blood—hissed at me as he threw his body weight against mine and tried to force me over the railing. My gun hand bent backward inch by inch, wrist trapped in his iron grip. His breath, hot and rancid like chicken left out to rot on a hot summer day, washed over my face. He was focused on my Glock. Apparently he hadn't been briefed properly.

I'm good with a gun, but I don't need one.

I gave my other hand a sharp twist, breaking his hold, and clamped my hand to his forehead. Then I spat the words of a banishing charm, an exorcism in bastard Latin intended to drive demonic intruders from a host's body. Against a cambion, it only does one thing: *hurt*. He shrieked as his blood boiled. He yanked away from me, my fingertips leaving black scorch marks on his twisted face. That bought me the second I needed to grab his forearm, turn my body, and execute an aikido throw. The cambion rolled up, off his feet, over my shoulder, and over the edge.

He plummeted to the bottom of the stairwell, hitting the railing on the small of his back. His spine snapped against the black iron with a sickening crunch.

Jessie's opponent was screaming, too—as best he could with her teeth in his throat, biting in deep while she shook her head like a terrier with a chew toy. She'd dropped her gun so she could get one of his arms in both her hands, breaking it like a twig and leaving naked, bloody bone jutting out from his tattered sleeve. One final clench of her jaw ended his struggles with a wet *crack*. The cambion fell still. She snatched up her gun, stood, and spat a gob of scarlet tissue onto the floor at her feet.

Luis's shoulders hit the wall. He looked between us, petrified.

"What . . . what *are* you?"

"We're from the government," I told him, "and we're here to help."

Jessie wiped the back of her hand across her bloody lips, leaving a ruddy smear along her cheek. She led the way—and jumped back as gunfire erupted from below, bullets pinging off ironwork and concrete. I leaned over the railing and snapped off a couple of quick shots, then took cover.

"Mistress," shouted a voice from below, "we've got them pinned on the second floor! Teams in both stairwells, holding ground."

Over the crackle of a walkie-talkie, Nadine's voice echoed off the tight concrete walls.

"Good. That filthy-clawed *peasant* is following us, but I'm splitting the convoy. Whoever she doesn't pursue is going to double back and bring reinforcements. Hold them until I get there. Oh, and throw them your radio."

"Beg pardon?" the man said.

"Throw. Them. Your. Radio."

Shuffling feet below. He called up, "Don't shoot, okay? I'm throwing you my radio."

"Totally going to shoot him," Jessie murmured. I shook my head at her.

The slim black box flew up in the air, sailing like an easy pitch at a softball game. Jessie snatched it and jumped back, out of the line of fire. She pressed the "Send" button and put the radio to her ear.

"Piss off, Nadine. We know who you're looking for—same as us—and he isn't here. Cut your losses and leave before more of your men get hurt. We've already dropped two bodies, and I don't mind making a few more before we go."

"*Bad* dog," Nadine snapped. "Dogs don't talk. Give the radio to Harmony."

Jessie stared at the radio, one incredulous eyebrow slowly lifting. I sighed and held out my hand.

"She isn't lying," I said into the radio. "He's not here, Nadine. And it doesn't sound like anybody else wants you around, either. Also, last I checked, that no-kill order was still in place. You could claim self-defense at the Bast Club. What's your excuse going to be today?"

A long, slow chuckle slithered over the radio, dragging a finger of ice down my spine.

"Oh, there won't be one, because you were never here. You're just going to disappear off the face of the earth. You remember our friendly chat at the club? What I promised I was going to do to you? I keep my promises. And tell your partner to get the last of her amusing little quips out. First thing I'm going to do when I arrive is cut her impudent tongue out and make her *eat* it. Wait for me, little girl. I'm coming in. And I'm going to greet you with a nice . . . long . . . kiss."

The memory of Nadine's lips and the torrent of her psychic poison made my brain spark like a misfiring battery. Whatever she'd done to me, it had played havoc with my mind and my magic, almost shutting me down completely. I was able to fight through it in Nevada, digging deep to save my partner's life. I'd gotten a little control back, but I could feel my grip starting to fail again.

"It's my job to protect people," I told Nadine. "To save them from monsters like you. I try to take the high road, I really do. I try to see the best in the world, to change things for the better—"

"There a point to this speech, Pollyanna?"

"Yes," I said. "The point is, this isn't the kind of thing I say very often, so listen up."

I brought the radio close to my lips, dropping to a whisper.

"I'm going to kill you, Nadine. You, your daughter, and everyone who stands with you. I'm going to burn your little house to ashes, and then I'm going to salt the earth it stood on. That's *my* promise."

I held the radio over the railing, opened my hand, and let it drop. I heard it clatter and break on the concrete below. Then I tapped my earpiece.

"Brain trust, we're pinned on two, and we need an evac route, us plus one civilian for extraction, *now*."

THREE

"We're going mobile," Kevin's voice said in my ear, buzzing with nervous anticipation. "Okay, okay, we've got a—yes! Fire escape. Go through the landing door on two, and make for the east side of the building."

Jessie and I breached the door, pistols covering the hall in both directions, checking for threats. Her hand tapped my shoulder. Clear. We turned right and ran down the corridor with Luis trailing in our wake. Around another bend, past door after numbered door, we hit a dead end. A dead end with a window overlooking the street and the railing of an old fire escape just beyond. I pulled at the window. It wouldn't budge. I cursed as my fingers traced the sill, feeling the seam where they'd painted it over.

"I got this," Jessie said. "Watch your face."

The window shattered under her elbow, chunks of glass falling and gleaming, reflecting the overcast sky. She used the butt of her gun to clear the rest, punching out the jagged remnants and clearing a hole. She was the first one through; I helped Luis up and over the sill, watching our backs, and followed.

The whir of propellers caught my ear. A quadcopter about the size of a bowling ball hovered a few feet away, the drone bobbing on a cold gust of wind as the black lens of a camera focused on me.

"Here I am," Kevin said in my ear. "Told you I was working on something new. After that dustup with the Xerxes drones during the Red Knight mission, I got inspired. I've been tinkering with this puppy in my spare time."

"Nice toy." Jessie thundered down the narrow iron steps, the scaffolding rocking under our shoes. "You know you can buy those off Amazon, right?"

"Not like mine. She's got a boosted transmitter for improved range, duplex ultralight battery setup for flight time, I'm patched into area navigation and traffic sys—*on your left*!"

I turned as a pair of gunmen burst out of the alley, left of the fire escape, guns raised and fingers on the triggers. I opened fire. Two slugs blossomed crimson in one shooter's chest and sent him to the concrete in a tangled heap. The drone swooped in, rotors screaming as it swarmed around the other man's face like a mosquito on steroids. Then it spun, graceful as a ballerina, and fired two tiny harpoons on a wire leash. The barbs dug into the shooter's neck. Then he went rigid, twitching, falling, his gun hitting the pavement a half second before he did.

"Also," Kevin said, "I added a Taser. You're welcome."

I was the last to touch down, jumping off the last three rungs of the fire escape's ladder and landing in a crouch. The drone whistled high to get a bird's-eye view of the tangled backstreets. Kevin called out our escape route over the earpieces.

"Okay, up this alley, then make a—wait, no, that's one of Nadine's cars about a block up; they're patrolling the neighborhood. Go the other way. I've gotta drive the van, so I'm passing the controls to April. Doc, please don't crash my drone?"

"If you'll recall," April said, "I've flown one of these before."

"I do recall. You crashed it."

April took over navigation, the drone zipping ahead and bobbing wildly. She sent us on a long and winding run through alleys and across side streets.

"Wait there," April said. "Right where you are. Stay out of sight."

I was grateful for the chance to rest. I crouched down behind a dumpster with my hands on my knees. Out of breath, with a painful stitch in my side that pinched every time I inhaled. Luis looked like he was about to throw up. Jessie wasn't even winded.

A car rumbled past on the street ahead. Nadine was in the backseat, and she didn't look happy. We stayed down, waiting until April gave us the all clear, then sprinted across the road. Two more turns and our race ended at the victory line: a white panel van advertising a local housecleaning service. The side door swooped open, revealing the electronic console and flickering screens of an FBI-grade surveillance suite. And Dr. April Cassidy, sitting regally in her wheelchair, her eyes cold behind steel bifocals.

"Quickly, please," she said. "We have a thirty-second window."

I shoved Luis on board and pulled the rattling door shut behind me. Sitting at the wheel, Kevin glanced back over his shoulder. The lanky nineteen-year-old gave us an expectant look.

"So? Yeah? Am I awesome?"

"You're awesome," Jessie said. "Now get us the fuck out of here."

He threw the van into gear. Luis bit down on his knuckles. "I don't understand any of this. Who were those people? Why were they chasing me?"

"They weren't after you," I told him. "They were looking for your roomie."

They would have gladly taken Luis and tortured him until they were sure he didn't know where Houston was—and then *kept* torturing him, just for fun—but he didn't need to hear that right now.

"He's not . . . he's not just my roommate," Luis said. His voice trailed off.

April tilted her head, looking close. I watched her eyes narrow as she studied him.

"You know, don't you, Mr. Perez?" she said. "You know there's more to your partner than he wanted you to see. More than just a skilled cardsharp."

His shoulders slumped.

"He never talked about his past. A year after we started dating, we got jumped by a mugger. Houston took his gun away, like snatching a rattle from a baby. Then he . . . took him apart—broke half the bones in the guy's body. It was like something from an action movie. Houston knew every move the guy was going to make; he blocked punches the mugger hadn't *thrown* yet. After, he just laughed it off, said he'd taken self-defense classes in college. Right. It was just little things, over the years. Things like that. I never confronted him—I didn't have anything concrete I could really confront him with, you know? And I just didn't want to rock the boat, I guess."

"I wish we had some concrete answers to give you," I said. "That said, I think that's a conversation you need to have with him, one-on-one."

Even through his exhaustion and fear, his face lit up.

"Can you save him? Can you bring him back to me?"

"We're going to try," I said. "I promise."

Jessie leaned against the console as the van swayed, taking a hard left.

"Right now," she told him, "you've gotta worry about you. You have any savings you can draw on? Fast?"

His head bobbed. "We're . . . we're pretty frugal. We were saving up, you know, thinking about . . . thinking about adopting a kid. That's expensive."

"We'll take you to your bank. You need to withdraw every dime you've got. Cash money. Then you need to get lost for a while. Stay off the radar and keep moving. A lot of people are going to be looking for Houston, and you don't want to be anywhere near when they come sniffing, got me?"

He got her. We took him to a strip-mall bank and waited while he withdrew every last dime. Our next stop was a no-tell motel on the edge of town, the kind of place that didn't demand photo ID and gladly accepted payment in cash. We checked him in under a false name and paid the clerk extra to develop sudden memory problems. I gave Luis the standard witness-protection spiel: Don't use the phone, don't reach out to friends or family, don't set foot outside if you absolutely don't have to.

If he followed the rules, he'd be safe, for a while. As safe as anyone could be after they'd dipped their toes into our world, willingly or not. We left him there, stranded, at the edge of an uncertain future. He was a civilian casualty, fallout from the war in the shadows. From there, he'd have to find his own way home.

# # #

"Right," Jessie said, "so we're going to New Jersey. Words I never wanted to speak. Kevin, get us to the airport. April, can you line up plane tickets? I want to stay under the radar. How's the Oceanic Polymer AmEx holding up?"

April reached for Kevin's laptop, resting it across her knees. "Uncomfortably close to the spending limit. If you plan on doing much more traveling, we're either going to have to tap FBI resources or find another source of funding."

Oceanic Polymer was a shell company, originally created for a long-abandoned DEA sting operation. Jessie snapped it up, dusted it off, and turned it into a civilian front for the team with a little help from Kevin's keyboard magic. We were reasonably sure not even Linder could trace Oceanic's finances, which made it the perfect cover for traveling right under his nose.

"We'll just have to rob the casino." Jessie smirked, catching something in my look. "Maybe not. Okay, probably not. We'll see."

"We're still FBI agents," I told her, crossing my arms.

"You are for the moment," April said. "There's a bit of a wrinkle. While you were off rescuing that civilian from Nadine's tender embrace—"

Kevin held up a finger. "On that note, is anyone else a little concerned that a psychotic succubus with her own hit squad has access to somebody inside the NSA? And Harmony, what was with the other one—Caitlin? She *wanted* you to get out safe?"

"While you were busy," April continued, "Linder called *me* this time."

"Oh, I can't wait to hear this," Jessie said.

April took out her phone, set it to speaker, and tapped the voice mail icon. Linder's voice—hushed, low, fast, and tinged with worry—flooded the van.

"Dr. Cassidy, I'm reaching out to you because . . . well, let's not mince words. Agent Temple is disregarding my orders, and I haven't been able to reach Agent Black. Considering the events of your last mission, what little I know of it, I'm starting to think Jessie is becoming a bad influence on her."

"Damn right," Jessie said. She held her fist out. Then she wriggled it at me until I halfheartedly bumped it.

"I know that you uncovered information about Glass Predator," Linder said. "I won't apologize for my part in that program. It was another time, and I did what I felt was best for the nation's safety. If that's what's keeping you from reporting in for debriefing, please disregard your feelings and listen to reason. We need to talk. Call me. Go behind their backs if you have to."

"I declined," April murmured, her voice dry.

"My superiors want a full report, and they want it yesterday," the recording continued. "There was an . . . an incident, involving Agent Temple's mother, in custody. Something she needs to know about—something you all need to know about. So come in, let me debrief you, and I'll have a full update for the team waiting and ready. Otherwise . . . look, things are being taken out of my hands. For your safety, for your team's safety, you *need* to call me immediately."

The recording beeped. April put her phone away, stashing it in the canvas tote bag that dangled from one arm of her wheelchair. I looked to Jessie. Her smile had vanished, replaced with a thousand-yard stare. Her turquoise eyes gone winter cold.

Facing Althea Temple-Sinclair and her pack of killers had pushed us all to the breaking point, but nobody more than Jessie. She'd fought the otherworldly infection in her veins, her own deepest instincts—and then fought Althea herself, taking a brutal beatdown that would have crippled or killed a woman without Jessie's supernatural resilience. As it was, I knew she'd earned some new scars from that battle. Some on her skin, some deeper down.

"He's full of shit," Jessie snapped.

"Jessie—" April started to say.

She shook her head. "No. He's got super-important information, but he won't just come out and say it? That's bait. He's trying to lure us in. My decision stands: we go for debriefing *after* we get to the bottom of this mess and find the truth. Linder's face was in Douglas Bredford's photo collection, circled with a bright-red bull's-eye. Whatever Cold Spectrum was, and whoever gave the order to kill Bredford's team, he was elbows-deep in it."

"Airport?" Kevin asked.

"Airport. So far we pulled off one rescue today. Let's break our record and go for two."

FOUR

Flying to Atlantic City was harder than it sounded. There weren't any direct flights from Portland International, and the best we could do was a red-eye to Philadelphia, then a SEPTA rail ride downtown, and finally another hour and a half crammed into a New Jersey Transit train.

"Gee," Jessie said, "it's almost like they don't want people to go here. We should take that as a hint."

The morning found us sleepless, aching, and looking for a fight. Cold rain drizzled down from a slate-gray sky over the Atlantic City boardwalk. A bankrupt casino on one side, its marquee rotting in the October wind, a span of empty beach on the other. Ice-cold waves rolled up on the dirty sand. We'd rented an SUV under civilian cover, and I cruised through sparse morning traffic on Pacific Avenue while April argued with an American Express rep on the phone, cajoling him into increasing our daily spending limit. Some covert agents had luxury jets and unlimited bank accounts; we just got by with what we had, improvised in the field, and somehow made it work.

The Diamondback was a quarter mile down, as lean and mean as its namesake. A diamond pattern glittered on the curving walls and curling metal canopy, tinted green and red like a harlequin's tights. A low-slung casino in front, a hotel tower rising behind it like a serpent's tail, twelve stories tall. The sign out front promised loose slots, single-zero roulette, and a happy hour that ran from 5:00 p.m. to midnight. A few veteran gamblers were already shuffling through the glass doors out front, clutching plastic cups for the slot machines in their grizzled hands, and none of them looked happy.

"Heading in to get their fix," Jessie said lightly, watching as we cruised for the parking garage ramp. "I know a junkie when I see one."

I wasn't sure she did. I was sitting right next to her.

She'd been there for me after Nadine's attack at the Bast Club. Sat beside me on a hotel roof while I screamed my frustration and my hunger into a bucket. Took the plastic room key—Nadine's room key—from my trembling fingers and pitched it over the side of the roof, banishing my temptation for one night and keeping me on the right path.

For one night.

But the hunger didn't go away. Neither did the incessant ache in my veins, or the way my connection to the currents of magic slipped and slid and sparked under my fingertips. I was a malfunctioning battery, a broken machine. And I knew what it would take to make me feel all right again.

April told me this wasn't my fault. That what Nadine had done, the occult drug-infused kiss she'd forced on me, was no different from forcing someone to smoke crack at gunpoint. Intellectually, I knew she was right. Emotionally, I felt . . . filthy. Used. And the only thing worse than the pain of withdrawal, the only thing more humiliating than what Nadine had done to me, was the fact that part of me wanted *more*.

One kiss . . . and I'd feel all right again. The itch and the ache would all go away.

I couldn't tell them that. Not now, not when we were so close to the truth, with so much riding on the mission. It didn't matter that I was still fighting it: an addict was an addict, and nobody trusts an addict.

I needed to be solid for my team. I needed to smile and pretend. Just for a little while longer.

The belly of the Diamondback smelled like stale cigarettes and cheap gin. Glass chandeliers that hadn't been dusted since the late '80s glowed over dirty diamond-patterned carpets. We skirted around a gambler with a walker—hobbling with his oxygen tank in one hand and his change cup in the other—and rented a room. Low in the tower, close to the exit.

"You two can set up base camp in the room while we do recon," Jessie said. "April, you're on background: I want to know who really owns this place and what kind of opposition we're looking at. Kevin, dig in to their financials. While I doubt they've got a file on their computer marked 'illegal activities and kidnapping'—"

"You might be surprised," he said.

Jessie and I stopped off at the cashier's cage and traded two fifties for a stack of colorful chips. Protective camouflage as we circled the casino floor, blending in the best we could with the sparse crowds. Banks of slot machines emblazoned with cobra heads jangled and flashed in our wake.

"They're really working the snake theme," Jessie murmured. "That's not sinister or anything."

I pretended to check my phone for messages, putting my back to a diamond-patterned pillar and tilting the screen close. I was really refreshing my memory. RedEye hadn't given us Houston's picture, but the envelope of photographs Douglas Bredford left behind for us had included—we assumed—snapshots of all his former teammates. Now we had them on digital, an electronic epitaph. If Houston stood numbered with the pictures of the condemned, I'd know him when I saw him in the flesh.

We played some halfhearted blackjack at the smallest-stakes table, five dollars a hand, and watched our chip stacks rise and fall for a while. The crowds filed in, tourists shuffling from the elevator banks in a slow and steady stream, but I had my eyes on the staff. Mostly Atlantic City lifers who would die with a deck of cards in one hand and a cigarette in the other. Nothing sinister, nothing unexpected.

That's when I spotted Houston Dalenta making his way across the casino floor with a bull of a pit boss at his shoulder. He looked like his picture, just older and with a few more wrinkles, his sparse blond hair going white and thin at the temples. He held a stack of chips, eyeing the tables as he passed.

I nodded. Jessie followed my gaze, her eyes widening. We tipped the dealer and pushed away from the blackjack table, quietly tailing Houston and the pit boss.

"Okay, something's weird here." Jessie murmured low, leaning close as we walked. "He tells his boyfriend that he got caught cheating, the casino's holding him hostage, and not to call the cops. Are we sure that wasn't just his twisted way of breaking up with him?"

"I'm not sure. He doesn't look happy. And check the guy with him."

His minder was never more than two feet from Houston's shoulder, and the thick bulge under his jacket probably wasn't a rolled-up newspaper. We stayed out of sight and watched close. They walked under an open arch, into a parlor set aside for high-limit games. Gamblers hooted and smacked the felt as black chips flowed in a serpentine river. Hand to hand, dealer to player, and back again. Judging from the shouts and high fives, the players at a horseshoe-shaped poker table in the heart of the lounge were on a hot streak.

Houston Dalenta took a seat. He anted up, nodded politely to the dealer, and started winning.

There wasn't anything subtle in his approach. Houston hit the table like a wrecking ball, turning the cheers to anguished groans as the cards turned his way again and again. He was a human vacuum cleaner, sucking all the luck and joy out of the room. Jessie sat at a slot machine near the archway, and I stood beside her, a good vantage point to watch the action from a distance. As one player threw down his cards and stalked out with a vintage Stetson in his angry fist, I put the pieces together.

"He's not a player," I said. "He's an employee. They caught him cheating, and they gave him a job."

Jessie pulled the slot-machine handle and glanced sidelong at the table, her brow furrowed. "Usually casinos toss you out for that. Or call the cops. Or break your fingers. Making you *work* there? That's a new one on me."

"Old gambler folklore. The story goes, casinos would have a guy on staff called a cooler—his whole job was to ruin a table's luck. Break a hot streak, turn a winner into a loser. I think that's what they did with Houston. See, he's pretending to be a player, mopping everybody up."

"And once he leaves the table," Jessie said, "he hands the chips he just 'won' back to the pit boss. He's cheating *for* the casino now."

"What do you do with a man who has an unbeatable system?"

Jessie fed another bill into the slot machine, barely glancing at the reels as they whistled and spun. "You put him to good use. Okay, so what's the scam? How's he pulling it off?"

I doubted a covert-ops program recruited him for his card-counting skills, and most of the obvious cheating techniques needed the help of a partner or even a corrupt dealer. Houston Dalenta worked solo. Even through the ache in my veins, I could smell the faint tang of magic clinging to his long-fingered hands as he tossed another black chip into the pot. Could he literally be stealing the other players' luck? I'd never seen a magician capable of that, but it would explain his unbreakable winning streak.

Then I thought back to when we rescued Luis, and how he'd described his partner in a fight. *Houston knew every move the guy was going to make; he blocked punches the mugger hadn't thrown yet.*

"He's a precognitive," I said.

"In English?" Jessie asked.

"He can see into the future. A friend of my mother's, when I was a little kid, she had the gift, too. When she'd concentrate just before making a decision, she'd catch glimpses of possible outcomes. The power was strictly short term, very hazy, and only a few seconds long, but she always knew the right choice—because she'd already seen all the wrong ones."

Houston flipped a card, responding to the table's groans with a casual shrug as he raked in another stack of chips.

"Every time he plays," I said, "he's seeing every move that everybody else at the table is about to make. He knows what the dealer's going to do and what cards are coming up next. In other words, if there's any mathematical way for him to win the hand—"

"He *will* win the hand," Jessie said. "Imagine how that would work in a gunfight. Hell, *I* want to recruit this guy. So how are they keeping him here? One pit boss with a gun isn't a big deterrent against that kind of power."

"Maybe they've got something on him. Come to think of it, he got a message out to Luis—we assumed he sneaked it out, but maybe they let him. He can protect himself with his ability, but that won't stop these people from going after his boyfriend."

"As long as he does what he's told, Luis is safe." Jessie nodded, adding it up. "Houston's been on the run for years, living under a fake name—he can't go to the authorities anyway, not without blowing his cover. He's all alone."

"He was alone," I said. "Now he's got us."

"How do you want to play it?"

We needed more information. We weren't sure who was running the Diamondback, or how many unfriendly pairs of eyes—and how many guns—stood between us, Houston, and the exit. Getting sloppy could get Houston killed, and considering the other Cold Spectrum survivor had vanished off the grid, he was our best and maybe our only connection to the truth.

"I've got an idea," I said. "I need a napkin and a pen. We're going to make Houston's powers work for us."

FIVE

A cocktail waitress had everything I needed. I tipped her and clicked the ballpoint pen, flipping a napkin over and writing on the back.

"If his ability works the way I think it does," I told Jessie, "he can see immediate near-future possibilities. Like, if someone's about to step in front of him—assuming he's concentrating—he'll know to move out of the way."

"So you're writing him a note?"

I had to keep this short and simple. *Houston Coe,* I scribbled, using his original name, *we know who you are. We are here to help.*

"That's the idea," I said.

Houston pushed his chair back. He'd left the opposition in ruins, and his stack of chips had grown from a cottage to a skyscraper or three. The pit boss with the gun eased around the table, looming over his shoulder.

"How are you going to pass it to him without the gorilla seeing you?" Jessie asked.

"If this works how I think, I won't have to. Or, that is to say, I will, but then I won't."

"You know, usually it's Kevin who makes my brain hurt. Also, I've been known to smack Kevin up the back side of the head every once in a while. You should contemplate these facts and how they may be connected."

I held up the note for Jessie. "If I approach Houston with every intention of handing him this note, then in some iteration of his future sight, he takes it and reads it a few seconds later, right?"

Jessie broke into a smile. "Which means he doesn't have to take it. Because he *did* read it. He'll know what you wrote without ever touching the napkin."

I added the final words: *If you can read this, give me a sign.*

"It's an experiment," I said. "If this works, we know we can get messages to him without his captors noticing. We can work out a plan from there."

"And if it doesn't work?"

"Then we may have to escalate things a lot faster than I'd like. Get ready."

I set myself on a collision course with Houston, two passing planes on a runway lined with dirty diamonds. A wall of slot machines let out an electronic cheer on my left, lights cascading in time with my footsteps. For this to work, I couldn't just hold the napkin: I had to approach with every intention of handing it to him. Which meant if I was wrong about Houston's powers, I was about to pass him a note in plain view of his minder. Bad news for everybody involved.

I never had the chance. As the gap between us shrank to five feet, then two, Houston locked eyes with me. He gave a short, firm shake of his head. "Uh-uh," he said under his breath. I pocketed the napkin and kept walking.

From behind my back, he spoke up. "Miss?"

I paused, turning. Under the pit boss's glowering stare, Houston crouched to scoop a plastic key card from the grimy carpet. He held it out to me.

"I think you dropped this."

I took the card. His minder gave him a nudge, steering him toward the elevator banks. Jessie fell in at my side as I quietly followed, trailing them at a distance, stepping behind a slot machine as they waited for the elevator doors to whisper open. Once they were on board, I watched the glowing orange numbers climb.

"Did you see where the card came from?" I asked Jessie.

"Yeah, it was slick. He palmed it from his hip pocket and dropped it down to his foot, out of the gorilla's eye line, and gave it a little kick for distance. I think we can assume he got the message."

The numbers climbed. First floor, second, third . . . all the way up to twelve, where the elevator paused long enough to let its passengers off. Penthouse floor. I twirled the key card in my fingers, one side solid black, the other embossed with the Diamondback's swirling logo.

"And we got his." I tapped my earpiece. "Kevin, are you in?"

"Eh, sort of? They've got crazy-good security on some chunks of their system, but the rest is a joke. If there's anything incriminating on here, they've got it locked down tight. I've got employee schedules, catering department, and the reservation system so far."

"Good. Hit reservations—pull all the room assignments for the twelfth floor. Looks like that's where they're keeping Houston, and he just slipped us a key."

"Probably not alone," Jessie said. "If they won't let him walk around without an armed escort, I guarantee they've got extra security up there."

"You'll need to do more than bypass a few thugs, I'm afraid." April's voice chimed in over the line. "I've traced the ownership records. While the Diamondback—and four other Atlantic City properties—is held by a trust, said trust can be traced directly to one Big Jim Ammandola."

Jessie scrunched up her face. "I'm guessing he's not an Eagle Scout."

"Regrettably, no. After a Bureau operation led to the arrest of most of the DeCavalcante crime family's associates, Mr. Ammandola stepped in to fill the power vacuum in Atlantic City. He holds strong ties to

New York's Five Families, is a ranking member of the local chamber of commerce, and donates generously to the police widows' and orphans' fund."

"In other words," Jessie said, "we don't need to get Houston out of this casino. We need to get him out of this *city*."

"That would be prudent, yes. Also, I'm not finding any indication of occult underworld ties, but one doesn't rise to a position like Mr. Ammandola's without some measure of supernatural support. I would prepare for physical and magical opposition."

Jessie looked my way. She turned off her earpiece. "You good for this?"

I felt angry, defensive. I bit it back.

"Sure," I said. "Why wouldn't I be?"

"Well, that thing with Nadine at the Bast Club, it hit you pretty hard—"

"We all took some hits," I said. "That's part of the job. We take it so other people don't have to."

She reached out and put her hand on my arm. I must have been bristling harder than I thought. Jessie softened her voice, fixing her eyes on mine.

"I'm just saying, we're in for a fight here. I need to make sure you're at a hundred percent."

What was I going to say, no?

If we had the luxury of time, if we had any choice at all, I would have told her the truth. But we didn't. So I had exactly two options. I could level with her, tell her that Nadine's psychic poison was like a serpent chewing its way through my veins, and go into battle with Jessie distracted and worried about me. A recipe for disaster. Or I could suck it up, put on a fake smile, and deal with my problems on my own time.

I put on the fake smile. My fingers brushed over hers.

"I'm fine. What's the plan, fearless leader?"

"Let's wait for tonight," Jessie said. "I want to move when the casino's at peak hours: the gangsters who own this place aren't going to open fire in a room crowded with civilian customers, and outside we'll have the cover of darkness. We go up to twelve, take out the security, and exfil Houston through the casino and into the parking garage. We'll drive back to Philly and . . . well, from there, I guess it depends on what Houston has to tell us."

I checked the time on my phone. "We should split up for a couple of hours. Less chance of attracting attention before we make our move."

"Good idea. I'm gonna take a stroll up to twelve, pretend to be a lost tourist, and get the lay of the land. Keep watch down here in case they trot Houston out for another dog-and-pony show; maybe he'll try to pass you a message."

She left me alone on the casino floor. Alone with the file on my phone, and the list of suspects and targets I'd requested from Vigilant Lock's archives.

An Assessment, the prim black type read, of Individuals Believed to Possess Incubus/Succubus-Class Abilities.

Scraps and rumors, mostly, partial write-ups of people who hadn't quite gotten high profile enough to join the Hostile Entities register. Potential targets for future investigation. And one of them was a local. A gigolo and a hustler with a reputation for leaving his clients inordinately satisfied.

Just one kiss. If he could do what Nadine could, that's all it would take. All I'd need to make the aching go away, to feel like myself again. To have my magic back, to be ready for the fight we knew was coming.

All it would take was making a mockery of everything I claimed to stand for. Becoming a hypocrite, trafficking with the powers I'd sworn to destroy, and putting my own life in danger behind my partner's back. That's all. Not much.

I argued with myself up and down the casino floor. I had a hundred reasons to say no. I just didn't know how to say it. Only one or two reasons to say yes, but they were big and loud and drowning out the others. I told myself it wasn't about the hunger, it wasn't about relief, it was about being reliable. We were about to go up against the Atlantic City Mob, with the life of an informant—a man who could crack open the mystery that had dogged our heels since our first mission together—hanging in the balance. I couldn't risk my powers fizzling out when I needed them most.

I was being a good partner. That's what I told myself as I logged into Atlantic City *Backpage* with a throwaway e-mail address and tapped out a private message. Five minutes later, "Romeo" pinged me back.

Sure, he wrote, always happy to meet new friends. Three hundred roses is the tribute for one hour. Where are you staying?

The Diamondback, I responded.

You won't be sorry, he told me.

I tried to make myself believe it, but I wasn't that good a liar yet. I found the ATM, used my cover identity's card, embossed with the Oceanic Polymer logo, and took out three hundred in cash. The money felt grubby under my fingers, faded and worn. Then I waited and I paced until my phone pinged again and Romeo was waiting for me in the hotel bar.

Last chance to turn back, I told myself, standing in the bar doorway. But that wasn't true, either. I'd already made my choice. Only one thing left to do.

I went inside.

SIX

Romeo sat at the end of the half-empty bar, cradling a glass of bourbon with his manicured fingernails. Roguish stubble, ruffled hair, and an orange sport coat slung carelessly over a shirt that looked like a kaleidoscope whorl. His peacock grace was so practiced it looked effortless: the loudest man in the room, without saying a word. He flashed a perfect smile as I walked his way.

"You must be Marilyn," he said.

"That's right."

"A beautiful name. Makes me think of Marilyn Monroe." He gestured to the empty stool on his left. "Why don't you have a seat? We don't need to be in a hurry."

I sat beside him.

"You didn't mention where you heard about me," he said. Gently probing as he looked into my eyes.

"A friend of mine . . . met with you once," I told him. "I don't think she'd want me to say her name."

He waved a hand. "I understand. I don't name names, either, in case you're worried. What's between us is between us, and that's where it stays. Nobody has to know. I do have to ask you one question, and I apologize for it."

"What's that?"

"Marilyn," he said, "are you a cop?"

I almost laughed. Never, in the history of law enforcement, has that question saved anyone from getting busted. I would have thought a demon-blooded hustler would know better. Then again, considering where I was sitting, I wasn't in a position to lecture anyone.

"No," I told him, "I'm not a cop."

"You seem nervous. It's okay, you know. I see clients who are in perfectly happy relationships; they just can't get what they need from their husband"—his gaze flicked to my hand, checking for a ring—"their boyfriend, but it doesn't mean they love them any less. I want you to think of me as your . . . fantasy facilitator. No judgment, just pleasure."

I forced myself to smile. The nervous edge in my voice—that was real.

"This is my first time doing something like this."

Romeo's gentle smile grew wider. "And you chose the best. Clearly you're a lady of impeccable taste. You won't be disappointed. All of my clients are repeat clients—once you get a taste of what I have to offer, I guarantee you'll be hungry for more."

I felt my veins squirming under my skin, empty and starving, moving in time to the jackhammer of my heartbeat.

"Would you like to continue this discussion someplace more private?" he asked. "Someplace we can get comfortable?"

"We can't use my room. It's . . . *he's* up there right now."

"Of course." That reassuring smile again. Knowing. "I have a room at the Starlite, just next door."

Romeo rose from the bar stool and held out his hand.

"Would you walk with me, Marilyn? Do me the honor?"

His palm tingled against mine. His fingers twined like the teeth of a warm steel trap, closing shut. He walked me through the lobby, out the door, down to the Starlite. His room was on the second floor, overlooking the boardwalk, and it smelled faintly of some musky cologne that made me think of the sea. He clicked on a lamp, spilling light across striped '70s-era wallpaper, and drew the heavy curtains shut.

I set the three hundred dollars on the nightstand. He gave the cash an appraising glance, nodded, didn't bother to count.

He slithered into the gap between us, stealing the air from my personal space. His voice dropped to a purr. "This is all for you. It's all about you. And don't worry—I'll be gentle. Unless . . . that's not what you want."

"What do you think I want?"

His brow furrowed, just a little bit.

"I'm usually good at reading people's desires," he said. "I've got a knack for knowing what they need, what they're hungry for. You . . . you're a tricky one. Tell me something, Marilyn: Do *you* know what you want?"

That was easy. I wanted this all to go away. I wanted to feel normal again. I wanted to stop remembering how Nadine had humiliated me, violated me, every single time I looked inside myself.

This was different. *Because I'm choosing this,* I thought. *Even if it's the wrong choice, at least it belongs to me.*

"I want you to kiss me," I told him.

And he did. And my world caught fire.

I felt the room burning around us, and I drank the smoke like some sweet summer wine. Then the room was gone, the hotel was gone, the universe was gone, torn away by a surge of pleasure so powerful that nothing else could exist in its presence. The pain and the hunger boiled away, and I fell backward into the wellspring of my own magic, splashing into the purest of rivers, letting it carry me to the heart of the universe.

# # #

Night fell over Atlantic City. The casinos and resorts lit up white-hot along the boardwalk, artificial suns and beacons glowing in the dark. I wound through the crowded lobby of the Diamondback, chin high, speed in my step. I had just left Romeo behind, returning alone, but I still felt the tingle of his lips. I tapped my earpiece.

"Full house down here. We gonna do this? Are you ready? I'm ready."

"Damn, girl." Jessie laughed. "Somebody's raring to go. Yeah, sounds about right. Come up and meet me on twelve. April, Kevin, clear the room and get down to the parking garage. I want you two in the SUV with the engine running. If we do this right, it should go quick and quiet. We'll be halfway to Philly by the time anybody notices their pet psychic is missing."

I was alone in the elevator. Bouncing from foot to foot as I punched the button for twelve, and feeling a tingle in my blood. I cupped my open hands, palms up.

The elevator took on a Halloween glow as swirls of orange flame ignited in my palms. I didn't even need the ritual words, my traditional call to the elements. The power came to me unbidden. I laughed—giddy—and snuffed the fires with a sudden clench of my fingers.

Jessie paced just outside the elevator door in a vestibule lined with tall mirrors. She greeted me with a curious tilt of her head. "What'd you do, chug a whole pot of espresso?"

"What? Why?"

"You're *vibrating*." She flashed a grin. "Let's go pick a fight with the Mafia. Our boy's in 1208—it's the only door with a couple of Jersey goombahs standing watch outside. I've been hanging out around the corner, listening to these idiots talk—it's like we walked into a *Sopranos* episode."

We eased up the hall, where the corridor broke into a three-way split. She held up a hand to stop me.

"Let's play it casual, get close, and take them down fast and quiet. I'll get the one on the left." She paused. Then she leaned in, and sniffed at me. "Harmony, were you . . . ?"

"What?"

Jessie shook her head, frowning, and tapped the side of her nose. "Never mind. This place is filled with weird smells. Downside of having hyperactive senses: with this much stimuli, not to mention the cigarette smoke, the sniffer gets a little confused. C'mon, let's do this."

We rounded the corner and strolled along, just another couple of tourists headed back to their room. Our targets stood dead ahead: two guys sporting gold chains and conspicuous bulges under their track jackets, looking bored and antsy. One stared us up and down as we got close. He gave me a reptile smile.

"Lookin' good, ladies."

"Thanks," I told him. Then I grabbed his wrist, spun him around, and shoved him off balance, sending him cheek-first against the wall. The barrel of my gun jabbed into the small of his back, and he turned into a statue. Jessie's dance partner hit the carpet. He let out a little yelp as she straddled him, twisting one arm hard behind his back, not breaking it but proving she could.

"Don't even think about yelling for help." I reached under his jacket, plucked the stubby pistol from his waistband, and tossed it to the floor behind me. "We're not here for you; we don't want you. Stay out of our way and you get to go home to your family tonight. *Capisce?*"

I slapped the cuffs on and sat him down next to his buddy, both of them glowering at us.

"You're making a big mistake," he said. "You know who owns this place? You got any idea who you're messing with?"

"Trust me," Jessie said, "considering the kind of people we usually go up against, you guys are minor-league at best. Still, you get an A for effort."

I waved the key card at the black box beside the door. It clicked, flashing a green light. On the other side, Houston was already walking up to greet us.

"Come on, we're getting you—"

"Out of here, I know, you said that already." Houston winced, fluttering a hand at his face. "I'm sorry. When I'm stressed, the visions get hard to handle. I forget which timeline I'm in."

We hustled him up the hall, back to the elevator banks.

"Your note," he said. "You used my real name. Who sent you?"

I hit the "Down" button and stepped back from the doors. "Douglas Bredford—well, sort of."

"Doug?" Houston's eyes widened. "He's still alive? No. Dead now, isn't he? I just asked you that."

"I'm sorry, as far as we know, the only survivors from your old team are you and Aselia Boulanger, and we're not sure about her. She's either dead or—"

"Underground. I talked to her a couple of years ago. Just once, that's all we could risk. She was our transportation specialist—if anyone knew how to move under the radar, it's . . . Damn it, *damn it*!" Houston pinched the bridge of his nose and squeezed his eyes shut. "Don't fight. *Don't* fight."

"What?" Jessie asked. "Fight who?"

"Just surrender. Watched it ten different ways, zero percent survival rate if you don't."

The elevators chimed. Two doors slid open at once, one on our left, one on our right, each one carrying a cargo of armed men. Suddenly the air bristled with guns aimed at point-blank range.

"That," Houston said, his face falling.

One of the gunmen stepped up, shaking his head. "What's the matter, Houston? You don't like the accommodations here no more? You got a problem with the room service?"

Houston suddenly flinched as if he'd been hit. He tucked his chin against his neck, staring meekly at the floor. The gunman snickered and looked my way.

"I love this guy. I can beat ten shades of crap out of him without bruisin' a knuckle. I just have to *think* about throwing a punch, and he feels it anyway. Security was watching him like a hawk on the casino cameras: they caught that move with his room key. We've just been waiting all day for you to go for it."

A rough hand plucked the Glock from my shoulder holster, then patted me down. The gunman gestured to the open elevator door.

"Mr. Ammandola requests the pleasure of your company, ladies. Please, right this way."

SEVEN

Being a witch means you're never unarmed. As they marched us across the casino floor, hissing a warning to stay quiet and keep our hands in plain sight, I ran through a dozen plans on the spur of the moment. I could cause a distraction, start a panic in the crowd, harness elemental fire, and take one of the gunmen down with brute force . . . but every option meant risking Houston's life. For now, until they put our backs to the wall—literally, I suspected—it felt smarter to go with the flow.

The Diamondback offered a number of dining options, but Tumicelli's was the only one that boasted a Michelin star. Also, the only one that wasn't snake themed. Double doors opened onto polished hardwood floors, ivory tablecloths, and candlelight, an old-world steak house where piped-in chamber music muffled the distant slot-machine chimes. A second-floor balcony ringed the room, hanging over the tables below, and long glass skylights in the ceiling opened up to the starless Jersey sky.

We didn't need an introduction to spot "Big Jim" Ammandola at a corner table, digging in to a bowl of Parmesan-crusted macaroni and cheese with a bib tucked into his tailored shirt. He was about as wide as he was tall, with fat lips and a jackal's eyes. His men ushered us over, pulled out chairs, and sat us down.

"This guy," Ammandola said, jabbing his fork at Houston. "Y'know, I'm nothing but fucking *nice* to this guy. Do I get any appreciation? No. Not one bit. So what's your story? Couple of hired guns? He get a message out, hire you to spring him?"

One of the gunmen leaned in, slapping my badge on the tablecloth.

"This says they're feds, Mr. Ammandola."

"This says, this says." Ammandola snorted and tossed back a swig of red wine. "My nephew, he's a computer whiz—give him ten minutes and he can print up creds that say *I'm* in the FBI."

"Afraid it's true," I told him. "You just abducted a pair of federal agents at gunpoint."

"Ain't the worst of my sins. Hell, probably ain't gonna be the worst tonight. But who said anything about abduction? We're just having a chat, that's all." He snapped his fingers at a passing waitress. "Hey, doll, bring another bottle of that merlot and a couple of glasses for my new friends here."

"We're not investigating you, if that's what you want to know." Jessie sat back and fixed him with a steely look. "We're here on a matter of national security. We need Houston's help, and it's in your best interests to give him to us."

The waitress set out glasses for us, splashing out dollops of burgundy wine that graced the air with a faint peppery scent. Houston, on my left, had retreated somewhere deep inside himself. Arms folded, head down. Crash position.

"I got a problem with that," Ammandola told Jessie. "See, this guy stole my money. Being the forgiving sort of person I am, I'm graciously allowing him the opportunity to repay me."

I leaned in. "How much does he owe you? Maybe we could work something out."

"It ain't a specific dollar amount so much as the general principle of the matter. C'mon, ladies, you know what this guy can do, right? When you've got a goose that lays golden eggs, you don't sell him."

"Sounds like we're getting close to an impasse," Jessie told him.

Houston rocked back and forth, his head twitching, eyes shut tight. I put my hand on his shoulder.

"Hey," I said, "are you okay?"

"Flip the table," he whispered.

"What?"

Houston's eyes shot open. He lifted his head and screamed, *"Flip the table!"*

I grabbed hold of the table's edge and heaved. Jessie followed my lead, shoving the big, round table like it was made of balsa wood. Glasses and plates flew as it crashed onto its side. The kitchen doors blasted open, and two men strode out, draped in long leather coats and motorcycle helmets with opaque visors. The bullpup rifles in their leather-gloved grips, stubby and black and modified for full auto, washed the room in steel fire. Bullets chewed into the table, the mahogany pillars, smashing plates and wine bottles. A waitress went down. She spun before she hit the floor, her white blouse torn and scarlet. One of Ammandola's men was the next to die, staggering backward and shrieking, with his jaw blown off and hanging by a thread of sinew as the others scrambled for cover. Tourists stampeded for the exit, cramming in at the doorway, one of them going down with a three-round burst to the spine.

The skylights exploded. I crouched behind the table and threw my arms over my head as shards of glass rained down, smashing in a glittering tide across the floorboards. A pair of black tactical ropes unfurled, and another pair of helmeted shooters rode them down, sliding along the lines with one hand while firing with the other.

Ammandola yanked a fat little .32 from his waistband. Jessie reached over and plucked it from his grip. Ammandola glared at her, then gave Houston a questioning look.

"Let her. She shoots better than you." Houston looked to Jessie. "They're wearing vests. Two shots to the head, then duck fast."

Jessie broke from cover, aiming at the men by the kitchen door. Her first bullet went wide, slamming into the wood and spitting splinters. The second crashed through the helmet's faceplate and straight into the gunman's face. He dropped hard and fast, finger squeezing his trigger in a death grip, spending the last of his magazine. Jessie hit the floor a split second before a hail of lead ripped through the air.

I was reaching to my magic, calling for a weapon, when Houston grabbed my forearm. He squeezed, hard.

"Listen. Aselia Boulanger was hiding in Louisiana. Des Allemands. Go to her. Tell her I said, 'Paris was nearsighted anyway.' *Remember* that, okay?"

"You're coming with us—"

"No," he said, his face contorted with grief. "I've seen forty-seven possible permutations of the next ten seconds."

"Houston—"

"I die in every single one of them. Thank you for trying."

For a moment, he seemed almost peaceful. The panic fading away, replaced by a quiet, sad resignation. A heartbeat of silence in the whirlwind of battle.

Then faint glowing embers danced on his skin. Flitting across his face, his hair, his arms, like tiny fireflies. My gut clenched. I'd seen that before. It could only mean—

Houston shrieked as his entire body caught fire. He went up like a Roman candle, stumbling away and flailing, leaving charred footprints in his wake. The only thing louder than the screams and the gunfire was the mad, gleeful laughter from the balcony above.

Mikki grinned down at us and raised her arms high in triumph.

"Hey, bitches! Did you miss me? I missed *you*! I thought about you two every single day I was locked in that—"

I didn't give her a chance to finish. I shot to my feet and flung out my open hand, calling to my magic. Fueled by rage, a lance of fire streaked from my fingertips like a razor-thin trail of burning gasoline. Mikki dived for cover, ducking behind the banisters, as the fire splashed across the wall behind her.

"Keep her head down," I shouted at Ammandola's men. "If she can't see you, she can't burn you!"

A couple of them were smart enough to listen, laying down covering fire and pinning Mikki in place. One of them got careless; Mikki's gunners flanked him, skirting the edge of the steak house, and dropped him with a burst that tore his throat out. He fell next to Houston's smoldering corpse. Jessie emptied her pistol and broke cover just long enough to snatch up the dead man's gun. She huddled next to me, gripping the weapon close to her chest.

"We are *leaving*," she snarled. She tapped her earpiece. "Forget the parking garage: get the SUV out front. We'll rendezvous in about two minutes."

"That voice," Kevin said. "Was that—"

"Move. Now." Jessie looked my way. "On three?"

I curled my open hand into a fist. Faint wisps of yellow light trailed behind my fingers, the idea of elemental air given form and life.

"On three," I told her.

Together, we leaped up from behind the table. Jessie opened fire on the run, forcing the shooters behind cover, while I waved my hand and laid out a shimmering trail of congealed air. A three-round burst raked toward us and slammed into my magical shield. The shells held suspended as they shivered, suddenly moving in slow motion.

We burst through the steak-house door and out into the casino. The place was empty, chips and spilled drinks and ashtrays littering the carpet, the smell of panic in the air and sirens wailing in the distance. Out front, the SUV screeched to the curb three footsteps before we got there, and we piled into the backseat. Jessie slapped the flat of her hand against Kevin's headrest.

"*Drive.*"

She didn't need to tell him twice. He veered into traffic, speeding down Pacific Avenue with red-and-blue lights flashing in the rearview.

Nobody spoke, not at first. Once we'd gotten clear, far from the lights and sirens, Kevin broke the silence.

"That was Mikki, wasn't it? She escaped."

"No," Jessie said.

I shot her a look. "He needs to know, Jessie. Yes, that was—"

"She did not," Jessie said, spitting the word out, "*escape.* Detention Site Burgundy is the strongest prison on Earth. It was built to hold the worst of the worst. Sorcerers. Demon cultists. People who can bend reality just by *thinking* real hard. They got a serial killer in there who has bones like cartilage. Guy can collapse his body and squeeze through openings small enough for a mouse. Got another guy who can step into a shadow and turn invisible. Know how close they've gotten to escaping? They *haven't.* Nobody escapes from Site Burgundy."

April turned her head, looking back at us. "Jessie? What are you saying?"

"The only way Mikki got out of that pit is if somebody let her out." Jessie's turquoise eyes burned cold, radioactive in the dark. "That was a Vigilant Lock team. We were just ambushed by *our own fucking people.*"

"On Linder's orders?" April asked.

Jessie took out her phone.

"Great question," she said. "Let's ask him."

EIGHT

"This is Special Agent Temple," Jessie said into the phone, "authorization ninety-three ninety-three. Get the director on the line. Oh, I guarantee he's expecting a call from me."

While we waited, Jessie ticked off names on her fingertips.

"Vigilant has three field teams besides us. Beach Cell, but they're all in deep cover at Diehl Innovations with Agent Cooper. Redbird Cell got wiped out in Miami right before the Red Knight incident, and there's no way Linder's trained up their replacements this fast."

"That leaves Panic Cell," I said.

"Yeah. The team that's always conveniently out of the country or otherwise unavailable every time we need backup."

"Looks like they cleared their schedule," Kevin said.

Jessie switched her phone to speaker mode. The sound of faint, rasping breath filled the car.

"Agent," Linder said, then nothing. Letting her make the first move.

"Oh, hey, buddy," Jessie said. "Want to hear a really funny story? So, there we were, enjoying a nice steak dinner, when one of our dining companions spontaneously combusted. And then a bunch of guys with close-quarters battle training tried to kill us. And I'm pretty sure—y'know, call me crazy if you must—but I'm pretty sure you sent them."

Linder sighed. "I told you to come in for debriefing."

"So you put out a contract on us? Fucking overreact much, *asshole*? And how long has Mikki been working with Panic Cell?"

"They weren't after—" He paused, taking a deep breath. "For the record, I was strongly opposed to releasing her. I was overruled. I promise you, Agent Temple, I am not your enemy. We can still iron things out, but your absolute best hope for survival right now is to come in for debriefing. I need to prove to my superiors that you're still reliable assets, that you haven't gone rogue. Trust me, things only get worse from here."

"Worse? Mikki and her pals just shot up a casino on the goddamned boardwalk, Linder! Civilians *died*, which is the exact *opposite* of what we're supposed to be doing here. Quantify 'worse' for me."

"For you," he said. "For you and your team, I mean. You still have your badges. You still have your reputations. All of that—all of it—can be taken away from you in an instant. This situation is still salvageable, but you have to come in."

Jessie stared at the phone, thinking.

"I'll call you back," she said. She stabbed her finger at the screen and disconnected the call.

We drove a little longer in silence.

"He tipped his hand," April mused.

I looked her way, leaning around the seat. "How do you mean?"

"What he said, just after Jessie asked how long Mikki had been working with Panic Cell. That defensive tic before he caught himself. 'They weren't after'—"

"Us," I said, finishing the thought. "They weren't after us. I'd figured Mikki murdered Houston because he was crouched next to us—she wanted to make a grand entrance and gloat before she killed Jessie

55

and me. But that wasn't it at all. They were there to assassinate *him*. We were just in the wrong place at the wrong time."

"Let's piece it together," April said. "Before Vigilant Lock formally existed, Linder was part of the RedEye program."

Jessie folded her arms. "And Glass Predator. Sending my mom and her murder buddies to hunt and kill 'domestic terrorists.'"

"Including Douglas Bredford and his team," I said. "We don't know if he gave the order personally, but *someone* decided everyone attached to Operation Cold Spectrum had to die. So . . . is Linder using Vigilant's resources to clean up his old messes?"

April put a finger to her lips, walking through it. She frowned and shook her head.

"I don't think so. The stress in his voice—he was legitimately regretful about Mikki's involvement."

"Man's not stupid," Jessie said. "The first time we tried rehabilitating her was a total disaster. Now she's loose, and we've got even more dead civvies."

Streetlights washed through the passenger window, casting a hard glow on April's face. Catching the downcast tilt of her chin, the weariness etched in the crow's-feet around her eyes.

"Shit," Jessie said. "Sorry. You know I didn't mean it like that."

"Why mince words? It was a disaster. Dozens of deaths, a near-global catastrophe." April turned her face, looking out the window. "And it was my idea. My hubris. If I was a religious woman, I'd be preparing to account for it before my creator. As it is, I've learned to shoulder that guilt alone."

"What happened tonight wasn't your fault," I told her. "Mikki was locked down. You didn't set her loose again."

"No. But the choice to try to weaponize her was entirely mine, and I've evidently inspired someone to re-create my experiment. That someone, I believe, *not* being Linder. Someone higher up in the chain of command."

Kevin flicked the turn signal. I caught his eyes in the rearview, looking back at me.

"What about his threat? Can they really pull your badges? Kick you out of the FBI?"

"Vigilant Lock technically doesn't even exist." I shrugged. "Not exactly bound by the rule of law. They can do anything they can get away with."

"They," Jessie said. "'They' was 'us' just a few days ago. Raises a good question, though. We know they can go scorched earth on us. Why haven't they yet?"

April shifted in her seat, looking back at her.

"Because every time we draw on Bureau resources, we essentially send up a flag letting them know exactly where we are. They weren't after us tonight, but now they know we're searching for the Cold Spectrum survivors. Just as they are."

"Aselia Boulanger. She's the last survivor." Jessie frowned, thinking it over. "If they don't know where to look, they'll just follow us right to her. Okay, we've gotta get off the grid, pronto."

"Agreed," I said. "They'll opt for soft leverage as long as they think they can follow us to Aselia. Once we throw them off our trail . . . *shit.*"

Kevin peered back at me. "What?"

I yanked my phone out and speed-dialed.

"Harmony," my mother said, "I didn't expect to hear from you tonight. Are you in town?"

Her voice was a blanket of warmth I wanted to wrap around my shoulders. I couldn't right now. Instead, I said a phrase I hoped I'd never have to speak.

"Wanted to catch you before you went on your vacation. I'm jealous. The Cayman Islands are nice this time of year."

She paused, but only for a heartbeat. "Y-yes. I'm looking forward to the trip. I'll see you when I get back."

My mother knew what I did for a living. What I *really* did for a living. My real vocation—as an agent for Vigilant Lock, under FBI cover—would be hard to hide from her. After all, everything I knew about witchcraft, I'd learned from her. And Vigilant knew about her. Linder had been to her house. We'd agreed, long ago, that there might come a time when my clandestine life went sour and she'd have to go to ground for a while, for her own safety. Referencing her "Cayman vacation" was our private warning signal for her to pack a bag and run.

"I love you, Mom."

"I love you, too, Harmony."

She hung up the phone. I cradled it in my hand.

"Escape routes," Jessie said. "We need options. All suggestions are welcome."

"We've still got the Oceanic Polymer cover," Kevin said. "That's secure."

"We *think* that's secure. Thinking and knowing could be the difference between life and death here. Let's get to the airport—I've got a way to put it to the test."

# # #

Despite the name, Atlantic City International Airport was about the size of a postage stamp. Down on the first level, bags slowly spun on a trio of luggage carousels. Jessie led the way to the Spirit Airlines check-in desk.

"What's the cheapest flight you've got?" she asked the attendant.

The woman squinted at her. "Well . . . where are you trying to go, ma'am?"

"Anywhere but New Jersey."

After a little more prodding, she offered us a seventy-nine-dollar shuttle flight into LaGuardia. We took it.

"Why are we going to New York?" Kevin asked as a printer spat out the tickets.

"We aren't," Jessie told him. "C'mon, let's go check out the gift shop. I want a souvenir. Maybe a nice plastic snow globe or something equally classy."

The gift shop looked out across the narrow concourse, a perfect vantage point and a place to hide in the clutter. All the same, I grabbed a newspaper and hid my face when Mikki strode right past us. Six men followed in her wake—no helmets, but they had to be the same men who had opened fire in the steak house. Their moves gave them away: smooth, precise, machines of lethal grace.

"Those beards, the cowboy look," Jessie murmured into my ear. "These guys aren't from the clandestine sector. They're pure special forces, born and bred."

"More elimination than investigation," I said. "It's a hit squad."

We slipped the desk clerk a twenty-dollar bribe. She told us they'd flashed FBI credentials and demanded to know our flight information. "Agent Mikki" was very insistent, she said. Once we were sure the coast was clear, Jessie hustled us back out to the parking garage.

"Well, we're burned," she said. "Our civvie covers are totally compromised, and so is the Oceanic AmEx account. On the plus side, obviously we're their only lead: they don't know Boulanger is hiding out in Des Allemands. As long as we stay under the radar, we can still get to her first."

"So we can't use our real identity or our covers," Kevin said. "Or withdraw money. Or use the card. We're kinda boned here, boss. Even if we had cash, you can't get on a plane or a train without ID these days. And we've gotta stay off cameras: they can tap image recognition, the Interstate Photo Service . . . they can do everything *we* can do."

"An intriguing conundrum," April mused. "How would we . . . escape from us? We appear to have become the villains of this story."

Jessie snapped her fingers. "Then we'll be the best damn villains anybody ever saw. Remember, we've hunted bad guys *nobody* could find. We know all the tricks they used. More important, we know how they screwed up. We just gotta learn from their mistakes. So: no planes, no trains. We're driving it. It's, what, eighteen hours from here to Louisiana? As long as Mikki and company are chasing their tails up in New York, we've still got a head start."

"The SUV was rented on the Oceanic Polymer card," April said. "They'll be able to trace its transponder."

"Not for long. Kevin, you still got that backdoor into the Budget car rental system? Can you scrub the receipts, like you did back in Oregon?"

"Gimme fifteen minutes," he said.

"You've got ten. Let's get rolling, team." Jessie took a deep breath and let it out in a sigh. "Apparently, we're gonna go pick a fight with Vigilant Lock."

"More like they picked one with us," I said.

"Yep. More like." She gave me the hint of a smile. "And, goddamn, are they gonna regret it."

NINE

We drove through the night along endless country back roads and desolate ribbons of highway, the deep and hungry American dark. Streetlights strobed in a hypnotic beat, lulling me, my slow-burn anxiety muffled under fatigue and the rhythm of the road. Eventually I had to pull over and swap places with Jessie. It felt like I'd barely closed my eyes when we were stopped again, her hand gently shaking my shoulder, waking me up for another shift change.

For a while, I thought I was the only one awake in the car. It was four in the morning, false dawn off to the left, and the radio faintly played under the sound of Jessie's and Kevin's snoring. Some local broadcast, an insomniac reading off farm-and-produce reports for an audience of nobody.

I glanced in the rearview. April was awake. Just silent. Staring out the window and watching the shadows of trees glide by in the dark.

"Are you okay?" I asked.

"Is there any reason I would be?"

I didn't know what to say to that.

April reached into the canvas tote on her lap and took out a small white plastic box. Three tiny pills bounced into her wrinkled palm.

She tossed them into her mouth one at a time and swallowed them dry.

"Prilosec, divalproex sodium, and chlortalidone," she said. "Thanks to a combination of paraplegia and advancing age. I have enough for a few more days."

"We can get you more," I said.

"Not without a prescription. And the moment I place an order, our location will light up for all to see. I'm a bit of an albatross around this team's neck at the moment."

"That's not true."

She arched an eyebrow at me. "Isn't it? Thanks to my medical condition, you're either going to have to risk capture or abandon me in the field."

"We aren't abandoning you," I said.

"No? If our roles were reversed, I'd abandon you."

I met her gaze in the mirror.

She looked back at me, cold and steely.

"What?" she said. "It's what's best for the team. Nothing matters but the mission. Isn't that your mantra?"

"I guess."

"You guess?"

I fell silent for a moment. Wrestling with the question. It felt like a serpent, slithering out of my grip, refusing to give me an easy answer.

"When I worked solo," I told her, "it was easier. I could throw myself into the job. Live the job. But now, with you and Jessie and Kevin in my life, the things we've all been through together . . . I'm seeing that there's layers to the world. Not everything is black-and-white. I guess I'm just asking more questions than I used to. Tell you what I do know, though—you're not a liability."

"Of course I am. I can't survive without my medication. I can't take a turn driving on this little road trip because my legs don't work. Tell me what I'm contributing, exactly?"

"You . . ." I trailed off, fumbling for an answer.

"You're about to say I inspire the team, aren't you? Grasping for some optimistic, feel-good platitude. You're very good at those."

I could have denied it, but we'd both know I'd be lying. So I didn't say anything at all.

"Do you know the worst thing about being disabled, Harmony?"

"No," I said.

"Everyone expecting you to be *inspirational*." April's lips curled in a smile of raw disdain. "The second you end up in a wheelchair, you're not a human being anymore. No personality, no dreams, no fears or hates or regrets. You're a sexless, faceless prop. A fetish for people's guilt, their need to show what *good people* they are, being nice to the poor cripple."

A rest stop was up ahead. A yellow sign advertised the local price for unleaded and diesel. I pulled in. We rumbled to a stop beside the pumps. I glanced back over my shoulder.

"Get out of the fucking car," I told her.

I heard her wrestling with her wheelchair on the other side of the SUV. I didn't help her. I popped the gas lid. After a minute or so, she rolled around the back of the car, looking up at me with a question in her eyes.

"I may be about to raise my voice," I told her, "and I didn't want to wake up Jessie and Kevin."

She stared at me, holding her pensive silence.

"I had a conversation with Jessie once," I said. "About you and this team. She said the only reason Linder made her the team leader is because she's half-feral. That in a kill-or-die moment, she kills without hesitation, and that's what Linder values most. She said you could lead this team. She said you usually pretty much do. She said you could do it from a cell phone, three states away from the action, if you had to. I agreed with her."

I hit the "Unleaded" button and squeezed the pump handle. The crisp night air carried the faint tang of spilled gasoline.

"When I say you're inspirational, that's what I mean. You. Dr. Cassidy, the profiler I wrote papers about in college. Jesus, I don't know if you're even aware of this, but I wrote you *fan mail* once. I didn't think we'd ever meet in person. Now? I've literally trusted you with my life more than once—with all of our lives—and you've never let us down." I looked over at her. "This isn't about your meds. It isn't about the wheelchair. It's about Mikki."

She rolled back an inch and looked away. Off toward the empty highway.

"You're right, and you're wrong. This isn't something I normally talk about. Not when Jessie's around."

"Because she was . . . responsible," I said. "For what happened to you."

April nodded. "She was another person then. Raised by a monster. Brainwashed. I've never blamed her for what she did to me, but I know she still carries the guilt. So we don't discuss it. Harmony, before that night . . . I climbed *mountains*. I competed in triathlons. Then, in one instant, one swing of an ax, all of that went away forever. It wasn't just a matter of acclimating to the chair. I had to change my life, my pursuits, but I never lost the drive to excel. To contribute. I had to find ways—mostly cerebral, now—of making a difference in the world."

"And you've done that, haven't you?"

"Not enough. Not enough to satisfy me. When Linder spoke to me about rehabilitating Mikki, turning her into an asset, he knew exactly how to stroke my ego. Reminding me what a stellar job I did with Jessie. I should have stopped him right then and there."

"Not really the same thing," I said.

"No." April frowned at the memory. "Jessie was raised by a psychopath. Mikki *is* one. But if I succeeded, if I refined a technique to draw some good from the most evil among us . . . Well, that's a moot point, isn't it? Because I failed. I failed, and innocent people died. Tonight, more died. And every one of those victims can be traced back to my doorstep. I didn't set her loose, but I certainly gave someone the idea."

The pump clicked, and the digital numbers froze.

April pursed her lips.

"It feels like I'm being mocked," she murmured.

I tilted my head at her. "How do you mean?"

"Anyone over Linder's head—the tiny handful of politicians and insiders behind Vigilant Lock—certainly knew the details of the case. They'd know about the first attempt to turn Mikki, how she faked her death and fled. They'd know the facts of the Red Knight incident, how she ended up working with Roman Steranko and Bobby Diehl. You know the old saw about the definition of insanity, right?"

"Doing the same thing over and over, expecting something different to happen?"

April took off her bifocals, wiping her blouse against a tiny smudge.

"Our masters in Washington may be cold, they may be ruthless, but they are not, to my knowledge, insane." April slipped her glasses back on. "I can see only one operational goal behind bringing Mikki into the field. To rattle us. And *me*, personally. Rattle us into making a critical mistake, or at least demoralize us. It's a calculated psychological attack."

"So they are after us. They didn't just free Mikki to go after the Cold Spectrum survivors—either now or later, we're on the menu, too."

"Indeed," April said. "We need more information. I want to see the face of our true enemy. Then we can formulate a plan to turn the tables."

I smiled. Her eyes were still hard and cold, but I could see the gears turning beneath the glacial ice.

"And that's what I mean. Right there. You were one of the best profilers in Bureau history. When it comes to data analysis, tactics, finding patterns under the chaos—you're ferocious. And that's what you bring to the team. Me and Jessie can do the heavy lifting." I tapped the side of my head. "We need your brain, and we need it now, because we've never been in trouble like this. We can't find the way out of these woods without your help."

I holstered the pump and turned the gas cap.

April nodded. Deep in thought, she turned her chair and rolled around the back of the car. Then she paused, coming back into sight.

"Harmony?"

I glanced her way. "Yeah?"

"I still have the letter you wrote me."

I laughed, feeling a twinge of embarrassment. "God, I was young. Whole other life."

"I honestly can't recall why I never replied. I believe I was on the lecture circuit then. Time slipped away from me. As it does."

"I didn't expect you to write back," I told her.

"I only mention this because I do remember what I thought when I read it. I said to myself, 'Someday, April, this young lady is going to make a fine agent.'" She tapped her finger against her chin, eyeing me. "I'm glad I was right about that much."

We got back on the highway. Danger on our heels, and somewhere up ahead, somewhere too far for our headlights to reach, one shot at finding the truth.

Too far for our headlights, but dawn was on the way.

TEN

We drove through the day and into the late afternoon. Kevin was behind the wheel by the time we rolled into Des Allemands, a sleepy town nestled in lush green and split on both sides of the bayou. Three bridges straddled the murky waters.

Louisiana took no notice of the fall: it was seventy-six degrees and sluggish, with a scent on the air like salt and some exotic, minty moss. As we crossed to the east bank, slowing down to scope out the street, the wind shifted and brought us the simmering aroma of catfish on an open grill.

"Don't know about you three," Jessie said, "but I could murder a plate or two of fish right now. How about we find someplace to stop, get something to eat, and find out if the locals are friendly?"

No objections. We pulled in at the Bait Bucket, a long shack in white clapboard. Painted alligators snapped at the logo on the sign, and Christmas-tree lights dangled, strung along the dirty eaves. Inside, a couple of slow overhead fans pushed the humidity around. A long and weathered bar stretched down one side of the room, tables on the other. We'd landed somewhere between lunch and dinner; the place was half-full, mostly on the bar stools, locals watching a grainy television and drinking long-necked bottles of beer. My stomach gurgled at the smell of fried fish, and my mouth started to water. I hadn't had anything on the road but convenience-store junk food and bad coffee.

A few trucker caps turned our way as we walked in. Curious glances, but welcoming enough. A woman in a faded calico dress came around to our table, passing out beige paper menus stained with a few years of random spills.

"Hey, folks," she said, "where y'at?"

"All right," Jessie told her with a smile. "But I think we're all starving. What's good?"

"Everything on the menu. But you are standing in the catfish capital of the universe, so that won't do you no wrong."

Jessie glanced at the list. "Catfish po'boy sounds like a winner to me."

"You want that dressed?" she asked.

"Put everything on it. Everything you can think of. I'm not a picky eater."

The rest of us followed her lead. As the woman left us, Jessie lowered her voice.

"So how are we fixed for weapons? They took our guns at the Diamondback, and we didn't exactly have time to ask for them back. I still have the nine-millimeter I grabbed off one of Ammandola's guys, but I've only got two shots left."

April reached into her tote bag, glancing over her shoulder. She slid a matte-black Glock 23 across the table. "Take mine."

Jessie made it disappear. Kevin looked between them.

"Probably a good time to talk about me getting a gun," he said.

Jessie lifted an eyebrow. "You've got a drone with a Taser on it. That's as close as you need to be getting to artillery."

"I'm *serious*. Jessie, Mikki tried to kill me once already. And considering I . . . kinda stood up to her . . ."

"There was no *kinda* about it," I told him. "Whoever let Mikki out *wants* us to be afraid right now. You and April, especially. They want us to be off our game, looking over our shoulders instead of keeping our eyes on the goal. Know the single best thing you can do about it?"

"What's that?"

"Don't give them the satisfaction," I said.

"We shouldn't tarry," April said. "Hopefully Panic Cell is chasing its own tail in New York, but we can't trust that we weren't picked up on a camera somewhere on the road. There's also the *other* party on this hunt."

"I might be able to dig up some information." I pushed my chair back. "Excuse me a second. Need to make a phone call."

I stepped outside. A pickup rumbled past, kicking up a cloud of dust, the sun starting to droop low over the bayou. A wet heat hung in the air, sticking in my lungs and making the shoulders of my blouse cling to my skin.

"Ma chérie," said the syrupy drawl on the other end of the line. "Seems you've been making quite a stir."

"Hey, Fontaine. What are you hearing?"

"Tales of intrigue and strife. Seems a certain noblewoman is most unhappy. She chased a couple of meddlesome humans clear from Portland to Atlantic City, just short of losing their trail. An embarrassing setback."

"Good to know." I paused. "So tell me about Caitlin."

He didn't answer right away. I heard a faint breath, pausing, as he weighed his options.

"Hound of Prince Sitri. Enforcer and whip hand for the Court of Jade Tears. They hold most of the West Coast."

"Considering my team hunts demons for a living, sounds like she *should* want us dead."

"Considering I am one," Fontaine said, "so should I. As it stands, you've got your own special ringtone on my telephone. Do I have one on yours?"

"She helped us in Portland. Played interference and kept Nadine busy long enough for us to escape."

"Like I told you before: she and her colleague Royce think you're useful. You can accomplish something they can't. I just don't know what that something is."

"Are you sure?" I asked.

"Am I sure I don't know?" He chuckled. "Reckon either I don't know or I'm lying to you. Answer's gonna be the same no matter how sweet you ask me."

"That's fair." I hesitated. I almost didn't want to ask the question. "How's Cody?"

"Heeding your sage advice for the nonce. He's in Los Angeles, spitting distance from Bobby Diehl's business but keeping clear for now."

"And he's off the grid?"

"Give the boy some credit," Fontaine said. "Just not too much, or I might start feelin' jealous. He knows how to keep his head down. Besides, nobody's looking for him. As far as Bobby knows, your beau met his sad demise in Talbot Cove. You worried somebody else is gonna come hunting?"

Vigilant Lock, for one, but I'd made a point of never registering Cody as an informant. During my last ill-fated trip to Talbot Cove, we'd explained my presence away as investigating loose ends from the Bogeyman case. As far as I knew, Linder didn't know Cody existed. I aimed to keep it that way.

"Probably not," I said. "But you've definitely got him under surveillance, just to be certain?"

"My apprentice, Rache, is keeping an eye on him. No worries."

"I think I met her in Vegas," I said. "She looks . . . kinda like Wednesday Addams?"

"I had a similar sentiment. I'd formally introduce you, but, well, she hates everyone, so there's really no point. Out of idle curiosity, where are you right now, exactly?"

I smiled at the phone. "Really?"

"What? Is there no trust between us, my dear? I'm wounded. Cut to the quick."

"Catch you later, Fontaine. And thanks."

"Take care of yourself, darlin'. I'm looking forward to seeing you again, and I'd prefer it *not* be on a mortician's slab. Corpses make for lousy conversation."

Back inside, lunch was on the table. Heaping sandwiches on crisp fresh-baked baguettes, fried catfish slathered in melted butter and pickle rounds. Jessie drowned hers in hot sauce. I tucked in, even hungrier than I thought I was.

"According to Fontaine, Nadine followed us as far as Atlantic City," I told them between bites. "If we lost her, good chance we lost our former colleagues, too."

"Then we'd best be on our guard," April said. "They won't wait long to escalate matters."

"You sure we can trust this guy?" Kevin asked me.

I was trusting Fontaine enough to keep Cody safe, a fact I'd decided not to share with the rest of the team. He had sworn vengeance after Bobby Diehl's terrorist attack in our hometown—Cody had almost opened fire on Diehl in Las Vegas, on a street crowded with police and federal agents—and it had taken everything I had just to convince him to stand down. For now. Fontaine's apprentice had two jobs: to keep anyone from hurting Cody, and to keep Cody from hurting himself.

A job I'd paid for with a favor to be named later.

Crossing demonic lines for information, or a temporary truce of convenience, was one thing. Swapping favors with the enemy was something else entirely. I didn't have a choice, the way I saw it, not if it meant risking Cody's life—but I couldn't tell my team that.

Between that and my visit with Romeo, I was keeping more secrets than I wanted to. Sooner or later I was going to pay a price for it. Just not right now. I was good for now.

"We can trust him when it comes to Nadine," I told Kevin. "She and her kid hate Fontaine almost as much as they hate us. Beyond that . . . I think we can trust Fontaine to do whatever's in his best interests at any given moment. And right now, that means helping us, or at least not getting in our way."

I laid my phone next to my plate, eating with one hand and flicking through pictures with the other. Thanks to Douglas Bredford's photo collection, we had a pretty good idea what the final living operative from Cold Spectrum looked like: there were three women on his team, and the photo stack had autopsy pictures for two of them. The third was a tall, willowy woman with rich brown skin and a sardonic smile. The photo captured her elbows-deep in the belly of a twin-prop plane, her gloved hands fiddling with its mechanical guts. I couldn't tell where it had been taken, but the mountains rising in the distance looked a dry and dusty world away from the bayou heat.

I caught the waitress's eye. "Excuse me, we're looking for an old friend of ours. We lost touch, but we think she might live around here. Her name was Boulanger, but she might have gotten remarried since then."

Or be using a complete alias, which was why I didn't drop a first name. Her surname, I could explain getting wrong. The woman leaned in. As she glanced to the phone, I saw the flicker of recognition in her eyes. And under that, a current of sudden suspicion.

"Aselia? Sure, she's a local. Sort of." She studied my face, hard. "What do you want with her?"

"Like I said, we're old friends."

"Well, that's funny," she said, "because she doesn't have any. She came to Des Allemands to leave her old life behind. And under no circumstances does she want it comin' back around again."

I put my phone away. "I'll level with you: trouble is on the way, whether she wants it or not, and we're trying to help her before it gets here. That old life just came back with a vengeance. You don't have to tell us where she is. If you can just get her on the phone—"

The waitress snorted. "She ain't got a phone. Look, Aselia helps out a lot of people around here. It's not something that gets talked about much, not the *way* she helps—but she helps. You're not gonna find many folks willing to let you or anybody else disturb her peace."

"We're asking," I told her. "The ones who come after us won't be asking. They'll be looking to hurt people. And they'll keep hurting people until they get at her. All we want to do is let her know what's coming and get her out of town before they show up."

She stared me hard in the eye. Hard and deep, looking for something she could trust. Whatever she saw there, she gave a nod and stepped back from the table.

"You want Beau's swamp-tour place. Up the Bayou Road, just by the Highway 631 bridge. Beau knows the way to find her. Not sayin' he'll take you, but he knows the way."

She headed back into the kitchen. Jessie splashed one last dollop of hot sauce onto the crusty edge of her sandwich and smiled.

"All right," she said. "We've got a lead, we're miles ahead of the competition—looks like everything's going our way for a change. I'm starting to feel good about this."

Kevin sat, frozen, staring off to the side. His mouth hung open. He reached over and tugged the sleeve of my jacket until I followed his line of sight, looking to the small, grainy TV set hanging over the bar.

We were on television.

ELEVEN

The television showed security-camera footage from the Diamondback. An angle on the casino floor, catching Jessie and me from above as we fled the gunfight. Distant and blurry, but definitely us.

". . . massacre at the Diamondback Casino in Atlantic City, which left twelve dead, has taken on a surprising twist," the anchorwoman said. "It appears that the thieves behind the bungled heist were a pair of federal agents on active duty."

Our photographs, scanned right from our credentials, appeared side by side on the screen.

"The two fugitive suspects, Jessica Temple and Harmony Black, allegedly used their FBI badges to gain access to the casino's counting room. When employees questioned their presence, an eyewitness tells us, they started shooting."

"Jesus," Jessie breathed. "They're pinning everything on us."

The camera shifted to a press conference. A podium on windy granite steps, cameras snapping, all eyes on a stone-faced man with a raptor-beak nose and an American-flag lapel pin on the breast of his suit. He held up a commanding hand to silence the gathered reporters as a title flashed at the bottom of the TV screen: FBI DIRECTOR BENJAMIN CROHN.

"Needless to say," he announced, "we are handling this situation with the utmost gravity. The alleged crime is a heinous one, involving the death of innocents and—if true—the deepest betrayal of these agents' badges and their oaths of office. A traitorous attack upon the American people. Warrants have been issued for Agent Temple and Agent Black's arrest, and they will answer these accusations in a court of law."

"They can't do this." Kevin's grip tightened on my sleeve. "They can't *do* this, can they?"

"They just did," I said.

The news anchor folded her hands on the studio desk as smaller versions of our photographs hovered over her left shoulder. "Director Crohn stressed that these fugitives should be considered armed and extremely dangerous. They are currently believed to be traveling with a pair of hostages, a young Caucasian male and an elderly woman. If you see them, do not attempt to approach. Instead, please call the toll-free number at the bottom of your screen—"

"What I said at the way-stop," April told me, "about seeing the face of our enemy?"

I looked her way, a question in my eyes.

"I believe we just did." She tossed a couple of bills onto the table and rolled her chair back. I followed her lead. We hadn't attracted any attention—yet—but sticking around felt like a bad idea. "Kevin, do you have a means of reaching out to Linder without risking a location trace?"

"Laptop's in the car," he said, hustling ahead of us and holding the door for her.

We piled into the SUV and hit the road. I drove slow and easy, watching the speed limit. The risk of a run-in with the local authorities loomed like a shadow over every move I made.

"They know we won't hurt the cops," Jessie growled, voicing my thoughts out loud. "They just turned every good guy with a badge in this entire country against us, and if they draw down, we *can't* shoot back."

Kevin fumbled with April's cell phone, hooking it by a USB cord to his laptop, typing fast and feverish. April sat beside him, her steady gaze as cold as an Alaskan sunset.

"And if someone reports us on that helpful tip line," she said, "Mikki and her team will have our location instantly. We won't even know we've been tracked. Which, of course, is the entire idea. They don't want us taken off the grid just yet: they want us to lead them to Aselia Boulanger first. The claim that Kevin and I are hostages will help in that regard. This will encourage local law enforcement to call the FBI for guidance first if they spot us—same result as a call to the tip line—or pin us in place until Mikki can get here."

"They called us traitors. On national television, they called us—" Jessie shook her head, clenched her jaw, and threw a punch at the glove compartment. The plastic buckled under her fist. It cracked with the sound of a gunshot, falling open, the broken lock dangling by a twisted pin. *"Fuck."*

I glanced at April in the rearview. "What did you mean back there, about the face of our enemy?"

"A theory I'm about to validate. Kevin?"

He hunched over the keyboard, working fast. "On it, Doc. Gimme thirty more seconds. I'm gonna bounce your signal to Siberia and back again, then bury it behind a half dozen proxies. Let 'em *try* to trace this."

"We knew Linder had juice inside the Bureau," Jessie muttered, "and half a dozen other alphabet agencies, but I never thought he had this kind of pull."

"I very much doubt that he does," April replied.

The phone, set to speaker mode, trilled. Kevin double-checked the cable link, rattled off a few more keystrokes, and passed it to April.

"Dr. Cassidy," Linder said, "I assume you're calling about the new development. I'm sorry, but as I told Agent Temple, this situation is out of my hands—"

"And firmly in Ben Crohn's," April said. "Tell me—how long has he been a part of Vigilant Lock's inner directorate?"

We knew about Linder's higher-ups, the shadowy figures in DC he reported to, in a general sense. There were a couple of senators, at least one retired military official, a few intelligence-sector officers—but we dealt in abstracts, not names. Everything in Vigilant Lock was compartmentalized to keep the entire illegal program safe from collapse in the event of compromise. The sole point of contact, from the bottom to the top, was Linder himself. The linchpin at the heart of the labyrinth.

"You know I can't discuss the identities of anyone who may or may not be associated with—"

"Cut the shit," April snapped. I wasn't sure if I'd ever heard her curse before. From the wide-eyed look on Jessie's face, neither had she.

"Excuse me, Dr. Cassidy?"

"You heard me," April said. "Every step of this debacle has Ben's fingerprints all over it. What did he tell you when he went over your head and brought Mikki onto the assault team? Let me guess: he wanted to rub my nose in my own failure."

"It wasn't—" Linder stammered. "I mean, I can't comment—"

"Did he tell you that he taught me everything I know?"

Silence.

"He was always fond of that line," April said. "What he didn't tell you is that I taught him something once, too. I want you to do something for me, Linder. I want you to deliver Ben a message. From me, with love."

Another pause. "I'm listening," he said, grudgingly.

"Ask Ben if he misses being a *real* FBI agent. He'll know what I mean."

She hung up on him.

Kevin blinked, unhooking the cable, lost for words. Jessie just stared at her, looking confused.

"You know the director of the FBI?" I asked her. "Like, *know* him?"

April sat back, easing against the headrest.

"A long time ago, and well before his presidential appointment. Benjamin Crohn started out in the Bureau just like I did: in the Behavioral Science Investigative Support Unit. He was my mentor. He was bright—no, brilliant. A giant in the annals of criminal psychology. And . . . a friend."

"Considering he just sent a whacked-out pyrokinetic and a hit squad after us," Jessie said, "I'm gonna guess that relationship went sour at some point."

"Correct."

We waited to see if April was going to elaborate on that. She didn't.

"So we know who's pulling Linder's strings," I said. "The important question is, what can we do with that knowledge?"

April rubbed her chin. "I'll be working on that. For now we'd best make the most of our lead time and get to Ms. Boulanger. Quickly."

# # #

SWAMP TOURS read the sign just off Up the Bayou Road, and the setting sun shone copper against the dusty windows. We parked out front, and I kept my ears perked for the sound of a television set as we approached the front door. I wasn't sure how much coverage we were getting, but I had to imagine "rogue FBI agents on a killing spree" would pretty much dominate the news cycle.

Jessie glanced sidelong at Kevin as he lugged a heavy black plastic case from the SUV. "Really? You're bringing your computer and your drone? You know we're probably getting on a boat, right?"

"I'm not leaving my stuff *here*."

The man inside the front door, his boots up on an empty desk, looked like he was born with the butt of a cigar in his mouth. He swung his legs down, sat up, and snuffed his smoke in a grimy ashtray as we walked in. When he smiled, sweat glistened on his whiskers.

"How y'at, folks! I'm Beauregard, owner and proprietor. Y'all lookin' for a tour?"

"We're looking for Aselia Boulanger," Jessie said. "Lady at the Bait Bucket says you can take us to her."

His eyes narrowed. "Can. Can don't mean will."

"She's got trouble coming," I told him. "We need to warn her before it's too late."

Beau's steady gaze swung my way. He looked me up and down.

"Could be. Could be *you* are the trouble."

"Tell us how we can prove it to you," I said.

"We don't mean her any harm," April said. "Just the opposite."

"Could be. All the same, trouble ain't a thing I like bringing into the bayou. See, Aselia's known in these parts as a miracle worker, though I suppose her miracles ain't entirely of the Christian variety. She works the gris-gris—get my meaning?"

"So do the people who are coming to hurt her," I said. "And they will, if we don't find her first."

"My reluctance, that's not for Aselia's sake." Beau looked past us, over my shoulder, his gaze going distant. "Few years back, some men from out west came asking around about her. They had guns and money and bad attitudes. So, I took 'em out into the swamp. They never did come back again. And the gators? They looked *fat*."

Beau locked eyes with me.

"I'll take you," he said, "but if you're lyin', I'm not the one you're gonna have a problem with. The bayou protects its own."

TWELVE

Beau's airboat was around back, an old and battered warhorse propelled by a giant fan mounted on the stern. The hull rocked under my feet, wobbling in murky olive waters. He passed out earmuffs, bulky yellow plastic headphones, and fired up the engine. The fan roared like the open belly of a truck engine, harsh and hungry.

We cast off. North. Into the swamp.

The airboat cruised slow and smooth between tangled clumps of oak trees. The trees stretched out twisted limbs, their boughs dripping with long spiderweb strands of Spanish moss. Beau pointed to a dangling branch up ahead. The dying sunlight shone off an antique key, heavy and forged from hammered brass, dangling from a gray string and slowly twisting in the breeze.

"Gotta follow the keys," he called out over the thrum of the fan. "Follow the keys, you find Aselia. Gotta watch careful, though."

I looked back over my shoulder as he steered the boat with a rudder, turning us to starboard. "Yeah? Why's that?"

"Sometimes the keys move."

We sailed through the bayou deeps. The sun was a smear of blood on the horizon now, shimmering and low, sending long shadows across the brackish water. Some of the shadows squirmed. A gator's head broke the surface, and the beast lazily undulated past us, eight feet of scale slithering in and out of the brine.

"Gonna see more of those as we get close," Beau said. "Gotta watch the snakes, too. We got cottonmouths, canebrake rattlers . . . you get bit out here, you'll be dead before you ever catch sight of dry land."

The oaks parted. Up ahead, the glow of lantern light. Soft fires mimicked the orange of the setting sun, washing the bayou waters in the colors of autumn and silence. The lanterns dangled from posts and eaves of an old gray shack, propped up on a lopsided, leaning pier. Beau killed the engine.

As the airboat glided in, the front door of the shack groaned open. Aselia Boulanger barely looked a day older than her picture, though her long raven hair had turned as gray as the worm-eaten wood at her back. The hem of a long and worn lavender dress swayed over her bare feet, and she cradled a double-barreled shotgun in an easy grip.

"That's plenty close enough," she said. "What are you bringing to my doorstep, Beau?"

"Say they're here to help," he called back. Ten feet of water lay between us and the pier. And the water was moving. Long, wriggling shadows, snakes under the surface, circling our boat.

"Help, huh?" Aselia said. "Read my cards this morning. Said a bad wind was comin' my way. Fire and death."

"Sounds like Mikki," Kevin muttered.

I stepped closer to the prow. "Houston Coe sent us."

Aselia's fingers curled a little tighter on the shotgun.

"Don't see him on the boat," she said.

"I'm sorry. He's dead. He was murdered in Atlantic City."

Her eyes narrowed. "Ain't that convenient."

"He said to tell you—" I paused, racking my memory. Remembering Houston's last words before he went up in flames. "He said to tell you, 'Paris was nearsighted anyway.'"

The ghost of some painful memory, some old heartbreak, swept over Aselia's face. Then she gave me a slow, wistful smile. Her hands relaxed.

"Old inside joke," she said. "We liked using those as pass phrases, back in the day. He figured anyone could torture a formal password out of you. We had a thing for that. If you came in here, telling me he said to say 'wormwood' or 'sigma fifteen,' it'd be a sign Houston told that to you under severe duress."

"And then?" I asked.

"And then I'd take this shotgun and blow your goddamned head off." Aselia shrugged. "But you said the right words, so I guess I gotta find somebody else to shoot. Knew this was coming. Heard about Douglas biting it up in Michigan. Once he was gone, only a matter of time before the dominoes started tumbling my way."

"He arranged it that way," I said. "He left a trail of bread crumbs for us to follow. I think he wanted us to find you. To warn you."

Aselia smiled. "Man had contingencies inside contingencies. He always did. And you are who, exactly?"

"We're with a—I mean, we *were* with a—" I shook my head. "It's a long story, and we should probably talk it out someplace safer than here. Will you come with us?"

"Let me get my boots on," she said.

We didn't have to wait long. She came back out of the shack with a pair of battered steel-toed boots on and a frayed duffel bag slung over her shoulder. Beau steered us in close, and she jumped down from the pier, into the belly of the boat.

"Gonna miss this place," Aselia said. "Still, operational dictum: never have a life you can't walk away from in thirty seconds; never care about anything you can't pack in a bugout bag."

I looked past her, at the smoke starting to billow from the shack's windows. Flames licked the inner walls, growing fast and hot.

"You set your own house on fire?" I asked her.

"Basic occult-forensic countermeasure."

Jessie flashed a broad smile and clapped Aselia on the shoulder. "Oh, I think you and me are gonna be friends."

Beau fired up the engines and turned us around. A little slower now, a little closer to the waterline, but we made good time despite the growing dark. Glimmering stars rose up to light our way. Steering us back to civilization, Beau put on speed as the tangled oaks broke and we hit the open swamp water.

He squinted into the dark and pointed up ahead.

I saw them, too. Another pair of airboats, headed straight for us.

"Go around!" I shouted, just before the first gunshot rang out. Beau yanked the rudder hard and veered left, my footing almost jerking out from under me as the boat careened. The twin boats turned like circling sharks. They came at us broadside, bullets peppering the water.

Aselia threw up her arm, pointing, and shouted to Beau. "That way, it's tighter over there—harder for 'em both to come at us!"

"Easier for me to wreck this damn boat, too," he shouted back.

She yanked a shotgun from the bag. Not the old pump action she'd brandished on the porch, but a nasty little sawed-off number.

"Do it anyway," she yelled and shouldered the gun.

To her left, Jessie dropped to one knee, steadying her Glock in a two-handed grip. One eye squinted as she took careful aim. I reached to the canopy of stars, gathering my power, as I strained to see our attackers in the dark. If Nadine had found us, we were about to battle an incarnate demon. If it was Mikki's crew, a pyrokinetic who could kill from a distance.

I got my answer in a heartbeat, as tiny fireflies danced across Aselia's flesh.

Line of sight. She couldn't burn what she couldn't see. On instinct, my mind brushed the face of the bayou. Ancient, brackish waters, teeming with life and secrets. And I *pulled*. A wall of water erupted into the air between us and the oncoming boats, eight feet high, roaring as it cascaded in a churning wave.

The fireflies died. One of the airboats crashed into the water wall at full speed, shattering it, the other veering hard to go around and slipping behind us. A bullet pinged into the fan grating. The drenched boat shot up on our right, a wall of tangled oaks coming up fast before us. I hit the deck as a gunshot cracked a few inches past my ear. Beau took the hit. The bullet splintered his skull, straight through the temple, and suddenly we were kicking up water and veering out of control as his dead hand yanked hard on the rudder. Aselia's shotgun roared. She staggered off balance, spent her shells to force the other boat back, then the empty piece clattered at her feet. She ran over and grabbed Beau's body, shoving him overboard and taking his seat. We spun hard in the other direction, the boat skipping hard and the engine redlining.

Jessie fired off a couple of rounds, staying low. "Can you drive these things?" she shouted.

"Not drive. Pilot," Aselia said through gritted teeth. "And I can pilot *anything*."

The airboats circled, both of them trying to get alongside us for a clean shot. We swung around, leaving a perfect opening as Aselia pointed us to the oaks. Digging deep, feeling my stomach clench into knots and a wave of heat washing over me, I conjured up another water wall. This one smaller than the last, crashing down twice as soon, my strength running out.

I shot a look to my left. A man stood on the prow of the second boat, bringing up the silhouette of a long-barreled rifle, locking us in the glint of a night-vision scope. Then a small matte-black .32 in April's clenched hands spat fire, three quick rounds, and the rifleman tumbled from the boat and splashed down into the brine.

Jessie looked at her, wide-eyed. "You carry a hold-out piece? Since when?"

"Since always." April glanced at her. "Why don't *you*? I raised you better than that."

We hit the gap between the oaks, the boat bouncing over brambles and tangled debris. Aselia jerked hard on the rudder and steered us through the shallows as more shots pinged off the fan at her back. Two more fast, tight turns, and the gunfire stopped, but I could still hear the whine of distant engines on our tail.

"This patch of the bayou's like a maze," Aselia called out. "I know it like the back of my hand. Doubt they do. You got an exit strategy?"

"We've got an SUV parked back in town, at Beau's place."

"Beau." Aselia shook her head. "Goddamn it. I liked Beau. He brought me beer sometimes. If your ride's still there, it's compromised, which means your exit strategy is shit. We'll use mine instead."

Kevin, clinging to the floor and looking nauseous, shot Jessie a look. "And you wanted me to leave my stuff in the car."

The pursuing engines faded into the distance. The sounds of the sultry night swept back in, the hoots of night birds ringing out over the thrum of our fan. Aselia slowed the boat, easing through tight bends in the tangled oaks. A mosquito landed on my cheek, drawn by the smell of sweat, and I brushed it away.

"Doubt you did all this out of the goodness of your heart," Aselia told me, "but I'm not ungrateful. Ready to hear that long story now."

I didn't see any reason not to lay everything on the line.

"We're operatives for Vigilant Lock," I told her. "It's a black-ops program designed to hunt and eliminate occult threats to the United States."

Aselia wore a poker face. She looked my way, nodding slow. "Go on."

"We crossed Douglas Bredford's path on an unrelated investigation. He pointed us toward an old and buried operation. Cold Spectrum. He was killed not long after that, but he left a trail of clues—photographs, a USB stick filled with old files—just enough to guide us."

"And what do you know," she asked me, "about Cold Spectrum?"

"We know that the project's members were targeted for assassination by our own government. That a clandestine op called Glass Predator, intended for eliminating domestic terrorists, was called in to make the kill. Before he took over Vigilant, a man named Linder—our boss—was the guiding hand behind Glass Predator. All three of these programs are . . . connected, somehow, and Linder is the common thread."

"That he is," Aselia said, almost too low to hear.

"You know him?"

"I do," she said. "Not sure *you* do, though. Hold on—we're almost clear. I want us off the ground and far away from here as fast as humanly possible. You and me, we've got a lot to talk about."

THIRTEEN

We put in at an empty dock somewhere north of the city. The prow of the airboat bumped a plastic buoy. Aselia was the first one out, jumping up onto the warped wooden planks.

"Don't bother tying her off. We're not coming back." She waved us along. "C'mon, I don't know how much of a lead we've got. Let's move."

We hustled along a grassy embankment and across a narrow strip of black tarmac. Up ahead, electric lights burned inside a small hangar, the curving arch of the roof just tall and wide enough for a single twin-prop plane. A man in greasy overalls was up on a stepladder and halfway inside the open canopy of the Cessna's engine, tools scattered around his feet.

"Marco!" Aselia shouted. "Marco, tell me she can fly. Tell me you fixed the intake manifold."

The man looked over at her and shrugged. He had the docile eyes of a cow and a big, wide mouth.

"It's okay," he said. "It's okay. Just fiddlin'."

"*No fiddling.* Seal her up. That thing I said might happen someday? It just happened."

Marco slammed the canopy and jumped down from the ladder.

"Okay," he said, placating. "It's okay."

Kevin looked around the cluttered hangar and out to the sparse landing strip.

"Wait a second," he said. "Small plane, unlisted runway in the middle of nowhere. Are . . . are you a smuggler?"

Aselia pursed her lips. "I'm an occasional purveyor of herbal medicinal remedies."

"You're a weed smuggler."

"Everybody's gotta pay the bills," she said. "Why are you here, anyway? Are you even old enough to shave?"

"I pulled him out of witness protection," Jessie told her. "Needed a hacker."

Aselia ran along the side of the Cessna, flung open the side door, and pulled down the boarding steps. She paused, looking back at Jessie.

"Yeah," Aselia said. "We probably are going to get along just fine. Okay, everybody on board. Marco, go to our safe house and stay there. I'll contact you at the dead drop in Baton Rouge once I'm clear."

"Okay, okay," he said, walking backward with his open palms raised.

I climbed into the back of the plane, sitting down just as the aftermath hit me. My guts cramping up, burning like someone shoved a branding iron into my belly. As April strapped in, Kevin folding her chair and stowing it with the luggage, her brow furrowed.

"You weren't hit, were you?"

I shook my head. "No, it's this . . . all that energy I was throwing around, keeping Mikki off us. It's the family curse. The more power I pull, the more I pay for it after. It'll pass in about fifteen minutes. I'm good."

I wasn't good. When I'd used my magic in Atlantic City, it had been effortless. Flowing like water from an open tap, clear and easy and not even a twinge when I was done. This time was a little harder—and as I slowly recovered, a too-familiar hunger started creeping in around the edges. The rush of power I'd stolen from Romeo's kiss was wearing off.

Aselia eyed her instruments and flipped rocker switches on the console, running through a preflight checklist at top speed. Jessie took the copilot seat, strapping in beside her.

"We're going to New Orleans," Aselia said. "We'll put in at a private airport—the owner goes deaf and blind if you kick him twenty bucks—and head for this place in the French Quarter. Restaurant with a sideline in moving contraband. They know me there. More important, they won't sell me out. Then we can plan our next move, which I imagine is gonna involve a lot of guns."

"Tell me you're single," Jessie said.

"Sorry, wrong team."

"It's true what they say," Jessie sighed. "All the good ones are straight or married."

Aselia jerked her thumb over her shoulder. "I figured you were with her."

"Harmony? Oh, no, she's straight, too."

Aselia paused. She turned in her seat, looking me up and down, taking in my suit and tie.

"Dressed like that," she said.

Jessie nodded, wide-eyed. "I know, right?"

The engine purred like a tiger, and the propellers began to spin. We rolled out of the hangar, taking a sharp left turn to line up with the runway, landing gear rumbling as we poured on the speed. Then we were airborne, lifting up into the starry night sky. Our hunters behind us and the answers we'd been looking for dead ahead. I thought I was ready to uncover the truth.

I wasn't. But that's the thing about buried secrets: when they emerge, you have to face them. Ready or not.

# # #

Raimond's was on Bienville, just off Bourbon Street. A touch of the old world, with white wood slats, ornate black ironwork, and windows tinted absinthe green. A black-tied maître d' swooped in and kissed Aselia on both cheeks. They spoke in soft Creole, the man's expression turning grave as he listened. He nodded and ushered us across the candlelit dining room, past tables draped in emerald cloth, and up a short hallway.

Beyond a locked door, a private dining room awaited. A single large table, big enough for a dozen people, beneath a glass chandelier. The deep-green walls, the same shade as the tablecloth, were festooned with old sepia-toned portraits of grave men in military uniforms. A few had names scribbled in faded margins, but I didn't recognize them.

"You'll be safe here," he said in English. "Have you eaten?"

"Best food in the city," Aselia told us, then looked to the maître d'. "Besides, no telling when we're gonna get another solid meal. Let's start with the *huitres thermidor*, *escargots à la Bordelaise*, and the *écrevisses cardinal.*"

He backed out of the room, shutting the door behind him. We took our seats at the table.

"We came a long way to find you," I told Aselia.

"I wasn't aiming to be found. I assume you know about the RedEye patch, right? When the kill order went out, Douglas couldn't save us all. He had to pick. Who would live, who would die."

"I think it broke him," I said. "When we met him in Michigan . . . he wasn't in good shape."

"*That* wasn't what broke him. It was just the cherry on top. Anyway, he picked the people he thought would have the best chance of survival. Houston was obvious: with that precognition trick of his, he could get out of almost anything. Always said nobody could take him down unless they boxed him in." Aselia sighed, her gaze going distant. "I guess they boxed him in, huh?"

"There wasn't any way out. He told us that right before he told us where to find you. I'm sorry."

"As for me," Aselia said, "I was Cold Spectrum's transportation and logistics expert. Air, water, land—I could move men and material in and out of hot spots all over the nation. Stealth mode. When it came to getting off the grid and digging in deep, nobody did it better than me. So Douglas figured I'd have a shot. I got my shot, and my friends, my teammates, people I trusted my life to . . . they didn't. RedEye tracked them, Glass Predator hunted them, and one by one they started filling graveyards."

She fell silent as the door opened. A pair of waiters swooped in with glasses, spreading them around the table, uncorking bottles.

"A 2013 Domaine la Chapelle," one told Aselia. "Compliments of the house."

Dollops of chardonnay, like liquid sunlight, splashed into the crystal glasses. Aselia raised hers, sniffed, took a sip, and nodded her approval. When the waiters got to Kevin's glass, he glanced left and right at April and me.

"So . . . nobody's stopping them? You're actually letting me have a glass of wine?"

Deep in thought, her fingers steepled and her glass untouched, April didn't reply. I didn't stop him, either. Right now, underage-drinking laws seemed like the furthest from anything I cared about. Maybe I just thought we were all about to need a drink.

The waiters left us. The door clicked shut.

"We know Linder was involved with Glass Predator," I said. "Was it him? Did he give the kill order?"

Aselia shrugged. "Maybe? Maybe not. He probably made the call, but not the actual decision. Linder's a middleman. That's his niche, the nice little spot he's carved out in the shadows of Washington, DC. He gets his hands dirty so other men—wealthier, more powerful ones—don't have to. We always reported directly to him. Never got a line on the people above him."

"Wait," Jessie said. "He was *also* part of Cold Spectrum? Linder was involved in all three operations?"

Aselia raised her glass. The wine glimmered in the candlelight.

"You're asking the wrong question," she said.

"Try this one, then," I told her. "Aselia, what *was* Cold Spectrum?"

She gave me a cold and ugly smirk.

"Cold Spectrum," she said, "was a black-ops program designed to hunt and eliminate occult threats to the United States."

I shook my head, hearing my own words from the airboat parroted back at me.

"Is this a joke? Aselia, that's . . . that's *us*. That's Vigilant Lock."

"Sure is."

She laid her palms flat on the table.

"You're just the latest flavor," she told us. "Vigilant Lock *is* Cold Spectrum. You've been chasing your own shadows since day one. Same covert program, same people in charge, with a shiny new coat of paint. And now you're learning what happens to Linder's people when they get too close to the truth: the exact same thing that happened to us."

FOURTEEN

A chill descended upon the room, the icy hand of an autumn midnight. The electric chandelier couldn't chase it away. Neither could the wine, as I tossed back a swig and swallowed hard. No warmth in the bottle, just more confusion.

"We weren't the first, either," Aselia said. "I did as much digging as I had time for, when the shit hit the fan. Far as I can tell, the original version of our little black-ops adventure started in the late 1960s. Lyndon B. Johnson was the first and *last* president to be kept in the loop. The original team lasted almost a decade on the job, with, of course, regular turnover in staff. Then the program was abruptly mothballed."

"What happened to the team?" Kevin asked.

Aselia made a gun with her fingers and pressed them to the side of her head. She let out a puff of breath as she pulled the imaginary trigger.

"There are two ways out of this life," she told us. "You die fighting the monsters, or you get to the little rotten nugget of truth at the heart of this whole mess. How clued in are you people? What do you know about the infernal courts?"

I thought back to our first meeting with Fontaine, in a bustling Michigan diner. How he'd laid out the map of the universe over a plate of pancakes he couldn't eat.

"At some point, a long time ago," I said, "there was a civil war in hell. After the dust cleared, the courts rose up. Each one has a prince and a hound—their right-hand agent on Earth. And, if everything we've been told is true, they've laid claim to territory here."

Aselia swirled her wineglass. "Every inch. From the Court of Jade Tears on the West Coast to the Court of Windswept Razors on Wall Street. Overseas, too. Every spot of dirt on the globe and most of the water."

"They're not united, though," Jessie said. "They just don't fight openly, and they've got rules they pretend to follow. What did Fontaine call it, Harmony? The Cold Peace?"

"Cold *war*, more like it," Aselia said. "Demons are almost as good as politicians when it comes to twisting words around. And, yeah, the courts hate each other, but full-on hostility would cause a dog pile. One court steps up, commits their troops to a battle, and suddenly five others would jump in and carve them up like a Thanksgiving turkey."

I reached for the bottle and poured myself another splash of wine. "So they scheme around. Stab each other in the backs, but not in a way that can be traced back to the source. It's just like Earth's Cold War, but between a dozen small nations who all hate each other instead of a pair of superpowers."

"We were on a mission in Utah when everything went sideways," Aselia said. "Our last mission. Linder called our target: a cult of cambion, demon half bloods, holing up in this desolate farmhouse. They were terrorists, he told us. Getting ready to launch a major attack on the East Coast. We found the cult, we found the explosives, we found the evidence. Mission successful. But Douglas, he smelled a rat. And he kept digging."

I remembered Bredford's drunken confession, his words to the director of RedEye.

"The last shot at the last battle," I said, my voice low as I echoed them out loud. "Douglas said . . . humanity lost."

Aselia's gaze went distant. Her hand tightened around the stem of her glass, turning her knuckles white.

"Sure did," she said. "See, we went down the rabbit hole. And what we found at the bottom was the truth. We found out who we were really working for."

An icy fingertip ran down my spine.

"Tell us," I said.

"The courts don't fight head-on, but they sure do love using proxies. Proxies and patsies."

Aselia sat back in her chair. Looking across the table, taking us all in one by one before looking me in the eye.

"Cold Spectrum, Vigilant Lock, every incarnation of the program, no matter what name they slap on it . . . it was created and sponsored by the infernal courts. There *is* no human resistance. There never was. You aren't fighting the powers of hell, Harmony. You *work* for them."

"That's not—" Kevin said, a stammer in his voice. "That's not true. That can't be true."

"This is an east side–west side feud," Aselia said. "The courts clustered along the East Coast are smaller, weaker than the heavy hitters out west. So they put their heads together and hatched a plan. A team of humans who believe they're fighting to protect humanity from the things that go bump in the night. And technically that's true. Except what they're really hunting is anyone the eastern coalition wants taken out. And when they do, well . . . who's to blame? Just some meddling humans. Hands clean. Every once in a while—like we did back then, like you are now—somebody figures out the game. So they scrub the program, sanction the operatives, and start it up all over again under a new name."

"She's making this up." Kevin looked to April, desperate now. "She is, isn't she?"

April's face was carved from stone. She sat perfectly still and silent.

Aselia looked him over. "Tell me something: How often have you been sent after a demon on the East Coast? Ever? Even once?"

The answer was written in Kevin's eyes. "Once," he said.

"Once. Out of how many missions? That one—I guarantee he pissed off people he shouldn't have. You were doing pest control for the courts of hell."

"We've done good work," Jessie said. "We've helped people. *Saved* people."

Aselia shrugged. "I'm sure you have. Doesn't change the tune you were dancing to, same as us. The purpose of this program is simple: weaken the western courts, strengthen the eastern coalition, take out anything that might cause trouble down the line. Human sorcerers who don't toe the line, independent factions—"

"The Network," I said. "Linder's obsessed with getting an inside man. We've even got a no-kill order on Bobby Diehl, in the hopes they can use him as a wedge."

"They're not demons," Aselia said. "I don't know what they are, but these Kings the Network serves are something on a whole different level. And the powers of hell are piss-scared of 'em."

"Your last mission. What did you find?" I asked.

The door opened. Waiters swirled in with plates and steaming trays, laying it all out across the emerald tablecloth. Louisiana gulf oysters served in tomato sauce with specks of bacon, crawfish tails in white-wine sauce, basted and baked snails drizzled with bread crumbs and cheese. The mingled aromas filled the air, savory and rich, but my stomach rebelled at the idea of eating right now.

They brought us another bottle of wine. That, I could have. I refreshed my glass and waited for the waiters to leave.

"The 'cult' was a faction of separatists calling themselves the Redemption Choir," Aselia said. "Half-breeds who believed they were born damned, and could be redeemed by fighting the powers of hell."

I sat up in my chair. "Redemption Choir? Wait a second, I crossed paths with them out in Nevada. Their leader, Sullivan—he was the first incarnate demon I ever faced."

"And I know about Sullivan," Aselia said. "Major whack job. The rank and file were a lot more reasonable, trust me. Well, as reasonable as fanatics get. This particular group had hived off from the main Choir: they thought Sullivan had gone around the bend and was going to get them all killed. Again, didn't know any of this until later. As part of the briefing, Linder gave us a dossier of their 'victims.' Once we dug in, we learned the truth: every last one of the dead was an agent for the eastern coalition. Half of 'em weren't even human. The Redemption Choir was innocent. They didn't hunt humans—they hunted monsters. Hell, they were doing our job better than we were."

"And you sanctioned them," Jessie said.

Aselia's voice dropped. Faint, distant, carrying the weight of memory.

"We murdered them. Bang, bang, bang. Shot first and asked questions later, just like we were trained to." She raised her wineglass, staring into it. "Just following orders, ma'am. And later, we found out just what we'd done. A big chunk of this splinter group—these guys were half magicians, half scientists. Eggheads working on their magnum opus. They called it Archangel."

Jessie squinted at her. "What was it supposed to do?"

"Kill incarnates. They were creating a weapon capable of destroying an incarnate demon. And it was going to work. That was the 'terrorist attack' they were planning: they were going to assassinate a hound. And me and Douglas and Houston and the others . . . we stormed into that farmhouse, and we gunned them down before they could do it. They could have built a tool to swing the fight against hell in humanity's favor for the first time in history. They could have saved the world. And we killed them for it."

The room fell into a dismal silence. The appetizers grew cold, untouched.

"So what happens now?" Kevin asked. The question hung in the air like the blade of a guillotine.

"Well, my cover's blown," Aselia said. "I'm in the same bag you are. We can run. We can hide. I'd love to give you a pep talk, kid, but I'm a realist. What happens now? We're probably all gonna die."

"No," April said.

It was the first thing she'd said since the meal began. She'd spent the entire time in rapt concentration, taking in every word, calculating. She laid her hands on the table.

"No," she said. "Now we fight."

Aselia's eyebrows lifted. "Are you kidding me? Look, every demon on the East Coast and all their human toadies want us dead. Washington wants us dead. They can send the cops after us. They can send the entire FBI. They can probably send the goddamn marines. If there's any way out of this rat trap, there's an entire army standing between us and the door."

Jessie looked to April. She nodded slowly, sharing her resolve. "I'll take those odds."

"We have avenues of information you never did," April told Aselia. "For instance, we know one of the men Linder reports to. Benjamin Crohn."

"The director of the FBI?" Aselia said. "Oh, even better."

"He's only a man," April said. "He can be manipulated. He can be turned. We also have allies. There's another Vigilant team, Beach Cell, embedded inside Diehl Innovations. If these eastern courts are so concerned about the Network . . . perhaps we can give them a fight to be afraid of. Or the appearance of one."

"We've also got a private military contractor in our back pocket," Jessie said, looking my way. "Assuming he's a man of his word—flip a coin and pray—Angus Caine owes us a favor for letting him walk last time we crossed paths. Xerxes is a shadow of what it used to be, but I bet they can still bring a little thunder."

"And then there's Senator Roth," I said. "We know his presidential campaign is being backed by demonic patrons, and we've still got that blackmail file hanging over his head. Maybe we could use it to pull some influence in DC."

Kevin nodded, fast. His fear giving way to nervous energy and the ghost of a smile.

"What about the western courts? I mean, if we could prove what Vigilant Lock really is, wouldn't that blow this whole thing up? God, we might be able to start another civil war. Demons fighting demons. That means humanity *wins*."

Aselia blinked. She shook her head, glancing from face to face, her lips slightly parted. "This is crazy—you're all crazy—but . . . this is the kind of crazy I can get behind. Fuck it, I'm on board. Let's do it."

"We need intel," Jessie said, "the inside scoop on the people at the top. And there's one place to find it."

She slapped her phone down on the table. She'd pulled up the picture of Linder from Bredford's photographs. Our former taskmaster surrounded by suits on the steps of the Capitol Building, his face circled by a bloodred bull's-eye.

"As of right now, we're starting a brand-new Hostile Entities list," Jessie said, "and our good buddy Linder is number one with a bullet."

She looked across the table and locked eyes with me.

"Let's *get* this motherfucker."

FIFTEEN

Kevin stared down at the phone. "Get him. Like . . . ?" He ran a finger across his throat.

Jessie folded her arms and shook her head.

"*Alive.* We kidnap him, we take him someplace nice and private, and we squeeze him dry. He's the middleman. He has to know the names of everybody at the top. Who they are, where they are, how we can take them out."

Jessie pushed her chair back. She stood, looming over the table. Her outstretched fingertips pressed against the emerald cloth as she leaned in.

"So we got hoodwinked. So we got used. I'll tell you something: I still believe in Vigilant Lock. The men behind the curtain might be full of shit, but the mission's true. So let's snatch Linder, force him to clear our names, and then *clean house.* We can take over Vigilant from the inside. We can turn it into the organization we believed it was."

"Linder's mobile," I said, "always. He never stands still, never stays in one place for more than a night. We'll have to lure him into a trap."

"He keeps telling us to turn ourselves in," Kevin said. "What if we do? I mean, what if we pretend to? Would he fall for it?"

April steepled her fingers, brow furrowed in thought.

"No. At this point it's obvious we're chasing the Cold Spectrum survivors and may have learned the truth. That makes us threats. Have you ever known Linder to react to a threat with anything less than overwhelming and deadly force? That said . . ." Her gaze drifted across the table, to Aselia. "It was dark, out on the bayou. Gunfire in all directions."

Aselia followed her lead. "I could have been shot. Killed. Meaning you don't know anything at all."

"We need to consider all of our primary actors." April ticked them off on her fingertips. "Linder will act out of self-preservation, above anything else. He's well trained, a seasoned covert operative and analyst, but predictable. Mikki is not. She's a narcissistic psychopath who kills for pleasure, meaning we can only trust that someone has her on a firm enough leash. If not, we'll be counting on Harmony to counter her magic."

"I've got it handled," I said. I hoped I wouldn't have to prove it.

April adjusted her bifocals. "The members of Panic Cell are either actively compromised, knowing they're working in hell's service, or they're indoctrinated to the point that it doesn't matter. They'll follow the orders they're given. They also have no qualms about civilian casualties, something we'll need to keep in mind when it comes to a direct confrontation. Which brings us to their master, Benjamin Crohn. Our most dangerous opponent and our most valuable potential prize. We have an edge, there. Me."

"Yeah," Jessie said, "what is it with you and Crohn? I know you didn't want to talk about it, but I think it's time to put all the cards on the table."

April reached for her wineglass. "He was my mentor. My partner."

"We got that part," Jessie said.

"He was also my lover. Until our . . . falling-out."

"So we've got Mikki, Crohn . . ." Kevin looked my way. "If you or Jessie have an evil ex, you should probably tell us about it right now before they come back for revenge. I'm sensing a theme here."

"Not evil," April said. "Vain. Greedy for the spotlight. As short-sighted as he was proud. We worked a case together: Otto Mars, the so-called Englewood Impaler."

"Heard about that," Jessie said. "Ugly business."

"A bit of ugly business who almost went free on a technicality. The arresting officers overreached. Critical evidence was obtained on a warrantless search and insufficient probable cause. Mars's lawyer had it thrown out—as well as all the evidence that followed. Fruit of the poisonous tree."

Jessie shook her head. "But he didn't walk, right? I thought that guy was still in a super-max, locked down until the second coming."

"He is. Because Ben followed up on his own and investigated a storage locker rented in Mars's name, with a scrapbook containing pho-tographs of the crime scenes. All the suppressed evidence was allowed back in under the doctrine of inevitable discovery, and the conviction was a cakewalk." April sipped her wine. "Only one problem. I'd already seen that scrapbook. In Mars's bedroom."

"Crohn tampered with evidence?" I asked.

"Otto Mars didn't rent a storage locker," April said. "His signature on the lease was a forgery. A good one. The employee who rented it developed an amazing strain of selective amnesia as well. Ben took the scrapbook from the sealed house, planted it in the locker, and used it to get a conviction."

Jessie winced. "Skeevy move, but still. I mean, we do some skeevy stuff, too. When you've gotta get the bad guy, you've gotta get the bad guy. At least Otto didn't go free."

"No. But I asked myself . . . Otto Mars was guilty as sin, but was he the only person Ben had done this to?"

"I'm guessing it wasn't," I said.

"I couldn't prove it," April said. "If I could have proved it, I'd have arrested him myself. But a long string of suspicious evidence tainted at least a dozen of Ben's arrests. His 'miraculously insightful profiles' bearing out as absolutely correct, thanks to some key clues he personally found . . . in already-searched crime scenes."

"Hell of a coincidence," Aselia said.

"Isn't it? And unlike Mars, none of those people—all of whom were tried and convicted on the strength of Ben's findings—were slam-dunk cases. Any number of them could have been innocent. I couldn't *prove* it, though. And I'll spend the rest of my life wondering."

"So what'd you do?" Jessie asked.

"I told him we were through. And I told him *he* was through. I gave him a choice: leave the Bureau of his own free will, or I'd go public with what I knew. I couldn't prove he'd committed any crimes, but the sheer weight of circumstantial evidence would destroy his reputation." April sank in her chair. "Granting that man any mercy at all was the greatest mistake of my entire life. I still had feelings for him, even then. So he resigned. He became a *political* animal after that. Two successful Senate runs, and eventually he wormed his way into a presidential appointment. Returning to the FBI in victory laurels."

"Running the whole show this time," Jessie said.

"With Vigilant Lock at his disposal, an entire black-ops unit to do his bidding, and the powers of hell at his back, it would appear. But he never forgave me. Fieldwork, that was his passion and his pride. I took that away from him."

"If he's still holding a grudge after all these years," Kevin asked, "why would he let Linder recruit you in the first place?"

"An excellent question, and one I look forward to asking in person." April offered a subtle nod. "I'm prepared to deliver my analysis."

"Please do," I said.

"Linder will accept an offer to meet. It will be a trap, a pretext to have us all killed. At this point—with Benjamin taking the field personally, racking up civilian casualties in Atlantic City, drawing potential attention to the program—Linder will be on the edge of panic. Also, the stress in his voice betrayed that Mikki really was freed against his objections; he's not that good of an actor. He's losing control of the situation, which is the one thing Linder absolutely cannot tolerate. It's his pressure point."

"Wipe us all out," Jessie said, "Crohn stops rampaging all over the place, Mikki goes back to prison, everything's nice and peaceful again."

April nodded. "Precisely. He'll take the most direct path to equilibrium, just as he always does. *But.* Director Crohn is in the field now. He didn't have to do that; Panic Cell could take their briefing via a long-distance video call, just as we usually do. They're obviously more than capable."

"He's making this personal," I said.

"Precisely. Mikki was released as a weapon against *us*, on Benjamin's orders. Specifically against me. His behavior is reckless. Blind to consequences. And I know what he wants." April raised her wineglass. "He wants what he's always wanted. To prove that he's better than me."

Aselia shook her head, not following. "Better? Better how?"

"We were always competitive, even when we were sharing a bed. Struggling to see who could follow a chain of evidence faster. Who could write the more accurate profile. Who could close the case first. You should have seen us play chess. And now he's seen the opportunity for the best and final game. Two teams, out in the field. His resources against ours, moving in the shadows, angling for the perfect attack. His mind against mine. And only the winner survives. How could he resist?"

"This isn't chess," Jessie said. "It's Battleship."

"Whatever the game," April replied, "he won't let it end without a chance to gloat. Benjamin will *need* to look in my eyes before he pulls the trigger. He'll need me to know that he beat me. That's our sole advantage: if I stay in hiding and you and Jessie go to meet with Linder,

Ben's people won't be looking to kill you. They'll want to take you alive so they can force you to reveal my location."

Jessie tilted her head. "Oh. So they'll want to torture us, *then* kill us. Great."

"It's your window of opportunity. It also means we won't have a repeat of Atlantic City: they'll be aiming for a quiet takedown, not a massacre. We can pick the venue of our choice without worrying about civilian casualties—at least, at the onset. You'll need to apprehend Linder and move him to a safer location quickly."

"So," Jessie said, "we need a place to meet, a plan to nab him, and a safe house to stash him in. We need transportation and guns—"

Aselia raised her hand. "Hello? That's what I do."

"We'll need an escape route," I said. "They're not going to let us just walk him out of there. I still want to focus on civilian safety: no matter what Director Crohn wants, there's no telling if or *when* Mikki might snap and start killing people just for the thrill of it. A distraction would be good: something nice and big to keep Crohn and his team busy while we make our getaway. Something like . . ."

I fell silent. Mentally assessing the pieces on the game board. Shuffling them this way and that.

Jessie pointed at me and looked to Aselia. "Just so you know? That's Harmony's 'got an idea' face. Get used to that."

"Alton Roth," I said. "Senator Roth is gearing up for a presidential run, and he's got demons on his side. His campaign manager, Webster Scratch—Calypso—he's holding Roth's leash. And Nadine is funneling money into his war chest."

"We've still got that blackmail file," Jessie said. "Proof that Roth was involved in Glass Predator. Just haven't figured out how to use it yet."

I smiled for the first time all night.

"I think we just did. Picture this: You're Roth. You get a call from us, demanding money, help clearing our names, whatever, doesn't matter. We want something, and if we don't get it, we'll release the Glass Predator file to the media. What do you do?"

April chuckled. She gave me a nod of approval. "I arrange a meeting. And then I call my powerful patrons for help."

"Nadine is already hunting for us. And thanks to Roth, now she'll know exactly where we'll be, supposedly waiting for a sit-down with the good senator."

"You wanna pit one faction of hell's stooges against *another* faction of hell's stooges," Jessie said. "Nadine versus Director Crohn."

"We grab Linder and escape in the chaos," I said.

Jessie broke into a grin. "You know that's gonna get messy."

"We can handle it."

"Yeah," she said. "You're damn right we can. What are we waiting for?"

SIXTEEN

We huddled around Kevin's laptop, poring over maps, while Aselia went shopping. She came back two hours later with an aluminum-sided briefcase.

She slapped it down on the table next to an empty bottle of wine.

"Called in some old favors," she told us. "Got a few goodies."

The briefcase's handles clicked in unison. She lifted the case open and swiveled it around. Inside, straps fastened a pair of matte-black Sig Sauer handguns to the inner lid.

"I know you Bureau types generally go for the Glock," Aselia told us, "but trust me: once you try the P226 TacOps, you'll never go back. Clean, sturdy, reliable."

"Sold," Jessie said.

Aselia reached into the case and set a pair of thin black tubes on the table. "Also picked up a couple of SRD9 sound suppressors. Titanium tube, stainless-steel baffles, all quality. Didn't know if you'd need 'em, but it's always better to have and not need than to need and not have."

I couldn't argue with that.

"We're going to need more than guns," I said. "Linder carries a bottled demon in his pocket. He showed it to me, back when he first recruited me for Vigilant Lock."

Aselia snorted. "He's still got that thing? Flashed it to me, too, on day one."

"His mutually assured destruction policy," I said. "The locals back in Des Allemands seemed to think you had some magic, too."

"Some," she said. "I know a little rootwork, and I can fix a charm or two. Nothing good for a fight, though. Most of the tricks I lay serve my specialty: getting from point A to point B with nothing hassling me in between."

"I'll take care of his pet, then. Any other goodies in that briefcase?"

"Your partner's special request." She handed Jessie a slim, flat case. "Folding tactical knife. Not the brand you asked for, but it'll do."

The blade, serrated and gleaming, unfolded from the slender hilt. Jessie turned it, catching the light from the electric chandelier on the steel. Her turquoise eyes shone. "Yeah, it will. Thank you."

"What's that for?" I asked her.

Jessie showed me her teeth. "Might feel like cutting on somebody."

"Also picked up ammo for the pistols and my shotty. Enough to take on a small army. Which is what we'll be doing if this plan goes sideways." Aselia slid a slim cardboard box toward April. "And some fresh rounds for your pocket .32. Hollow points. He threw that in as lagniappe, just a little something extra."

"Much obliged," April said. She reached into the canvas tote dangling from the arm of her wheelchair, slipping out the revolver, quietly reloading while Kevin typed beside her. He looked over, one eyebrow slowly lifting.

"So . . . what did you bring for me?" he asked.

"Got a couple sticks of chewing gum," Aselia said. "Spearmint. You want 'em?"

Kevin sighed. "Pass."

He tapped a few keys. The map on his screen, streets drawn in streaks of neon green, slowly turned and zoomed in.

"The National Mall in Washington DC," he said. "Roth's schedule is public info; he's in DC this week. And Linder is there, more often than not. Now, traffic around the Mall is tight, but you've got all these footpaths and decent cover for a lot of it. You could get out on Constitution, Independence, Seventeenth Street Northwest . . . basically, if something goes *really* wrong, at least you won't get cornered."

Aselia came around to stand at his shoulder.

"We're gonna need two exfil vehicles. One to leave the scene with, and one to swap once we've thrown off anyone on our tail. We could stash it . . . here," she said, tapping a blunt fingernail against the screen. "I think that's an overpass. Gonna need to scope it out in person."

"Maybe we only need one," I said. "Linder hates getting more than fifteen feet from that damn limo of his."

"Meaning it'll be on the scene," Jessie said.

I nodded. "Nice and close. We steal him *and* his car."

Aselia rubbed her chin. "Not gonna be winning any car chases in a stretch limo."

"No," I said, "but I guarantee it's been armored. Less chance of us getting shot on our way out. Or *him* getting shot. If Linder dies before we can question him, this will all be for nothing."

"Could work," Aselia said. "Could work. Still, we'd better have a diversion somewhere along the route to the switch car. I could handle that, if you and Jessie can take Linder on your own."

I gazed at the glowing lines on the screen. A labyrinth of streets in neon green. I had dreams about labyrinths, sometimes. Running, turning corner after corner, hearing the Minotaur's hooves pound as he closed in on me.

This time, I was the Minotaur.

# # #

Aselia's Cessna cut through the murky night sky like a hot knife, skimming over storm clouds. The airframe shook, rattling as she fought the wind. Jessie and I sat side by side toward the back of the small plane, Kevin's laptop open and paired to my phone, forest-green lights glowing on his anti-trace program. We wore bulky headphones to cut the chop of the engine. The dial tone was a tin whistle in my ears.

It wasn't hard to get hold of Senator Roth, even in the small hours of the night. All it took was finding the right intern and saying the right words.

"Tell him we're calling about Glass Predator. He'll know what that means. And if he doesn't get on the line in the next five minutes, our next call is to the *Washington Post*."

He got on the line.

"This is Special Agent Harmony Black," I told him. "Do you recognize my name?"

The sleepiness in his voice faded fast. "You're that . . . that rogue agent. You murdered those people out in New Jersey."

"Can't trust everything you see. Of course, you know that all too well. We e-mailed you a page from the Glass Predator dossier, so you know what we have. Enough evidence to burn you at the stake."

"Nobody will believe it," he said, blustery.

"You won't end up in handcuffs, if that's what you mean, but even if it gets debunked by your hired experts, that document will haunt the rest of your career. A little question mark in the minds of the electorate. Bye-bye, White House."

He fell silent for a moment. Then he grunted, "What do you want from me?"

"My partner and I are fleeing the country. Going permanently dark. We need funds to make that happen. You're going to be at the Washington Mall at 8:00 a.m. sharp with a briefcase containing one hundred thousand dollars in nonsequential bills. We'll text you the specific location just before the meeting."

"I can't—that's unreasonable! I need time to gather that kind of money."

"I think you can make it happen if you need to," I said. "And you need to. One hundred thousand dollars and we're out of your life forever. Not a high price when you think about it."

I hung up on him and gave Jessie a questioning look.

"Now that's some quality bait." She held her palm up for a high five. "The second Nadine hears we might be about to disappear for good? She *has* to show up."

"That's one fish," I said, slapping her palm. "Let's go for two."

Vigilant's inner switchboard routed me to Linder. I wasn't surprised to find him awake and on the move. I wasn't sure when or if he ever slept.

"Mission accomplished, I suppose," I said.

"Meaning?"

"You know what we were after, Linder. Cold Spectrum. There were two survivors, the only two people—beside Douglas Bredford—who escaped your assassination order. And now they're both dead. So congrats. You win."

"Aselia?" he said. I heard the tone in his voice perk up. Halfway between curious and hopeful.

"Gunned down on the bayou. She died before she could even tell us what Cold Spectrum *was*. So there you go. You wanted the truth buried forever. Now it is."

"This wasn't any of your business in the first place," Linder said. "Agent, I . . . I tried to warn you. I didn't want this. I didn't want any of this."

Time for the real gambit. I had to lure him in and make him believe it. I had to help him set us up for the kill.

"You owe us," I said. "Again and again we've risked our lives for you, for this program. You *owe* us."

"What do I owe you?"

"Protection. From Benjamin Crohn and Mikki. Look, whatever Cold Spectrum was about, it's over now. The only reason to silence us was to protect the secret. It's protected. We're good agents. The most reliable team you have. Are you really going to let Crohn sanction us and throw that all away?"

He went quiet. Weighing his options. I gave him a little nudge.

"Meet with us," I said. "Just us. Let's talk it out in person."

"I . . . think I can convince Director Crohn to call off the dogs. Possibly. I'll need assurances, though. You've put me in a difficult situation here."

"I understand," I said.

Then he told me exactly what his intentions were.

"Bring your entire team. I want everyone there, in person."

"Of course," I said. "It's a debriefing."

"Where are you now, please?" he asked.

"En route to DC. Meet us at the Washington Mall, 8:00 a.m."

"Specifically where?"

"I'll text you just before the meet," I said.

I hung up on him.

"Yep," I told Jessie, "he's planning to kill us."

"Glad to hear that."

I glanced sidelong at her. "Yeah?"

She was playing with her tactical knife. Unfolding the blade from the hilt, running the ridges of her thumb along the edge, tucking it closed again.

"Given what I'm probably gonna have to do to him," she said, "I'd hate to think he was trying to do the right thing for a change."

We coasted down into the heart of the nation, chasing dawn, over a field of shimmering scarlet lights.

SEVENTEEN

Washington was in motion before the sunrise. A clockwork beast with a paper heart, its gears strung with red tape. Dawn's light shimmered on the Mall's great reflecting pool, with the spire of the Washington Monument rising up at its back. A spear built to pierce the heavens. Jessie and I walked side by side along a crowded path, stepping to one side as a pack of joggers in reflective windbreakers hustled past. I tapped my earpiece.

"Status check. April."

"At the overpass," she said in my ear. "The swap car is acquired and in place. I've just verified that the interrogation site is clear; I contacted the bank, posing as a prospective buyer, and they confirmed the foreclosure took place four months ago. Nobody has been or will be setting foot in there, except—if all goes well—us."

"Good. Aselia."

"Positioned at the distraction point. My timing's going to have to be perfect for this to work, which means *your* timing is going to have to be perfect. Don't screw it up."

"Not planning on it," I said. "Kevin?"

"I'm on overwatch. Drone's airborne and running initial sweeps. By the way, just thought I'd point out that DC is the most restricted airspace on Earth. Like, what I'm doing right now is *super*-illegal."

Jessie adjusted her dark glasses, her turquoise eyes concealed.

"Harmony and I are wanted for murdering about a dozen innocent people, and they're calling us traitors on national television," she said. "You wanna switch places?"

"No, no, I'm just saying, the longer I'm flying this thing, the more attention it's gonna get."

I checked the time. Fifteen minutes to the meet.

"Shouldn't be much longer," I said. "Are you patched into the fire-suppression system?"

"Done and done," he said.

We walked.

Up the winding path, past the rippling sheen of the reflecting pool, the towering steps of the Lincoln Memorial awaited. A Greek temple with white marble columns over forty feet tall. And beyond, in the vast memorial chamber, the statue of Abraham Lincoln sat silent and titanic upon his graven throne.

We walked into the south chamber, where the words of the Gettysburg Address stood engraved upon the wall, flanked by marble eagles. Above the text, a mural spanned the wall, the only splash of color in the white stillness beyond the amber skylights. An angel spread her wings over the emancipated.

"You're quiet," I said.

"I'm angry," Jessie told me.

I reached out and touched her arm. She didn't pull away. She stared at the inscription, her eyes hidden behind her shades.

"My glasses aren't rose tinted," she said. "Let's get that right. America isn't perfect. I wasn't considered a human being until the Thirteenth damn Amendment was ratified. Neither of us could vote until the Nineteenth. We have fought and we have struggled and we have bled for every inch of ground we've ever got."

She turned, facing me.

"But we're *getting there*. And now we find out that the director of the FBI is in some demon's hip pocket. And Alton Roth, *that* motherfucker—he's bought and paid for by the powers of hell. And he's probably gonna be our next president. But that's nothing compared to the cherry on top. Vigilant Lock, the organization that's supposed to stop all this from happening, *my* organization, was nothing but a con game all along."

"Now we know," I said.

"Now we know."

She folded her arms. Her jaw set, resolute.

"Not having this, Harmony. I'm not having it. Maybe our country isn't perfect, but we're trying, and it's *ours*. The American experiment isn't gonna end like this. Our *freedom* isn't gonna end like this. And if the courts of hell think they can take what we built and put us back on our knees . . . they're gonna have to get through me first."

"Us," I told her. "Through us first."

My earpiece crackled.

"Multiple incoming," Kevin said. "Linder's limousine dropped him off on Independence Avenue. Looks like the driver's been told to keep circling the Mall. Meanwhile, spotted Mikki—from a mile away, with that hair—and Ben Crohn coming in from the reflecting pool."

"Just them?" I asked.

"I don't know. I mean, the best description I have of these Panic Cell guys is beards and Oakley sunglasses, either of which could be different now. Spec-ops soldiers are trained to fade into crowds—they could be anywhere."

"What about Nadine?" Jessie said.

"Don't see her."

That was bad. Our plan depended on pitting our enemies against one another. If one decided to sit the fight out, we were already sunk.

"Doesn't make sense," Jessie muttered. "Why wouldn't she take the bait?"

I touched my ear. "Kevin, stay on the limo. We'll improvise something, but when the fireworks start, we'll need to know exactly where that car is."

"You got it."

Nothing to do now but wait. I read the writing on the wall.

Linder arrived first. He moved politely, silently through the growing throng of tourists, dressed in a bland gray suit. Even in Washington, in the seat of his power, he was a forgettable shadow. He stood before us, five feet apart.

"You said you were going to bring the rest of your team," he told me.

"Guess that makes us all liars." Jessie rolled her neck, joints popping, and stretched her arms behind her back. Her prefight warm-up.

"We know everything," I said. "Aselia survived. We know what Cold Spectrum was. We know what Vigilant Lock *is*. And we know what you've done."

His thin lips tightened.

"I just have one question." I pointed past his shoulder. To the chamber exit, and to the colossus on his marble throne. "When you walked in here and saw Lincoln staring down at you . . . did you feel any guilt at all for the things you've done? For selling out our entire nation? Our entire *species*?"

A wave of emotions passed over his face. Anger, denial, fear. Then his eyes turned to frozen steel.

"No," he said.

"You traitorous piece of *shit*—" Jessie moved in, her fingers curling into claws, and I put my hand on her arm to hold her back.

We had new arrivals to deal with. Director Crohn sauntered into the south chamber with Mikki at his side, both of them looking like cats with a fresh saucer of cream.

"Kevin," I murmured, "fire alarm. Now."

Tourists milled, confused, as a warning Klaxon rang out. Officers from the park police rushed into action, herding them out and down the memorial steps. We held our ground. So did the enemy. Mikki gave a theatrical eye roll.

"Aw, can't have any innocent people getting hurt." She looked to Crohn, then glanced upward. "She pulled this same move in a shopping mall once. Probably got her pet hacker tapped into the sprinkler system, thinking it'll stop me from burning anybody. Hey, Jessie, guess what?"

Jessie tilted her head, not saying a word. Mikki beamed and opened her jacket. She flashed a fat .45 automatic and a badge clipped to her belt.

"I brought a *gun* for your ass, just in case. Aw, yeah, that's right: I'm a federal agent now."

"Provisional," Crohn sighed.

A paunch-bellied park officer walked up to us from the left. "Everyone, please, gotta have you move along—that's the fire alarm. I'm sure everything will be sorted out and we'll be open again in a few minutes."

Then he got a good look at my face. His gun slapped from his holster, wavering in his shaky hands.

"You're—you're them! From the television! On your knees, now—hands where I can see 'em, both of you!"

Crohn's lips curled in a hungry smile. "You should do as the officer says, Agents. Please, take them into custody."

"That is already being handled," said a voice at his back, laden with a thick Russian accent.

Nadine had gotten the message from Senator Roth, all right. I guess she was busy elsewhere at the moment.

She'd sent Nyx instead.

Nadine's daughter, in her human guise, looked like a Nordic goddess. A long ponytail, blonde and braided, draped down to the waist of

CRAIG SCHAEFER

her black leather jacket. With a pair of men in dark suits and mirrored glasses at her back, both of them sporting holster bulges under their suit coats, she flashed laminated credentials.

"Svetlana Tkachenko," she said. "Federal Bureau of Investigation. We will be taking the fugitives now."

Crohn furrowed his brow. "That badge is a cheap fake."

"How would you know?" Nyx asked.

"I have a bit of professional experience. You have no idea who I am, do you?"

The park cop was still aiming at Jessie and me, his gun shaking hard and his finger tight on the trigger.

"This one does not care who you are. This one will be taking them, regardless," Nyx said.

Mikki blinked at her. "Which one?"

"*This* one," Nyx said, giving her a frustrated grimace.

I glanced to the park officer. "You don't want to be in the middle of this, trust me—"

"S-shut up," he stammered. The muzzle of the gun swung my way. "I said, on your knees! Now!"

Linder, trapped between the warring camps, let his guard down for one fleeting second. A second was all I needed to grab his wrist in one hand and draw my nine-millimeter with the other. I spun him around and yanked him close, pressing the barrel of the gun to the side of his head. Jessie grabbed the cop's pistol and ripped it from his hand before he could pull the trigger. *"Run,"* she growled at him.

Mikki laughed, delighted, and pulled her own gun. So did the two men flanking Nyx, their aim swinging wildly, not sure whom to cover. I patted Linder down fast with one arm around his hip, searching for his bottled demon. Nothing on him but a wallet and a phone.

"Oh, shit," Mikki crowed, "it's popping off now!"

"Please stop talking," Crohn told her.

Mikki aimed at me, squinting one eye.

"Hey, if I accidentally shoot Linder in the face while I'm trying to kill Harmony, do I get in trouble for that? I'd feel so bad if I mistakenly shot him. *So* bad."

"*Director,*" Linder said through gritted teeth. He held his hands up and open.

"Don't you dare pull that trigger," Crohn said in a low voice. "Not until we find out where April is."

Nyx stepped up to him. "No triggers will be pulled at all. This one will be taking Black and Temple. Alive."

Crohn inched closer to her. His nose wrinkled as he leaned in. Sniffing.

"I don't know who you are," he murmured, "but you're a long way from home. Go back where you came from. Before you get hurt."

Nyx smiled. Her lips parted, revealing a mouth lined with shark teeth.

"*Hurt,*" she said, "is this one's favorite word."

Earth, air, water, fire, I thought, the trigger phrase calling to my magic. *Garb me in your raiment, arm me with your weapons.*

I knew every move everyone in that chamber would make. The cop, cowering with his back to the wall since Jessie had grabbed his gun, was out of the fight: he'd run, I hoped. Nyx was about to tear Director Crohn into bite-size pieces. Good riddance. Mikki, not knowing Nyx was an incarnate demon, would be taken by surprise. She'd hesitate, and one of Nyx's gunmen would take her out. She was powerful, not bulletproof. We'd need to move fast, skirting the pack, summoning a shield of air to hold off the gunfire and get us down the steps. Once we were out of the memorial and on the street, it'd all depend on whether Nyx wanted to risk a public confrontation—

I was still planning the battle when everything went wrong.

Crohn's hand shot out, and his fingers clamped around Nyx's throat.

"I agree," he said, his voice effortless, casual. And Nyx let out a strangled gasp as he hoisted her a foot off the ground, his arm outstretched, lifting her up by the neck as if she was weightless.

EIGHTEEN

Nyx's body ignited. She kicked and flailed against Crohn's iron grip as the flames licked along her skin, but he didn't let go. Mikki backpedaled with her eyes wide. The cop had the right idea: he broke and ran like all hell was on his heels.

"I didn't do that," Mikki said. "Who the—*who set her on fire?*"

"She did it to herself," I said.

Nyx's human guise melted like candle wax. Skin knitted and hardened to plates of black insect chitin, the armor of an infernal knight. She wore the face of a desiccated corpse, her black lips pulled back in a permanent grimace, and a barbed tail like a razor-lined bullwhip uncoiled from the base of her spine. Blue flames licked at Crohn's hand, but he simply held her aloft, effortless, and stared her down as she clawed at his wrist.

We'd seen Nyx punch holes in a car with her bare fists. Crohn barely flinched.

Her men opened fire. Bullets shredded Crohn's shirt, knocking one shoulder back as the rounds chewed into him. His hand spasmed, and he dropped Nyx. Her hooves hit the floor, and she spun fast, lashing out with a brutal kick to his stomach that sent him flying as her tail whipped the air. His back hit the wall with a *crack* of marble and bone.

"Oh, *fuck* this," Mikki hissed. She put her fingers to her forehead, a vein pulsing in her temple as fireflies of light danced around one of the gunmen. I rammed my pistol into the small of Linder's back and gave him a hard shove, Jessie racing just ahead of us, making for the exit. The gunman screamed as he ignited, his body engulfed in broiling flame. The second turned his aim onto Mikki, but he was a split second too late: she had her own pistol out, and she emptied her clip into his chest.

As I looked over my shoulder, Crohn was pushing himself away from the wall. Chunks of splintered marble fell to the floor at his back. He tilted his head, his neck cracking, and closed in on Nyx with his fists clenched.

We burst through the chamber arch, fleeing for the steps under Lincoln's silent gaze as the battle raged behind us.

I held Linder close and tried to conceal my pistol as we wove through crowds of confused tourists and upraised cell phones. If they hadn't heard the fire alarm, they'd certainly heard the gunfire. Park cops held the throng back, arms upraised, calling in for emergency backup. Sirens wailed in the distance, fire and police closing in fast.

Jessie tapped her earpiece. "Aunt April? You maybe forget to tell us something?"

"Meaning?" her voice crackled.

"Your ex-boyfriend's a *goddamn incarnate demon.*"

"That . . . that can't be," she said. "I assure you, Benjamin Crohn is quite human."

"Really? Because he's in there trading punches with Nyx, and it looks like he might be winning—"

I cut her off. No time for arguments. "Kevin, we've got the package, and we're on the move. Where's the limo?"

"Still circling the Mall," he said, "coming close to Henry Bacon Drive. Hard left from where you're standing—head toward the Vietnam Veterans Memorial."

I made sure Linder could feel the muzzle of the gun against his spine. "Get out your phone. Call your driver—tell him you're ready to be picked up. No tricks. We want you alive, but pulling this trigger is just fine by me."

He reached into his breast pocket, slow and easy, taking out his phone with two fingers.

"How cold-blooded of you." He tapped the speed dial. "A shame it took a situation like this to bring out your best qualities."

He made the call, his voice calm as glass. I listened for any signal words, code phrases to hint at trouble, but the entire point of a good signal word is that it's undetectable. If he'd secretly told his driver to flee the scene, we'd have to improvise.

"There." Jessie pointed up ahead. The jet-black stretch limo had pulled up to the curb and out of the sluggish flow of traffic. The driver sat behind smoked glass, impassive. Jessie ran ahead of us. She grabbed the handle for the back door, pulled it—and froze, petrified, as fifty thousand volts coursed through her body. She collapsed to the sidewalk, twitching and stunned.

The driver-side door burst open. Linder's chauffeur leaped out, clenched hand held high. I turned, keeping my grip on Linder as the driver hurled his weapon to the pavement: a slender glass vial that shattered as it hit the stone, spilling a rancid cloud of black gas. The cloud rippled and swirled like a mass of angry hornets. Then it streaked right toward my face.

I shoved Linder down, hard, brought up my open hand in a warding gesture, and hissed the first words of a banishing chant. The infernal smoke slammed against my hand, washing it in blistering heat and psychic poison, then bounced off and veered in the other direction.

Straight toward the chauffeur, driving like a fist between his parted teeth. He screamed and clutched his mouth as Jessie pushed herself up to her hands and knees, still dazed. The chauffeur's head jerked, spasming, then turned my way. Blood vessels burst behind his eyes, flooding them with blooming scarlet as his irises faded to frosty white. He shrieked as he lunged for me with his hands hooked into claws and going for my face.

Linder was scrambling, on the move. Jessie latched on to his pants leg. "No, you fucking *don't*," she grunted, hauling him in. She grabbed him by the scruff of the neck and smacked his head against the limo door. The fight and the fireworks had drawn a crowd, some tourists watching from a distance, others running for help, shouting for the police.

The driver threw himself onto me, still shrieking, a mindless vessel of hate. I put my pistol under his chin and pulled the trigger twice. The gunshots rang out over the screams of tourists, a full-on stampede now, fresh panic washing across the Mall, and sirens closing in. I dropped the body and holstered my gun. My face was wet, sticky. Ears ringing. All I smelled, when I breathed in, was copper and death stench.

No time. I jumped behind the wheel as Jessie hauled Linder into the back.

"We're in," she shouted through the open partition. "Go, go, go!"

Horns squealed as I lurched into traffic, yanking the wheel hard and forcing the limo into the flow.

"Where are you two?" Aselia said over my earpiece. "What's taking so long?"

"Asshole's just *full* of surprises," Jessie replied.

"We're on the move now," I said. "ETA five minutes."

I glanced in the rearview. Jessie had Linder down on the limo's floor, one knee on his stomach. Her tactical knife, unfolded and deadly sharp, gleamed as she held it under his chin.

"Are you chipped?" she demanded.

"What?"

"Are you *chipped*? You're hell's pet bitch, Linder. Gotta figure they might have put a tracker under your skin, like any other dog."

"No." He glowered at her. "They wanted to. I said no."

He seemed just sullen enough, insulted by the very idea, that I believed him. Jessie looked like she was on the fence. The knife swayed in her hand, but she didn't start cutting. Yet.

The limo swayed like a drunken rhino on a rampage. Swerving lanes, cutting through traffic, horns blasting all around us. A pair of black sedans was on our trail and closing in fast, and they didn't have sirens or lights. A man in mirrored shades leaned out the passenger's-side window, dark steel in his hand. The steel spat fire, and a three-round burst of bullets raked across the trunk of the limo, pinging like hail on a tin roof.

I tapped my earpiece. "We've got pursuers. Not sure whether they're Crohn's people or Nadine's, but they're closing in fast."

"I'm ready," Aselia said. "Just give me a ten-second warning, and make sure you get the distance right."

The limo veered hard, wheels thumping as we hit the corner of a curb and bounced. Its nose barely cleared a brick wall as we shot down a narrow side street. Rough, choppy gravel rumbled under the tires. The two sedans stayed right on our tail. Another burst of gunfire rattled against the back window, the reinforced glass crackling but holding fast.

"Approaching now," I told Aselia. "Lead chase car is about thirty feet behind us."

"Speed?"

I glanced to the speedometer. "I'm doing forty-eight."

"Hold that speed."

I tapped the cruise control and gripped the wheel.

We shot past the wide mouth of an alley, the other side of the street lined with flat brick walls: the back end of a strip mall. The sudden scream of an air horn rang out. A cement-mixer truck lunged from the alley right behind us, engine roaring as Aselia redlined it. It smashed into the first sedan, T-boning it, crushing it between the truck's nose and the wall. The second sedan was following too close: the driver spun out, turning too hard and too fast, and slammed into the mixer. The shriek of tortured metal and shattered glass split the air, steam hissing from shattered transmissions, hoods crumpled and windshields streaked with blood spatter.

I braked, hard, screeching to a stop. Aselia clambered out of the truck, cradling her sawed-off shotgun and wincing as she limped toward us.

One of the gunmen wrenched his way from the twisted metal, his scalp torn and blood in his eyes, taking aim at her. She turned and gave him both barrels. The roar of the shotgun forced his head down long enough for her to shove herself into the back of the limo. She draped herself across the bucket seats, clutching her left knee, breathing hard.

I hit the gas, one eye on the rearview as we left the carnage behind. "You okay?"

"Had worse," Aselia breathed. "Crashed a cargo helicopter once, and that wasn't even on purpose. Oh, hey, Linder. Remember me?"

Linder didn't say a word.

"Yeah," she said. "You remember me. Got that poker face going, just like I remember. But I gotta tell you . . . if you're not scared right now? You really, really should be."

I tapped my earpiece. "We're coming in hot, and we've got Aselia. Is the switch car ready?"

"Ready and waiting," Kevin said.

Two miles up, in the shadow of an overpass, a grime-streaked panel van sat with its engine purring. We'd stolen it from the same construction site as the mixer, rubbing a little fresh mud on the license plate. Not the greatest camouflage—by now, it had to have been reported stolen—but we only needed it to take us a little bit farther. Kevin threw open the back doors as we pulled up behind the van. Jessie marched Linder out at knifepoint, shoving his head down and throwing him in back. I helped Aselia out. She threw one arm around my shoulder, leaning on me and hobbling the distance.

Ten seconds later we were off. Our trail clean and our prize in hand. I should have felt triumphant, but all I could see were the walls closing in around us. At least we'd captured a bargaining chip.

Now we had to figure out how to use him. A choice that would make the difference between life and death for all of us.

NINETEEN

We left the city behind for the solitude of the suburbs. Marlow Heights, a quiet sprawl of strip malls and gas stations, stoplights dangling over empty four-lane roads. Kevin drove, steering us into the parking lot of a boarded-up Kmart. Then around back, to the loading docks.

With the van out of sight, we jimmied open the back door. The store had been shuttered for months, the alarm system long gone and nothing left to steal. The stockroom was bare, only the skeletons of built-in shelves left behind. I poked my head out into the main floor: there, they hadn't even left the shelves. A vast span of empty and yellowed tile floor, the only illumination seeping in from cracks at the edges of the covered windows. Dust danced on razor blades of light.

Jessie grabbed a folding chair from the back of the van and slapped it dead center in the empty store. Then she sat Linder down and zip-tied his hands behind his back.

"I shouldn't have to tell you this," Jessie said, "but we picked this spot for a reason. You can scream all you want. Nobody's gonna hear you."

Linder stared at her, impassive. Then he let out a tiny, amused snort.

"Empty threat, Agent Temple. You're not going to torture me."

She took her glasses off so he could see her eyes softly glowing in the dark. Then she unfolded her knife. Her voice was a deadly soft murmur.

"You know what kind of skills my father taught me," she said. "You know what I've done and where I've been. You better think about that."

"Oh, I'm sure *you'd* be quite happy to," he replied. Then he looked my way. "But your partner has an excess of moral certitude. Isn't that right, Agent Black? You've never tolerated the use of enhanced interrogation techniques. You're not going to start now."

I weighed my options and then looked over at Kevin. "I think your drone took a little damage out there."

"What? No, it's fine. It worked totally—"

"No. You need to run some diagnostics." I nodded to the stockroom door. "Take it out back."

He caught my meaning. Nodding slowly as he stepped outside.

I looked to April next. She fixed me with her steely gaze.

"April, I need to go over the mission plan with you." I turned to Jessie and Aselia. "We'll just be a bit. Maybe . . . ten, fifteen minutes. You can watch Linder while we're gone, right?"

Aselia's lips slowly curled in a vicious smile. "Sure. We'll be right here. With the man who murdered my friends. Don't worry. We'll be angels."

April and I were halfway to the door when Linder spoke up.

"All right," he said. "All right. Point made. There's no need for this. I'll cooperate."

We turned back.

"Incidentally, Agent Boulanger, you do realize that I didn't personally assassinate your former teammates, yes?" Linder nodded at Jessie. "Agent Temple's *mother* pulled the trigger."

Aselia's hands tightened on her shotgun. She looked to Jessie. "That true?"

"She's no mother of mine," Jessie told her.

"You may have to tell her that in person," Linder said. "That matter I wanted to talk to you about at your debriefing? Althea Temple-Sinclair escaped from Vigilant Lock custody. It's a shame, really. Agent Boulanger's one real chance for justice, and your refusal to terminate Althea when you had a chance may have stolen that from her forever."

April cleared her throat. She gave her wheels a hard shove, her chair rolling close.

"What our former patron is doing," she said, "is an attempt at pitting us against one another. Staving off his own fate while we fight among ourselves and question our loyalties. And it will not succeed."

Linder half smiled. "Now why would you be worried about that, Dr. Cassidy? Are you concerned these fine agents might find out you shared a bed with Benjamin Crohn? Or that you blackmailed him into leaving the Bureau, the entire reason for his current enmity toward you?"

"No," she replied, "because I already told them everything. Are there any other dirty little secrets you'd like to share, or can we proceed with the interrogation?"

Aselia was still staring at Jessie. Looking at her like a stranger.

"Swear to God," Jessie told her, "I thought my mother was dead until a few days ago. She abandoned me when I was a kid. What she did has nothing to do with me."

"It's true," I said.

Aselia nodded, slow. Swallowing, like drinking down some old pain just to get the taste out of her mouth. She circled Linder's chair.

"Still sore, after all these years," she said, her voice faint. "Guess it's not something you really get over, watching all your friends die."

"And if you had followed orders," Linder said, "they would still be alive today."

The butt of the shotgun cracked against the side of his head. Linder's scalp split open, the cut spitting blood as he tumbled with the chair and landed hard on his side. Aselia stomped her shoe down on his hip and stood over him with both barrels aimed in his face, her face twisted in sudden rage.

"Give me one reason not to pull the trigger," she roared, "*one fucking reason!*"

"Because he wants you to," April said.

Aselia froze. We all did. Wrapped in the dusty stillness of the abandoned Kmart, one trigger squeeze between life and death.

"He wants you to kill him," April said. "Because he believes that's the best and only option left to him. If you pull that trigger, he wins. Don't give him the satisfaction."

The shotgun drooped, Aselia's hand going limp, her anger deflated and squandered. Jessie grabbed Linder's shoulders and hauled him back up. A steady trickle of blood ran down his cheek. It dribbled onto the shoulder of his bland gray suit.

"Astute as always, Dr. Cassidy," he said.

"All this time," Jessie said, "we were out there hunting the enemy, when the enemy was you all along."

"Not true," Linder said.

"You work for the courts of hell. The eastern coalition. Vigilant Lock is nothing but a con game."

"Everything you've said is correct," he replied. "And none of it makes me the enemy. I am a patriot."

"You sold out the human race. You've murdered your own field agents. How can you *say* that?"

"Can you do math, Agent Temple? I can do math."

Jessie loomed over him, hands on her hips. "Explain."

"I started as an Agency man. Clandestine ops, graduated to case manager by my late twenties. I was stationed in this little backwater hellhole in South America. One of our assets needed an urgent face-to-face meeting; normally I avoided that, but the information he'd acquired was just that explosive. We made contact in a back alley about a block from the United States Embassy."

His gaze went distant. Lost in the gloom, grasping at the threads of a memory as blood pattered down onto his shoulder.

"Children made their living selling chewing gum to the cruise-boat tourists," he said. "They'd walk up to you with their hands out. *'Chicle? Chicle?'* Now, this boy—couldn't have been more than seven or eight—made a wrong turn. He stumbled upon us. He couldn't have known what was in the folder, but he knew enough. He knew he'd just seen a local handing over important-looking documents to a gringo. He knew our faces. And he knew he was hungry. The soldiers, you see, paid for information on rebel activity."

"Linder," I said softly, "what did you do?"

"I did the math, Agent Black. Exposure meant my asset would be arrested and killed. Everyone he named under torture would be arrested and killed. And so it goes. Our entire local network would be dismantled overnight. Twelve lives, at least. Twelve is a larger number than one. That's what I was thinking as I put my hand over that boy's mouth and snapped his tiny neck."

He met my gaze, subdued now, almost serene.

"When I was brought into this organization, they told me the truth. What was at stake. And just like they knew I would, because that's why they chose me . . . I did the math. The courts of hell have infiltrated every stratum of our nation; they have operatives in our government, our military, our courts and schools. The only thing that's kept them from openly conquering the earth is the state of cold war: they all dream of a takeover, but no prince wants to share his throne. Keeping the shadow war in motion, the constant flux of espionage and soft betrayal, is the sole factor ensuring humanity's survival."

"Liar," Aselia said. "The entire point of this program was to tip the scales."

Linder regarded her like a college professor with a particularly slow student.

"Consider the forces in play," he said. "The Courts of Jade Tears and Night-Blooming Flowers hold vast amounts of territory. Between the two of them, their domain extends from California through almost the entire Midwest. The eastern coalition is tiny by comparison. Waging war through deniable human assets gives them a survival advantage. Yes, Vigilant Lock—and Cold Spectrum before it, and Directive Nine before *that*—was a false-flag operation orchestrated by infernal operatives. Yes, I deceived you. But look at the effect. Seeding turbulence, perpetuating the cold war, all of it leads to the ultimate objective: keeping the courts fighting each other and sparing humanity in the process. Do. The. Math."

Linder looked my way. His tone steady and cool as he held my gaze.

"And can you say you've done anything you wouldn't have if Vigilant Lock really was the organization you thought it was? Look at just the last few months. Your team stopped the Bogeyman kidnappings. You kept the King of Silence from being unleashed on Earth. You prevented a terrorist attack on Las Vegas. Regardless of who backs it, this organization does good for the world."

"Tell that to the Redemption Choir," Aselia said through gritted teeth. "Tell that to *my team*."

"What happened was . . . regrettable. I underestimated Douglas Bredford's tenacity."

"You put a bomb in his trailer," Jessie said.

"No," Linder said, "actually, we didn't. It's my assessment that Bredford committed tactical suicide."

"Pardon?" I said.

"He was dying. Cirrhosis of the liver and God knows what else. When you and Agent Temple made contact with him in Michigan, he must have seen the chance to strike back at me from beyond the grave. A string of clues and bread crumbs carefully placed and designed to lead you to the truth."

"He could have just told us up front," Jessie said.

Linder cracked a humorless smile. "Would you have believed him?" She didn't have an answer for that. Neither did I.

"You needed to uncover it for yourself," he said. "From RedEye, to Glass Predator, to . . . me. And, just as he likely intended, doing plenty of damage along the way. So here you are. All the lies banished, the truth unveiled. And, unfortunately, like Icarus, you've flown too close to the sun and doomed yourselves in the process. As it stands, I give you two days, four at most, before you're taken down. You'll be arrested by law enforcement, brought in and then assassinated in custody before you can talk, or tracked and eliminated by Panic Cell. You'll be remembered as murderers and traitors for a week or two, and then you won't be remembered at all. The news cycle has a very short attention span."

Aselia pressed the barrels of her shotgun against the back of Linder's head.

"On the bright side," she said, "you'll land in hell before we do."

TWENTY

Nobody moved.

We froze in the stillness. Dust floated on blades of sunlight. A strong wind rattled the vacant store. The exposed scaffolding above, like the bones of some vast dead beast, groaned and clanked.

"I don't hear any objections," Aselia said. The shotgun's muzzle pressed in, forcing Linder to bow his head. "Any last words?"

"Yes," Linder replied calmly. "What if I offered you an alternative?"

She frowned, uncertain. Her eyes flicked to Jessie.

"Hear him out," Jessie said. "You got thirty seconds."

Aselia eased back.

Linder raised his chin. "What if there was a way to restore your names and reputations, strike back against Benjamin Crohn and his allies, and subvert Vigilant Lock from within? I propose a coup."

I put my hands on my hips. "With your help, I assume."

"Of course, Agent Black. It would hardly be the first regime change I've orchestrated."

"No way," Aselia said. She paced behind his chair, her free hand balled into a fist. "No way this asshole gets to live. No way we can trust him. Tell me this, Linder: If you had a way to take over from inside, why haven't you *done* it by now?"

"I didn't have the resources. Going to war against the courts of hell is not a matter to take lightly, Agent Boulanger. You succeed or you die. You—"

He paused, stumbling over his words. A flicker of something passed over his normally impassive face. Something like regret.

"I have a family," he said, softer now. "A wife, a little girl. Her name is—"

Aselia jammed her shotgun in his face. "Don't. Don't you even *try* that 'humanizing yourself to your captors' bullshit. That's hostage-survival 101, and we've all had the same training. Didn't have the resources, my ass. You had *my team*."

"I did. And when Benjamin Crohn ordered me to have your team liquidated, I didn't have the time to arrange a plan. He was also watching me far more closely than he does today. I hadn't yet earned his trust. As it was, I saved as many of you as I could."

Her jaw dropped. "*Saved?* You made the call to have us all wiped out."

Linder took a deep breath. He let it out in a faint sigh.

"Yes. And Douglas Bredford found RedEye, made contact with the administrator, Burton Webb, and arranged to have as many of you shielded from detection as possible." He tilted his head, looking her way. "Did you ever ask yourself how Bredford found out about RedEye in the first place?"

"You?" Aselia asked. "You . . . told him?"

"Not directly. He never knew it was me; I simply made sure he 'stumbled across' enough back-channel intelligence to make his way to safety." His head gave a tiny shake. "I hoped more of you would get clear. It was out of my hands. As is this. Director Crohn is out of control. I believe his sanity is slipping."

"About that," I said. "April says he was as human as we are, back when she knew him. But we just watched him get into a fistfight with Nyx and hold his own, not to mention getting *shot* three or four times."

"Even among Vigilant's directorate," Linder said, "not everyone knows who they truly serve. Crohn is the main intermediary between our organization and the courts of hell. As such, he's been suitably rewarded."

"Rewarded how?" Jessie asked.

"He's paid in bound demons. Captives from the western courts. He . . . ingests them. Eleven or twelve by now. He's human, yes, but at this point he has the physical power and speed of an incarnate. Possibly more—it's not a thing I'd like to test."

April leaned on the armrest of her wheelchair with her chin cradled against her curled knuckles.

"So if we could immobilize him long enough for Harmony to perform an exorcism," she said, thinking out loud.

Linder shook his head. "I wouldn't count on it. They're not possessing him. He's possessing *them*. It's a bit of a Damocles sword, too. His masters hold the contracts that bind them to service. Do you know what happens when you burn an infernal contract, Agents?"

"The demon goes free," I said.

Linder gave me a nod.

"And considering they've been bound against their will, their reaction would be . . . unpleasant. Essentially, Crohn is a slave of the eastern courts: they can kill him at any moment, from half a world away, with the flick of a lighter. Ample incentive to stay loyal."

"We need those contracts," Jessie said. "We could force him to clear our names. Go on TV and say this whole manhunt was a big mistake."

"A laudable start." Linder eased back in his chair, flexing his bound wrists. "Of course, he'll still need to be eliminated once he's served his purpose. You have a more pressing problem to deal with: the eastern coalition can't afford the risk of exposure. Once Vigilant Lock declares its independence, they'll react like any other self-respecting kingdom does in the face of a rebel colony."

"Send an army," Jessie said.

"They'll come after you—*us*, actually—without mercy," Linder said. "They can't risk their enemies finding out that Vigilant was their brainchild. The blowback would be devastating."

My thoughts drifted back to Portland. Caitlin, the West Coast hound, showing up just as we needed a distraction. And before that, Fontaine's insistence that there was something she wanted Jessie and me to do—something she couldn't get done on her own.

"I think . . . maybe they already know," I said. "Is there any kind of paper trail? Communications between Director Crohn and the eastern courts?"

Linder turned his head. His gaze dropped to the floor as he thought it over.

"I imagine there's *something*," he said. "The binding contracts alone would be proof of collusion. Why do you ask?"

"Caitlin helped us out by stalling Nadine." I looked to Jessie. "Why? Because she needs us alive, to do something she can't."

Jessie snapped her fingers. "Proof. She might *know* Vigilant Lock is a scam, but knowing and proving aren't the same thing. And if we expose the eastern coalition . . . what was that you were just saying about blowback, Linder? Hell, get the courts openly fighting each other, and they might be too busy to even think about coming after us."

"The enemy of our enemy," April mused. "Well, the enemy of our enemy is still our enemy, but that doesn't mean they can't serve a purpose."

"Our first priority has to be those contracts," Jessie said. "We can't do a damn thing with our faces on TV and half the cops in the country hunting for us. We get the contracts, then we blackmail Crohn into clearing our names."

Linder nodded. "Then your next stop is New York. The Court of Windswept Razors rules that region, and they're Director Crohn's point of contact. I wish I had more for you to go on; you'll have to improvise in the field. Meanwhile, I'll be running intelligence on the rest of Vigilant Lock's directorate. They're a mixture of the ignorant and the venal; the ignorant can be taught. Some of the venal ones, those willingly serving the courts in exchange for money and power, can be swayed to our cause. The others, we'll have to eliminate."

The room went silent. Aselia stood over him, the shotgun cradled in her hands.

"You're assuming a lot," she said. "You already gave us all the intel we need. What you haven't given us is a reason to keep you alive."

"You disappoint me, Agent Boulanger. I thought it was obvious. Once this fight is over and the dust settles, Vigilant Lock still needs to be able to function. I have access to the alphabet agencies. You don't. I have the ability to generate funding. You don't. I can misdirect the authorities and keep our existence concealed. You can't. Your fieldwork is superb, but no covert operation survives without signals intelligence and supply. You don't want me alive—you *need* me alive."

Jessie held up a finger. "Excuse us a minute. Team? Conference out back."

We gathered on the oil-stained loading dock, leaving Linder alone in the boarded-up store, and brought Kevin up to speed.

"I really hate to say this," he told Jessie, "but Linder's got a point. I can scrounge for rumors and leads on the net, but all our big cases, the real trouble spots, come down from him. He's got access to intel I can't even dream of. If we go it alone, we'll be letting a lot of bad guys slip under the radar."

Jessie paced the dock. She clasped her hands behind her back and stretched her arms out, sighing.

"And then there's the funding," she said. "None of us does this for the paycheck, but we still need to eat. And buy plane tickets. And guns."

Aselia leaned back against the scuffed brick wall, apart from the group. She'd been lingering in silence. Now she raised one hand. "Do I get a say?"

Jessie glanced over at her. "As far as I'm concerned, you became a part of this team the second we flew out of Des Allemands. If you want to be. So, yeah, you get a say."

Aselia shoved herself away from the wall. She walked over, joining us.

"I can't even tell you how much I hate that man." She jerked her head toward the loading-bay door. "That thing about trying to save my team, leaking the RedEye info to Douglas? Maybe true, maybe not. Linder breathes lies like other people breathe air. Doesn't matter if it *is* true; he still sent our team after innocent people, and then we died for asking questions. Doesn't matter if he was only following orders. That excuse didn't fly for the Nazis, and it damn sure doesn't fly for people working for the courts of hell."

"You voting we kill him?" Jessie asked.

"No." Aselia's shoulders sagged. "Because he's right. For now, at least, we need him. The question is, can we trust him?"

She looked to Jessie. Jessie looked to April.

"Let's consider his drives," April said. "Survival, first and foremost."

"And his family?" Jessie asked.

"If he has one. That mention of his wife and daughter may have been real, or it may have been crocodile tears. Ultimately it doesn't matter. If we subvert Vigilant Lock from within and allow him to retain his post—as well as his life—it means more security for him. He'll have more power and influence without Ben Crohn standing over his shoulder, too. On the other hand, what does he get if he betrays us?"

"Ben Crohn standing over his shoulder," I said. "Forever. And a lot more work. He'll have to recruit yet another new team, put up with more meddling from above, and probably deal with—and it makes my skin crawl just saying this out loud—Special Agent Mikki."

Jessie winced. "Yeah, let's not make that a thing."

"Supporting us is the path of least resistance and greatest reward," April said. "Linder's not political. He's barely moral. He has no ideology, beyond patriotism, to interfere with his self-interest. This makes him dangerous, but it also makes him predictable. We can't trust *him*, but we can trust his pattern of behavior."

"So that's a vote for letting him walk," Jessie said.

"A reserved yes."

"Harmony?" Jessie asked me.

I had to think about that.

Linder wasn't the only one with survival on the brain. We'd been hunted, hounded, and it felt like the entire world was closing in over our heads like the teeth of a bear trap. I was tired, more than anything, and I didn't see anything but more danger, more struggle, more death ahead of us. Putting a bullet in Linder's brain would be quick. Easy. One obstacle done and gone. Nobody could say we wouldn't be justified.

But I'd been around long enough to know one thing for certain: the easy choice is almost always the wrong choice.

"We're taking a risk, keeping him alive," I said, "but I think we're taking a bigger one if we don't. I say we let him live."

"I hear you," Jessie told me. "Kevin?"

Kevin shrugged. "He can do things we can't. I'm not joining the guy's fan club anytime soon, but I think we need him. It's your team, boss. Your call."

Jessie hooked her thumbs in her pockets, nodding slow, taking everything in.

"Linder gets to keep breathing. For now." She glanced at Aselia. "So, you staying on board? No obligation. Once we take out Crohn and his buddies, nobody's gonna be hunting you anymore."

Aselia spread her open hands. "What am I gonna do, get a *civilian* job? It's not like I can put 'clandestine ops and pot smuggling' on a résumé. Besides, for all the shit we saw in Cold Spectrum, all the horrors we had to wade through . . . I'd be lying if I said I didn't miss it a little."

"You're gonna fit right in," Jessie said. "Welcome to Circus Cell."

She arched an eyebrow. "Wait a second. Circus? That's your team designation?"

"Yeah, it's . . ." Jessie's voice trailed off. Then her eyes lit up. "You know what? *We're* calling the shots now. Time for a name change."

"Dragon Cell!" Kevin said. Jessie clapped his shoulder.

"Bless your nerdy little heart, but no. C'mon, let's go back inside and break the good news. We've got a mission to plan."

TWENTY-ONE

"We did the math," I told Linder.

He raised his slumped head, his face still a stoic mask, but he couldn't hide the glimmer of relief in his eyes.

"I had every confidence that you would," he said.

"We're going to New York," Jessie said. "Chasing those contracts down so we can force Crohn to call off the dogs. There anything else you can tell us? Anything that might help?"

"I don't know where you'll find the contracts," Linder said, "but I know who's on your heels."

"Panic Cell," April said.

Linder nodded. "When we reformed this program as Vigilant Lock, we intended each cell to be highly specialized. Beach Cell was primarily intended for scientific field support, for instance. Investigation fell to you and Redbird Cell. Panic Cell was for . . . heavy removals. They don't investigate—they eliminate. It's a twelve-man team—though I believe you've already cut down their numbers a bit—all culled from US special forces. They operate from a mobile base: a C-130 cargo plane outfitted with a command-and-control suite."

Jessie loomed over him, her mouth hanging open. "We have to rent compact cars and submit receipts for motel rooms, and you're telling me you gave these motherfuckers their own *jet*?"

"*I* didn't, no. Unlike the other cells, Panic's members were hand-selected by Director Crohn. They enjoy considerably more funding than the rest of you." Linder gave a wry smile. "Benefits of being the teacher's pets."

"C-130 isn't a jet," Aselia muttered. "It's a turboprop with optional jet-assisted takeoff. Still a dick move, though."

"Unlike you," Linder continued, "and the members of Beach and Redbird, the operatives in Panic know exactly who they serve. They're incentivized and highly motivated."

"Satanic special forces," Jessie said.

Linder shrugged. "Hard to be afraid of death when you know you have a lucrative job waiting in hell. They've been promised treasure in the afterlife—and unlike many who have been offered such glory over the ages, they've actually *seen* theirs. They can't be bought or turned."

"That leaves elimination," Jessie said. "Them, Crohn, Mikki—they've all gotta go. First things first, though. They know we took you. How do we put you back without raising suspicions?"

"I'll handle that part myself," Linder said.

He wriggled in his chair, took a deep breath—then wrenched his face in pain as a loud *pop* crackled behind his back. He twisted his arms like he was turning a stubborn screw, then finally brought his hands around in front of him. An empty cuff dangled from one wrist, and the other was free, skinned raw and bleeding, the flesh purple where the heel of his thumb folded in like a broken accordion.

"You left me alone to confer over my fate," he said, his voice strained. "I dislocated my thumb to escape the handcuffs, then escaped on foot. I'll find a phone somewhere nearby and call for help. In a half hour or so, of course, to give you a head start."

Kevin bit his knuckles, looking green. Jessie just shook her head.

"God *damn*, Linder. We probably could have come up with a less painful story."

He forced a smile, still catching his breath. "They wouldn't have *bought* a less painful story, Agent."

"We'll be in touch." Jessie turned, then paused, looking back. "Just so you know? You work for *us* now. We're gonna be making some changes around here."

Linder cradled his hand against his chest and grunted an acknowledgment.

"Time for that later," he said. "For now, just try to survive."

# # #

Storm clouds trailed like wispy streaks of black ice under the Cessna's shuddering wings. We were mobile and heading north, straight into a patch of bad weather. Two days from Halloween, and the holiday dogged my thoughts like a bad omen. Nothing to do for it, though. Nothing but steeling myself and preparing for the road ahead.

Nothing to do but fight.

We skirted New York City, past the spires of granite and glass, and put in at a small airfield about an hour upstate. "These are good folks," Aselia told us. "They'll keep quiet and give us breathing room."

"Is there anyone you *don't* know?" Kevin asked her.

The props spun down as we taxied into a vacant hangar, the plane rumbling over uneven asphalt. A man in oil-stained coveralls waved us in, and Aselia gave him a thumbs-up from the cockpit window.

"My transport network's a shadow of what it used to be," she said. "Was a time when I had somebody reliable in all fifty states. Still, I got us this far. The rest is up to you."

"We're making this our base camp," Jessie said. "Me and Harmony are going to hit the pavement. April, I want you running media sweeps. That scrap at the Washington Mall is probably on every channel: check

144

out the coverage, read between the lines, and see if we've been tied to it. Also, if Ben Crohn shows his face, he might let something useful slip."

"If we're lucky, Nyx killed him," Kevin said.

"We're never that lucky," Jessie told him. "I want you scanning police-band radio; we're gonna be as low profile as we can, but if some eagle-eyed local spots us and calls the cops, I want to know before the SWAT team rolls in."

"I'll be doing maintenance on my baby." Aselia patted the plane's yoke. "I didn't like some of those sounds she was making when we landed. Don't worry: when we need to leave, we'll be ready to go on five minutes' notice."

"Can you cut that down to three?" Jessie asked.

Aselia gave her a wan smile. Then she looked away.

Jessie put her hand on Aselia's shoulder. "What?"

"Douglas used to say that all the time." Aselia stared at the console. "You met him at his worst. At his best . . . damn. Sorry. Last couple of days dug up memories I thought I'd buried a long time ago."

I wriggled a finger through the knot in my tie, loosening it, slipping it off. I needed to look inconspicuous. Still, I didn't like going to battle without a tie on. It wasn't magic, it wasn't bulletproof, but it reminded me of my father. Buttoning his uniform shirt, putting on his polyester tie and sheriff's star before heading out to save the day. He was immortal, until the night he suddenly wasn't.

The tie reminded me of everything he stood for in my six-year-old eyes. Law. Order. The right way. Maybe it was just as well that I was taking mine off. We weren't going to get out of this mess by fighting fair. I rolled it up and passed it to Kevin.

"We're doing this for Douglas," Jessie told Aselia. "And for Houston, and the rest of your team. We can't bring 'em back, but we'll make sure they get some justice."

"Crohn," Aselia said. She took a deep breath, steadying herself, and looked Jessie in the eye. "Find that son of a bitch before he finds you."

"That's the plan." Jessie glanced back over her shoulder at me and slipped her dark glasses on. "You ready to roll, partner?"

I was ready.

We took a commuter train into the city, bound for Queens. Winter had come early, caking windows with morning frost, turning breath and bus exhaust into curlicues of white smoke. My suit coat wasn't heavy enough to cut the chill, and I rubbed my arms to stay warm as we hustled along a bustling sidewalk. Our first stop was a thrift shop on Greenpoint Avenue: we needed camouflage, and we needed warmth, in that order.

When we emerged, I'd swapped my suit for a sturdy windbreaker, battered jeans, a knit stocking cap, and a cheap pair of sunglasses. Jessie opted for a gray flannel hoodie, her wiry bun tucked under the pulled-down hood. We weren't unrecognizable, but at least we didn't mirror the photos they were flashing on television. We'd chosen gray-and-beige colors, bland styles, nothing for anyone's memory to latch on to. There were eight million people in New York City; sometimes there's anonymity in numbers. We blended in with the herd and kept our heads down.

Our next stop was the Crystal Crow. The window display was all stocked up for Halloween, a broomstick and a jack-o'-lantern sharing a dusty shelf with glass "crystal" balls and a plethora of paperbacks promising the secrets of real witchcraft. Inside the cluttered shoe box of a store, Vlad was putting on his fortune-teller routine for a couple of giggling hipster girls. He stroked his Rasputin beard, gold-plated rings glimmering on his sausage fingers, as he pored over tarot cards on a black velvet mat.

"Ah, yes, you see. Zhis is the Vheel of Fortune, a very fortuitous card. It says you maybe find love, yes? Maybe with handsome and mystically powerful older man—"

Standing by the door, Jessie coughed into her hand. He looked up, his face falling.

"Sorry, sorry, ladies, but Vlad must close ze store. The spirits, zhey call him. Zhey are awed by your natural psychic abilities and think you should sign up for Vlad's spiritual-development course, meeting every other Zhursday night—"

We waited as he eased them out the door. He clicked the lock, flipped the **CLOSED** sign, and put his back to the glass. When he spoke again, the bold Russian mystic magically transformed into a native of Yonkers.

"You're killin' me here. Swear to God, you're killin' me. Ain't you been watching the TV?"

"Good to see you, too," Jessie said. "And no, why? See any good shows lately?"

"Yeah. Like the one about the two FBI agents who shot up a casino. Top ratings. I hear the next season's gonna be set in a prison."

"We're working on a happier ending. We need some local intel. And seeing as you're our local-intel guy . . ."

Vlad tugged at his beard. "Just make it quick, okay? I've stuck my neck out for you plenty. I don't need to get busted for harboring known fugitives."

"Help us out, and we won't *be* fugitives. We need info on the Court of Windswept Razors. Who's the court's hound, and where can we find her?"

Vlad gaped at her. He waved his hands, shooing us away from the window and closer to the heart of the store. The cramped shelves stank of old, dried herbs and cheap incense.

"Are you"—he paused, lowering his voice—"are you kidding me? You want me to give up a *hound*?"

"We think the hound has some contracts we need," I said. "Or at least knows where they are."

"Contracts." He stared up at the ceiling. A stuffed dragon dangled from a wrought iron chandelier. "I'm gonna get torn into itty-bitty pieces and scattered across the Hudson so you can ask a demon prince's right hand about *contracts*."

"They're special contracts." Jessie flicked her fingers against his brocade vest. "C'mon, Vlad. The Razors claim New York as their turf. Don't tell me you don't know where they hang out."

He bristled. "Believe it or not, Agent Smarty-pants, I don't. The Razors are old-school, old money. They keep their business on the down low. If they need to reach out and hurt someone, they generally use a proxy."

"Who's the proxy?" I asked.

He looked at me like I'd asked the dumbest question imaginable. "They're called the Mafia, sweetheart. The Five Families? You mighta heard of 'em? Not everybody on the wiseguy scene is hooked up with the Razors, but they've got enough influence to take care of business. The hound doesn't make personal appearances, at least not the kind anybody lives to talk about. I don't even have a name to give you, let alone a face or a place."

"A hound's job is taking care of their prince's business," Jessie said. "That's no career for a hermit. *Somebody* talks to this person."

Vlad stared at his curly-toed shoes. We let him wrestle with himself in silence.

"I might have something," he said. "It's a reach, but it's something. And you gotta keep my name out of it."

"Vlad who?" Jessie said. "Now dish."

"Guy named Tonino Giannetti. Tony Four-Ways. He's *allegedly* a made guy, captain of a Genovese crew."

"Allegedly," I echoed.

"Allegedly. Now here's the facts." Vlad tapped the base of his wrist. "He's got a tat, right here, with the glyph of Prince Berith. Humans who are high up in the Razors' esteem get those; it's a get-out-of-jail-free card, if you flash it at the right kind of cop. It means 'Hell's property, do not touch.' Word is, Tonino is an informant for Berith's hound. Acts as his eyes and ears out on the street."

"Meaning they have to meet now and then," Jessie said. "Where can we find this guy?"

"If you want to catch him alone, away from his crew? Try Dashwood Abbey. Clubhouse for New York's occult-underground scene. Watch yourself in there: that particular party gets a little too freaky for my liking."

Jessie patted him on the shoulder.

"Trust me," she said. "Until we show up, the party hasn't *begun* to get freaky."

TWENTY-TWO

We sat at the tail end of a half-empty subway car on hard-backed seats. A cold breeze ruffled through the train, carrying the odor of stale sweat. We kept our faces turned and our hands in our pockets. I was still worried about being spotted, but one truth about New York worked in our favor: it was the kind of place where everybody minded their own business.

"How do you want to play this?" I asked Jessie.

"I was thinking we could ask for a meeting."

I peered at her. "I don't think the Razors' hound is going to just hand over the contracts. Even if we ask politely."

"I said we'd *ask* for a meet," Jessie replied. "Didn't say we'd really show up. If we can get a line on the hound from a distance, we can follow 'em back to wherever they rest their head at night. Then we come up with a distraction, some pretext to get them back outside, and we snoop around their lair a little bit."

"*Lair?*" I asked. I couldn't help cracking a smile. "It's probably a mansion in the Hamptons."

"Still counts as a lair," she said. "It's not the quality of the real estate—it's the monster inside."

My phone vibrated against my hip. I held it between us so Jessie could listen in. "Yeah."

"Good news and bad news," Kevin said. "Good news is, Linder just contacted us on an encrypted channel. They bought his story. He's back in Vigilant's good graces, though Crohn's pretty much frozen him out of the hunt at this point."

"Good enough," I said. "What's the bad news?"

"Linder's tracking Panic Cell's plane. It just touched down in New York."

A cold hand gripped my spine. The walls of the subway car closed in around us, and suddenly it felt like every other passenger was staring right at us. Every cell phone in every tight hand tapping out our location.

"What?" I said. "*How?* We were careful."

Kevin lowered his voice to a muffled whisper. "Our new teammate is *pissed*. Aselia thinks Linder snitched on us."

I frowned. Easy conclusion, but it didn't scan.

"No," I said. "If he betrayed us, he wouldn't call to warn us about it: he wouldn't want us to know Crohn was on our tail. His hands are clean—this time. What about Aselia's buddies at the airstrip? She's positive we can trust them?"

"As positive as she can be, but she's still working double time on the plane in case Panic Cell shows up here. Harmony, if they do—"

"Leave without us," Jessie said.

I heard Kevin swallow, hard. "Boss?"

"That's an order. If you spot anything that looks like it might *possibly* be trouble, I want you, April, and Aselia out of there immediately."

"We're not abandoning you—"

"Kevin." Jessie's voice was as firm as a hand on the back of his neck. "I said it's an order. Hopefully it won't come to that, but if it does, you can and you *will* fly out of here. Now give April the phone."

We waited as he passed it over.

"Jessie," April said, in a tone I couldn't quite read.

"I assume you heard that."

"I caught the gist of it from Kevin's end. You don't want us to wait for you if Crohn's men come poking around."

"I expect he'll try to disobey that order," Jessie said. "I expect you won't."

"You expect correctly. Be safe, Jessie."

"You, too." Jessie nodded at me, and I hung up the phone.

We listened to the rattling of the subway wheels. Lights strobed in the tunnel dark, flashing off grimy windows.

"We messed up," Jessie said. "Obviously. Just can't see *where*."

"Could have been a street camera. We've been as careful as we can be, but New York is blanketed with them. If Crohn's got people running traffic cams through facial recognition—"

"Every cam in every city in America? Not even the Bureau can do that. No, it's got to be something else." She bit her bottom lip, thinking hard. "We'll figure it out. Let's just keep moving, and cover our tracks as best we can."

Once we got off at the Twenty-Third Street station, our tracks led for six minutes through Manhattan's skyscraper canyons. They ended a stone's throw from Broadway. Vlad gave us the secret lay of the land: our final destination was Wycombe's, a two-story bookstore built into the gray brick facade of the Saint Francis Building. We camped at a table in the Starbucks down the block, watching the clock and watching the street. Dashwood Abbey didn't open its doors until moonrise, as a rule.

I sipped my hot coffee—black, one cream, one sugar—and waited. The shadows grew long, sunset dipping below the skyline, the streets choked with taxicabs and blaring horns. The commuter stampede was still under way by the time Jessie slurped the last dregs from her plastic cup through an oversize straw. She'd opted for some mocha monstrosity under a boulder of whipped cream and sluiced in caramel sauce. Then she'd had a second one with double the caramel.

"I have been adequately caffeinated and sugared," she said. She eyed my paper cup. "And you have been . . . bored."

"Nothing wrong with classic black coffee." I pushed my chair back and stood on weary legs.

"Sure, if Joe Friday is your role model."

"Just the facts, ma'am," I deadpanned, following her to the door.

Jessie stopped in her tracks. She looked back at me, wide-eyed.

"What?" I asked.

"I've just . . ." She clapped her hands to her chest and batted her eyelashes at me. "I've never actually heard you say that out loud. And I didn't know how much I wanted to until this very moment. Harmony . . . you complete me."

I grinned and gave her shoulder a push. "C'mon, let's get to work."

Wycombe's revolving door drew a stark dividing line between the night chill of the street and warm, soft ambience. Piped-in chamber music swallowed the muffled traffic noise, and the smell outside—musty cardboard and car exhaust—gave way to the scent of lavender. Track lighting cast sleek circles along the polished hardwood floor and wide, welcoming aisles. The bookstore kept late hours—the sign out front said they didn't turn off the lights until midnight—but I only saw a handful of shoppers browsing the stacks.

"Even if I didn't *know* this place was off," Jessie murmured at my side, "I'd still know it."

"How do you figure?"

Jessie nodded at the shelves. "You tell me."

I put my detective hat on. There weren't many *New York Times* bestsellers on display. No popular authors, or authors I recognized at all, really. Wycombe's specialized in foreign translations and imported hardcovers, scholarly dissertations, entire sections on high cuisine and musical theory.

"Cultured," I said.

"Mmm-hmm. And cultured doesn't pay rent on two floors of Manhattan real estate, one street down from Broadway. Judging from the lack of customers, they've got champagne tastes and a ginger-ale budget."

"They're making their money elsewhere." I approached one of the clerks, a rail-thin woman in a black turtleneck sweaterdress. "Pardon me. Have you seen the abbot?"

Her eyes widened, just a bit. Recognizing the pass phrase Vlad had taught us.

"They say he's gone away," she replied, glancing left and right to ensure we were out of her customers' earshot.

"How far has he gone?" I asked.

"Too far, perhaps."

I shook my head and folded my arms. As I did, I pressed my index and middle fingers together, tapping my elbows twice.

"You can never go too far."

She favored us with a smile, and I lowered my arms. The ritual exchange complete. She pointed toward a short hallway in the back of the shop, under a plaque reading EMPLOYEES ONLY.

"Just through there," she said. "Please, enjoy yourselves."

Jessie looked over her shoulder and dropped her voice as we crossed the sales floor.

"Thing about these occult-underground types," she said, "they *love* their complicated, stupid-ass passwords. That was just embarrassing."

"Yeah," I said. "I noticed you made me do it."

She rubbed my shoulder. "I wouldn't have kept a straight face. You're good at being stoic. It's your superpower. Now, what do we have here?"

At the end of the hall, past a sharp left turn, an elevator door with a single button waited for us. A pale stone plaque hung over the door, engraved with the words *Fais ce que voudras*. Jessie leaned in, punched the button, and glanced up at the carving.

"What do you think that means?"

"My high-school French is rusty, but . . ." I thought back, knowing I'd seen those words somewhere before. "Oh, right. It's a quote from Rabelais. Means 'Do what you will.'"

The door rumbled open. Beyond, a small and empty cage with stainless steel walls awaited us.

"Thank you," Jessie said to the plaque. She stepped into the elevator. "Don't mind if I do."

The panel offered a pair of buttons, 1 and 2. I tapped 2. Nothing happened.

"Looks like we're going down," I said, and hit 1. The door shut, sealing us in, and the elevator shuddered as it slowly descended.

"Ominous."

"I assume it's supposed to be," I said. "So, what we've got here is basically the New York City version of Chicago's Bast Club. On the plus side, it couldn't possibly be more obnoxious than the Bast Club."

Jessie turned and gave me a long, hard look.

"Why do you have to go and tempt fate like that?"

The elevator chimed.

TWENTY-THREE

The elevator door opened onto darkness, and the music washed in. A thrumming bass line, deep and sinuous. It rumbled through the floor, up my legs, and straight into my spine like a writhing serpent made of sound. The walls beyond the door were painted midnight black, the only illumination coming from a tiny white plastic pyramid set into one corner of the floor where the hall bent to the left.

Another bend, then another, and the serpentine hall opened onto a murky lounge half-lit in pale blue. Knife-scarred tables sat at odd angles with mismatched chairs. Sofas ringed the room, all upholstered in fraying velvet. Couples sat here and there; others lingered by a bar. The shelves behind the bar were lined with empty bottles, foreign brands with names I'd never heard of, and the barflies pantomimed sipping from dry and dusty glasses. Some of the couples, most dressed in tailored suits or haute couture, whispered under the thrumming bass. Others stared at one another in perfect silence. A few wore masks, pale white and sculpted to resemble the faces of animals.

"What was that you were saying a minute ago?" Jessie whispered in my ear.

There were no rules posted, but raising my voice instinctively felt like a bad idea. I whispered back, "Let's keep moving."

The lounge had three exits, open archways spaced at random along the walls. We chose one and navigated between walls of bare wood slats. Up ahead, beyond a closed and unadorned door, a cry of pain rang out. Then another, along with a muffled *crack*, as my shoulders tensed and I reached for my holster.

Jessie stepped ahead of me, the hall barely wide enough for two people to move side by side. She paused at the door. She opened it, barely an inch, and peered inside. Then she closed it again. She looked back at me and shook her head as she whispered, "Nobody's getting hurt. Well, they *are*, but—" She shook her head again. "It's a play party."

I blinked. "What's a play party?"

Jessie patted my shoulder. "Dear, sweet, innocent Harmony. Sweet, impressionable, naive—"

"It's a sex thing," I whispered. "Isn't it?"

"C'mon." She nodded ahead. "Y'know, normally I might check this out . . ."

"There are things I don't need to know about you, Jessie."

"My safe word is *Oklahoma*." She winked and kept walking.

We skirted through a small octagonal room filled with dangling glass wind chimes. Underground, in heat that grew more stifling the longer we lingered, there was no wind. Yet as we turned our backs, they chimed anyway. Jessie opened a random door, and we stared into a lightless chamber, squinting to see. Someone was in there, huddled in the farthest corner, clutching their arms and slowly rocking from side to side as they faced the wall.

"Uh-uh," Jessie said. She shut the door.

Another archway opened onto a second lounge. Unlike the first, this one had full bottles behind the bar and an actual bartender— dressed in red suspenders and his cuffs rolled up to show off his tattoo sleeves—to serve them up. His golden septum piercing glittered as he gave us an inviting nod from across the room. This was the real lounge, I assumed, as far as anything in Dashwood Abbey felt real. The room thrummed with low conversation, partygoers casting smoldering glances, dark laughter and clinking glasses. Everything—the tables, the benches, the bar—was gray. Draped in gray velvet or painted the colors of smoke, fleeting, like the world around us could vanish under my fingertips.

"Ladies," the bartender said. A light strip along the bar shone up and onto his face from below, like a counselor about to tell a ghost story around a campfire. Jessie slid onto a padded stool. I stood at her shoulder.

"Evening," Jessie said. "Quite a place you've got here."

He gave us a knowing smile. "First-timers, huh? Thought so. From out of town?"

"Chicago," I said. "Traveling on business. Some friends of ours at the Bast Club said we had to check this place out."

Never hurts to drop a name or two. Our credentials established, his smile grew a bit more familiar. He reached for a tumbler behind the bar and wiped it out with a storm-gray terry cloth.

"I like to think we have a little something for everyone," he said. "Patrons come to us with healthy desires, and we try to . . . facilitate them."

"What about the unhealthy ones?" I asked him.

He chuckled and picked up a smoked-glass bottle. The label, scarlet with black letters, was in Cyrillic. "Those, too. But let's start where we start. Drinks?"

"How about a manhattan?" Jessie said.

The bartender gave her a patronizing look. "Oh, your friends didn't tell you."

"Tell us what?" Jessie said. "Is a manhattan called something different *in* Manhattan? Like how french fries are called *pommes frites* in France?"

"Drinks at Dashwood Abbey don't work that way. You order by flavor or feel, whatever your palate is craving, and I mix something to suit. Perhaps you'd like something fruity and cold, something tangy and hot? Maybe something recklessly erotic, but with an aftertaste of next-morning regret. Something mournful, perhaps."

"How can a drink be mournful?" I asked.

He turned to regard me, his face underlit by the bar, and the hint of a dare dancing in his eyes.

"Ask for one," he said, "and find out."

"Spicy," Jessie told him. "Spicy sounds good."

He flipped the bottle, catching it in his other hand, and gave it a shake. "Spicy like dancing the tango with your lover, or spicy like a back-alley knife fight?"

"Let's go with the knife fight."

He poured from unrecognizable carafes, shaking thick cubes of ice in a tumbler, and looked my way. "And you, miss?"

I wasn't sure. As I thought it over, he took another long look at me.

"Those aren't your usual clothes," he told me.

I glanced down at my thrift-store disguise. "Oh?"

"They fit you fine, but you wear them like they're made of burlap. Your every move, chafing." He snatched up another bottle. "No, you . . . I see you in a battered trench coat, the kind that fits you like an old familiar song. Leaning against the bar in some low-rent dive, marinating in bourbon and misery, contemplating the dame who did you wrong."

I forced half a smile, even as his gaze dug a hole straight through me. He poured the contents of the tumbler into a cocktail glass without even looking at it, not missing a drop.

"You've mistaken me for an old private-eye movie," I told him.

"Have I? I get impressions about people." He tapped the side of his head and swapped bottles, reaching for a blue glass decanter.

The label bore characters in a language I couldn't even recognize, a disjointed mash-up of Chinese letters and Nordic runes.

"Definitely a trench coat. Alone, your back to the wall, coming around to the terrible truth that every noir hero must eventually face."

"Which is?" I asked.

"That the world as you wish it to be, and the world as it is, are two very different things and always will be. That happiness is fleeting, that pain is the human condition, and that life is a string of short-lived ports of solace in one long, dark storm."

He slid two glasses toward us. Jessie's was lobster pink and speckled scarlet, bits of red pepper bobbing on the surface. Mine was umber brown, served in a lowball glass with an octagonal stick of ice leaning to one side like a garnish.

"Cheers," he said. I raised my glass and took a sip.

It tasted like a saxophone melody playing in a cold summer rain. Smoky and swirling and pulling me down, a little come-hither, a little lonely.

Jessie blinked at her glass, wide-eyed.

"This is . . . really damn good," she said.

The bartender just whistled, wiping down another tumbler and looking smug.

"You must know your clientele," I said.

"I'm a bartender. People tell me things, with their words or their faces. I listen."

"We're looking to meet up with a friend of a friend. Tonino Giannetti."

He glanced up from his work. "Tony Four-Ways? Now, why would a couple of nice ladies like you want to talk to a nasty piece of work like that?"

"Like I said," I told him, "we're traveling on business."

The bartender's gaze dropped to my side. I cut a slim profile, but his eyes still latched on to the gun under my windbreaker as if he could see through the cheap fabric.

"Word of advice," he said. "I don't know what your line of business is, but if you're into hostile takeovers, Dashwood Abbey has ways of protecting itself. And our valued clientele."

"You make it sound like Tony has enemies."

"Tony likes the ladies," the bartender said, "and he likes dropping names to make himself sound more important than he is. Names that certain people might not want dropped. Play gangster games, win gangster prizes."

"We just want to talk to him," Jessie said. "We're basically friendly people."

The bartender gave a casual nod over my left shoulder. Steering my attention to the back of the lounge.

"Far sofa, against the wall," he said. "Wears his hair in a side part, under a fistful of grease. Powder-blue suit."

I paid for the drinks with cash. We carried our glasses across the lounge, winding between tables and murmured conversations. Giannetti's voice rang out over the rest, drenched in alcohol-infused bravado.

"So then I said," he laughed, "you ain't apologized to my *other* fist yet."

The women to his left and his right—a blonde and a brunette in minidresses the color of smoke—giggled politely. He had a chubby arm around each of their shoulders, leaning back on the sofa with his knees spread. His gaze swung our way, hungry, taking us in from head to toe.

"Hey, hey, what do we have here?" he said. "Ain't seen you two around before."

"We're new in town," I said. "Looking to make new friends."

His hands massaged the women's bare shoulders, fingers wriggling like centipedes. They wore plastic smiles in silence.

"You came to the right place. I'm a friendly guy."

"This is more business than pleasure," Jessie said. "Opportunity knocks."

"That's one door I always open." He patted his companions' shoulders. "You wanna excuse us for a moment? Don't go far."

The women in the smoke-colored dresses rose as one, sharing a knowing glance, and stepped around us. Not sure why, but I turned to look behind me.

They were gone.

"Care to have a seat?" Giannetti patted the vacant cushions.

"We'll stand," Jessie said. "We understand you're a big man in this town. The kind of guy who gets things done."

His smile could have lit up the lounge. We didn't need April's help to crack into Giannetti's brain: he walked around with a user's manual tattooed on his forehead.

"You heard that, huh? Where at?"

"Everywhere," I said. "Where *don't* they talk about you? Back home, everybody told us the same thing: when you get to New York, you'd better look up Tony Four-Ways. Nothing happens without his say-so."

He ducked his head and gave an expansive shrug, a picture of false modesty. "I wouldn't go that far, but yeah, I got some juice. Where do you call home, doll?"

"We used to call it Los Angeles, but we're looking for a change of lifestyle," Jessie said.

"You could do a lot worse than New York, if that's what you're thinking. This is the place to be."

We'd rehearsed our approach on the subway, concocting a story that would get the hound's attention. Now I just needed to sell it.

"I wish it was that easy," I said. "We have certain ties back home. Ties we need help cutting."

"This a family thing?" He gave me a closer look, squinting. "Nah. Capital-*F* family thing. Lemme guess: You got a jealous boyfriend? Guy with connections? I could make a few phone calls—"

"Different kind of underworld," Jessie said. "We hear you know people in the Court of Windswept Razors. Powerful people. They say you've got their hound on speed dial, and when you talk, the hound listens."

He nodded, appraising her. "True. True. But I'm not entirely sure what you're asking me for. Lay it on the line for me."

I stepped closer to the couch, voice low, and dangled my baited hook.

"We're agents for the Court of Jade Tears," I said. "We want to defect."

TWENTY-FOUR

Giannetti's eyes glittered like he'd opened a pirate's treasure chest. Before, he'd been appraising our bedroom potential. Now we were commodities.

"The Jade Tears don't employ many pure-bred humans," he said, "and you don't have the cambion look . . ."

I held my drink in one hand and cupped the other, raising my palm between us. Then I reached to my magic. A swirling spark became a marble of flame, casting shifting shadows across our faces. His eyes widened. Then I curled my fingers and snuffed out the light.

"We have talents," I told him.

"So you do. Now, when you say 'agents'—"

"We work with Caitlin," Jessie said. "Her personal staff. And yes, that means we know where the bodies are buried—figuratively and literally."

"We took three terabytes of files from her private server before we left," I said.

We had no idea if Caitlin even owned a computer. Still, modern age, modern tools, and the agents of hell we'd met mostly seemed as tech savvy as we were, so it felt like a safe gamble.

Giannetti rubbed his greasy chin. "That's a big number."

"I imagine certain people would pay a big number to get it, too," I said. "But the files aren't for sale. We're looking to *give* them away. They go to the first court that offers us new jobs and new identities. Any chance you could swing an introduction to the hound for us?"

"Have to think there'd be a reward involved," Jessie added.

From the look on his face, Giannetti was thinking the same thing.

"Let me make a couple of phone calls, real quick." He pushed himself off the gray velvet sofa and stepped between us, going out of his way to brush his hand across my arm. I forced myself to smile. Once he was out of earshot, Jessie leaned in close.

"We shoot, we score. Sounds like he bought it."

"Now we just need to see if the *hound* buys it," I murmured back. "Are defectors even a thing with these people? We need more intel on how the courts operate."

Of course, now we knew why it had always been so hard to get that intelligence. Vigilant Lock had been kneecapped from day one. We were meant to be disposable weapons of the eastern courts all along, skilled enough to be a thorn in their enemies' sides but never informed or strong enough to pose a real threat. I wondered how many field reports were quietly dustbinned instead of being disseminated to Vigilant's other teams. How much data on the monsters we fought—critical, lifesaving information—had been deliberately swept under the rug?

I thought about the *Wunderkammer*, Vigilant's storage facility for captured artifacts and dangerous manuscripts. The lockup was firmly under the eastern coalition's control, all that power at hell's fingertips. The relics we'd captured, the demons we'd trapped in soul bottles . . . we'd *given* it all to them. Signed, sealed, and delivered.

"We've got a lot of work to do," I said.

"Amen." Jessie sipped her cocktail, then glanced at the glass in my hand. "You gonna finish that?"

"We're on duty."

"Yeah, but they're damn good drinks. Besides, no telling when we'll be back here again." Jessie's gaze swept across the room. "I don't think we're hip enough for this place."

"I don't think *anyone* is hip enough for this place."

Giannetti came back, all smiles, arms spread wide like he was hoping for a hug.

"Good news. Prospero—that's the Razors' hound, good guy, *great* guy—is very interested and would love to have a sit-down with you ladies. He wants to hear what you're bringing to the table, then hopefully he'll be making you an offer. Call it a job interview."

Jessie ran her fingers up his arm like she was playing a piano. "Everything they said is true. You're the man, Tony. The real thing."

"Hey, don't you forget it." He flashed a couple of gold-capped teeth as he basked in her approval. "And don't forget me when you find yourself moving up in the world, yeah? We're gonna be neighbors now. Anyway, he doesn't see any reason to wait on this: the meet's tonight—I'll give you the address. It's on Bridge Street in Vinegar Hill. That's Brooklyn, out by the waterfront."

"Well, then," Jessie said, tossing back the last of her cocktail, "we'd better not keep him waiting."

# # #

Brooklyn was a subway ride away. The train rattled through the night, the frigid tunnels like veins under the city's stone skin. We rode in silence. The subway doors hissed open, and a gust of cold wind washed over us. We stepped out onto the platform, following the sparse late-night crowd to a staircase blanketed in harsh white light.

I called April.

"Do we have any information on a demon calling himself Prospero?"

"Prospero, as in Shakespeare's *Tempest*?" April asked. "I don't have much in the way of research material here, but I'll see what I can dig up. Are you—hold on, Kevin is wildly gesticulating in my direction. Ah. Linder's calling in."

"Can you patch him through?" I asked. We stepped off to the side, hovering on the platform's edge.

I waited, listening as a string of clicks echoed across the line.

Then Linder's voice, an edge of tension under his usual calculated dispassion. "Agents."

"What have you got?" I said. "Any idea how Panic Cell found out we were in New York? And how are they tracking us?"

"I'm not remotely certain. Director Crohn's behavior has grown increasingly . . . erratic since you escaped him in Washington. His body is intact. His pride, grievously wounded. At any rate, he's shutting me out of the pursuit, and given the circumstances, I can't risk drawing attention by asking too many questions."

"*He's* intact," Jessie said, almost cheek to cheek with me as she leaned into the phone. "Any chance he killed Nyx?"

"Negative. Street cameras show her injured but fleeing the scene. In human form, thankfully. I called to update you on my end of things. I'm making inroads with Dick Esposito, the Bureau's deputy director. He's motivated, ambitious, he hasn't been compromised by our enemies—oh, and he and Crohn despise each other. I think we can turn him into an asset."

"Can he clear our names?" I said.

"Not yet, so keep your heads down. Esposito's completely in the dark when it comes to Vigilant, and I'd like to keep him that way for as long as possible. That said, if we were to pave the way for his career advancement and earn his gratitude . . ."

"Like proof that Crohn is shady?" Jessie asked. "Not occult-underground stuff—details on bribes, crimes, anything that we can put in front of a news camera."

"It's an option. One way or another—burn the contracts or burn his career—Crohn's removal is our top priority. But we have to think about follow-through. If he suddenly drops dead, it won't magically make the charges against you go away. If anything, considering he fabricated them, it could be even harder to prove your innocence. I'll keep grooming Esposito. Dig deep, Agents. Bring me leverage."

He disconnected the call.

I put my phone away and looked sidelong at Jessie. "If there's any dirt to be found, this Prospero guy's gonna have it."

Jessie nodded. "Along with the contracts, if we're lucky."

"If we're lucky," I said.

"Not even gonna bother crossing my fingers," Jessie said. "Okay, so . . . two options. One, we do a covert pass-by on the address Tony gave us, check it out, see if we can get eyes on Prospero from a safe distance. Then we tail him and hope he leads us to the goodies."

"And the other?"

"We keep the ruse going," she said. "Show up for the job interview. If we play this right, he might walk us right into his office, or wherever high-ranking demon creeps happen to keep their important files. If we go for stealth and then lose this guy, we're right back at square one."

"And if we go face-to-face and he thinks we're lying, we'll be a lot worse off than that. Hounds are supposed to be the best of the best. I mean, we barely fought Nadine to a draw, and you saw her back in Portland—she was *scared* of Caitlin. Whatever this Prospero is capable of, I think we need to be better prepared than this."

"Danger is my middle name," she said.

"Georgeanne is your middle name."

She stopped walking, tugged down her dark glasses, and glared at me.

I shrugged. "What? I looked at your driver's license once."

"Harmony," she said, "there are things you don't need to know about me."

New York hummed electric at night. Even long after dark, in the cold hours past midnight, the streets were alive with people and traffic. Up in Vinegar Hill, with the lights of the Brooklyn Navy Yard in the distance, a soft and steady thrum from a power plant filled the air. We walked down side streets where old worlds and new stood shoulder to shoulder, a five-story condo pressed between antique carriage houses. Belgian blocks, vintage bricks shaped like cobblestones, clacked under our feet.

We'd gone far enough off the beaten path to leave the pedestrians and the late-night taxicabs behind.

I checked the address Giannetti gave us. It was an apartment complex up ahead, a squat U-shaped antique in dirty white brick with a central courtyard. Half the windows dark, the rest draped with bedsheets or cheap and mismatched blinds. Jessie lowered her glasses and squinted.

"He gave us the place but no apartment number," she said. "What are we supposed to do, knock on doors?"

Our answer came in the full-throated growl of a motorcycle engine. Then another, and another, until seven more joined the chorus. Bikes rolled out of the courtyard and onto the street like a military convoy. Headlights washed over us, pinning us where we stood.

"I think he's coming to *us*," I said.

"Huh." Jessie's right hand curled into a fist. "Looks like we're trying my plan, after all."

TWENTY-FIVE

We stood in the middle of the street as the caravan of motorcycles circled us, closing ranks, swirling like slow and hungry sharks. The riders, decked out in black leather and patches, looked like sharks themselves as they flashed gnarled, jagged teeth. One pulled up his tinted goggles to show us a pair of runny-egg-yolk eyes.

"Cambion biker gang," Jessie breathed. "Great. You wanna take the four on the left, I'll take the four on the right?"

A ripple of unfocused magic sent a nervous shiver up my spine, ready to be called upon. I kept my hands easy and open.

"Wait for it," I said. "When it comes to the courts of hell, cambion are errand boys at best. We want the *big* boss."

The convoy rumbled to a halt.

One of the bikers, the one with the goggles, looked our way. "You girls look lost," he said. One of his buddies, behind us, let out a wolf whistle.

Giannetti had written the address down on a smoke-gray napkin, along with a squiggle that looked like some kind of personal sigil. I held it up, the ink glossy black in the streetlight.

"We're right where we're supposed to be," I said. "We've got an appointment with Prospero. Don't think he'd like it very much if we were late."

The biker locked eyes with me. I held his gaze, counting under my breath. One, one hundred, two, one hundred—

"That's where *he* meets Prospero." He made a gun with his fingers and pointed it the other way. The far side of the street, the door to a second-floor walk-up above a repair shop with a dirty yellow awning. "That's where *you* meet him."

"Does he own the whole block?" Jessie asked.

"He owns the whole city. You'll remember that if you're smart."

The circle of bikes parted. They walked their rides back, opening a hole just wide enough for the two of us, aiming us at the door. The battered metal knob wriggled under my hand as it turned, and the rickety wooden door yawned wide.

"Be seeing you," the biker called out behind us. "Or not."

A narrow staircase waited beyond the door, bare and dusty steps that groaned under our feet. We knew Ben Crohn reported directly to Prospero. The way I saw it, there were two possibilities. Either Prospero was a hands-off manager, or he was in the loop. If he was in the loop, he'd know who we were on sight. Crohn's pride and his sense of self-preservation were our best allies right now. Would he admit what was going on and risk his boss's wrath, or try to keep it hushed up and handle it himself? I knew what I would pick, considering Prospero could kill him with a single lit match.

My hand brushed the Sig Sauer under my windbreaker. The other called to my magic, feeling the faint and flickering current like a wave of static electricity.

I felt Jessie's palm against the small of my back. "Hey," she murmured. "We can do this."

"Do I look tense?"

She tapped the side of her nose and gave me a lopsided smile.

"Right," I said, "wolf senses."

"Just remember, we've got two goals here: get as much intel as we can going in; do as much damage as we can on our way out."

"Sounds doable," I said.

"Very doable. Especially the damage part. After the shit we've been through these last few days, I *really* want to break some stuff."

She wasn't alone there. At the second-floor landing, a bare wooden door awaited. No sign, no number. I knocked twice.

The figure who opened the door, standing on the threshold and gazing at us from behind tortoiseshell glasses, didn't look like my idea of a demon prince's right-hand man. More like a moderately successful accountant, with his ash-colored hair in a wispy comb-over, and spearmint-green suspenders holding up his slacks. His eyes were a little too big for his face, his chin a little too small. If I'd seen him out on the street somewhere, I would have looked past him without a second glance.

Up close, though, what I felt clashed with what I saw. Waves of power rippled off him like a heat mirage in the desert. He was an open gas main, turning the air around him toxic, just waiting for the flick of a lighter to drench the world in flame.

"My new friends," he said in a nervous, uneven voice. "I hope we'll be friends. Won't you please come in?"

He ushered us into his office, a staid room that smelled like mothballs. Books on law and accounting lined floor-to-ceiling shelves, and a lamp with a green shade sat on an immaculately clean desk. Behind the desk, off to the right, a narrow window looked out onto a back alley.

"I hope the welcoming committee didn't give you any trouble." He let out a high-pitched giggle. His left eyelid twitched. "Cambion. So boisterous. Eager to please, eager not to please—they can hardly make up their minds."

When he turned his back, stepping behind the desk, Jessie shot me a look. She twirled one finger around her ear. I didn't disagree. Something was just *off* about Prospero. Then I looked past Jessie and nodded at the bookshelves. One section of books, right in the middle, didn't match the rest. Unlabeled covers, squeezed too tight and too evenly together, and filling the shelf from top to bottom. Fakes. Like a concealed lid for a wall safe, possibly.

We sat in low-slung chairs on the far side of the desk. Prospero looked from me to Jessie and back again. He pointed his fingers at us, then slapped his palms on the desk in an erratic little drumbeat.

"I," he said, "have seen you on television. I just can't quite remember where. Was it an episode of *Law & Order*? No. Wait. A Western. An old rerun of *Gunsmoke*, perhaps."

Weird mirth danced in his eyes. He was playing with us—I just wasn't sure what kind of game. Or how much he really knew. In the corner of my eye, Jessie shifted in her chair. Bringing her concealed gun a half inch closer to her hand. As my mind raced, I settled on a gamble. A big one.

"That's why we're here," I told him. "We're deep-cover operatives for the Court of Jade Tears, inserted into the Federal Bureau of Investigation on a long-term mission. What you saw on the news, that so-called robbery, was actually an attempt on our lives."

His eyebrows lifted. "Atlantic City is a long way from the West Coast. Caitlin knowingly sent operatives outside her prince's territory?"

"We've been investigating a serious threat—not just to her court, but to all of them." I took a deep breath and rolled the dice. "We've become aware of an illegal black-ops program, buried deep inside the government. It's called Vigilant Lock."

Prospero's cheek twitched. The ghost of an "I know something you don't" smile. "And the . . . purpose of this program is what, exactly?"

My phone vibrated against my hip, a call coming in. I ignored it and looked Prospero in the eye.

"It's a band of humans who have somehow become aware of the courts' existence. Their mandate is to detect, intercept, and kill our people by any means necessary."

"You say 'our people,'" he replied, "but I don't smell a whiff of *my* blood in your veins."

Jessie followed my lead. "We've been loyal to the Jade Tears. They took us in. Gave us a purpose."

"A purpose?" Prospero gave her a shy smile and another high-pitched giggle. "Ooh, are you *idealists*? Most humans just want cash in exchange for betraying their own species."

"The cash is nice, too," I said. "But we thought loyalty was a two-way street. Vigilant operatives attacked us in the Diamondback Casino. We had to shoot our way out—idiot civilians got in our way. Next thing we know, our faces are all over the news. We called Caitlin for extraction. Know what she told us? 'You're useless to us now. You're on your own.'"

"They burned us," Jessie grumbled.

My phone started buzzing again, insistent. Prospero shot a pointed glance downward.

"Do you need to get that?" he asked.

"No, it's fine."

"Really," he said, "this is *only* the most important job interview of your mortal lives. I can wait."

"I'll call them back."

He drummed his palms on the desk again. "Right answer. So. You're in the wind, cast aside like yesterday's rubbish. I wish I could tell you that our rivals didn't have a reputation for that sort of thing. You arguably should have known better."

"We hear you treat your people with more respect than that," Jessie said. "We're looking for new faces and new identities."

"Hmm. Your usefulness as assets in the FBI is over—I'm afraid she was right about that much. What else can you do? What can you do for *me*?"

"We're trained in infiltration, abduction, interrogation, and assassination." I spread my hands, trying to sell the role. I thought back to the first time I met Mikki. Channeling her movements, her speech patterns. "We've also both been diagnosed as clinical psychopaths, which, let's face it, is an asset in this line of work. We're the complete package."

"Try us out," Jessie said. "Call it an audition. Point out a problem—or a problem person—and we'll eliminate it for you. Free of charge. Once you see the results, pretty sure you're gonna want us on your team."

Smart move. An audition would get us out of this office and away from the weirdly giggling toxic-magic-leaking demon on the other side of the desk. We could come back, break in, and crack his safe once the coast was clear.

"Try before I buy?" Prospero tittered. "If the murder business doesn't work out, you should think about getting into sales. You know, there is something. A reporter for the *Times* has been digging in to a shell company owned by friends of mine. Could be a scandal brewing, or legal trouble."

"You want us to take him out?" I asked.

He stared across the desk at me. His dimples faded; the giggling stopped. His voice became cool and measured.

"He's been useful to me in the past, so I want you to send a message instead. I would like him to wake up and find the corpse of his five-year-old son. I would like the boy to be skinned, and his entrails placed to spell out something amusing. Is that a problem?"

My guts clenched, and I fought to keep the revulsion from showing on my face. If I slipped, if I gave him any reason not to believe my act, we were both dead. I felt my cheek muscles tightening—and went in the opposite direction. Instead of struggling for a poker face, I burst out laughing and gave him a lunatic grin.

"A kid? I thought you were going to give us a *hard* test." I looked over at Jessie. "And you were worried."

She shrugged like she couldn't care less. "Whatever, give us the address and we'll be back in an hour."

Prospero beamed at us, his palms slapping a staccato beat on the desk. "Eager beavers! Now remember, I want *lots* of pictures—"

A phone trilled. He glanced down, suddenly irritated, and arched his eyebrow.

"Sorry, I do have to take this." He put the phone to his ear. "Ben, what have I told you about calling me? This number is only for emergen—what? Wait. Wait. Slow down and take a deep breath—you're babbling."

My stomach plummeted harder than the first drop of a roller coaster. Jessie and I shared a sidelong glance.

"Wait, you're *here*? *Here* here, or . . . I'm not going to tell you again, *take a breath.*" Prospero shoved his chair back, cupping his hand over the phone. "I'm sorry, I'll be right back. Please, make yourselves comfortable. There's coffee, if you'd like."

The door swung shut behind him. The only door. And from the sound of it, he was standing right on the other side, listening to a man who was about to blow our cover.

TWENTY-SIX

We jumped to our feet. *"Desk,"* I whispered, pointing as I padded over to the bookshelves. Every passing second dragged us closer to a fight with an angry demon, a fight we weren't equipped for, but we had to grab whatever intel we could. I felt along the fake row of books, fingers searching for a seam or a catch, while Jessie riffled through his desk drawers. On the other side of the flimsy door, I heard Prospero talking on the phone.

"What do you mean, a cell's gone rogue? So what are you calling me for? Kill them and replace them. It's not the team investigating Diehl, is it? Ben, we *need* a way to take down the Network. You're not the only person who's accountable for results. I promise you, my boss is a lot tougher on me than I am on—okay, then stop babbling and explain it to me."

I found the catch. The panel swung open on a concealed hinge, exposing a recessed steel safe with an electronic keypad mechanism. I took out my phone and snapped pictures. Nothing we could do right now, but once we had time to regroup with the team, we could come up with a strategy for cracking it open. Having the make and model might help. Behind me, Jessie dug through old files and receipts, shaking her head.

"Does this have something to do with that Vigilant operation in Atlantic City?" Prospero said. He giggled. "How do I know about that? Oh, you're going to love this. Those Jade Tears agents your people were after? They're *here*, looking for safe harbor. I'm probably going to hire them. They actually came to warn me about—wait, slow down. What?"

Jessie ran to the window. I shut the safe panel, leaving it exactly as I'd found it: if Prospero figured out his safe was our target, he might empty it out before we came back for the break-in.

Optimistic thinking. First, we had to survive the next five minutes. Jessie flipped the clasps, hauling the window up and open. The hall had gone silent. Then, as Jessie swung one leg over the sill and looked down to the alley below, I heard Prospero's voice drop to a slow and venomous growl.

"Ben. Listen to me. It is very, very important that I understand you correctly before I do something irreversible. Your rogue operatives are *who*, exactly?"

Jessie shoved herself out the window. I was right behind her. I leaned out to take a look, and my breath caught in my throat.

No fire escape. It was a straight drop to the alley, maybe fifteen feet down. I saw Jessie land with a thud, dropping to a crouch, then rolling on her shoulder with supernatural grace. She jumped to her feet and dusted off her sleeve.

I didn't have any occult-infused blood to ease my landing. My bones were all too human and breakable. Still, I hooked one leg over the sill, looking back at the office door. I froze for the space of a heartbeat, trapped between a demon and a long, hard drop.

"Come *on*," Jessie whispered, waving her hands at me. "I'll catch you, I promise!"

I sat on the edge and took a deep breath. Then I shoved my palms against the sill and let myself fall. Behind me, the office door exploded.

I heard the wood shatter, the door blasting open on a torn and tortured hinge, splinters and sawdust flying above my head like shrapnel as I plummeted. My heart lurched into my throat, night wind whistling in my ears—

Then Jessie's arms caught me, scooping me up before my feet hit the alley floor. She set me down and hugged me tight just for a second. Above our heads, a guttural bellow of rage boomed from the office window.

"I've got a great idea," Jessie said.

"Run really fast?"

She nodded and pointed up the garbage-strewn alley, toward a distant streetlight. "It's like you read my mind."

We broke into a sprint, footfalls pounding. I glanced back over my shoulder. If Prospero was coming after us, he wasn't taking the window. I tried to figure the distance between the front door and the alley. How fast could he move?

And what would he look like when we saw him?

A headlight flared up ahead, punctuated by the roar of an engine. Prospero had called for backup. A motorcycle blazed toward us, its front wheel lifting off the ground, charging full throttle down the middle of the alley. I grabbed Jessie's arm and yanked her to one side, taking cover beside a dumpster. Electric light glinted off chrome in the rider's gloved hand. His front wheel slapped down on the broken pavement as he took rough aim and squeezed the trigger. His machine pistol's muzzle flashed hot white, and bullets chewed into the dumpster, twisting steel.

As he veered past us, I was already down on one knee, Sig Sauer in my hand and my eyes on the sights. I fired one shot. The back of his helmet ruptured like a crater on the moon, and he spun out, falling from the saddle and rolling, dead. His bike skidded across the alley in a shower of sparks. We ran after it. Jessie grabbed hold of the handlebars and hauled the motorcycle back upright while another headlight blazed at the opposite end of the alley.

I summoned my magic as I swung into the saddle. Jessie got on behind me, her hands tight on my hips. I revved the engine. At the far end of the alley, straight ahead of us, so did they.

I gunned it.

We lurched forward, wheels bouncing, charging toward the oncoming headlight. I couldn't see the riders in the glare, couldn't see if they were taking aim. Only intuition could guide me now. I counted down—three, two, one—then flung up my hand, drawing a shimmering wall of air in front of us just a heartbeat before they opened fire. A trio of rounds hung frozen in the air, one aimed right between my eyes and six inches away, slowly boring through the magical shield. The speedometer read thirty, thirty-five, and the gap between our bikes closed by the second as we charged down the narrow alley on a collision course.

I dug deep, drawing up every last reserve of energy, and mentally *shoved*. The air shield tugged, pulled, then snapped like a rubber band, sending the bullets winging back where they came from. The oncoming headlight shattered. The bike wobbled, but the rider, unhit, kept on coming.

"You want to play chicken?" I breathed. "Okay. Let's play."

I gritted my teeth and went hard on the throttle, picking up even more speed, holding the bike on a spear-straight course right down the middle of the alley. Close enough now to see the look of the cambion biker's face in the wash of my high beam. I looked for the flicker of fear on his face, any indication that he wasn't on a suicide mission.

There it was. Three seconds to impact, his mouth opened wide as he realized I wasn't going to stop.

He yanked his handlebars hard to the left, veering out of our path, careening into a pile of garbage bags. His front wheel hit the debris, and his bike flipped. He went flying, hitting the asphalt face-first and skidding across the alley while his ride crashed and burned behind him. A gasoline fire glimmered in our rearview mirror as we burst out of the alley mouth and onto the street.

I swerved, got my balance, and hit the throttle. Up ahead of us, a lone figure stepped into the middle of the street.

Prospero.

He hadn't shifted into his true form. Still just a weird-eyed, twitchy accountant, and somehow that made him all the more threatening. Like he couldn't even be bothered. He fixed us with a glare of pure venom and slowly raised one open palm, fingers curling.

The pavement in front of us erupted. The street burst open, chunks of rock flying like fist-size bullets, as a two-foot-deep pothole sprouted straight ahead. I veered left, almost hard enough to lay the bike down, and swerved around it. A second pothole erupted. The front wheel missed it by a scant inch as I dodged at the last second. I realized what he was doing: forcing us closer to *him*. And unlike the rider in the alley, he wasn't going to flinch.

I knew what incarnates were capable of. If we hit him full-on at fifty miles an hour, he'd be the only thing left standing.

Heart pounding, magic all but drained, I dug deeper into my center. Down to the last flickering sparks of energy, scooping them up in my hand and turning them into alchemical fire. One chance, one shot. I pointed my finger like an accusation and let it fly. Another thing I knew about incarnates: they might be faster, stronger, and harder to kill than humans, but they could still feel pain.

A stream of fire, like a lit trail of gasoline, streaked through the cold night air. The fire dart hit Prospero square in the eye. He yelped, clutching his face, his concentration shattered.

I yanked the handlebars, careening around and past him, leaving him in our dust. I hooked a right at the next intersection and streaked through a red light. Then another turn, and another, until I was sure he wasn't running after us. As sure as I could be. I slowed down and pulled the bike over to the curb.

"You okay?" Jessie said. "You didn't get hit, did you?"

"No, I'm—" I doubled over, pale and shaking, as the first wave of cramps hit me. My body reacting to the volume of raw energy I'd just forced through it, protesting being used as a tool of the universe. "Bill's due, that's all. Switch with me. You drive, I'll ride."

We found an all-night diner in Bensonhurst, halfway down a street lined with butchers' shops and pizza parlors. I was still shaky, but a mug of black coffee had me feeling human again. Jessie sat across from me in a booth with padded vinyl benches.

"It wasn't a total wash," she said. "We've ID'd a hound, which is good intel. And we know about two pieces of property he supposedly owns. Once we get Vigilant under control and back on its feet, we can start digging in to the paper trail."

I smiled faintly into my coffee. "These eastern courts . . . they never had to be careful. Vigilant wouldn't target them, period. How much you wanna bet they've got all *kinds* of weak spots we can exploit?"

"Silver linings." Jessie clinked her mug against mine. "Didn't find anything useful in his desk. How did the safe look?"

I fished my phone out, remembering the calls I'd gotten during our "job interview."

"High quality. Electronic lock, though. Hopefully Kevin can work some magic on it. This might be . . ." I looked at the screen. Two missed calls, two voice mails—both from Burton Webb, the director of the RedEye program.

"What?" Jessie asked.

"Trouble." I set the phone on the table and played the first voice mail.

Burton's voice was a strained whisper edged with fear. Beyond his heavy breathing, a distant clatter punctuated his words. Muffled gunfire.

"Agent Black, I'm . . . oh fucking God, I'm in trouble here, and you're the only person I can trust. Can't get hold of my NSA handler, the hotline's down, they cut the Internet. These people, they . . . they stormed the building, killed the receptionist. I ran to my office and barricaded the door. I'm hiding under my fucking desk, but it's only a matter of time. Please, *help* me!"

TWENTY-SEVEN

Jessie stared at the silent phone on the table.

"We had it wrong," she said. "We thought we screwed up—that Crohn was in town because he figured out we were in New York."

I cued up the second voice mail. "He doesn't know where to look. But he knows how to find us. Linder used to run the RedEye program; of course Crohn would know it exists."

The second message started with a rhythmic thumping. Thudding steel against wood, and from the jarring, splintering sounds, the wood was losing fast.

"It's me again," Burton breathed. "I don't have much time. Think I'm the only person left. I was watching the security feed on my desktop. This woman, she just *stared* at one of my IT guys and lit him on fire from ten feet away. I don't know who these people are, what they want. I'll try to get out one last—"

The sound washed out in the crash of a door bursting open, and the thudding of hard-soled boots rushing in fast. Burton's message ended with a click and a beep.

"He's insane," Jessie said. "Crohn is completely batshit insane. He just attacked an NSA facility."

"Exactly." I raised my mug and took a swallow. I needed the caffeine more than ever. "A facility housing a totally illegal program, run by a company that doesn't exist and is paid for by siphoned taxpayer money. What's the NSA going to do about it? It's like ripping off a drug dealer: they can't exactly go to the cops and complain."

"If we're lucky, Burton's dead."

"Jessie." I stared at her over the rim of my mug.

She gave me a halfhearted shrug. "You're the moral compass here, Harmony. I'm operating in survival mode right now. Or did you forget I'm a wolf on two legs?"

It was easy to, sometimes. Jessie was my friend. My best friend. I could honestly say I wished I'd known her my entire life, because I'd spent too many years alone, without one. She was quick with a joke and a smile, and sometimes I let myself forget who and what had raised her. Human empathy didn't come naturally to Jessie. But she was working on it.

"You have a point," I said grudgingly. "Burton packed RedEye with biometrics and code triggers to make sure he was the only person who could operate the system. The ultimate in job security. If Crohn doesn't know that, we're safe."

"And if he does . . . " Jessie said.

I finished the thought for her. "If he does, he's gonna let Mikki go to work on Burton. How long do you think he can hold out under torture?"

Jessie curled her lips back, showing her teeth as she grimaced. "An hour, tops. Burton's not a field operative—he's a bureaucrat with a marshmallow spine. And Mikki's good at what she does."

"We've got to warn the team." I picked up the phone, flipping through my dialing directory. "What do you think? Fly 'em out of here and finish this on our own, or bring them into the city?"

Jessie took a deep breath. She let it out between her clenched teeth.

"I want to send them away. Realistically, though? Neither one of us knows jack about cracking an electronic safe. April's intel, Kevin's toys, Aselia's transport know-how . . . we need them. Besides, RedEye's got nationwide reach; if they unleash that system on us, it'll be biting all of our heels no matter *where* we go. Might as well get comfy in the belly of the beast."

"Agreed. I'll ask them to—"

I froze as a text message came in from Burton's number. One stark line.

RedEye is hunting you. I bought you five minutes. Use it wisely.

I set the phone back down, gingerly, as if it was packed with nitroglycerin.

RedEye was designed as the ultimate in fugitive pursuit technology. It was the Echelon program on steroids, a system monitoring nationwide cell-phone traffic in real time. Listening for keywords and phrases, text-message scanning and voiceprint recognition, instant triangulation of its targets. Back in the day, the Glass Predator team had used RedEye to stalk its targets. Not one of them, Burton told us, had ever survived more than a week on the run.

And that was with a whole country to flee across. We were snuggled up close and personal with our would-be killers, in the very same city.

"Well," Jessie said.

I squinted at the phone. This wasn't right. I sipped my coffee, grim, as the answer came to me.

"Burton didn't send that text. And we don't have five minutes—the tracking is already live."

Jessie glanced over at me. "How do you figure?"

"We know how they operate. Crohn's men captured Burton, and Mikki hurt him until he agreed to sic RedEye on us."

"Right," Jessie said. "But if he got a chance to send us a warning—"

"A warning that RedEye would pick up on instantly. Just saying or typing the word *RedEye* on any phone in America is an instant security flag. And Burton knows that—he *built* the damn thing. If he somehow got access to his phone—and I don't see that happening, once they took him prisoner—he wouldn't have worded the message like that."

"So what is it? A bluff?"

"No," I said, "impatience. They know how we operate, too. You and me in the field, April and Kevin on logistical support. Crohn knows we're in town, after our little run-in with his boss."

"And April's the one Crohn wants more than the rest of us," Jessie said.

"Bingo. See, we're supposed to panic now. We think we've got a five-minute window, we make a quick, desperate call to warn the team, RedEye locks in on *both* of our phones, and Crohn sends Panic Cell to round us up. So, what do you think? Travel back upstate by train and collect the team in person?"

Jessie rubbed her chin, thinking. "Now that Crohn knows we're here, he's gonna tap all his local resources. FBI, NYPD. There's, what, six thousand street cameras running twenty-four-hour surveillance and another four thousand in the subways? We've gotta go on the offensive, and fast. Every minute counts."

"We've gotta warn the others, though. If they make a phone call . . ." I trailed off, thinking it through. "Okay. So we *do* make a call. Then we get the hell out of here, fast. We've got to tell the others where to meet us without letting Crohn in on the secret."

I sipped my coffee. Then I picked up the phone.

April answered on the second ring. "Harmony, I—"

"Listen carefully," I told her. "Burton Webb just sent us a warning: Crohn is about to activate the RedEye program and use it to hunt us down. I know you and Jessie were opposed to this, but Kevin was right: you and the rest of the team need to get out of New York, right now. Leave us behind."

The exact opposite of the argument they'd had when we arrived. There was barely a hitch in April's voice as she picked up on my meaning. She knew we were being listened in on.

"If you insist," she said, "but I'd really rather stay and fight."

"Just keep doing what you're doing, *looking for the pattern*. We'll meet up with you when we can, once you're *deposited safely* elsewhere."

A slight pause. Then: "Understood. Be careful." She hung up.

I popped the back of my phone, pried out the SIM card, snapped it in half, and dropped it into the last half inch of my coffee. The black plastic pieces bobbed on the surface like shipwreck debris. Then I tossed a couple of rumpled bills onto the table.

"Let's go," I said. "They'll meet us in Manhattan."

Jessie gave me a lopsided smile as she figured it out. "The National Equity Bank."

Our last mission had started right here in New York City, at the scene of a bizarre bank robbery. April had walked me through the puzzle, looking for an intentional pattern in a wall of "randomly" drilled safe-deposit boxes. That hunt had brought us head-to-head with Jessie's own mother and her pack of killers: it was fresh in all our minds. I knew April wouldn't need more than a tiny nudge.

We hustled out of the diner, jumped on the motorcycle, and I revved the engine while Jessie hopped onto the saddle behind me. She was right: playing defense would just delay the inevitable. Soon enough, with the electronic dragnet closing in around us, we'd run out of hiding places.

Time to go on the attack.

# # #

We found an alley near the National Equity Bank, stashed the bike, and loitered in a patch of shadow. Watching every passing car and taxi, my shoulders tensing as a patrol car cruised on by. A surveillance camera hung from a nearby lamppost, its dark eye turned away from us. One slipup, one moment of carelessness, and we were as good as dead.

Jessie stifled a yawn behind her hand. I felt my own yawn rise up to greet hers and covered my mouth.

"Sorry," Jessie said. "Contagious yawn."

When had we slept last? I'd caught a nap on the flight to New York, but since then we'd been on the move nonstop. Now the sunrise was coming, turning the eastern horizon to muddy gold, and our biggest fight was still ahead of us.

"Well," I said, "look at it this way. We're being hunted by the government, the law, at least one infernal court, a team of satanic special forces operatives, a psycho pyromaniac, and the director of the FBI. Who has something like a dozen or so demons inside him. Oh, and they've got the NSA's magnum opus hunting for us along with the NYPD's real-time surveillance camera system. And we're all in the same city. On the bright side? Things can't possibly get any worse."

Jessie stepped up behind me. She put her hands on my shoulders and gently turned me to face the sunrise.

"G'morning, Harmony." She leaned in and whispered, "Hey, it's the thirty-first. Happy Halloween."

I sighed. "Goddamn it, Jessie."

A Cadillac Escalade, deep ocean blue with tinted windows, rumbled up to the mouth of the alley.

The driver-side window hissed down, and Aselia leaned out.

"Get in. Fast."

I blinked. "Where did you get this car?"

"I stole it. Get *in*."

Kevin was in back, hunched over his laptop, typing so fast I expected to see smoke rising from his fingers. Beside him, April pored over a foldout gas-station map of the city. She'd drawn circles here and there, x-ing off certain streets. The second we were on board, Aselia hit the gas. I fell back into an open chair and reached for the seat belt.

"Glad you found us," I told April.

She adjusted her bifocals, keeping her eyes on the map. "I have been known to put clues together, now and then. Goodness, I could have been an FBI agent."

"I'm on police band, monitoring comms traffic." Kevin waved a flustered hand at his screen. "Tracking Bureau movements the best I can, but I can only do so much from here."

"RedEye," Jessie said. "We need to go in there, kick some ass, and take that system *down*."

"Crohn's entire team is most likely on-site," April replied.

Jessie folded her arms. "I've got two legs, and I can kick all day long. The morning is young."

"I doubt the NSA will be happy if we hurt their pride and joy." I paused. Frozen in midthought.

"Uh-oh." Jessie looked my way, lips curling into a slow smile. "I think Harmony just got an idea."

"I think I did."

I looked across the seats, taking in the faces of my teammates. Putting together the pieces to save all of us—our lives and our freedom.

"Jessie was right. Benjamin Crohn knows he can get away with hijacking RedEye because the NSA can't admit it exists. They'd rather sweep the whole thing under the rug than risk a scandal."

I glanced out the window, watching the city glide by. Vast concrete canyons, teeming with life—and under the surface, the digital machine sweeping, combing, hunting for the five of us.

"Smart move," I said. "Except in doing so, he just showed us how to take him down. Crohn's got one massive weak point, an Achilles' heel of his own creation, and that's precisely where we're going to hit him."

TWENTY-EIGHT

"The first thing we need to do is get a message to Linder," I said. "*Without* being detected by RedEye. Any ideas?"

Kevin shrugged. "I can still set up an encrypted channel and bounce it from Istanbul to Prague and back again, but that won't stop the system from running voiceprint matches or listening for keywords."

"No reason they'd be monitoring for Linder's voice," Jessie said. "*He* thinks he sold Crohn on his innocence, anyway, and for all his countless flaws, the man knows his tradecraft. So we just need to worry about our voices and making sure neither side of the conversation says any naughty words that'll flag the call."

Aselia glanced at her in the rearview as she drove. "Voice changer. There's software for that, yeah?"

"Like in *Scream*," Jessie said.

"Consider it done," Kevin said. "Give me ten minutes."

It took him five. I squeezed in next to him as he hooked my phone to his laptop, juggling open windows on his screen.

"Okay," he said, "say something."

"Testing, one, two—" I paused, thrown as my voice bounced back at me, gravelly and distorted.

"Exactly like in *Scream*," Jessie said. "Kevin, you're my favorite geek."

He tipped an imaginary fedora. "M'lady. Anyway, I don't know exactly how RedEye runs voiceprint checks, but it's a safe bet they're using existing architecture, probably bought the code wholesale from a commercial firm. Burton Webb's claim to fame is cracking cell-phone encryption: everything else the system can do on top of that is just gravy. This ought to throw your scent off."

I took a deep breath, steeling myself. All I had to do was tell Linder what our plan was without saying any trigger words that'd draw RedEye's attention. And make sure *he* didn't, either.

"Let's do it. Patch me in."

Kevin rattled off a command string. I watched a thin green line snake across a wire-frame map of the globe, side windows reeling off connection statistics and upload times. Then a click echoed from my phone, and Linder's voice filled the SUV.

"Yes."

"Choose your words very carefully," I said, hearing my distorted voice echo back at me.

"Who is this?" he asked, a steel edge of suspicion in his voice.

"No names. You know us. Your employer has taken control of your old workplace and turned it against us."

He fell silent. *Don't say the word,* I thought. My nails dug into my palms. *Don't say RedEye.*

"I understand completely," Linder said. "Can you tell me your status?"

"Ask him if he likes scary movies," Jessie whispered. I shot her a look.

"We have a lead on the legal documents. Changing mission parameters to deal with the present situation before we're boxed in."

"I'm not in a position to assist with that," Linder said. "I have no access or authority at my former workplace."

"I'm calling about our last discussion. Specifically, the man in position to replace our mutual problem."

"I'm still working on winning his support," Linder said.

"We may have a way," I said. "Make sure he's in the city where we are, as soon as possible. The window of opportunity will be very tight."

"Acknowledged," Linder said. "And . . . be careful out there."

He disconnected the call.

Jessie whistled under her breath.

"Be careful?" she said. "Wow, coming from him, that's positively human."

I saw Aselia's hands tighten on the steering wheel. "Still not one hundred percent convinced we shouldn't have sanctioned his ass in DC. But I'm open to being convinced. Someone want to tell me where I'm supposed to be driving?"

"The Lower East Side," I told her. "Let's get eyes on the target and hash out a battle plan."

RedEye Infometrics stood at the end of a crowded block, next door to a temp agency and a cell-phone store. The building stood two stories tall—and ran far deeper, we knew from our last visit inside. Anonymous beige brick and glazed windows. It was the kind of place designed to slide right off the eye and out of memory; you could pass it every day for years and never notice it, let alone think it was a top-level government black site.

Our first drive-by, I was focused on the pedestrian traffic. The facility had permanent spotters out front, men in coats a little too heavy for the weather, keeping an eye on the street. Operative word: *had*.

"No watchers, no shooters," Jessie murmured. She leaned close to the tinted passenger window and slouched low in her seat. "Crohn's guys took 'em out in the middle of a crowd in broad daylight, didn't even raise a fuss. That's . . . impressive."

Aselia drove around the block. Our second pass, we focused on the front door.

"Looks like . . . two guys in the lobby?" Jessie said.

I nodded. "One close to the door, one back by the desk. The rest are probably deeper inside."

"Too many. We've gotta thin the herd before we charge in there. Any ideas?"

"If the system picked up our location, they'd have a reason to come out and look for us," I said. "Problem is, they know that we know RedEye is active."

"So if we expose our location, it's an obvious trap," Kevin said.

"We need to make it look like an accident." I furrowed my brow. Thinking about our enemies. "Or a necessity. A situation where we just have to risk it. April, is it safe to say Crohn's been studying you from a distance?"

She lifted an eyebrow. "Is that a polite euphemism for 'obsessing over'?"

"I was just thinking about the conversation we had, back at that rest stop on the way to Des Allemands." I nodded at her tote bag. "How's your supply of medication holding up?"

"I have two days left." She gave me a wry smile. "But he doesn't know that. I think we're about to have an emergency on our hands. Kevin, what can you do with a pay phone? Can you make a call look as if it's coming from a different location?"

"A real, actual pay phone? No." He gestured to the window. "Fortunately, they're going the way of the dinosaur. LinkNYC's been replacing the old infrastructure with public Wi-Fi hot spots. Now *those*, I can play with."

We got some distance between us and the black site, prowling the congested streets at a slug-slow crawl until we found the holy grail: a hot spot with no street cameras in sight. The kiosk was over on East Twenty-Fourth Street, next to a pawnshop. Kevin took April's phone and jumped out at the red light.

"Just keep circling," he told us. "This is gonna take a little doing. I'll give you a wave when I'm done."

Our eighth time around the block, Kevin flagged us down like he was hailing a taxi. Aselia slowed down just long enough for him to jump in back. He passed April's phone back to her and grabbed his laptop.

"Okay," he said, "now we need a different public hot spot. Preferably one nowhere near here."

"As close to RedEye as we can get," I told Aselia. She gave me a thumbs-up and flicked her turn signal.

We found one a couple of blocks away. Kevin ran a few last-second checks while Aselia pulled the Escalade over, tapping the emergency blinkers. Once everything was ready, April made the call.

"Yes, hello. This is April Cassidy, calling for Dr. Sokoloff. I'm afraid I'm in a bit of a pickle. I neglected to pick up my divalproex prescription before leaving on a trip, and, well, I'm in Manhattan, all out of pills, and I can't go without it. Could you please arrange for a refill? As quickly as possible?" She paused, listening. "The Duane Reade at 250 Broadway? Wonderful, I'll be there as soon as I can. Thank you so much."

We rolled past the RedEye office just in time to see Ben Crohn striding across the street toward the nearest parking lot, the tails of his gray trench coat rippling at his back, followed by Mikki and four men in Oakleys and heavy fleece coats.

"I suspect half of them are heading for the drugstore," April said, "and half for East Twenty-Fourth Street."

Aselia glanced at the clock on the dashboard. "By the time they figure out they've been had, they're gonna be neck-deep in traffic. That bought us a little breathing room."

"Not as much as I'd like," I said, "but under the circumstances, I'll take what we can get. Okay, next up, we need an electronics store. Someplace local, with a dumpster we can get at."

It took about an hour to find what we needed. All the while, going over the plan and April's street map, rehearsing every single step until all five of us knew it by heart. We'd only have one chance to pull this off. If it all went like clockwork, no surprises, no mistakes, we might actually live to see tomorrow. Jessie caught my eye.

"You think we can pull this off, Mayberry?"

I didn't answer right away. You don't lie to your friends.

"I think we've got a shot," I told her. "I'll tell you what I know. I know we're all going to try our best. I know we're gonna give 'em hell. And if that isn't good enough to win . . . well, we'll leave them some scars to remember us by."

Aselia pulled over to the curb.

"That's good enough for me," Jessie said. "This is our stop."

TWENTY-NINE

The RedEye lobby didn't offer much in the way of concealment: just an open span of clean ivory tile between the front door and the reception desk at the back of the room. So we brought our own cover.

We pushed through the front door, Jessie in front and me right behind her, carrying the cardboard box for a seventy-inch Sony television set. We'd scavenged it from the dumpster of a Best Buy, nothing but chunks of loose white polystyrene inside, but a little body language and a little droop in our knees made it look heavy enough to be real. Jessie cantered to the right as we walked in, keeping the box between our faces and the two sentries on guard.

"'Ey, got a delivery!" Jessie called out in a bad attempt at a Brooklyn accent. "Delivery for Mr. Burton Webb, gotta get his signature, a'ight?"

Both men moved in on us, fast, somewhere between confused and annoyed.

"You can't—" one said as he moved to stand in Jessie's path. "You can't bring that in here. No deliveries today. Turn around, *now*."

"Hey, I'm *walkin'* here," she said.

Jessie paused as the first sentry rounded the edge of the box. He came face-to-face with her, freezing, the glimmer of sudden recognition in his eyes.

"More accurately," Jessie added, the accent gone, "I'm punchin' here."

We shoved the box, throwing it at the second sentry. He backpedaled, fast, expecting a hundred pounds of TV set to come crashing into him. The empty box bounced off his upheld arms, harmless, as Jessie threw a brutal right cross and splintered his partner's nose. He dropped to the floor, staining the ivory tile with a trickle of scarlet. The second man recovered fast and went for his sidearm. I was faster. I drew my pistol and held it in a two-handed grip, aiming the muzzle right between his eyes. He froze on the spot.

"Good choice," I told him. "Keep those hands nice and empty."

Jessie disarmed both men, tossing their weapons to the far corner of the lobby, then we got them on their bellies and zip-tied their wrists and ankles. I glanced sidelong at her as I yanked the ties tight.

"What was that supposed to be—John Travolta?"

Jessie's lips parted, momentarily speechless. "Dustin Hoffman. *Midnight Cowboy.* C'mon, get with the program."

"I'm just saying, *if* you were doing Travolta, it would have been a passable Travolta."

The sentry with the broken nose had woken up. He jerked at his bonds and squirmed.

"You're dead," he seethed. "Both of you, your whole team, everybody you know, everybody who ever knew your names. *Dead.*"

"Wow," Jessie said in mock dismay, "tough room. Everybody's a critic. Hey, don't suppose either of you upstanding gentlemen want to tell us how many of your buddies are here and where they've been stationed? How about you help us out a little?"

His partner, pinned under Jessie's knee, craned his neck. "How about you choke on my dick instead?"

Jessie's eyelashes fluttered. "Wow. I'm impressed. That's tough talk from a man with a concussion."

"What concu—"

Jessie grabbed him by the back of his head. His forehead slammed into the floor, spattering blood, leaving a crack in the ceramic tile as his body went limp. She dusted her hands off and stood up, whistling innocently. She glanced my way.

"Aren't you going to lecture me about unnecessary brutality?"

I thought about it. Then I shrugged. "Just this once, under the circumstances . . . nope."

The receptionist was behind the front desk. On the floor, her white blouse stained spilled-wine red, her glazed eyes wide-open. After our last two visits, I knew she had a weapon hidden out of sight; there it was under the desk, a short-barreled Mossberg shotgun dangling from leather straps. She hadn't gotten off a single shot. I helped myself to the Mossberg. Had a feeling we could use some extra firepower. Jessie patted the two invaders down, coming up with her key card on a blood-streaked lanyard.

I shouldered the shotgun, covering the door behind the desk. Jessie waved the key card past the handle. It clicked. Pistol braced, she swept to one side and shoved the door wide.

Nothing. Just a clear, pristine hallway, industrial eggshell white under softly buzzing fluorescents.

I took point, with Jessie at my shoulder. Rounding each corner clean and smooth, ears perked, our footsteps as soft as we could manage. Halfway to the elevator, a man lay facedown in a pool of his own blood, the back of his sweater perforated by bullets. I crouched beside him and pressed my fingertips to his neck.

"Dead," I whispered. "It's not Burton."

Jessie nodded to the elevator door. "What do you think? Downstairs, in the server room?"

"It'd make sense. They need Burton to operate the system. Whole party's probably down there." I didn't like the idea of going in blind. From the look on Jessie's face, neither did she. Then I snapped my fingers. "Wait, we might have an edge."

Jessie followed me to the elevator door. "Whatcha thinking?"

"When he left those voice mails, Burton said he was watching the security feeds from his computer in his office. Crohn's people might have left the feeds active. They took the building and everybody in it, so why bother cutting them after the fact?"

Jessie waved the receptionist's key card at the elevator panel and hit the button. It lit up pale yellow. A moment later, the door slithered aside, opening onto a cramped, closet-size cage. We squeezed on board and hit the button for the second floor.

"This is how you know it's a government facility," Jessie grumbled. "Cheap, cramped, and *not* built for comfort."

Two more corpses littered the hall leading to Burton's office. Security, by the looks of them, wearing navy-blue body armor over their dress shirts and ties. One still held his revolver in a death grip, half his bullets spent. Impact holes marred the elevator door and the walls around it like bloodless craters. We stepped over the bodies and eased through the open office doorway.

No sign of Burton, but judging from the papers and pens scattered across the threadbare carpet, they'd bounced him off his own desk a few times before dragging him away. His bulky monitor, shoved to one side, showed a slate-gray screen. I stepped around his capsized desk chair and clicked his mouse. The screen woke up. It flickered to life, showing grainy black-and-white feeds from cameras around the facility. The lobby, the first-floor hall, more corridors, and more dead bodies.

Jessie leaned in over my shoulder, pointing to the feed in the bottom left corner. "That one. Can you enlarge that?"

One click, and the window blossomed to fill the screen. We knew that room: the server farm in the sub-basement, aisles of flashing lights and softly whirring boxes. RedEye's heart, brain, and nerve center. Burton Webb stood at a terminal, a Panic Cell gunman standing right behind him and watching him like a hawk. Other figures prowled the aisles, pacing forward and back, armed for battle and looking sharp.

"What do you think," Jessie asked. "Four guys in all?"

"Yeah. Three roamers, plus the one on Burton. As far as I know, the only way into that room is right through the main door. Straight shot from the elevator, down a short hall. They might have somebody stationed in the hall, too; camera doesn't cover that angle."

"So. Four, maybe five, guys, they're ready for trouble, and we absolutely have to make sure Burton survives or our entire plan is screwed." Jessie rubbed her chin. "Okay. I'll take those odds."

"Thought you might."

She rubbed my shoulder. "You know me so well."

As we waited for the elevator, side by side, I braced myself for the fight. These weren't low-rent mercenaries or bottom-feeding mobsters. Panic Cell was the real deal: special operators trained to terminate any threat, human or superhuman. And Crohn had called them in just for us.

In my peripheral vision, I saw Jessie looking my way. I tried to keep the tension from my face. Then I caught her eyeing my shotgun.

"You, uh, like the Mossberg, huh?" she said.

"It'll help downstairs," I said. "Narrow aisles between the server racks. It's a good tactical choice."

"Mmm-hmm."

She fell silent for a second.

"You know," she added, "I'm *really* good with shotguns."

"Jessie." I glanced her way. "Do you want the Mossberg?"

"No. I mean, not if *you* want it."

I sighed and pulled back my windbreaker, baring my holster.

"You can have the shotgun if you'd like it," I told her, *"or . . ."*

Her eyes went wide. She plucked the Sig Sauer from my holster, clutching a matching pistol in each hand.

"Aw, *yes*." She beamed at me. "Now everybody's a winner. Except those guys down in the server room. They will never be winners."

The elevator chimed, and the door slid open, inviting us to the showdown.

"Won't even know what hit 'em," I said as I stepped into the cage.

That was bravado, not confidence. Trying to pump myself up for the fight. As the elevator descended with a faint whir, though, I realized I didn't need to. I found that cold center inside myself, that quiet, peaceful place that wraps its arms around me just before the bullets fly and the blood flows. When Cody confronted me, back in our hometown, he said there was something wrong with me. That on some fundamental level, I didn't react to violence like a normal person should. Bad wiring in my head.

I tried to feel bad about that. I knew I should feel bad about it. I just didn't know how.

In moments like this, I recognized it for what it was. Survival instinct. The men in that server room wouldn't hesitate to kill us. They wouldn't show mercy. No, for men like them, mercy was for the weak. They only knew one way to prove their strength: by hurting people, just because they could.

It wasn't just Panic Cell. Wasn't just Benjamin Crohn, or his masters in the courts of hell. I'd seen it time and time again since the day I put on a badge: men who saw themselves as predators and the entire world as prey. They saw other people, innocent people, as nothing but objects to use, plunder, and break as they pleased. Our civility was their shield. They counted on the fact that they could act like barbarians, take what they wanted, and hurt who they wanted, while the rest of us yearned for peace and moral victories. Lines protected them: lines they knew "good people" wouldn't cross.

For a long time, I'd wanted to be a good person more than anything else. I still tried. But in these quiet moments of truth, I faced myself and understood the facts. The things I'd done and the things I knew set me apart from the society I'd sworn to protect. I wasn't a sheepdog watching over the flock. I was like Jessie, a wolf hunting wolves. And I would cross any line, do whatever it took, and pay any price to protect the innocent and the weak.

"Penny for your thoughts," Jessie murmured, her eyes on the elevator door as we glided downward.

"Just remembering who I am," I said.

"Yeah?" She glanced sidelong. "Who's that?"

I racked the shotgun.

"I'm the woman who makes the monsters go away."

The elevator stopped with a jolt. A chime rang out. The door rattled open.

THIRTY

A short hallway stretched out before us, lit in soft-blue LED light and ending in a sliding door of frosted glass. The air was cold and smelled of industrial antiseptic, like the antechamber to some frozen and long-forgotten hell. We moved in silence, our footsteps whispers on the ivory tile, weapons raised and ready.

Jessie held up the key card, glanced to the small black square beside the door, then to me. I took a slow, deep breath. Four seconds in, four seconds out, steadying my grip on the shotgun. Then I gave her a nod.

The door hissed open. Jessie dropped the card and drew her second pistol. The server room, washed in deep blue and the faint amber glow from a hundred flickering electronic eyes along the server racks, stretched out before us.

We moved in.

I swept left, and she went right. Normally we'd announce our presence, flash a badge, give our suspects a chance to surrender. Not today. A Panic Cell hitter stepped out in front of me as he rounded a bend in the aisle. Just for a split second, he froze.

I pulled the trigger. The shotgun roared, shattering the silence like the sound of an avalanche, knocking him off his feet and into a server rack. Pellets shredded flesh and metal, electronics sparking as he fell to the rubber-mat floor in a cloud of blood. To my left Jessie moved like lightning, raising one pistol and firing off two quick shots, dodging around a stack, bringing up the other and blazing away. Dancing a bullet ballet and daring them to try to keep up.

Where she was a whirlwind, I was a slow and steady juggernaut. I marched down a narrow aisle, shotgun shouldered, listening to running footfalls all around me and staying crouched. A gunman came at me from behind. I spun fast, lowered the Mossberg, and opened fire. He staggered backward as his Kevlar caught the brunt of the blast. I racked the pump and hit him again, then again, the third volley hitting him in the face and shredding half the skin from his skull. He collapsed, still twitching, the ravaged servers at his back igniting with a half dozen pinprick fires.

Out of ammo. I tossed the empty shotgun to the rubber mats and called to my magic.

Another trooper charged at me from the left, a screaming blur with a tactical knife, steel gleaming as he swung with deadly precision. I unleashed a torrent of congealed, twisting air from my fingertips. The stream snaked around his wrist, lashing like a thorny vine, grabbing hold. Something in my mind twisted. So did his wrist. The leash of air yanked taut and whipped his knife hand back. He slashed his own throat from ear to ear.

Arterial blood spattered the servers, turned the blinking amber eyes dark crimson. It splashed hot across my cheeks, my mouth, my windbreaker. I stared, wide-eyed, as I watched him fall to his knees and die at my feet. I'd never done that with my magic before, never even considered it, but in the heat of the moment—

"Harmony," Jessie shouted from behind me. *"Down!"*

I dropped to one knee as a three-round burst chopped above my head. Another Panic Cell gunman stood behind me—and behind him, Jessie had both her pistols raised and ready. A muzzle flash left stars in my eyes as she unloaded on him, pumping bullets into his back until he hit the floor. I was bookended in dead bodies.

I wiped my sleeve across my face, feeling the sticky smear of fresh blood.

Our work wasn't done. I'd counted six operatives on the security feed. Two to go. One rounded the corner and locked Jessie in his sights, the Magnum in his grip booming. She was moving before he pulled the trigger, dropping her pistols, lunging in for the kill with her turquoise eyes blazing. The round blasted the faceplate off a server at her back, right where she'd been standing a second ago. She slapped the gun from his hand and drove a knuckle punch into his throat. He fell back, gagging, drawing his combat knife. Jessie flashed a toothy grin and beckoned to him. I knew that look. Her adrenaline was pumping, her inner wolf coming out to play, and that meant one thing.

He was a dead man. He just didn't know it yet.

He lunged with perfect precision, going for the kill. She side-stepped, crouched low, and threw a punch. The trooper howled as his kneecap shattered like a porcelain plate. She caught his wrist as his leg went out from under him, twisted his arm, and drove the edge of her hand down against his elbow. His arm snapped and bent double. His hand spasmed against the back of his elbow as he convulsed on the floor. She crouched over him, with her back to me, and leaned in.

I heard the wet crunch of throat cartilage, and he stopped moving.

"Jessie?" I said, my voice soft. "You okay? You keeping it together?"

She gave a tiny nod. Taking deep breaths to keep the wolf in check and her human mind in control. She picked up her guns.

A strangled yelp from Burton Webb echoed across the chamber. The last Panic Cell gunman had one arm wrapped around Burton's throat, his other hand pressing a fat-barreled revolver to the side of his head. He'd backed himself into the farthest corner of the room, eyes bulging with panic.

Feeling shaky in the aftermath of my spellwork, I paused just long enough to snatch up a pistol from a dead man's hand. Jessie and I split up. We came at Burton and his captor from right angles, closing in on two sides.

The trooper's head turned wildly. The gun at Burton's head pressed hard enough to leave a welt. Both men were on the verge of panic. We couldn't have that. People do stupid things when they panic. And we needed Burton alive.

"I'll kill him," the gunman shouted. "I will!"

"And then we have no reason to let you live," I said. "Be smart about this."

I aimed for his head, but I didn't dare take the shot. Not with my hand unsteady, between my exhaustion and the adrenaline still pumping through my veins. Not with his finger a heartbeat away from squeezing the trigger. If I missed by half an inch, in any direction, we'd be scraping two bodies off the floor instead of just one.

"I'm taking h-him with me," he stammered. "We're leaving. Don't try to stop us."

I took a step forward, pistol raised and ready. "Can't let you do that."

From the other side, a shadow between the stacks, I saw Jessie moving in, too. We pressed closer and pinned him into the corner.

"Let him go," Jessie said, "and we let you go."

"I'm not *stupid*," he snapped at her.

Burton whimpered as his head bent to one side, pressed by the weight of the muzzle.

"No," I told him, "you're not. So use your head and consider your options. Burton dies, you die. That's a fact. You're not leaving with him. That's another fact. Here's a third: we want him more than we want you."

His finger tensed on the trigger. "I'll kill him," he shouted again. Fear had its fangs in deep. He was nothing but a broken record now, with a chance of sudden gunfire every time the audio skipped. Reasoning wasn't going to work.

My new trick might, if I could repeat it. I already felt the familiar ache in my stomach, and the too-familiar gulf of growing hunger.

Normally I wouldn't try to call on my magic again, not this soon, not this strong. I didn't see any choice.

"Jessie," I called out, "you got a clean shot?"

"The *cleanest*."

"Good," I said.

Then I flung out my hand, streamers of air snapping out like heat-mirage whips, coiling around the gunman's wrist. His hand yanked upward, the muzzle swinging away from Burton's face. The trigger jerked, and a chunk of ceiling tile exploded, raining down on the black rubber mats.

Jessie fired. Her bullet caught him between the eyes and dropped him cold.

Burton stood mute, wide-eyed, his mouth opening and closing like a fish on a dry dock. Jessie walked over and threw an arm around his shoulder.

"Hey," she said, "you called. We came. Be happy."

He stared around the chamber. Taking in the blasted and twisted server racks, the pinprick fires and acrid gray smoke, the fallen bodies.

"My baby," he breathed. "What did you do to my baby?"

I sighed. "About that. Good news and bad news, Burton. We're about to take down some really bad guys—I mean, worse than these bad guys, and that's saying something. Good news is, you cooperate, and they won't come after you again."

"Okay," he said, still looking shell-shocked. "What's the bad news?"

Jessie clasped his shoulder. "Well, first we have to live long enough to get the job done. And you're about to undergo a sudden and dramatic career change. So, do you have to supervise this system, or can Ben Crohn access it remotely?"

"Remote access. Until midnight. That's when access resets and I have to reenter my personal passwords. I mean"—he flailed a hand at the damage—"if it's even still working. Do you want me to lock him out?"

"Get it back online, pronto. I'll grab a fire extinguisher. And no. Leave his access exactly as it is. We *want* him to have it." Jessie looked my way. "You . . . should probably wash the blood off before we go outside."

# # #

No time to spare, but I darted into an employee restroom while Jessie told Burton the facts of life. I scrubbed the blood from my face, pumping out gritty soap by the fistful, leaving my cheeks raw and ruddy. The windbreaker I took off and reversed. The fall of my hair covered the bare tag in the back; the exposed seams, I couldn't do anything about. Still, it was better to look like I'd dressed in a dark closet than to walk around Manhattan with blood-drenched sleeves.

I shoved open the door and darted into the lobby, where Burton looked like he was about to throw up. I looked to Jessie. "He's on board?"

"I don't have a choice," he said. "You didn't *give* me a choice."

"Sure we did," Jessie said. "You can do exactly what we tell you, or you can spend the rest of your life behind bars. Or dead. See, that's *three* choices. We're so nice."

I led the way to the front door. We stood out on the sidewalk, anonymous in the urban foot traffic, washed in traffic noises and the smell of diesel fumes. A cold wind ruffled past as Kevin's drone zipped overhead and then out of sight over a low-slung roof. It bobbed twice in passing, acknowledging our arrival.

"April's on an encrypted channel with Linder right now, hashing out the logistics." I took out my phone. "Aselia should be on her way to our location, fresh from dropping Kevin off a few blocks away. Now we up the stakes."

I dialed the FBI tip line.

When they picked up, I put an edge of panic in my voice. "Yes, those—those killer FBI agents, the ones from the television? I saw them, just a minute ago! In Manhattan, the Lower East Side. I saw them get into a blue Escalade. I only have a partial plate number—the last three digits are three-eight-four."

Aselia pulled up to the curb. I hung up, then tossed her my phone. She didn't say a word before lurching back into traffic and away, northbound.

"You . . . you just told them where we are," Burton stammered. "And we had a getaway ride. Which we *didn't* take."

I started walking, fast, and he scrambled to keep up. "Yep. And now, thanks to his remote access, Crohn's getting an automated heads-up from RedEye. He'll know it was my voice, and he'll figure it was some kind of a ruse, but now that he has a way to track my phone, he'll have to follow up just in case. Aselia's running a distraction play: she's gonna drive around and draw as much heat as she can."

"What if they catch her?"

"They won't," Jessie said.

"I don't get it," Burton said. "Why draw attention at all?"

"Because we want Crohn to chase us," I told him. "We just can't let him *catch* us until we're good and ready."

"Speaking of good and ready." Jessie eyed her own phone, a call coming in. "Speak. Okay, yeah, we're on the move. Do it."

Burton shook his head. "Wait, wait, do *what?* Phones are bad, okay? Phones are really, really bad right now."

"Kevin is patching April through to my line," Jessie said. "It's going to look like her call is coming from my phone. We'll be able to listen in from here."

She held it close enough for me to hear the faint, tinny ringing.

Then a woman picked up, her voice nasal. "Federal Bureau of Investigation, how may I direct your call?"

"Dr. April Cassidy, calling for Benjamin Crohn," April said. "He's in the field at the moment, but you should reach out to him as quickly as possible. I believe he's expecting my call."

THIRTY-ONE

We listened in, walking briskly along the sidewalk and getting lost in the city crowds, as the hold music suddenly died.

"April," Benjamin Crohn's voice said, "it's been . . . a long time."

"I'd say I missed you," April replied, "but we both know a lie when we hear one. We just missed each other at the drugstore."

"Apparently I'm a bit faster than you these days. That's the nice thing about having functional legs. Sorry you weren't able to get your prescription filled."

"Dirty pool, Ben. You know I need those medications."

He chuckled, a low and ugly sound.

"Is that why you're calling? Hoping to wave the white flag of truce? It's a little late for that, April. We know exactly where you and your team are. I'm so close you should feel my breath on the back of your neck. I'm a little disappointed, to be honest. I hoped you'd at least give me some kind of a real challenge before all was said and done."

"Oh, *that's* why I'm calling," she said. "I'm sure you've figured out we have access to a private aircraft."

"Bet yours isn't as nice as mine. So?"

"I'm taking myself out of the game. As we speak, I'm on my way to turn myself in to local law enforcement."

"But—" He paused, thrown off his stride. "But you weren't even named in the warrants for Temple and Black. We called you a hostage—"

"You're not the only one who can spin a story," April said. "I'm going to confess to being an accessory. Once my lawyer arrives, I imagine we can keep the NYPD tangled in red tape for a good twenty-four hours or so, during which time they'll be obligated to provide me with medical treatment and the drugs I require to survive. Oh, you'll swoop in and try to take me into federal custody, but you'll still have to file papers, argue with the locals . . . it's going to be quite a mess. A loud mess."

"What's your game?" he growled.

"Only that I'm all alone in the big city," April said. "While I play the lone wolf, I've sent the rest of my team to the plane with orders to abandon me. They're going to vanish, Ben. They're good at vanishing. And now that we know you've commandeered RedEye, they know exactly how to stay under its radar while they work to expose you and your 'patrons' in the eastern infernal courts. So now you get to choose: Who do you chase? Let me go and I end up with police protection, media attention, and all kinds of ways to make your life difficult. Let them go and I imagine you'll be getting a very unpleasant phone call from your superiors by tomorrow night. I wouldn't want to be you right now. Then again, I never did."

I listened to the pulse of Crohn's heavy breathing.

"You think I can't round all of you up at once?"

"I think you're a once moderately talented investigator who let his skills go to seed, choosing to prop up his egotistical 'legend' by planting evidence and framing suspects. These days you're a second-rate amateur at best. A washout who couldn't hack it as a *real* FBI agent, so you had to worm your way into the bureaucracy. A paper pusher with a pedigree."

"You're going to regret that," Crohn seethed. "You know, it's funny. I was vehemently opposed to recruiting you into Vigilant. The only reason we took you is because we wanted your pet science project."

"Jessie isn't a *science project*. She's the best thing that ever happened to me. And as far as regrets go, my sole regret is that I was once young and naive enough to share my bed with you. But we live and we learn. When it comes to fieldwork, Ben, you're a pretender. I'm the real thing. Come at me if you think you've got the chops for it."

She broke the call. A second later, Crohn did the same, leaving the phone in Jessie's hand broadcasting dead air. She put it away.

"What . . . what just happened here?" Burton said. "So, wait. RedEye is tracking both of your phones now."

"Right." I pointed into the distance. "Except Crohn thinks *our* phone is the one Aselia is driving all over Manhattan."

Jessie gave him a lopsided smile, walking with a breezy stride. "And he thinks the one we're carrying is April's. See, he can't risk us getting away and blowing the whistle on him, and April just guaranteed he can't let her get away, either. His pride won't let him. So he's gonna split the team he has left."

"Great," Burton said. "So we'll only have *half* the psycho killers coming after us. Crazy idea here, but maybe it would have been better to, say, *not* paint a giant moving target on our backs in the first place?"

We moved south on Clinton Street, toward East Broadway—then I held out my hand, bringing us to a dead stop. A block ahead, a black sedan cruised by, its occupants in shark mode. Watching the sidewalks from behind dark glasses, checking every face and being obvious about it.

"Jessie. Bureau?"

She nodded and pointed right. "Let's cut across."

"Locals," I told Burton. "Crohn can't tell them *how* he knows where we are, without exposing RedEye, but he can use 'tips' to send them in our path and slow us down until he gets here."

We darted into Seward Park, a little patch of green, the worn concrete paths strewn with dead autumn leaves. We rounded a dried-up fountain, water stained and leaf choked, while off to the side, kids were screaming and laughing on swing sets. I looked over my shoulder, double-checking that we hadn't been spotted. Or at least that they weren't chasing us. Yet.

"And to answer your question," I told him, "we want Crohn on our heels. That's the entire point of the switch: he won't be able to resist being there when April is captured. If we play this right, he won't know until the last minute that we're the ones he actually caught."

"Uh-huh. Operative word being *caught*. Did you see the woman he's got with him? You know, wears her hair like a My Little Pony doll? Sets people on fire with her brain?"

Jessie grinned. "Yeah. See, Mikki hates us. She hates us a lot. So guess who's gonna volunteer to lead the second team, the one chasing Aselia's SUV?"

"Oh, good," Burton said. "So she's out of the picture, and we only have to worry about the spec-ops guys, the FBI, and the NYPD. No sweat."

"Exactly." Jessie clapped him on the back. "Now you're getting in the spirit of things."

Close to the street corner on the southwest side of the park, I crouched low behind a clump of scraggly bushes. The foliage was half-dead and half-brown in the October chill. A bus stop stood about twenty feet away, a few commuters listlessly waiting, pedestrian traffic drifting by. Twenty feet, and half of it was wide-open. The black sedan had pulled over a little farther up the block. Waiting. Watching. RedEye couldn't pinpoint our position to the square foot, but it could triangulate off local cell towers—and the longer we stayed in one place, the tighter the noose became.

Five minutes felt like an eternity. Then I saw the M9 bus chugging down East Broadway, spitting a plume of smoke toward the slate-gray sky. I tapped my earpiece, twice.

We'd worked out a signal before the operation began, shorthand that didn't require us to use our voices on an open line. Kevin's response came back immediately: three quick splashes of white-noise static.

"Distraction's primed and ready," I said. I watched the bus, judged the distance, counted under my breath.

"Now?" Jessie asked.

I held up my hand. "Wait for it."

Three seconds, two, then—"Now!" I led the way as we broke from cover, racing past the bushes and toward the bus stop. The bus chugged to a halt, doors hissing open. Up the block, Kevin's drone swooped in. It circled the sedan, bounced off the windows, wriggled up and down in front of the driver. The doors swung open, and men in black suits and clunky shoes boiled out, confused, all eyes on the dancing quadcopter. The drone did an elegant pirouette just before firing a pair of barbs on wire lines. The barbs nailed one of the agents in the shoulder, and he went rigid, twitching as the Taser kicked in, then crumpled to the sidewalk. I was the last one on the bus. I looked back, watching another agent knock the copter out of the sky with the butt of his gun. His foot stomped down, shattering Kevin's handiwork under his heel.

The door hissed shut, and the crowded bus rolled into city traffic.

It took ten minutes to go a single mile down East Broadway. Stop-and-go, more stopping than going, and I held my breath with every jolt of the brakes. We were packed into the crowded bus like sardines in a tin, and I didn't want to think about what would happen if Crohn's men boarded us. We had to worry about civilian lives. They didn't. It felt like bliss when we got to the Worth Street stop and I could finally step outside and breathe open air again.

"Let's go," Jessie said, pointing up the street. "Third of a mile between us and the endgame. Not too far at all."

We weren't alone. Kevin scurried out of a Starbucks doorway, his laptop case tucked under one arm.

"Thanks for that," I told him. "Sorry about the drone."

He shrugged. "It was a heroic sacrifice. I was already working on the model-two version anyway. I'll have it ready in time for our next mission. Assuming, you know, we don't all die in the next fifteen minutes."

Burton gaped at him. "Are any of you people *not* crazy?"

"Yeah," Jessie said. "April. But she's not here right now. Don't worry about it; this is almost over."

Almost. Except that was the moment some sharp-eyed locals in a squad car got a good look at our faces. A siren squawked at our backs as the car veered up to the curb and the cops jumped out.

"Hey!" a gruff voice shouted at our backs. "You! Stop right there!"

Didn't have to ask whom they meant. Didn't have to hold a meeting to decide our next course of action, either. We ran.

We barreled along the sidewalk, shoving through the crowds, one cop hot on our heels while the other called for emergency backup. At least the police wouldn't open fire and risk civilian casualties—we couldn't shoot at them, they wouldn't shoot at us—but that didn't mean they weren't going to come at us with everything they had. Fresh sirens wailed from a side street up ahead. A second squad car swerved hard, tires squealing, blocking off traffic as we darted across the intersection.

They weren't alone. An unmarked car coming the other way almost spun out as it lurched to a stop. The thrum of rotors split the air as a white-and-blue helicopter flew overhead, veering over the rooftops to double-back again. I kept my eyes dead ahead. Pushed aside the hammering in my heart, the burning in my legs and my lungs and my back. Nothing but the mission.

"Don't stop," Jessie hissed through gritted teeth as Burton and Kevin started to fall behind. "Whatever you do, *don't stop*."

THIRTY-TWO

I looked back and wished I hadn't. Pedestrians stampeded, jumping aside and racing into doorways, as a mob of uniforms raced after us down the sidewalk. A police wagon kept time like a pace car, cherry lights flashing, clearing traffic for the three squad cars behind it.

Foley Square loomed ahead. The end of the line.

Monuments to law and justice ringed the open park like grand Greek temples, their ivory Ionic columns soaring tall and flags rippling in the crisp autumn wind. The United States Courthouse, the Thurgood Marshall Courthouse, the New York County Municipal Building—and not far away, the beige-and-black tower of the Manhattan FBI field office. Seemed as good a place as any to make our last stand.

A fountain stood at the heart of Foley Square, waters rippling around a black granite monument like stylized antelope horns. The polished stone caught the sunlight. We ran to the fountain's edge—and stopped.

The cops didn't get a chance to take us down. Three more unmarked sedans screeched to a stop at the edge of the square, hoods pointed toward us like spearheads, and Bureau agents jumped out with guns drawn. They crouched behind their doors, taking careful aim, every eye on the four of us. The police formed a cordon. They waved pedestrians back as more squad cars screeched up to block side streets, closing the square and cutting off one escape route at a time.

"Why are we stopping?" Burton stared at me, bug-eyed. "They're going to kill us. Or worse."

"Wait for it," I murmured.

I wish I felt as calm as I sounded. We'd done everything we could, and it was out of our hands. Everything depended on April now. The police helicopter circled overhead, hovering, pinning us in the rotor wash.

"Keep your hands where we can see them," a voice shouted through a bullhorn. "Do not attempt to run."

"Wouldn't dream of it," Jessie called back, holding up her open hands.

Crohn sauntered to the edge of the square, wearing a cocky grin, flanked by a couple of his own men.

"Where is she?" he said. "We'll find her eventually, you know. Might as well save yourself some trouble and start talking now."

I glanced back over my shoulder and smiled.

"Right here," I told him.

Another four unmarked cars screeched to a halt at the opposite end of the square. Bureau men helped April out of a backseat and into her wheelchair while Crohn stared, eyes slowly widening, at her companions.

Linder, along with Deputy Director Esposito. Dick Esposito marched in like a man on a mission, a sheaf of papers clutched in one angry hand.

"Deputy Director?" Crohn said. He blinked at Linder like he was a piece that belonged to a different puzzle. "What . . . what is this?"

Esposito pointed at the agents behind Crohn. "Stand down. Stand down *right now*."

Crohn looked back over his shoulder, confused. "Ignore that order. Eyes on the fugitives! *I'm* in charge here."

April rolled over to us, and I made room so she could sit beside Jessie. She squeezed Jessie's hand, smiling thinly, but her eyes were locked on Crohn. Crohn went toe-to-toe with Linder and Esposito as his face turned beet red.

"The hell do you think you're playing at? What is this?" He turned to Linder. "What do you think you're doing, besides diving headfirst into a world of shit?"

"You've read my classified jacket," Linder told him. "You know my specialties, the things I've done for this government, the things I'm *good* at. You should have paid more attention. Also, while I fear this may sound petty . . . you should have been nicer to me."

We had incoming. New arrivals pulling up behind Esposito's pack of agents. First came the local vans, their livery advertising ABC Channel 7 and CBS New York. CNN and Fox News weren't far behind, bringing cameras and pole-mounted lights into the square. Their colleagues from the press, lanyards for the *Times* and the *Post* dangling around their necks, crowded as close as the cordon of agents would let them.

Esposito preened, smoothing back his hair, straightening his tie.

Someone must have called off the police helicopter. It veered away, the air settling, an expectant silence flooding the square. Nothing but the burble of the black granite fountain, the popping of flashbulbs, and the faint electronic clicks of digital cameras. Esposito turned to address the gathering.

"I've called you here today," Esposito said, "to address a grievous wrong. These women, Special Agents Jessica Temple and Harmony Black, have been accused of a murderous rampage. In truth—and I deeply regret that I could not reveal the facts until today—they are not only innocent, but they were working on a special, secret assignment directly under my authorization."

He pointed an accusing finger at Crohn.

"An assignment to expose Benjamin Crohn, the director of the FBI, as a traitor to the American people."

Crohn took a step back, his jaw dropping. I squinted in the blinding hail of camera flashes.

"That's—that's preposterous," Crohn stammered. He waved a shaking hand at us. "These women are federal fugitives, and I want them arrested *now*."

None of the agents on the scene, or the gauntlet of uniformed officers at their backs, made a move. They watched in uncertain silence.

"These agents were framed for crimes committed by Mr. Crohn's associates when they came too close to the truth," Esposito told the press. "The truth being that Mr. Crohn illegally siphoned taxpayer dollars to pay for a top-secret program, operated without the knowledge or consent of the Bureau. This program, code-named RedEye, carried out a shocking and unconstitutional level of surveillance. Breaking into citizens' cell phones, harvesting private data, all without any judicial oversight."

As the press erupted, shouting questions and waving hands, I leaned close to Linder. "Tell your buddies in the NSA we said 'You're welcome.'"

He glanced sidelong with a thin, humorless smile. "RedEye is effectively dead as of today. That system cost millions; they're hardly going to jump for joy over this."

"They ought to be happy," I murmured. "It was going to get exposed eventually, one way or another. Now their hands are clean, and the whole mess gets pinned on a rogue FBI agent. Well, almost all of it. Now for the cherry on top."

Jessie was whispering in Burton's ear. He looked at her like someone had just kicked him between the legs. "Do I have to?"

"Do you want immunity from all charges?" she asked in return. His shoulders slumped.

Crohn's henchmen from Panic Cell had faded into the crowd and turned invisible. He stood alone and abandoned on an empty patch of concrete, hands trembling at his sides.

"He didn't do this alone," Esposito said. "His chief engineer, who was blackmailed into working for him, has agreed to turn state's evidence. Sir, please tell them the rest."

Burton stepped forward to stand at the deputy director's side. He swallowed hard, eyes at the reporters' feet.

"Um, hi. I'm, uh, Burton Webb, and, well . . ."

Esposito said in a low voice, "Just tell them the truth, son."

"Director—Director Crohn needed technical help to make RedEye happen," Burton stammered. "So he approached Bobby Diehl. Of Diehl Innovations. My, um, former boss. Mr. Diehl agreed to help, so long as he could use the system to gather people's personal information for targeted advertising and get a cut of the government money that Director Crohn was stealing."

I basked in grim satisfaction as the press exploded, shouting over one another to be heard. This was small recompense for the damage Bobby Diehl had done, the lives he'd taken, and the innocent people he'd destroyed, but it was a start.

Killing him was too easy. I wanted to hurt him first. And the man who thought he was untouchable just got backhanded, long-distance, in a way he'd never forget. Meanwhile, Crohn was melting down on camera. His jaw, tense as steel cord, twitched as his hands curled into fists.

"This is . . . this is all a criminal conspiracy. He's in it with them!" He looked to the agents at his back, pointing furiously at Esposito. "Arrest them, and arrest him, too. *All* of them."

"You have no authority here, sir," Esposito told him.

"I am the director of the Federal—"

"Not anymore." Esposito unfurled the papers in his hand, holding them high for the cameras. "An administrative order from the White

House, as of forty minutes ago. Benjamin Crohn, you have been relieved of your office pending your investigation and trial."

He looked behind him, to his own agents, and nodded at Crohn. "Cuff him."

I braced myself as the agents moved in. Crohn might have looked like a man on the ropes, but that didn't change the fact that he had the proportionate speed and power of an incarnate demon. We'd seen him in action against Nyx. If he wanted to, he could kill his way out of here. Just start tearing off limbs and running like a freight train, probably shrugging off bullets while he did it.

But he'd be doing it in front of live television cameras. Exposing his true nature—and the reality of the occult underground—for the entire globe to see. His masters in the eastern courts might find a way to forgive this mess, but *that*? That, they'd never forgive. Neither would every other monster, sorcerer, and shadow-lurker on Earth. The underground survived by an unspoken pact of secrecy; if he blew that, there'd be nowhere in the world to hide.

Was he smart enough to bide his time and play it cool? I held my breath, waiting to find out.

The cuffs slapped on. Rough hands shoved him forward, pushing him toward the backseat of an unmarked car. I let myself relax, just a little.

"I'm expecting the former director to have an unfortunate and fatal accident in custody," Linder murmured in my ear. "We've got a line on his demonic contracts?"

I nodded, subtle, and answered out the side of my mouth. "We've identified the Windswept Razors' hound and his place of business. Pretty sure the contracts are in his safe. We're going in tonight. One lit match and Crohn's a bad memory."

"I'll send flowers to his holding cell."

Esposito waved Jessie and me forward. The camera flashes turned my vision into a blotchy forest of white and fading afterimages.

"The Bureau wishes to extend its deepest thanks to these agents, who sacrificed so much, who risked so much, to uncover the truth." He threw his arm around my shoulder. "These are American heroes."

I tried not to flinch under a fresh hail of flashbulbs and shouted questions.

Esposito leaned close, speaking low through clenched, grinning teeth.

"C'mon, damn it, smile for the cameras. Make me look good here."

THIRTY-THREE

Linder stepped in as soon as he could, gracefully extricating us from the press conference, and had his aides ferry us out of the square in an unmarked car. We ended up in a private meeting room on the seventh floor of the FBI field office. Windows along the wall looked down over the street below—and not far away, the press scrum was still going on at Foley Square.

Jessie paced along the windows while April, Kevin, and I sat scattered around a long beechwood conference table. Kevin was huddled over his laptop, poring over electronic safe schematics. April jotted lines in a notebook, her handwriting tight and precise. I just slumped with my chin against my curled knuckles, staring out the window.

"American heroes," Jessie muttered. "Not that I object to the title, but he didn't need to drag us right in front of the damn cameras and make us field questions."

"Doesn't do much for our value as *covert* assets," I said.

April didn't look up from her pad. "You're both being melodramatic as well as seriously overestimating your own importance."

I lifted my head, looking her way. "How do you figure?"

"We live in a twenty-four-hour news cycle. An engine that requires perpetual feeding. You'll be household names until tomorrow, two days at most. That was your first *and* your last show-pony experience. Yes, media outlets will be calling for interviews. Said calls will be patched through to SAC Walburgh's office. Seeing as SAC Walburgh does not exist, those calls will never be returned."

"But what happens when Crohn goes on trial—" Kevin started to ask. He withered under April's silent stare. "Oh. Right. He's not going on trial."

"He'll be dead by dawn if we do our jobs properly," April told him. "The real story here isn't us, and it isn't even him. It's RedEye. And even that, one month from today, will barely be more than a poorly annotated Wikipedia entry. A year from now it'll be a five-hundred-dollar question on *Jeopardy!* There's no need for elaborate cover-ups when the public has the collective memory of a goldfish."

The door swung open, and Aselia strode in, all smiles. She tossed my phone over, and I snatched it out of the air.

"All good?" Jessie asked her.

"They never even got close. I had fun listening to the local news on the way back, too." She put her fist to her mouth, clearing her throat, and lifted her chin high as she imitated my voice. "It is the sworn duty of every federal agent to pursue the truth and uphold the law. Our nation's Constitution is powerful, but at the same time, as defenseless as a newborn child. It falls not only upon our shoulders but upon every American citizen to rise up, to be ever vigilant, and to fight in its defense—"

I waved my hands at her. "Okay, okay."

Aselia snickered. "Seriously, did you have that speech memorized?"

"No. I don't know." I shrugged. "There were a lot of cameras. I just said the first thing that popped into my head."

"You're like that . . . what's his name, that eagle from *The Muppet Show*."

I got up and ambled over to the credenza, pouring myself a paper cup of water from a half-full pitcher, and tried to change the subject.

"Kevin, where are we on the burglary? What do you think—can you open Prospero's safe?"

He rubbed his forehead, wincing. "It's theoretically possible to engineer an auto-cracker. I mean, they exist, and I can lift the code-lock schematics from the company's servers since you got the model number for me, but . . . actually wiring one isn't something I've ever done on my own. I reached out to this West Coast hacker, a friend of mine, for advice—I know she's built one before—she just hasn't gotten back to me yet."

I glanced out the window, to the amber light of the setting sun.

"Well," I said, "we have to go in *tonight*, so either you find a solution in the next hour, or we start shopping for explosives."

Jessie held up her hand. "I vote for explosives."

"You always vote for explosives," I said.

"You should praise me for consistency. That's what my therapist does."

The phone on the conference table trilled. I leaned over, sipping my ice water, and hit the button for the speaker.

"Agents," Linder said, "we have a problem. I need you mobile, immediately."

Jessie turned from the window, hands on her hips. "What? Esposito wants another press junket?"

"Benjamin Crohn is missing."

The water in my stomach turned into a cold lead weight.

"How?" I said. "They only had to drive him two damn blocks. Who was in charge of the transfer?"

"The wrong people. Crohn was placed in a reinforced police truck. Probably not capable of holding someone with the strength of an incarnate demon, but it would have slowed him down. We were counting on his reluctance to reveal his true nature in public view. The truck had four escort units, two in front and two behind."

"So what happened?"

"Halfway to the detention facility, the truck suddenly made a hard right turn and escaped down an alley. The primary agents driving the unit dropped smoke grenades out their windows for cover. By the time the escorts sorted out the chaos, they were long gone. The GPS tracker on the truck shows it currently stopped in the Bronx: Clason Point, on the edge of the East River. I pulled an emergency requisition for the primaries' personal bank accounts. Both agents received five-figure cash deposits in the last hour."

"They took a bribe to let him go." I closed my eyes, feeling like I was sinking through the floor. "We needed one thing from you, Linder. *One thing.*"

"Considering I've just added myself to Crohn's personal list of enemies, Agent, I assure you I'm equally displeased."

I thought fast, running down a list of his assets. "His team's plane. The C-130. You've gotta find it and make sure it stays grounded—"

"Unfortunately, it took off half an hour ago, piloted by two of the surviving members of Panic Cell. Their flight plan was falsified."

"But he wasn't on it?" Jessie asked.

"No," Linder said. "Crohn, Mikki, and the rest of Panic Cell are at large and presumably still in the city."

Kevin squinted at the phone. "Doesn't make sense. These guys are supposed to be super loyal, right? Why would two of them take off with the getaway ride and leave their boss behind?"

April sat back. She gently drummed the eraser of her pencil against the notepad.

"Because they were ordered to," she said. "We're witnessing a contingency plan in motion. Jessie, Harmony, I recommend you get to that vehicle as quickly as possible. See if he's left anything behind we can use."

# # #

What he'd left was scorched steel and the stench of burned pork. The secure truck sat on a dead-end drive at the river's edge, an icy wind rippling off the water and pushing wispy clouds of black smoke over our faces like funeral veils. Broiled inside and out, the vehicle was only identifiable by what remained of its license plate. The arresting agents, still in the front seat, would only be identifiable by their dental records.

Bile rose up in my throat as I stared at the twisted, agonized corpses. This was what their treason had really bought them. I was sure they thought they were in for a hell of a payday—until Mikki arrived.

"Damn." Jessie threw a punch at the blackened metal, tortured steel buckling under her fist. "So he cons them into delivering him here, Mikki and the rest of his crew show up, they kill the only witnesses—"

"This was all preplanned," I said. "April is right. No chance they thought this up on the fly, with no way of communicating while he was in cuffs. Crohn had a worst-case-scenario contingency set up, and this was it. A couple of his men leaving him behind and taking the plane was part of it."

"Where would they be going without him?" Jessie asked.

"I'm more concerned with where *he's* going. Okay. Let's put ourselves in his shoes. His brilliant plan to use RedEye against us just backfired. He's been arrested, dishonored, humiliated in the press, and he's looking at prison time."

"Can't salvage his old life," Jessie said. "Who he was, his job, his control over the Bureau—that's all over now."

"So he needs a brand-new life."

"Prospero," Jessie said.

"You think he'll help?" I asked. "Crohn just lost control of Vigilant Lock. His program—his *bosses'* program—has been hijacked from inside, and there's nothing they can do to get it back. The fake weapon just became a real one. They've gotta know we're coming for them next. I can't imagine the former director is a popular guy right about now."

"Any port in a storm. Can he afford *not* to ask for help?"

Good question. We knew exactly where to find the answer. Aselia drove us out to Vinegar Hill.

No motorcycles prowled the Belgian-block streets. No sound in the gloomy twilight but the hum of the power plant. Inside the walk-up to Prospero's office, we found one of the cambion bikers. His head was at the foot of the staircase. His arms and legs, twisted and torn from his body, haphazardly strewn across the steps. Wide arcs of crimson, still sticky wet, decorated the narrow walls as if someone had used the man's severed limbs as paintbrushes.

Not *someone*. Crohn. He'd been here, and he hadn't been looking for help. I breathed through my mouth, fighting past the overpowering stench of copper and rotten meat. We stepped over the scattered limbs. Past the ruined door on the second-floor landing, tatters of shattered wood clinging to a single twisted hinge, fresh horror awaited us.

If I'd had any doubts that an infernal hound could be killed, Crohn laid them to rest.

Jessie hovered in the doorway. She tugged her glasses down, her eyes glinting as her nose wrinkled in disgust. "What . . . *is* that?"

A glistening, gelatinous goop the color of melted flesh covered the desk and drenched the thin carpet. It splashed the bookshelves, dripping down in ropy strands to land on the floor with wet, squelching spatters. A few bits and pieces still held their shape: a finger on the desk, still twitching, its nail black and rotting. A handful of yellowed teeth, scattered across the sodden floor. And from the edge of a knocked-over chair, a human face dangled like a discarded Halloween mask. Prospero's face.

THIRTY-FOUR

I dug out my glasses. Black, with chunky Buddy Holly frames and clear glass lenses. They'd been a weapon once, a bugged Trojan horse given to us by a mole, but we'd turned them into an asset. Two clicks of the pen in my pocket, activating the concealed Bluetooth link, and the pinhole camera in the glasses' frame began transmitting back to the team.

"Holy—" Kevin breathed over my earpiece. "Is that a *face?*"

"It's Prospero. What's left of him after Crohn paid a visit." I turned my head slowly, taking in every inch of the grotesque aftermath. "Record this footage and save it for the files. I also want a sample of the . . . remains . . . for later study."

"Incarnate demons are walking tanks," Kevin said, "and hounds are supposed to be the most dangerous of them all. So that means . . ."

Jessie finished the thought for him. "It means Ben Crohn isn't screwing around. He's been eating his demon Wheaties. Speaking of."

She gestured to the bookshelves. The false front hung open, and so did the safe door, ripped from its hinges and tossed to the corner of the room. The reinforced-steel compartment sat empty, not even a speck of dust left behind.

"The contracts," I said. "He knew how badly he screwed up, and he knew there was a chance Prospero might just burn them and cut his losses. So he went on the offensive."

Jessie stood beside me. "Makes sense. If someone had a bundle of papers that could kill me from the other side of the world, getting those back would be priority one. The one weapon he's afraid of, and now it's in his hands. If I was Crohn, I'd be looking for a fresh hiding place."

"But then what? He's a wanted man. The law's going to hunt him, we're going to hunt him. Then there's the eastern courts: if he wasn't on their hit list already, murdering Prospero just made him infernal enemy number one."

"What about the *other* courts," Jessie said, "the ones Vigilant Lock was created to mess with? You think he'd try running to them?"

Any port in a storm. Still, it didn't feel right. They had no reason to open their arms to the man who'd spent years working against them, not unless he had something to offer. Something valuable enough to make amends for his crimes. And I didn't get the impression that these were forgiving people.

"I know a way we can find out," I told her.

Jessie stared at me over the rims of her glasses. She caught my meaning.

"Portland," she said.

"Do we have any other leads?"

"You know this is gonna be insanely dangerous, right?" Jessie asked. "I mean, even by our usual standards."

"It's not only about the intel." I took off my glasses and killed the audio feed. This discussion was just for Jessie and me. "As of today, Vigilant Lock is out from under hell's thumb. As of today, we're the outfit we were *supposed* to be, the outfit they conned us all into thinking we were signing up for."

"Independence Day," Jessie said. "And the eastern courts aren't gonna take that gracefully. They're gonna come at us with everything they've got. We have to be ready for it."

"Now we're making our own rules. The old playbook, such as it was, is out the window. Where we go from here, the alliances we make, the enemies we target . . . it's all up to us. And there aren't any small choices. Every move we make has life-and-death consequences."

Jessie nodded. She stared across the office, her gaze distant.

"It was easy, being a weapon. Letting Linder and his bosses call the shots, make the big decisions."

I put my hand on her shoulder.

"Linder works for us now. What's left of Panic Cell is an enemy force, what's left of Beach Cell is embedded in deep cover, and as far as I know, the new Redbird Cell hasn't even been on their first mission yet. Jessie . . . you aren't just heading up this team anymore. This is a field promotion. You *are* the leader of Vigilant Lock."

"No," she said, meeting my gaze. She put her hand, soft but firm, over mine. "*We* are. And we'll get the job done." She took a deep breath. "Make the call."

Fontaine picked up on the third ring. His syrupy drawl filled my ear.

"*Ma chérie.* Saw you on the five o'clock news. Points for style, but aren't you supposed to be a *covert* operative?"

"Getting my fifteen minutes of fame over with," I told him. "I need something. A professional introduction."

"My, you've just piqued my curiosity. You and I don't run in the same social circles, after all. Who were you looking to trade handshakes with?"

"Caitlin," I said. "I want to meet her."

I heard his slow hiss of breath on the other end of the line. His voice, slow and sly and curling around my brain like a rattlesnake's tail.

"Are you . . . sure about that, darlin'? It's important that I know: Are you asking of your own free will? Are you ready to accept the consequences of your request, whatever may befall?"

"She's been waiting for this call, Fontaine. And while I don't expect you to admit it, I think you have, too. Two words: Cold Spectrum. We know the truth. So does she. But we've got something she doesn't."

"That being?" he asked.

"Proof. Call her. I want a meeting. Face-to-face."

He fell silent for a moment, calculating. "And what does good old Fontaine get out of this deal?"

"One hell of a scoop. Guess where I'm standing right now?"

"In your boudoir," he mused wistfully, "wearing a French silk negligee and a smile."

I arched an eyebrow at the phone.

"I'm more into flannel pajamas, but no. I'm in Prospero's office in New York."

"And you're jawing on the phone while you should be slipping out the back door?" Fontaine asked. "Reckless, darlin'. He's not much of a gentleman."

"He's not much of anything." I snapped a photo of the goo- and gore-streaked room and sent it over. "He's dead."

I heard the hitch in Fontaine's breath. "You tellin' me true? Who else knows about this?"

"Nobody but his killer. Now, if I understand how the courts work, a human killing a hound—that's the sort of thing they call out the Chainmen for, right? Like you."

"Like me," he said. "With a bounty worth ten times his weight in gold. A human just layin' hands on a hound is a mortal insult—unforgivable. *Killing* one . . . well, over five hundred years on the job, and I've gotta say that's damn near unprecedented."

"Then it's a good thing that our favorite bounty hunter just got a head start on the competition. Ben Crohn did it, and we're going after him. If we get him before you do, you're welcome to take full credit for the kill."

"Far be it from me to tell you your business, but you might want to leave this job to the heavy hitters. A man capable of taking down a hound—"

"Hasn't seen what me and my partner are capable of," I said. "So. Does that buy us an introduction to Caitlin?"

"You just rubbed my back so nicely, it'd be an absolute pleasure to rub yours. I need to make a few phone calls. I'll get back to you in about an hour."

An hour gave us time to rally the troops. We picked up April and Kevin, swapping out Aselia's stolen SUV for a Bureau-issued one. Down in the motor pool, Jessie stood and stared.

"What?" I asked her.

"They gave us a recent model, no dents or scrapes, bumpers intact, windshields unbroken . . . it's been *washed*." Jessie held the keys high, dangling from a stamped paper tag. "This is a new era."

We drove north, heading for the airfield. Linder got back to us before Fontaine did. I put him on speaker, and we heard the steady thrum of a helicopter's rotors in the background.

"I'm herding cats," he told us. "You might imagine, Vigilant's senior directors are a bit—to put it charitably—*anxious* about today's events. I've been reaching out to them and explaining the way of the world."

"And the verdict is?" Jessie asked.

"Seven people, besides myself, are charged with overseeing the program. These are the government officials who secure our funding, cover our paper trails, arrange access to the information we need, and so on. Most of them were as firmly in the dark as you were, and now that they know Crohn manipulated them, they're all too happy to come to the side of the angels."

"Most," I echoed.

"Two or three are going to need special handling. At least one I can swing with financial incentives. Another is on the fence. The third is, unfortunately, a true believer in the infernal cause. I'm on my way to pay him a private visit right now. I'm giving him his severance papers."

We didn't have to ask if that was a euphemism.

"There's something else," he said, and I caught a hesitant edge in his voice. "I expect it's part of Crohn's exit strategy. In the last hour, Vigilant's private servers were targets of multiple cyberattacks. I've taken our entire network off-line until we get this mess sorted—pulled the physical plugs, literally—but it looks like he may have copied large chunks of our database."

I leaned over the phone. "What kind of information did he pull?"

"A little of everything. Hostile Entity records, financial transfers, operative dossiers—"

"On us? Linder, *specifically* what did he get? How much data was Vigilant keeping on us?"

"Only what was considered necessary, to pair up operatives with the missions they're most qualified for. Basic skill assessments and field reports."

"Naturally," April said, her voice dripping with sarcasm. She was thinking the same thing I was: Until now, Vigilant Lock's agents were disposable, meant to be discarded when convenient—and terminated when we weren't. Any intelligence they kept on us—intel in Crohn's hands, now—was for the purpose of making us easier to kill.

"Once Crohn's been put down and Vigilant is back on its feet," Jessie said, "I'll be expecting full access to that database. *Full* access."

"Understood," Linder said. "I'm going airborne. I'll be in touch as the situation develops."

Jessie leaned over the armrest and hung up the phone.

Aselia clutched the wheel, staring dead ahead. "We got rid of Crohn, kicked his bosses to the curb, and Vigilant is *still* screwing us."

"Short term," Jessie said. "Let's just keep our eyes on the target. Plenty of time for cleaning house later."

Fontaine rang in. I snatched up the phone. I didn't put it on speaker.

"Against my better judgment," he said, "the bargain is struck. Caitlin wants to meet you, too. Her home turf, if you'd be so kind. Las Vegas. Call me when you land—I'll give you the specifics."

"*Her* turf? Seems a little lopsided, Fontaine. She's not exactly trying to make us feel assured of our safety, is she?"

Fontaine chuckled. "No, darlin', it's a sign of respect for your intelligence."

"How's that?" I asked.

"Because you know perfectly well that no matter where you meet, the only way you're walking out alive is with her permission. She's not gonna insult you by pretending otherwise."

THIRTY-FIVE

Access to a private plane beat flying coach, but the six-seater Cessna wasn't built for cross-country hauls. We had to land and refuel twice, putting in at tiny airfields in the middle of nowhere, and I checked in with Linder each time while Aselia ran her maintenance checks.

I called my mom. Three rings, a hang-up, then calling back thirty seconds later. That was our signal, letting her know it was really me and that I wasn't under any duress.

"It's not safe yet," I told her. "Safer than it was, but stay hidden just a little while longer. We've got a loose end to wrap up."

"I saw you on the news. At the press conference."

"Yeah?"

"Your father would have been proud."

Memories welled up, and I shoved them back down, down into the padlocked box of my heart. No time for emotions, not on a mission. Besides, thinking about Dad made me think about the crawling, itching gnaw in my veins, getting worse by the hour, and the incubus gigolo I had on speed dial. Dad was a man of the law, down to his bones. He didn't have a lot of regard for junkies.

I needed to work past this. We were about to go toe-to-toe with a man capable of ripping an infernal hound to shreds. No chance we'd survive without my magic, and the addiction Nadine left in my system was like a wall rising up around it. Romeo's kiss, back in Atlantic City, had smashed the wall down. Now it was coming back, brick by iron brick.

If I could find a way to top off, just get a little hit to see me through until the crisis was over . . . I squeezed my eyes shut. *No.* I'd find another way.

We flew through the night. I slept when I could. It was air sleep, that fuzzy, floating place that mimicked the real thing, tossing me back to the waking world with every shudder of the Cessna's wings.

The sun rose over the sleeping city as we landed at North Vegas Airport. Linder had called ahead and arranged a car, an unmarked sedan from the local FBI office. An agent was on standby to hand over the keys along with a message from the Vegas Bureau chief, SAC Brannon.

"She hopes you have a wonderful visit to our city," he recited, "and also please don't destroy anything while you're here."

Jessie took the keys and tossed them over to me.

"That's not up to us," she told him.

After he left, she rallied the team. The sedan's tinted window caught the reflection of the rising sun, turning the glass to shimmering amber. It gleamed in the corner of my eye.

"Me and Harmony are going in alone," Jessie said. "Based on what we've seen so far, this Caitlin has an interest in keeping us alive. We're kinda gambling on that still being the case."

"You're betting the whole damn house," Aselia said.

April pushed her bifocals up on her nose. "I think it's a reasonable risk."

"Reasonable?" Aselia stared at her. "You've seen what these things are capable of, right? You don't sit down to chat with an incarnate demon, especially not a damn hound."

"They just did, back in New York," Kevin offered.

"They had to *jump out a window* in New York," she shot back. "And before that, Prospero had no idea who they really were. Caitlin knows. She's got their number, and she knows they're coming."

"I said 'reasonable risk,'" April replied. "I didn't say 'no risk.' But there are times when politics makes for strange bedfellows, and this may be one of them. Ben Crohn is as much her enemy as he is ours."

Aselia threw her hands up. "Do what you want. I'll be working on the plane."

"Good," Jessie said. "Get her ready—we may have to leave in a hurry. Kevin and April, I want you monitoring Internet traffic and prowling media feeds. If you see anything that remotely *looks* like Crohn or Mikki poking their heads out of hiding, flag it."

"The one nice thing about Mikki," Kevin muttered, "is that she isn't exactly subtle. Sounds like the two of them deserve each other."

"Sure do," Jessie said. "We'll buy 'em side-by-side cemetery plots."

Fontaine gave us the destination: an address in the 18b, Las Vegas's arts district. This patch of town was a rough little bohemian enclave, set apart from the slick, polished sheen of the Strip and trying to wriggle out from under its neon shadow. Vintage clothes stores and remainder shops shared space with tiny theaters, dive bars, and corner bistros, every other wall adorned with swirling murals and street art.

Just off Coolidge Avenue, a squat two-story office building in white stucco basked in the desert sun beside a postage stamp–size parking lot. Going by the sign in the lobby, business wasn't great: beyond a resident dental office and a couple of accounting practices, three-quarters of the building was vacant.

"Office 2C," I said, trailing my finger along the sign. "According to this, nobody's there."

Jessie tapped her earpiece. "Kevin, check the building's tenant records. I've got a hunch we're gonna find out 2C was rented out just for today, with untraceable money, but it's still worth a look."

A man in mirrored glasses stood at the foot of a curling staircase, a dusty gold runner stretching up to the second floor. As we approached, he gave us a once-over and spoke into his sleeve.

"Ma'am. They're on their way up."

"You gonna search us for weapons?" Jessie asked.

His lips curled into a reptilian smile. "Would it matter?"

We climbed the stairs. The entrance to 2C didn't have a label, just a blank holder for a nameplate beside the windowless door. Another man snapped to attention, pulling the door wide and holding it for us.

"You sure about this?" Jessie murmured.

"Nope," I said. "Let's do it anyway."

She nudged me with her elbow. "That's *my* line."

I wasn't sure what to expect beyond the door. The only hound we'd ever encountered up close and personal was Prospero, a giggly, twitching train wreck. Half accountant, half serial killer. He'd been capable of playing at being human, short term, but the sheer sense of *wrongness* around him was overwhelming, and I wasn't sure if it was just his personal nature or part of the territory when it came to being a demon prince's right-hand man.

At the end of the hall, 2C was a conference room with floor-to-ceiling windows. The polished glass stretched along one wall, flooding the office with warm desert light. An oval table in soft, pale wood shared space alongside a credenza stocked with polished glasses, a carafe, a French press, and packets of sugar. The air smelled faintly of cinnamon.

Caitlin rose from her seat at the head of the table and greeted us with a pomegranate-lipped smile. She wore a black pin-striped pantsuit, raw silk tailored perfectly to her frame, and her Louboutin heels clicked softly on the checkerboard-tile floor as she stepped toward us.

"Good morning, and thank you for coming. Can I interest you in refreshments? We have Voss water, Seattle coffee, an assortment of herbal tea blends." She looked my way as she spoke, her voice tinged with a faint Scottish burr. "I asked that the minifridge be stocked with

Diet Coke—I understand that's your preferred brand. Also, ginger ale, in case either of you has an unsettled stomach. Did you have a good flight?"

"I'm . . . good, thanks," Jessie said, sounding as off balance as I felt. "The flight was fine."

Caitlin held out her hand. I wavered for a moment, unsure, then decided diplomacy was my best move. She shook with a firm, professional grip. After she shook hands with Jessie, she strode over to the credenza.

"Change your mind later if you like. *I'm* having coffee. Been on the move for something like forty-seven hours straight at this point, and I have six more meetings scheduled for later today." Caitlin glanced over her shoulder, tossing her scarlet hair, and waved a hand at us. "Please, sit—sit anywhere, the room's ours. Make yourselves comfortable."

I pulled back a seat at the far end of the table, the plush tan leather chair rolling on freshly oiled casters.

"You . . . aren't what I expected," I said.

Caitlin chuckled, favoring me with an impish smile. "Not surprising, given what I know about your previous encounters with my kind. You will find that I'm considerably easier to negotiate with than the late and unlamented Prospero. And much more pleasant than Nadine. I'll let you in on a little secret: *nobody* likes Nadine."

"You helped us out," Jessie said, "back in Portland."

"And she was deliciously furious." Caitlin walked back to her seat at the head of the table, cradling a steaming mug of coffee. "Wasn't the reason I did it, but any time I get a chance to tweak her nose, I'm hardly going to pass it up. And . . . really?"

I shook my head at her, not following.

Caitlin waved her arm across the table, drawing the space between us. "You're going to sit all the way over there?" She arched a sculpted eyebrow and wriggled her fingers. "Come on. Closer."

I felt like I was being invited deeper into a lion's den. I shared an uncertain glance with Jessie. Then I rose from my chair and moved up a couple of seats. Not within arm's reach, but closer. She did the same.

"If I brought you here to kill you," Caitlin said, "I wouldn't have paid for catering. Honestly. I'd bring my own coffee, and that would be it. Also, there'd be plastic tarps on the floor, because the cleaning deposit for this building is *absurd*."

"Pragmatic," I said.

"I am. There's something else you should understand about me: I like this city. I like the earth. I like humans! I even own one."

Jessie yanked her glasses off, curling her fist around them as she glared across the table. "*Excuse* me?"

"My point is, I'm not some cackling comic-book villain looking to destroy the planet. I am charged with maintaining my prince's territory, keeping the wheels of politics and finance spinning, and paving the eventual path to his triumph. It's not a part-time job."

"That territory belongs to humanity," Jessie told her. "You can understand why we've got a problem with that."

"Do you like Howard Jones?" Caitlin asked.

I blinked. "The . . . the musician?"

"I *adore* Howard Jones." Caitlin clasped her hands, all earnestness. "Duran Duran, the Pet Shop Boys, Spandau Ballet. I could never destroy a world that had Howard Jones in it. Something you may not be aware of: I'm loath to admit it, but my people are . . . not good at art. We can appreciate it, cherish it, but we lack some primal spark required to make it for ourselves. Humanity has that spark. We can inspire you, though. All throughout history, wearing countless names and masks, *we* have been your muses."

"Sounds like you're trying to sell us on a kinder, gentler hell," I said.

She chuckled into her coffee mug.

"I am neither gentle nor kind," Caitlin replied. "I'm a business-woman. And I see no need for fire and bluster when cooler heads can prevail. So, yes, I provided a distraction in Portland for you. Why do *you* think I did that?"

I laid my hands on the table, feeling the warm wood grain under my fingertips.

"Cold Spectrum," I said.

She inclined her head. "Proceed."

"I think you knew the truth. That Vigilant Lock—and Cold Spectrum before it—was a con game. The eastern infernal courts created it as a deniable weapon to target you and your allies. But knowing it and proving it aren't the same thing. You needed us alive so we could get to the truth in a way you couldn't: from the inside. If we give you absolute proof, that's justification to go to war against them. The Cold Peace is over."

"Close," Caitlin said. "Very close. Except for one thing: a justification for war is the absolute *last* thing I want. And while I'm sure you're quite enthused at the prospect of my people taking tooth and claw to one another, it's the last thing you want, too . . . at least, if you enjoy this planet as much as I do."

THIRTY-SIX

I felt like a rookie detective wrestling with an unsolvable crime. I had locked down the means and the opportunity, but the motive unraveled under Caitlin's patient, sly smile.

"From what we're told," I said, "the eastern courts of hell are tiny. They're shrimp compared to the West Coast and the Midwest. That's the whole reason they created Vigilant Lock: so they could attack you through a proxy. Why *wouldn't* you want a reason to take them out?"

"Because stability is good for business. Good for everyone, really, and that includes humanity. Come now, Harmony: if open hostilities erupted, do you think we'd fight that war in *our* world? No. The battle lines would be drawn here, on Earth. Once our agents and our human servants mobilize, no one will be able to stop the dominoes from tumbling. Assassinations, bombings, mass atrocities disguised as terrorist attacks. The death toll will be breathtaking. And if I may be so bold as to remind you . . . my people don't age. Yes, my court would win the war, eventually—that is a foregone conclusion. The time it would take, however, would be measured in human generations. Not long at all, from my perspective, but you and your children and your children's children would endure a world of unrelenting violence and horror."

"What about Nadine?" Jessie said. "She was after the truth behind Cold Spectrum, too. What's her angle?"

Caitlin rose from her chair. She stood at the window, basking in sunlight as she sipped her coffee.

"Beyond being an incessant irritation? She wants a promotion. You see, one variant or another of your little monster-hunting team has existed since the 1960s. We only recently became aware of it, and even more recently ferreted out the real backers behind it. Some would consider that an embarrassing lapse of duty. *I'm* fine—I've already confessed to my prince and done my penance for failure, but my ally in the Midwest wouldn't be quite so fortunate. If the truth about Vigilant Lock emerged, my colleague Royce would likely be shamed and stripped of his position, and Nadine, next in line for it, would become Prince Malphas's new hound."

Jessie stared at her. "She'd start a war . . . for a *job*?"

Caitlin glanced back over her shoulder, her lips curled in distaste. "Not a mere *job*. Houndship is the highest honor a demon can earn. One heartbeat removed from a prince's throne. And I suspect she wouldn't be satisfied there. Believe me, if you think a hundred-year war sounds unpleasant, just wait and see what Princess Nadine would do to this planet."

I shuddered. "I can imagine."

"Trust me," Caitlin said. "You can't. I've known her for centuries. However horrid you think she is, she's worse than that. And given that you two have made yourselves enemies of her family, it's in your best interests to keep her far away from the reins of power."

I eased my chair back. My mouth felt like it was packed with cotton. "Think I will have something to drink now."

"Try the chocolate-raspberry coffee blend. I brought it for Jessie, but you'll enjoy it."

"How do you know what kind of coffee I—" Jessie paused, shaking her head. "Never mind. Okay, so you don't want the truth exposed. I can follow that. But if that's the case, what do you want from us?"

Caitlin turned her back to the window. She gave a tiny shrug and a satisfied chuckle, her voice like prickly velvet.

"What I want is exactly what you're in the process of doing. A coup. If Vigilant Lock is successfully freed from the influence of the eastern courts and becomes exactly what it pretended to be all along—an organization run by and for humans—there's no scandal to conceal and nothing to go to war over."

"But we'll still be out there," I said. "We're still a threat."

Caitlin put her hand to her mouth, covering a sudden smirk.

"I'm sorry." She fluttered her hand, her cheeks turning pink. "I'm sorry, but you are *adorable*. I'm not trying to denigrate your talents— I'm really not. But let's consider the odds. By the law of averages, the majority of your operations will either target people I don't care about, people who annoy me, or my actual enemies in the other courts. That's a win for me, across the board."

"And if we come after you?" I asked.

Her smile vanished. Caitlin's face became an expressionless mask. Watching me—*studying* me, like a virus under a microscope. The temperature in the room dropped. The sunlight at the windows became cold and barren, a stray cloud drifting in front of the sun and draining the color from the room.

"Then I would destroy you," she replied, "without hesitation and without mercy."

Caitlin set down her mug. She clapped her hands once, sharp and strident. Her pleasant smile returned, and the warmth came back with it, as if the sunlight had been waiting for her permission to enter the room.

"And we don't want that," Caitlin said, "now do we? But let's speak to our shared concern: Benjamin Crohn. He's a link to the truth. He's also living, breathing evidence. I would like him to *stop* living and breathing, as soon as possible."

"Feeling's mutual," Jessie said.

"Good." Caitlin sat back down at the head of the table. "I can't move against Crohn directly—*officially*, he's nobody to me, and any overt action would betray my hand to the eastern courts. But you can."

"We have to find him first," I said. "He killed Prospero, stole the contracts for the demons he's got bound up inside his body, and went on the run. We were wondering if he'd come to you, actually."

"No. He'll find no succor at the gates of hell, not from my court or any other. His offenses and his failures are equally unforgivable."

I poured myself a mug of coffee. The steam, scented faintly raspberry, wafted through the warm office air.

"In my experience," I said, "when a criminal burns his bridges in the underworld, he usually goes looking to make a deal with the authorities."

Caitlin leaned back and stretched her arms over her head. Languid, like a cat.

"What a pity that they don't exist," she said, stifling a yawn. "I hope I'm not the bearer of bad news, Harmony, but if you're insinuating that he might go looking for the guardians of the pearly gates . . . there aren't any. There is no heaven, there are no bearers of holy light, there is no primal force of good watching over you. Your species is quite alone in the universe."

She sipped her coffee, smiling at me contentedly over the rim of the mug.

"Well, not entirely alone," she added. "You have us, to keep you company in the dark."

I wasn't sure if I believed her. I wasn't sure I wanted to think about it. Bad time for an existential crisis.

Besides, I was thinking about Crohn. My experience with crooks of all stripes, mundane and supernatural, still held: when their backs were up against the wall and every ally turned enemy, the bad guys generally went looking to make a deal anywhere they could. Crohn wouldn't survive on his own. He wasn't stupid—he had to know that.

"He had a contingency plan," I said, thinking out loud. "A backup in case Vigilant Lock turned on him. He couldn't go to you, obviously couldn't go back to the eastern courts—hell's not an option, period."

"He stole as much data as he could off Vigilant's servers," Jessie said. She looked to Caitlin. "Would *he* know that exposing the truth would start a war?"

"Unquestionably, and he could certainly anticipate the chaos that would result. Not that it would save his life. He'd just be giving us more reasons to punish him."

"No," I said, "that might be part of his game, but he still needs allies. A safe harbor."

Then it came to me.

"Excuse me," I said, taking out my phone. "I need to verify something."

Linder's voice was hard to hear, muffled by the chop of helicopter blades. "Agent Black? What is it? I'm in transit at the moment."

"This is important," I said. "The no-kill order on Bobby Diehl. Was it your idea or Crohn's?"

I listened. Then I hung up the phone and slumped in my seat.

"I know exactly where Crohn is going," I said. "He's defecting. He's joining the Network."

Caitlin leaned in, eyes flashing. "Tell me everything."

"The eastern courts were leaning hard on Crohn to find a means of attacking the Network," I said.

"Right," Jessie said. "Bobby Diehl's the way in. We hang back until he gets his full membership, the embedded agents from Beach Cell get the info, and we take the whole outfit down in one fell swoop."

"Linder wanted to accelerate the timetable. He felt like the surveillance wasn't getting anywhere, and he was worried about keeping Beach

Cell undercover while we knew Diehl's suspicions were growing. Only a matter of time before they were exposed. Crohn told him to stay the course."

Jessie's mouth hung open. "Motherfucker was hedging his bets. He knew he could pack up and run to Bobby if things went south—and bring Vigilant's files as a peace offering. The Network exposes the truth, sparks a war between the courts—"

"And while we weaken ourselves," Caitlin said, "bleeding in battle, the Network grows fat and strong. Ready to ambush whoever's still standing when the dust settles. *Unacceptable.*"

"What do you know about the Network?" I asked her.

"Until a short time ago, we knew what everyone else knows: that they were an urban legend. A myth of the criminal underworld. Recent events have proved otherwise. Their members are self-proclaimed servants of the so-called Kings of Man." Caitlin stared at Jessie. "I believe you know that much."

Jessie put her sunglasses back on. She pushed the tinted lenses up over her turquoise eyes, shrouding them from sight. "We're aware."

"These Kings aren't demons," Caitlin said. "No part of our courts or our kind, and they're as hostile to us as they are to humanity. Their ultimate goals . . . unknown, but unquestionably toxic. You need to stop Crohn and, just as importantly, delete the data he stole. Every shred of evidence, anything he could use to provoke a war. Don't do it for my people: do it for yours."

She put her fingers to her lips and let out a short, shrill whistle. The office door opened. One of her men stepped inside, silent as he approached the table. He leaned in and dropped eight thick stacks of money on the pale wood. Hundreds, in tight-packed bands. He left without a word.

"Seeing as you're currently rebuilding your organization from the ground up," Caitlin said, "this should cover your mission expenses. Fifty thousand dollars. Untraceable and clean."

"We're not taking your money," Jessie told her.

"Access to liquid assets," Caitlin said patiently, "could make the difference between failure and success. Time is not on our side here. Please. Accept it as a gift. No strings attached."

Jessie shoved back her chair.

"I was born on a Tuesday. Not *last* Tuesday. And I've never seen a free lunch that didn't have a fishhook buried in it."

She turned to leave. I followed her to the door.

"As you wish," Caitlin said. "It's been a pleasure meeting you both in person. I do hope that if and when we meet again, it's not as mortal enemies, but that's really up to you. Oh, and . . . Harmony?"

I paused, glancing back over my shoulder.

"Could I speak to you a moment?" she asked. "Privately."

Jessie had the door halfway open. She shut it again, hard enough to rattle the frame, keeping her hand on the knob.

"Anything you have to say to my partner," Jessie said, "you can say in front of me."

A faint twinkle played in Caitlin's eyes.

"I could," she said, "but that might be awkward for everyone involved. Please. Just two minutes of your time."

I didn't know what game she was playing, but she'd been straight with us so far—at least, as straight as I could expect from a demon. And if she wanted to kill us, she'd have already made her move. My intuition told me to take a chance.

I looked to Jessie.

"Two minutes," I said.

She nodded, slow, and turned the knob. "I'll be right outside."

Then she stepped out and shut the office door behind her. Leaving me alone with Caitlin.

THIRTY-SEVEN

"You're fighting a revolution," Caitlin told me. "Striking out against the eastern courts, demanding sovereignty. An interesting time. All of history—yours and ours—is bookmarked by revolutions."

"Sounds like you're talking from experience."

She chuckled. Her hips swayed as she walked to the credenza, refreshing her mug of coffee. My gaze flicked to her shadow, cast in the light from the tall office windows.

Her shadow had a tail. Thin, serpentine, moving in time with her footsteps.

"I was in New York City in the summer of 1775," she said. "I wasn't a hound then—I wasn't *anything* then, really—just an ambitious traveler, exploring this world and its pleasures. Passing an evening in a public house, I listened in on a band of young men at the next table as they spoke of revolution, egging each other on with their boasts and their dreams. I was charmed, utterly charmed. They had the perfect combination of daring and naïveté."

"What did you do?" I asked.

"Bought them a round of drinks and subtly encouraged them, as I do. I wanted to see what would happen." She sipped her coffee.

"Much as I do now. Are you prepared for what happens *after* the war's won, Harmony? It's not enough for Vigilant Lock to be independent. You'll have to nurture it, shape it, decide its mandate and its purpose. Following orders is easy; giving them is considerably more complicated, especially when you're deciding matters of life and death. Other people's lives and deaths, people who are counting on you to make the right call each and every time. Take it from me—I speak from experience."

"I think we'll do all right."

She set down her mug and approached me.

"I know what Nadine did to you in Chicago," she said. The words hung between us, expecting an answer I wasn't sure how to give. "And now I can smell the lingering cologne of another of my kind on you. Not her perfume. You've indulged, haven't you?"

My pride stung, my weakness on full display like the centerfold of a dirty magazine, but lying felt like a waste of time.

"Once," I said.

"I assume your partner doesn't know, which is why I wanted to speak to you privately. You felt more than relieved after you gave in, didn't you? Energized. I imagine your magic flowed like water through a broken dam. For a little while, anyway. Now the hunger is coming back, worse than last time."

The weight of my guilt dragged my gaze to the floor. "Yes."

"Like Nadine, I am a daughter of the Choir of Lust. I'm familiar with your condition. I've inflicted it myself a time or two, as a means of control and coercion. Or simply for the pleasure of torment. Never on a magician, though, for good reason. Harmony . . . your magic didn't flow."

I looked up, furrowing my brow. "But it did. It got us through a fight back in—"

She closed the distance between us.

"It wasn't your magic," Caitlin said.

I fell silent. Not sure how to answer that.

251

"You were simply processing the demonic energy imbued by the kiss. It wasn't *your* magic. It was ours. If you go back for more, you'll do it again and again, gradually losing connection to your own powers. It isn't just the addiction; eventually, you'll be utterly incapable of working a simple spell without the touch of my kind to fuel you."

She put her hand on my shoulder.

"You have to quit," she told me. "Entirely. There will be pain. You will most assuredly crave the bliss of death before Nadine's curse has worked its way out of your system. The hunger will be unimaginable. But you have to do it."

"Why are you helping me?" I asked, my voice softer than I intended it to be.

"Because you are that rarest of gifts—an enemy I respect. I predict two possible eventualities. Either you'll come to your senses, realize that my prince offers the best future for your species, and willingly serve me, or we will meet in honorable battle. In no case do I wish to see you as Nadine would have you: broken, hopelessly mired in addiction, and cut off from your power forever. That serves no good purpose."

Her hand tightened on my shoulder.

"We are warriors, Harmony. When next we meet, it may be with spears in our hands, but today we share a battlefield. If you won't take my money, take my advice, from one soldier to another: Fight this sickness while you still can. Don't let Nadine have the last laugh."

"Thank you," I said, looking her in the eye.

"Good luck with your revolution."

# # #

"So what was that all about?" Jessie asked as we pushed through the front door of the office building, out into the desert sunlight.

"Trying to get me to take the money," I told her. I hated lying to Jessie, hated myself for doing it, but I didn't see an alternative.

Caitlin was right. I needed to quit, to go cold turkey, to get the toxic remnants of Nadine's attack and Romeo's kiss out of my veins once and for all. With the clock ticking down and our enemies on the move, not to mention a war about to begin, the timing couldn't possibly be worse. I needed the fuel, another hit of energy from Romeo's kiss, to get through this fight. I needed to never touch him again, or I'd be risking a downward spiral with no way back.

I needed to decide what was more important: me . . . or the mission.

Even I could only deny basic human needs like food and sleep for so long. We needed a team meeting, so we killed two birds with one stone by calling April, Kevin, and Aselia downtown for lunch. We ended up at Tiki Pete's, a strip-mall Thai place a few blocks from the Vegas Strip. A reporter recited sports scores from a ceiling-mounted TV over the bar, across from empty tables and booths where strips of duct tape covered the cracks in the vinyl seats.

"You know we've got a standing invitation at the Monaco, right?" Kevin asked as he gave the restaurant a dubious look. "Like, actual gourmet food? For free?"

"No time, and this is closer to the airport." Jessie led the way, grabbing a table and giving the hostess a wave. "We gotta eat and run. Los Angeles is the hub of Bobby Diehl's empire, and that's probably where Crohn is headed. I want us camped on Diehl's doorstep before sundown. We make our move *today*."

We gave them the rundown in between poring over faded, grease-stained menus. I ordered the lunch special, pad thai and a Diet Coke for $3.99. I made a mental note to buy antacid on the way back to the plane.

Aselia rubbed her forehead like she was staving off a headache. "So now we have to *stop* the demonic courts from going to war. And, I'm sorry, who are these Network assholes? That wasn't even a thing, back in my day."

"It probably was; you just didn't know about it," I told her. "From what we can gather, picture the Mafia on occult steroids, buried behind five layers of whispers and urban legends. They snare their foot soldiers with magical *geises* to compel their silence. Nobody talks, and anybody who gets close to exposing them is killed before they can go public. That was the only reason we were keeping Bobby Diehl alive: he's in line for a membership, and we have agents buried deep inside his organization. His personal assistant is a Vigilant operative."

"Yeah, that no-kill order?" Jessie chopped the air with the flat of her hand. "*Rescinded.* We've got three mission objectives, gang: One, take out Benjamin Crohn. Two, find and destroy the data he stole from Vigilant's servers. Every scrap of evidence, anything the Network could use—it's gotta be scrubbed off the face of the earth. Three, safely extract Agent Cooper and the rest of Beach Cell. They've been in deep cover at Diehl Innovations for months, and the second Crohn makes contact with Bobby, they're gonna get burned, and they're gonna get dead. Can't let that happen. Optional objective: terminate Bobby Diehl."

The waitress came around with our drinks. Kevin cracked open a can of Mountain Dew and unwrapped a fat paper straw.

"The tower in LA is the hub of Diehl's business empire," he said. "So it's networked with every plant, every satellite office . . . What if we shut it all down?"

"Whatcha thinking?" Jessie asked.

Kevin gestured with his straw. "I could write up a worm to freeze their network. Wouldn't take too long if I use preexisting code, just a few tweaks . . . we shut down their e-mail servers, communication apps—basically, the only way Crohn's gonna deliver Bobby those files is if he prints them out and walks them in by hand. It's a short-term solution, but that could buy you time to get the job done."

"Are you sure you can pull it off?" I asked him. "We've seen what Bobby Diehl is capable of. Blending magic and high technology is kind of his thing."

"Yeah, his thing, but the flunkies in his IT department don't know they're working for an evil mastermind. Unless he personally built their e-mail server from the ground up, *he's* not the brain I'll be facing off against. It's probably a bunch of off-the-rack code with a custom upgrade or two. I can handle it."

"I like it," Jessie said. "Let's do it."

"Only issue is, to pull this off we're gonna need on-site access. You need to break into the physical server room at the tower."

"If we could get word to Agent Cooper, seeing as she works a heartbeat away from Diehl's office—" April paused, her eyes on the television set. "Ah. Speak of the devil, and he shall appear."

It was the first time I'd seen Bobby Diehl on a television set without his ubiquitous used-car-salesman grin. Red-faced and flustered, he stood at a press-conference podium, flanked by grim and silent lawyers. The ticker across the bottom of the screen read: NASDAQ: DIEHL INNOVATIONS STOCK DOWN BY TWENTY-EIGHT POINTS.

"These allegations are . . . *outrageous*," Diehl stammered. "I have never met these people, I have never heard of this RedEye program, and I categorically deny the accusations against me. Not only will I be fully vindicated, I promise that my legal team will see that those slandering me are punished to the fullest extent of the law. That's . . . that's all. That's all I have to say. Thank you."

The camera cut back to a dubious-looking anchor. "While no official charges have been filed against Robert Diehl, sources inside the FBI indicate that an exploration is ongoing, and we may see a formal indictment by the end of this month."

"Not gonna lie," Jessie said. "Watching him squirm is the best part of my week. Somebody's starting to figure out he's not as bulletproof as he thought."

My gaze slid from the television to the rumpled paper place mats. I wasn't focused on anything in particular as I thought things over.

"Still walking around free, though. It's understandable; Esposito has to tread carefully until he officially gets the nod and becomes the Bureau's new director. He's already kicked up a tidal wave, arresting Ben Crohn on national TV, and Bobby Diehl's one of the richest men in America. You don't hunt big game without lining up some big guns first."

"Looks like they didn't release the news about Crohn escaping from custody," April said. "Once we resolve the situation, I imagine Linder will concoct an appropriate story to explain his untimely demise. I'm guessing suicide in a holding cell."

"Can't beat the classics," I said. Then I paused, tilting my head.

"Uh-oh." Jessie poked me. "We have Idea Face. Warning. Warning. Idea Face spotted."

"Like I just said. The classics. We don't need a new tactic—we need an old and time-tested one." I smiled. "Jessie, call Esposito. April, get in touch with the LA Bureau office, and coordinate for our arrival. I'm gonna call an old colleague of mine, back from my forensic-accounting days. I know exactly how we're going to ruin Bobby Diehl's life. Legally, publicly, and *very* old-school."

Our plan secured, we headed for the airport. Aselia rented a shower and changing room intended for pilots on long hauls. We didn't have long, but five minutes of hot, clean water and the chance to run a brush through my hair felt like paradise. The thrift-store outfit I'd bought in New York sat discarded. With our names cleared, no need to hide in a crowd any longer; it was time to put on my real clothes. The tie, sea-foam green, looped around the collar of a fresh ivory blouse. The black jacket slid over my shoulders like a second skin. I looked at myself in the mirror, brushed my bangs to one side, and gave myself a nod of approval.

I'd already stabbed Bobby Diehl from a distance, but it wasn't a mortal wound. Now it was time to give that blade a twist and drive it in deep.

THIRTY-EIGHT

The autumn sun simmered through the amber fog, just another late afternoon in Los Angeles. The Diehl Innovations tower rose up like a silver spike, a needle of chrome and glass surrounded by manicured lawns and sculpted hedgerows. Employees on break lingered along the paved walking paths and relaxed on bamboo benches. It was a modern corporate mecca, pristine and tranquil.

Horns blared as a convoy in black surged up the avenue, sirens and lights shoving traffic aside. SUVs jumped the curb, wheels tearing up the grass and spitting loam as they screamed to a halt outside the tower's glass doors. The back doors of a pair of police trucks burst open, and SWAT officers boiled out like armored wasps. They took the lead and hit the doors with clockwork precision. They streamed into the lobby in two columns, boots pounding on Italian marble floors as they fanned out.

I strode into the lobby with Jessie at my side and a pack of suits at my back. Jessie held up a walkie-talkie, barking orders. "Alpha team, you're on doors—nobody comes in, nobody leaves. Send some people around to lock down the service entrances and the loading dock. Bravo team, secure the elevators and emergency stairwells. Get somebody into that maintenance room, and lock the whole damn system down."

Some of the employees milling in the lobby froze, uncertain. A couple tried to run for it. They landed hard and sprouted steel bracelets. I held my badge high above my head like a crusader's sword.

"FBI," I shouted. "This is a raid. We have a warrant to search these premises. Cooperate and we'll be done in no time."

One of the receptionists was hunched over his phone, whispering in a panic. I pointed at him.

"You calling your boss? You'd better be. Get him down here. *Now.*"

The man who came down from the executive floor, flanked by a pair of SWAT troopers, wasn't the fish I wanted to catch. He was in his seventies, dressed in Armani, his hair slicked back, and streaks of gray showing through his dye job.

I didn't wait for an introduction. "Bobby Diehl. Where is he?"

"I'm Harold Linkletter, senior counsel to Diehl Innovations, and Mr. Diehl's personal attorney. This is—this is an inexcusable witch hunt, and don't think there won't be consequences. Do you even have a warrant?"

I shoved a stack of paper in his face.

"Signed by Judge Morris half an hour ago," I said. "You will also find a list of employees we want for questioning. Consider yourself added to that list. You will escort these officers through the tower, and help them find the people we want, then bring them down to the lobby. You will do this now."

"You don't need to disturb Mr. Diehl's employees. I can answer any questions you have—"

I stood toe-to-toe with him.

"Five seconds. If you're still standing here when I get to zero, I'm arresting you for obstruction of justice, and you can spend the night in a county lockup while we look for your inexplicably missing paperwork."

"This is unreasonable," Linkletter sputtered, "and if you think this showboating is going to—"

"Four," I said. "Three. Two."

He flung up his open hands. "Fine! Fine. Going. But you haven't heard the end of this."

"Believe me," I said, "we're just getting warmed up."

He didn't know it, but he was partially right: we didn't need to talk to all the people on our list. I'd compiled it from the company website, picking random managers from random departments, twelve in all. The officers brought them down in small batches, sitting the nervous-looking bureaucrats along the designer sandalwood benches.

The one we really wanted was lucky number thirteen. Agent Cooper, dressed in a prim skirt and blouse and keeping her poker face on tight. Jessie and I stood over her.

"Cooper," I said. "You're Bobby Diehl's personal assistant, correct?"

"That's right," she said, pretending not to know me.

"Then you know this building better than anyone. You're our official tour guide. On your feet."

Linkletter was pacing, gripping his cell phone with one hand and plucking his hair out with the other. He stopped hissing into the phone long enough to look my way. "Are any of these people under arrest?"

"Not at all," Jessie said, surveying the glum and worried faces. "As soon as we finish executing our search, you're all free to either talk to us or leave. Of course, if you leave, you're gonna look *super* guilty. You should probably consult a lawyer. But not this one—this guy looks shady to me."

"Take us to your IT department," I told Cooper. She rose, scowling at me, and led the way.

I walked at her side, close, while Linkletter and a squad of local agents filled the hall at our back.

We got a little distance, and Cooper leaned in close, her voice a hard murmur. "The hell is going on? Are you *trying* to ruin my operation?"

"Change of plans," I told her. "The rest of your team: Where are they? Do you have a way to send them underground?"

"Scattered around Diehl's other facilities around the country. We've got a go code for mission abort—I can send a burst transmission from our safe house in Lincoln Heights. Only four left. Bobby's been hunting for traitors. I've lost two of my teammates in the last week."

I raised an eyebrow. "Captured? Interrogated?"

"Suicide." Her lips formed a hard, tight line. "*Before* they could be interrogated. My people know their duty, Agent Black."

"Benjamin Crohn escaped custody, and he's on his way to Bobby with a peace offering. Vigilant's database, including dossiers on you and your team. We're trying to stop him, but no guarantees. Here's what's going to happen: as soon as we're done here, you're going to be placed under arrest and moved to a secure federal facility."

"Meaning, if you manage to salvage what's left of this op, I've got perfect deniability, and I can be reinserted." Cooper nodded once, sharp. "Thank you for that."

"And if not, you can disappear cleanly. Send the rest of your team underground, Agent, that's an—"

Linkletter barged ahead of his escort, getting in between us. "You don't need to tell these people anything, Ms. Cooper. I strongly recommend you hold your silence."

"I plan on it." Cooper frowned, throwing up an imperious hand. "This is insane. Have you notified Mr. Diehl yet?"

The lawyer brandished his cell phone. "Working on it."

"Work harder. He is *not* going to be happy."

Down a short flight of stairs, the IT department was part cubicle farm, part tomb, the lights dimmed and the air just shy of freezing. Our band of agents swept through the room and took control—herding the employees into the aisles, covering junction boxes, physically dragging a few of Diehl's techs away from their keyboards before they could delete anything. Behind a long wall of glass, tall server banks hummed and strobed in silent harmony.

I tapped my earpiece. "We're in."

"Okay," Kevin's voice said, "just get to the head of IT, grab his computer, and slot the USB stick I gave you. I'll take it from there."

We already had the IT department's supervisor. He was one of the "suspects" we'd called up to the lobby for questioning. His empty office was a technophile's dream: fractal screen savers played on three ultrawide monitors arrayed on steel arms around a skeletal steel desk. Two more oversize screens hung on the back wall of the room, the Diehl Innovations logo animated and spinning in gold. Jessie and I walked Cooper inside, the lawyer hot on our heels. I pulled back the director's ergonomic chair.

The dangling screens bloomed to life. Bobby Diehl stared down at us, his face mirrored on both displays. He forced a humorless smile. Judging from the bags under his eyes and the bristle on his cheeks, he hadn't been having a good couple of days. Or sleeping.

"Hey, folks, Bobby Diehl here." He gave up on the smile. "Cooper? Linkletter? Why are these people in my tower?"

"I'm very sorry, sir—" Cooper started to say as Linkletter talked over her.

"They . . . they have warrants." The lawyer wrung his hands. "I'm working on it. The rest of the firm is inbound."

"*Working* on it," Bobby echoed. "Is this what 'working on it' looks like?"

I sat at the computer and tapped the space bar, banishing the swirling fractals. The director's monitors flashed a password prompt. Jessie stepped over to the hanging screens and looked up at Bobby.

"Our paper's in order," she told him. "We've got a warrant to search these premises and seize any evidence relevant to our investigation, as well as freeze any bank accounts related to Diehl Innovations and put an indefinite hold on any financial transfers."

"What?" Bobby gaped at her. "You can't . . . you can't *do* that! Linkletter, tell her she can't do that."

"Actually, we can," I told him. "Burton Webb alleges money from the illegal RedEye program was paid not directly to you, but to Diehl Innovations. That makes Diehl Innovations a criminal enterprise under the RICO statutes. Which, in turn, means its assets are frozen, pending investigation. We don't need to indict you personally; we're going after your company. Ready for the fun part?"

"Harmony," Jessie said as she pointed at the screen, "look at that face. This man is *ready* for the fun part. Hit him."

"As established by the Supreme Court in *United States v. Sullivan*, 1927, *James v. United States*, 1961, et cetera, illegal gains are still considered taxable income. As we speak, a good friend of mine in the IRS special-investigation unit is getting the green light on a full audit of you and your company. We're talking floor to ceiling, every penny counted—"

"—up to the elbow with no lubrication," Jessie finished for me. "You wanna act like Al Capone? We're gonna *treat* you like Al Capone."

I pointed at the monitor. "I need a password to access this system."

Cooper stared at her shoes. Linkletter stared at anything but Bobby's frowning face.

"Don't tell them *anything*," Bobby seethed.

"Ms. Cooper?" I said. "You're his right-hand woman. Don't tell me you don't have access to every computer in this building. I can and will arrest you for obstruction if you refuse to cooperate."

I caught the faintest glimmer of recognition as she looked my way. She saw exactly what I was doing: giving her a chance to strengthen her footing with Bobby and look like a loyal subject, in case we had to send her back inside undercover when this was all over.

"Cooper," Bobby said, "don't do it. Don't you dare."

"I'm running out of patience, Ms. Cooper."

She wavered on her feet, pretending to be torn—then she snapped. She screamed like a madwoman, charging at me with her fists flailing. I grabbed her wrist, locking her arm and throwing her over my hip, slamming her down onto the carpet. I wrenched her arms behind her back and slapped the cuffs on.

"Congratulations," I told her, "you just assaulted a federal agent, which officially makes you the dumbest person in this building. What'd she win, Jessie?"

"Shiny new bracelets and a taxpayer-funded vacation," Jessie said.

Bobby clapped his hands. "Bam! You see that? *Loyalty.* That's what I pay the big bucks for. Don't worry, Cooper, I'll have you out in time for dinner. Hey, Linkletter—you might want to take some notes. You know what? Even better idea: how about you go and scrub the toilets by the mail room? That might be more your speed. Incompetent *ass.*"

I pointed at Linkletter. "Your turn."

He edged backward. A pair of local agents hit the door, hearing the commotion. They grabbed Cooper and dragged her outside, still kicking and screaming.

"I . . . I don't know any passwords," the lawyer said. "That's not my job."

"Then go find someone who *does*," I said. "You've got five minutes before you join Cooper in the back of a squad car."

He hustled out and shut the door behind him. Leaving Jessie and me alone with Bobby Diehl.

THIRTY-NINE

Up on the double screens, Bobby's twin visages twitched. His bottom lip curled as he stared down at us.

"All I did was kill your boyfriend," Bobby pouted. "*Overreact* much, you crazy bitch?"

Bobby was too flustered to lie, so that was a minor relief. The story we'd spread about Cody dying in Talbot Cove had apparently taken root just like we hoped it would.

"It's that time of the month," Jessie deadpanned. "We've been working together long enough that our cycles are synchronized, and we get *really* mean for a few days."

"It's true. We get these hormonal urges to tear down corrupt corporations and send entitled billionaire assholes to prison." I shrugged. "Women, right?"

Bobby held up his hands. "Okay, okay, no witnesses—it's just us now. Let's cut the bull and get down to brass tacks. What do you want?"

"Just told you," I said. "You, behind bars, for the rest of your life."

"We'll also take 'you, dead,'" Jessie added. "In fact, I'm really leaning toward dead. We just thought we'd drag your name through the mud, destroy your career, and make your life a living hell first. Even you've gotta admit: you had it coming."

"No," Bobby said, "what else do you want? What's it gonna take to make this all go away? You want money? I've got money. You want an island? I literally just bought my own island. You can have it."

"You ever seen a problem in your life you couldn't buy off?" Jessie asked.

"No," he said. "Because there's no such thing. Everybody has a price."

I shoved my chair back. I stood up and walked to stand before the screens, my chin high.

"I don't," I told him.

"You—" He flailed, fumbling for words. "You *started* this fight. You came after me first, remember?"

"You were trying to unleash an alien god from outer space," Jessie said. "So, yeah. We felt a strong inclination to intervene. We get touchy about things like that."

"No. No. That was my *birthright*, and you stood in my way." He jabbed his finger at the screen. "You started this fight. And everything that happens now is on your heads. Your fault, not mine. And you tell Burton Webb—you tell that worthless little snitch that there's nowhere in the world he can hide from me."

I spread my hands, taking in the room.

"I'm not a big fan of gambling," I said, "but I'll make you a bet. I bet we find you before you find him."

He moved close to the camera. First his face filling the lens, then just his eyes, burning a hole in the screens. Close enough to see the beads of sweat on his brow, the tangled strands of his eyebrows. He didn't blink.

"After I'm done with him," he whispered in a gravelly hiss, "I'm coming for you."

The feed went dead. The office fell silent.

"I think we shook him up," Jessie said. "What do you think? Did he seem shaken?"

The door rattled open. A young man in his twenties, dressed in a sweater-vest, sheepishly poked his head in.

"Uh, hi. Dude outside told me you needed my boss's passwords?" He held up a yellow sticky note, affixed to his index finger. "I'm his backup when he's on vacation, so I've got 'em all written down."

"Come on in." I gestured to the computer. "Where's Linkletter?"

He shrugged as he trudged in. "The lawyer? Don't know, he just told me to bring you the passwords."

I didn't like that. From the look on Jessie's face, she was feeling the same.

"Find him," I told her. "I'll take care of this."

She darted out of the office. Every exit was covered, but if he was wandering the building looking for evidence to destroy, we needed to know about it. I took the sticky note from the kid's finger and sent him out, too. A few taps of the keyboard, and I was inside the supervisor's system. I slipped a slender black USB stick from the inner pocket of my jacket and slotted it into the PC. A moment later windows sprouted on the screen like mushrooms, screens filling with colored code. The text spooled out faster than the reels of a slot machine.

I tapped my earpiece. "Okay. Payload delivered, what now?"

"You see it working?" Kevin asked.

"I see *something* happening." I squinted at the screen. "Lots and lots of really fast text whipping by, and windows opening and closing themselves?"

"Sounds about right. Give it one more minute, just to be safe, then yank the USB. The worm'll take care of itself. Not only will it snarl up net traffic inside the building—then spread to any other network that *that* network is connected to, hopefully clogging up the works until they get it under control—I added in a little search-and-destroy algorithm just for kicks and giggles."

"What's it do?" I asked.

"It hunts for anything that might be Vigilant's proprietary data. Then it copies those files to a hidden sub-directory so I can retrieve them later and scrubs the original data clean. The worm looks for specific keywords that don't have any business being on Bobby's computers— specifically, your names, and Crohn's name, too. Downside is, if you've got any Diehl Innovations appliances at home, your warranty's probably about to disappear."

"I threw out my Diehl coffeemaker. Jessie, do you have eyes on the lawyer?"

Jessie's voice crackled in. "No, and it's pissing me off. Meet me in the lobby?"

I gave it another minute or so. Kevin's worm kept chugging along, pouring syrup in the company network, so I turned off the monitor and headed upstairs. Jessie was over by the elevator doors, talking to a pair of bored-looking SWAT officers.

". . . seventies, black dye job, around my height?"

One of the officers nodded. "Yeah, saw him pass by a couple of minutes ago. He didn't try to go upstairs, though—we've got the whole place on lockdown. Nobody goes up without a police escort and your say-so."

"Did he try to leave?" I asked.

"Nobody's leaving, Agent. Like I said. Lockdown."

"I shouldn't be worried about this joker," Jessie said, giving me the side-eye. "And yet."

"And yet. He's up to something. He knows he can't get out past the police cordon. He knows he can't get up to the floors where they keep the company records, so he's not trying to throw a paper-shredding party . . ."

I thought back to the IT office and Bobby's words. Bobby was a murderous, self-entitled narcissist, but he was also a genius. I couldn't imagine he didn't have some kind of a fallback, just in case of disaster.

Then it hit me. I stormed over to the front desk and grabbed a receptionist's attention.

"Mail room," I said. "Where is it, and does it have its own bathroom?"

"Up the hall," she told me, pointing. "Not its *own*, exactly, but there's a unisex bathroom just across from the entrance. Is there something I can help wi—"

I was already moving. Jessie scrambled to catch up, matching my stride.

"Whatcha thinking?" she asked.

"He wasn't insulting Linkletter," I said. "That reference to the mailroom toilets was way too specific."

"He was giving him orders."

I jiggled the door handle. It gave, the door swinging open on freshly oiled hinges.

"Bingo." My gaze swept slowly across the pristine bathroom. "Now let's figure out what they were."

There wasn't much to look at. Three stalls with beige dividers, each one open and empty. A couple of sinks facing a long mirror, harsh white light bars over our heads. A hand dryer on the wall and a jumbo-size trash can in garish orange plastic shoved into the back corner. Nothing out of the ordinary.

Nothing but the garbage can, which was big enough to hold a couple of bodies. Way too big for a small office bathroom. I yanked up the lid. Nothing inside but crumpled paper towels. Then I grabbed the rim and hauled it back a few feet, away from the corner.

A square patch of tile underneath it, about three feet wide and almost as long, wasn't the same color as the rest of the floor. I lifted my foot and stomped my heel down on it. It thumped. Hollow.

I dropped to one knee and felt around the edges of the square. A section of tile gave under my fingertips, pivoting back on a concealed hinge to expose a pewter keyhole. I poked my head out into the hallway.

"Sergeant," I called out, "we've got a spider hole here."

The SWAT troopers brought up a breaching shotgun. Two deafening blasts, roaring like cannon fire and echoing off the tiled walls, and the concealed hatch yawned back on shattered hinges. The rungs of a ladder led down a concrete tube into a tunnel below.

"Must run parallel to the IT department," Jessie said. She jumped in, clambering down the rungs and looked up at me. "I'm gonna see where it goes, but my best guess is out. Go find Cooper—see if she's got any idea where Linkletter would run."

They hadn't taken Cooper for processing yet. I found her in the back of an unmarked car, cuffed for safekeeping. She grimaced as I gave her the update.

"Son of a—" She shook her head. "I had no idea. That's one of the reasons Bobby's organization is so hard to infiltrate: he compartmentalizes this stuff like crazy. There's probably three other escape routes in that building, built special for the only three people who know about them. Why the hell would he run, though? He wasn't under arrest, and even if he was, Linkletter knows better than that; he'd sit tight and wait for Bobby to get him out."

"I don't think he's running *from*, I think he's running *to*. Bobby told him he should be 'scrubbing.'"

"Destroying evidence," Cooper said. "At the very least, covering Bobby's trail. The raid, the media blitz, an indictment on the way—trust me, I know Bobby. I know how he thinks, how he reacts to problems."

"He's going into hiding."

"Deep underground," she said. "He'll bury himself in lawyers and red tape until this all blows over. Right now, Linkletter's job is to kick dirt over his footprints and make sure you can't track him down."

"That's my hunch. Diehl Innovations has plants and offices all over the country, but there's no reason to send Linkletter on a long haul when he's already got people on-site there. He has to be headed someplace close. Maybe the Spearhead facility, out in Santa Monica?"

Cooper shook her head. "No. After the Red Knight debacle, Bobby stopped keeping anything important at Spearhead. That whole place is squeaky-clean now. Maybe . . . damn. He's going to one of Bobby's houses. That has to be it."

"Where?"

"Closest one is near Pacific Coast Highway, west of Topanga Beach." She rattled her cuffed wrists. "Get these off me—I'll text you the directions and the entry codes."

Jessie's voice came in over my earpiece. "Yep, 'out' was the direction. Escape tunnel ends at a one-way door, locked and concealed on the far side, opening onto a drainage culvert about a hundred yards from the building."

"I've got a line on Linkletter," I told her. "I'm near the parking lot with Cooper. We need to rally the troops. Looks like we're doing *two* raids today."

Cooper's eyes went wide. "You can't. You can't bring police in there."

"Why not?"

"Traps. Remember those brain-burner curses from Spearhead? He's got them in his house, too. That's also where he keeps his ritual room. He's got stuff we can't allow people who aren't us to lay eyes on."

I sighed and tapped my earpiece.

"Cancel that, Jessie. It's just you and me." I looked to Cooper. "Don't suppose he's still slipping warding sigils inside your employee ID cards?"

She plucked off her ID, dangling from a black lanyard, and pressed it into my hand.

"This will keep you safe from the curses. Can't say the same for anything else he's got creeping around in there. That's where he does . . . personal experiments." She gritted her teeth. "You should get going. Not good if anyone sees us talking right now."

I recuffed her wrists and left her in the backseat. Jessie met me in the parking lot. As I walked, I peeled open the glued sides of Cooper's

ID card. The thin cardboard separated, exposing the secret hidden inside: a razor-thin silver disk, its face etched with faintly glimmering runes. I plucked out the talisman and passed it to Jessie.

"Hang on to that," I said.

She turned the disk between her fingertips, catching the fading sunlight. "Brain burners, huh?"

"And possibly other surprises," I said.

"Good times." She punched my arm. "Let's roll."

FORTY

We took a Bureau SUV and drove west along Pacific Coast Highway. Straight into a golden sunset, between the glimmering ocean waters and the rise of the Santa Monica mountains. It was nightfall by the time we reached the long and winding private drive to Bobby Diehl's estate. A sliver of waning moon hung in a starless sky.

Cooper was a regular visitor to Bobby's house. We had the passcode for the automated gates out front, cold iron bars humming open as Jessie tapped the keypad. A second passcode, down a long and sloping concrete canyon, for the garage door. Steel shutters rolled up, and white LEDs flared to life, guiding us inside.

Bobby's garage, lined with diamond-patterned rubber flooring, was a showroom of extravagance. He collected cars like some people collected shoes, each one waxed and buffed to a mirror sheen. Hard-winged Italian sports cars that looked like spaceships, vintage Detroit muscle, even a Packard from the Roaring Twenties. He had three stretch limousines—black, white, and silver—lined up side by side. Jessie whistled, moving from car to car, peering into the tinted depths of a cherry-red Lamborghini.

"The odometers. Half of 'em are under ten miles. He doesn't even *drive* these beauties—he just keeps them locked up in his damn garage." She looked over at me. "I didn't think I could hate him any more than I already do, but he keeps giving me reasons."

My eyes were on another ride, over by an elevator door. I pointed. "One of these things is not like the others," I said.

It was a slightly battered Lincoln, and from the road dust and dead bugs on the grille, this one definitely got driven. I put my palm on the hood. Still warm.

"Linkletter beat us here." I drew my pistol, the textured grip of the Sig Sauer firm against my desert-dry palm. "But not by much."

Jessie took the lead. We only had the one warding talisman, which meant I'd have to rely on my magical senses to steer clear of any invisible traps. Bobby had used his brain burners to protect his inner stronghold at the Spearhead facility: dormant and invisible curses that waited for the unwary, disintegrating neurons with occult fire. There was nothing left of the guard we'd seen fall prey to one—nothing but the pain centers in his nervous system, leaving him in mindless and endless, screaming agony. That was Bobby's idea of a funny joke.

A sleek, mirrored cage ferried us up to the main floor of the house on silent pulleys. The doors opened onto a mahogany-walled corridor, lit by softly glowing electric sconces crafted to look like Victorian gas-lights. No sound but the whisper of the air conditioner as a cool breeze flowed through the labyrinth of halls. I caught a strange, peaty scent, like fresh-churned soil.

We didn't have a floor plan, though Cooper had given us a sketchy guide to finding Bobby's office. Left, left, then a right, down corridors laid out with no rhyme or reason. Halls dead-ended with no doors, at least none we could see. A coat closet opened onto another, smaller coat closet.

Jessie moved a half pace ahead of me, gun drawn and ready. "His architect's as crazy as he is," she murmured.

"I think he was his own architect." I squinted at faint carvings along the rich crown molding, carefully cut scars in the wood. "There's a whole school of occult design theory. Building houses as spirit traps, as psychic funnels or resonators. The layout becomes a sigil; the place becomes a spell."

"And what's this spell meant to do?"

I tapped her shoulder, pulling her back from a darkened threshold. I sensed the razor-barbed coils of a mystical trap, the curse laid into the rococo flooring and waiting for a victim.

"Nothing good," I said. "C'mon, let's go around."

The odor of churned soil grew stronger down one narrow passageway. And underneath it, something foul and cloying, like a bed of rotten flowers. I took the lead now. My magical senses pounded a red alert up and down my spine, a piano hammering a jagged, electric chord.

On the other side of an open archway, a stone altar stood at the heart of an octagonal chamber. I held up my phone and clicked on the light, strobing a thin beam through the gloom. Catching the sheen of the scarlet-and-black altar cloth, the pages of a fat and yellowed book. The light trailed across the floor of the ritual room. Soil, rich and black as a moonless night.

"Is this where he does his sorcerer thing?" Jessie said, standing at my shoulder. She pointed at the altar. "We should grab that book. Grab it or burn it."

I shook my head, keeping the tiny light trained on the soil floor.

"There's something in there," I said.

Jessie leaned in, squinting. "I don't see anything."

The soil burbled. A solitary bubble rose up to the light and popped, the stench of excrement wafting through the air.

"*Underneath,*" I said. I pulled away from the threshold. "Leave it alone."

Jessie paused halfway up the hall. She tugged out her softly vibrating phone. Linder was on the line. I leaned in close.

"Can't talk right now," Jessie whispered. "We're inside—"

Linder's voice was terse, even by his standards. "Don't speak. Listen. I miscalculated. I'm about to be taken or killed. If I'm taken, expect that they'll use me to snare you: do not trust this line, or anything I say or do, until you have eyes-on verification that I haven't been compromised."

"Taken by who? Crohn's men? The eastern courts?"

"If I'm killed, it was an honor serving with you." I heard thumping in the background, wood splintering. "Have to go—just enough time to erase this call and cover my tracks. Good luck, Agents."

The line went dead.

"Damn," Jessie breathed.

"Last we heard, he was on his way to take out one of Vigilant's directors. A loyalist to the courts of hell. Think he got smart and saw Linder coming, laid a trap for him?"

"If he did, we're screwed. Linder's our only point of access to the rest of the directorate. Even if we figure out who they are, we won't know which one's the bad apple." She shook her head. "One problem at a time. Linder's a survivor; he can take care of himself. Let's get this done."

We took another turn. Jessie pointed left.

"I hear him," she said. "Linkletter."

I didn't hear anything but the air conditioner's hum, but her senses were sharper than mine. I followed her to an open door and pressed my back to the cool mahogany wall, ears perked.

"You are completely useless," Bobby was saying, his voice pumped over a high-resonance sound system. "You're like . . . what's the saying? Tits on a bull?"

I crept a little closer and peeked around the threshold. Bobby's office was a tech fetishist's paradise. Cool LED lights shifted colors, bathing liquid-cooled computers in shades of luminous green. A massive screen dominated the entire back wall. Linkletter stood before the video feed of Bobby's glaring face, wringing his hands, head bowed.

"I . . . I'm not sure," he said.

"You're not sure because you're useless. Are you sensing a theme here?"

I tapped my earpiece and whispered, "Kevin? The systems at Bobby's house aren't affected by the worm. Why?"

"Probably not connected to the corporate network." His voice crackled. "Trust me, I'm watching the status in real time. The Diehl Innovations plant in *Shanghai* just went dark. They're gonna be unclogging this thing for a week, easy."

"The entire firm will be working on your case around the clock," Linkletter said. "We've put all other business on hold. You're in good hands, Mr. Diehl."

"Good hands? Have you noticed I'm being pilloried in the media right now? Have you seen our fucking *stock price* today?" Bobby held up his phone. "Oh, and my e-mail is frozen. I mean, seriously, what is this? Are we not a tech company? I'm pretty sure we're a tech company."

"I really can't comment on your e-mail, sir. I'm not an IT professional—"

"Maybe if you were, you wouldn't be *useless*. Forget it. Look, I need you to do something for me. The FBI hasn't frozen my Grand Cayman account yet. You need to wire a hundred and twenty-five thousand dollars to the Concierge. Same account as usual. He's running a pickup job for me—gonna grab my new friend and bring him to safe harbor. He's got all the details; he just needs the money. Contact him when the transfer is under way with confirmation; the man won't move until he sees the green. At least I think he's a man."

"Understood, sir."

"Great." Bobby gave him two thumbs up. "Oh, and start working on an alibi for me? A bunch of people are about to die horrifically. Between that and the media hounding me and the FBI on my doorstep, I really need a rock-solid trail of deniability here. And get some good

PIs hunting for Burton Webb. I'm putting a bounty on that traitorous little prick."

"I wish you wouldn't tell me these things, sir."

Bobby tilted his head. He leaned closer to the camera. "Client-attorney privilege," he said. "Stop whining and handle my business. And remember one thing, Linkletter, I've still got the video from your little sex-tourism adventure in Thailand. If I go down, *you* go down. I'll land on my feet. You won't."

He killed the feed. The video screen flickered to black.

Jessie glanced at me. I answered her unspoken question with a nod. We moved in. When Linkletter turned around, he found us standing right behind him. He stumbled back, resting a shaking palm on Bobby's desk to steady himself.

"Thailand, huh?" Jessie asked. "You a pedo, Linkletter? Like 'em young?"

"That's—that's not—" He swallowed, hard. "Do you have a warrant? This is a private domicile—"

Jessie pressed the muzzle of her gun to the lawyer's forehead. And kept pressing until he sank to his knees on the polished mahogany floor.

"It's written on the barrel," she said. "Can you read it now, or do you need a closer look? By the way, I *really* hate people who fuck with kids."

"What my partner's trying to say," I added, "is that this is no longer a by-the-books situation. Who's the Concierge?"

"I don't know," he stammered. "Even Bobby doesn't know for certain. He's an independent contractor, a professional smuggler. He moves people, money, goods. He's a ghost."

"Where's Ben Crohn, and where is the Concierge supposed to take him?"

"I *can't*," Linkletter said. "Look, you don't understand. Bobby Diehl isn't some run-of-the-mill tech magnate with a fat stock portfolio. The man's a monster. You have no idea what he's capable of."

I loomed over him. I thought back to Talbot Cove and tasted bile in the back of my throat.

"I don't know? I was at ground zero when Bobby unleashed a mutagen in my hometown," I told him. "Right in the middle of Main Street. He was gunning for me. A dozen innocent people died instead. Want to see what they looked like when the gas cleared?"

I took out my phone and called up the crime-scene photos. Arms twisted in spirals, bones gone to rubber. Corpses with distended jaws and tumor-bloated eyes. I shoved the screen in his face. He tried to turn away, and I grabbed his hair and yanked hard.

"*Look* at it, you son of a bitch! This is Bobby's handiwork. This is the man you're protecting. And if you don't talk, he'll just keep hurting people and keep getting away with it. Do the right thing for once in your life and *help* us."

The lawyer squeezed his eyes shut. "I don't know where Crohn is, I swear to God. I just know where Bobby is probably taking him. Xanadu."

Jessie squinted at him. "Xanadu as in the Coleridge poem, or Xanadu as in the Olivia Newton-John movie?"

"His new retreat. After the mess at Spearhead, he needed a new facility for his . . . special projects. That's where he is right now. He won't even tell *me* where Xanadu is. It could be a mile from here; it could be halfway across the world."

"But the Concierge knows," I said.

I shared a look with Jessie. Her eyes narrowed as she caught my meaning.

"On your feet," she told Linkletter. "You've got a chance to live through this. Just a chance, and you'd better do exactly what we tell you, to the letter. You screw up, Bobby has to put out a want ad for a new lawyer."

He rose, petrified, still staring at her pistol. "What do I need to do?"

"Exactly what Bobby told you," I said. "Transfer the money to the Concierge. Then get him on the phone."

FORTY-ONE

Linkletter hunched over Bobby's console, tapping out strings of commands and shuffling money like Kevin shuffled code. Strings of numbers flew by with more commas and zeroes on the end than anyone could dream of spending in a lifetime.

"How many secret accounts does Bobby have?" Jessie asked him.

"Five that I'm aware of. Undoubtedly others that I'm not. Your freeze of his corporate accounts will be an impediment, but not a lethal one, I'm sorry to tell you."

"Probably don't wanna use words like *lethal* right now. Oh, and we'll take a list of what you *do* know. Account names and numbers, routing details—write 'em all down."

"None of this will be admissible in court—"

"You believe this guy?" Jessie asked me, still covering him with her gun. "He actually thinks Bobby's gonna live to see the inside of a courtroom. You oughta be more worried about yourself right now, Linkletter."

He rattled off a few final keystrokes. I watched confirmation numbers scroll on the screen, blocks of crisp black font.

"It's done," he said. "The Concierge has been paid."

We moved off to the side, out of the camera's eye, and Jessie gestured to the video wall. "Good. Call him up. When you do, we want to know where the pickup location is at, and where Xanadu is."

"I don't normally ask questions. What if he gets suspicious?"

Jessie chopped the side of her hand in front of her throat. "If I go like this, back off. Just do your best."

He made the call. A blur filled the video wall, resolving into the outline of a face. The person, their background, everything was covered in digital camouflage. Thousands of pixelated squares shifting and shimmering as a distorted voice emerged from the sound system.

"Yes," the voice said.

Linkletter tugged at the knot of his tie. "Um, yes. Mr. Diehl wanted me to notify you when the wire transfer was under way."

"Confirmation numbers, please."

"Just—just a second," the lawyer said. "I need to make sure the details are right. Where, exactly, is the pickup location?"

A pause. The blurry figure sat motionless on the screen.

"Details already confirmed with the client," the Concierge said. "You don't need to be involved."

"And where are you taking them?"

"Them? I only have one package for transit. Again, details have already been confirmed with the client."

"But the address—" Linkletter said, flustered.

Jessie chopped her hand near her throat, warning him off.

"This is not how we do business," the Concierge said. "Provide wire-confirmation details, or I'm terminating our agreement."

Linkletter caught Jessie's frantically waving hand. He coughed, clearing his throat, and turned to the monitor.

"Bank confirmation is as follows," he said. "One, nine, D as in Denver, A as in apple, six . . ."

When he finished, the Concierge terminated the call without speaking another word. Linkletter leaned against the desk, looking pale.

"He'll kill me," he said. "If Bobby finds out I cooperated with the authorities, he'll kill me. Or worse."

I wasn't concerned about his feelings or his well-being at the moment. More frustrated that we hadn't gotten anything out of Bobby's smuggler. No idea where Crohn was holed up, no idea where he was going. And if he escaped to this Xanadu, he and Bobby would both be out of our reach.

One package, though—that was strange. As far as we knew, Mikki and the soldiers from Panic Cell were still doing Crohn's dirty work. What was their exit strategy?

"What do you think?" Jessie asked me. "Drop him or take him with us?"

"He's Bobby's lawyer. Whatever he knows, we can use it. I bet he can give us more than bank-account numbers."

"I . . . I will not be illegally detained," Linkletter protested. "You're going to answer for this."

"Shut it," Jessie snapped. She glanced sidelong at me. "Good thinking. Let's take him with us, find a place to put him on ice, and we can squeeze him dry later."

We marched him out ahead of us. Navigating the twisted halls by memory, making our way back toward the parking garage. I tapped my earpiece.

"We're on our way back, and we've got a prisoner. Are we ready to get airborne?"

"Aselia says the plane is fueled and ready," April's voice replied. "Where are we headed?"

"That's the problem," I sighed. "I'm not sure—"

Linkletter, two feet ahead of us, crossed an open threshold. His palm shot out and slapped a chunk of the wood paneling. It sank like a stone under his hand. I jumped back as a steel grate whistled down between us, chopping down through the archway and sealing the hall.

Jessie cursed and fired off a round at his back. The bullet pinged off the grate, sparking as it ricocheted, tearing into the mahogany wall.

"Damn it, get back here!" she shouted. The lawyer couldn't run fast, but he was putting his all into it. I pointed left.

"Through here," I said. "We'll go around and cut him off."

We sprinted as fast as we could, faster than I dared—Bobby had studded the house with his psychic traps, and I hadn't charted them all coming in. Jessie and Linkletter had the employee ID cards with concealed warding talismans. I didn't. My senses in overdrive, my mind raced five feet ahead of my pounding footsteps.

We caught up to him just as he darted into Bobby's altar chamber. His expensive shoes sank two inches into the muddy loam. He turned, wide-eyed, and hit another concealed panel.

Bars slammed down between us. He fumbled for his phone, standing in the dark. The odor of wet dirt and rotting flowers grew stronger, curdling in my nostrils.

"Linkletter," I said, my heart pounding as I caught my breath, "you need to come out of there, right now. Open this gate."

He shook his head, trying to dial with shaking hands.

"I have to tell him," the lawyer stammered. "If I warn Bobby, it'll be all right. He'll forgive me."

A shadow rose up at his back.

It was a figure, a man, emerging from the mud. His featureless head crested from the soil, then his shoulders, rising up silently behind him. Jessie saw it, too. She shook the bars, the grate rattling in her grip.

"Come on," she said, "get *out* of there."

I clasped my hand over my mouth. The rotten stench stole my breath, my stomach churning. Linkletter fumbled his way through his contacts list. His sweaty, panicked face glowed in the light of his phone's pale screen.

The faceless muck man clamped a wet hand on Linkletter's shoulder. The phone fell from his grip and into the loam as it spun him around.

Then, just before he could scream, it plunged a curled fist into his wide-open mouth. Shattering teeth, cracking bone, Linkletter's neck bulging as the muck man forced his putrid arm down the lawyer's throat one brutal inch at a time. He gurgled, drooling blood. Pressed to his knees in the rippling black soil.

"Linkletter?" Bobby's voice echoed from the fallen phone. "Is it done? Did you make the transfer? Hello?"

The creature ripped his arm from Linkletter's throat. A spray of liquid filth spattered across the silken drapes on Bobby's altar, glistening black in the shadows. The lawyer fell, dead, his white face and broken jaw an inch from the phone.

"Hello? I can't hear anything," Bobby said. "Your connection is shit—call me back on a better line."

The screen went dark. The muck man descended into the loam, dragging Linkletter's corpse down with it. The soil rippled with one final squelching *pop*, then fell still and silent.

"Okay," Jessie breathed. "That just happened. Let's get out of here. *Carefully.* I was thinking we'd come back and search this place after we got done dealing with Crohn. Now I'm leaning more toward bombing the entire house from orbit."

"Bombing has my vote," I said. We were almost out, stepping off the elevator and jogging through the parking garage, when April's voice cut in over our earpieces.

"Are you near a radio?" she asked.

"We're almost back to the SUV," Jessie said. "Why? What's up?"

"Turn on the news. Any channel."

We jumped into the car, and Jessie fired up the engine. I tapped the radio presets until we found a news broadcast. It didn't take long.

"—apparent violent abduction of Senator Susan Cheng from her home in Columbus, Ohio. While authorities refuse to release details, this is the third such abduction of a senior government official to be reported this evening. Officials have declined to comment on whether these disappearances have any connection to the arrest of former FBI director Benjamin Crohn and his alleged illegal surveillance program, and have only said that they are pursuing this matter with all due—"

Jessie threw the SUV into reverse and spun us around. We jarred to a stop on screeching tires. Then she hit the gas, and we tore down the private drive, aiming for Pacific Coast Highway.

"Not three abductions so far tonight," she said. "Four."

"Linder."

"And more coming, if my guess is right. Crohn's buying his safe passage to Xanadu, and he's bringing more than stolen data. He's gonna serve up the entire Vigilant Lock directorate on a silver platter."

"Makes sense," I said. "Bobby gets his revenge, and Crohn cuts all ties with his past. That's why he scattered his team, back in New York: he gave them a target list. They're rounding up hostages and bringing them someplace for safekeeping."

Jessie fixed her eyes on the road.

"They won't be safe for long. You heard the Concierge. He's bringing *one* person to Xanadu. Those hostages are living on borrowed time."

"Yeah," I said. "And we've got no idea where to look for them."

# # #

We regrouped with the team in a private hangar, Aselia's plane polished and ready to fly in the shine of harsh white work lights.

"So that's where we are," Jessie said. "I figure Crohn's gonna round up all the Vigilant directors, including Linder, and kill 'em all at once. Probably film it as proof, or maybe he'll do it while Bobby watches on a video feed. His token of sacrifice, to join the Network."

Kevin hunched over a workbench, surrounded by a scattering of half-assembled electronics. He peered through a magnifying glass on a boom arm as he twisted a screwdriver.

"We lose them," he said, "we pretty much lose Vigilant. No funding, no intel, no inside connections."

Aselia grimaced. She leaned against the bonnet of the Cessna with her arms crossed tight. "And then Crohn skips off on his merry way and vanishes forever. Can't believe we actually have to save these assholes, but the kid's right. So what's the plan?"

Jessie's face fell. She took off her dark glasses. Her turquoise eyes stared out at the empty runway.

"I don't have one," she said. "Trying to get info out of Bobby's smuggler was a bust. The raid at Diehl HQ threw a wrench in the works, but we didn't get any actionable intel . . . it's a dead end. We've got nothing."

"Maybe not," April said.

She rolled across the smooth concrete floor, over to Kevin's workbench.

"How fast can you build a GPS transmitter, and how small can you make it?"

"Real fast and real small." He nodded at the bench. "I already have one. Supposed to build it into the new drone. It's light, about the size of a gum ball."

"Good," April said. She patted her armrest. "These parts unscrew fairly easily, and the armrests are hollow. Build the tracker into my chair and get it online, if you would, please."

Jessie turned around, furrowing her brow. "Aunt April? What are you doing?"

"If Ben Crohn is on a kidnapping spree, I see no reason not to join the party."

She pulled down her bifocals, gazing at Jessie over the gray steel frames.

"We're going to give him a target he can't resist. Me."

FORTY-TWO

"No." Jessie paced the hangar, shaking her head. "No, absolutely not, nuh-uh, no way."

"It's the only way," April said.

"It's the insane way, was that what you just meant to say? They're not kidnapping these people for ransom. They're going to *kill* them."

April took a deep breath.

"Not until he has them all in one place. Otherwise the news would be talking about bodies, not abductions. Crohn doesn't know that *we* know Linder's been taken. If we send a mission report with our locations, and I appear to be alone and unguarded, he won't be able to resist. We let him kidnap me, take me to the location with the other hostages, then you and Harmony can move in."

"While you're unarmed," Jessie said. "And in the line of fire."

"I've been in worse situations. We need to know where Crohn's infernal contracts are. If I can get him talking, I think I can burrow my way into his head. Manipulate him into giving up the location so you'll have a chance to retrieve and destroy the documents."

"Isn't getting into people's heads what he does, too?" Kevin asked.

"Yes." April favored him with a thin, humorless smile. "I'm better at it than he is."

Jessie floundered, grasping for an argument. "What if they leave your chair behind? No GPS means we don't have any way of knowing where they're taking you."

"Put yourself in their shoes," April replied. "I weigh a hundred and never-you-mind pounds, and I can't walk. If you had to take me prisoner, would you really want to carry me off—making a scene in the process, and discovering there's nothing wrong with my fists—or just leave me in the chair and roll me to my presumptive doom? If there's one thing we can trust, it's the human tendency to take the path of least effort."

Jessie's gaze snapped my way. "Harmony, back me up here."

"I'm sorry, Jessie." I shrugged, helpless. "I don't like it, either. It's a dangerous plan, and there's no telling how many ways it could go wrong. But the clock's running out, and I don't see another way."

Jessie fell silent. She stopped pacing.

"Kevin," she said, her voice softer now, "this transmitter of yours. It's long-range? Reliable? One hundred percent reliable?"

"Yeah, mostly. I mean, it's tech, nothing is ever a hundred—"

"*Kevin.*" Her eyes flashed, softly glowing. "I'm asking if you're willing to bet April's life on it. Yes or no."

He swallowed, hard. "Yes."

"Fine," Jessie said. "Then we're doing this. Get her chair rigged. April, find us a staging ground. Then Harmony can make the call."

# # #

"Agent Black." Linder was a good actor. I wouldn't have caught the strain in his voice, the rough edges of his breathing, unless I'd been listening for it.

"Reporting in," I said. Every word from my lips going straight to Crohn's ears. "Jessie and I finished our raid on Bobby Diehl's mansion.

287

We found some actionable intel. Financial irregularities at a Diehl Innovations subsidiary in Berkeley. We're going to check it out now."

The line went mute for a few seconds, the sound cutting out as Linder was given his orders, probably with a gun to the back of his head.

"Excellent work," he said. "And the rest of your team?"

"Since we're staying in California, Kevin and Dr. Cassidy are holing up here in LA. No need to relocate them—they can provide mission support from the motel."

"Agreed." Another pause. "I haven't seen an expense request for the motel room yet. That's not standard procedure. Usually you're much more prompt with your receipts."

He effortlessly established the lie. I feigned contrition and passed on the intel: the address of a Red Roof Inn on a rough stretch of road by the airport. Room five.

Jessie and I were in room four, huddled by the adjoining door with the lights out and the curtains drawn. Waiting. Kevin was across the street, keeping his head down and his eyes peeled. April waited alone in her room.

An hour passed, then two, then three, the minutes creeping by like slow drops of molasses.

"I hate this," Jessie told me.

I put my hand on her shoulder. "I know."

"We should just jump whoever shows up to take her. Force 'em to tell us where Crohn and the other hostages are."

"They won't talk."

She glared at me. "Bullshit they won't. I can *make* them talk. You know I can."

"You remember our briefing. These Panic Cell troops are true believers. They don't mind dying: they've got cushy jobs waiting for them in hell."

"So why are they helping Crohn defect?" Jessie shook her head, brow furrowed. "Caitlin said these Network creeps aren't demons."

"I doubt *they* know that. Who knows what excuse Crohn gave them? Point is, by the time we get through to them—the easy way or the hard way—those hostages will be dead."

Jessie's head slumped. She stared at the adjoining door.

"I hate this," she said.

"Movement." Kevin's voice crackled over my earpiece. "A car just showed up. Looks like one of those Panic Cell dudes and, uh . . . Special Agent Mikki."

Jessie put her fingertip to her ear. "We are *not* making 'Special Agent Mikki' a thing, Kevin."

"Well, she's at the check-in desk and flashing her badge like she's on a TV show. Okay, now they're headed up the walk by the parking lot. She's twirling a room key around—must have gotten it off the manager. Get ready, Doc."

"I'm prepared," April's voice said. "Taking my earpiece off now. I'll toss it under the bed so you can pick it up after I'm gone."

"April—" Jessie started to say.

"They'll take it from me anyway and likely destroy it. No sense wasting good electronics."

We heard the door to her room rattle open, then the muffled sound of voices through the adjoining door.

"Mikki," April said, pretending to be surprised, "how did you find me?"

"Because I'm smarter than you. Where's Kevin?"

"He's not here."

Then we heard the crack of a backhand slap. Jessie lurched for the door as April cried out. I held her shoulder, firm, pulling her back.

"I can see he's not here, you stupid bitch," Mikki snapped. "Where *is* he?"

"Jessie and Harmony," April said, her voice strained. "They needed his help on-site. He's on his way to join them in Berkeley."

"Y'know what? I don't think I believe you."

Whatever she did next, it made April squeal like a kicked dog. Jessie strained against my grip, her eyes squeezed shut and her hands curled into fists.

"That's enough," said a man's gruff voice. "The director wants her in one piece."

"I want Kevin."

"I don't care what you want," he told her. "We have our orders. Cassidy is the priority target—anyone else on the list is gravy. Let's go."

Mikki started for the door. Then her footsteps stopped. I could feel her mind stretching out, tickling at the back of my brain like an anxious gnat. For once, Mikki's prowess as a one-trick pony worked in our favor: her magic was great for lighting things on fire, and that was about it. She gave up, failing to sense us crouching ten feet from her, and walked out. They wheeled April to a waiting van. Jessie and I sat beside the door, breaths held, waiting for them to leave before we broke cover.

She opened her eyes. Luminous in the dark, faintly glistening.

"If we made the wrong choice," she whispered, "if we *lose* her—"

"It was her choice, Jessie, and she knew the risks. She's trusting us to have her back. So let's get out there and do our job."

# # #

"Refueling?" Jessie said as the Cessna's wings rattled under a buffet of wind. "Again?"

"Yeah, again," Aselia told her. "This isn't a 747, okay? I'm pushing her as hard as I can, but unless your witch buddy here has a spell to magically conjure fuel, we've got to land. I've been flying low, zigzagging, pulling off then pouring on the speed—anything to keep them from noticing they've got a suspicious blip on the radar. It's not as easy as making a beeline."

Kevin huddled over his laptop. Two strobing beacons pinged in neon green across a wire-frame map of the United States. We'd been flying east by northeast for hours, through rain and black clouds, chasing a point of electronic light.

"Tracker's holding steady," he said, "and we're not far behind. They've had to stop a couple of times, too."

"Let's just make it fast," Jessie said.

A rainy morning gave way to a drizzly noon under a cold bronze sky. We ate cheap sandwiches on rye bread at a regional airport while Aselia ran flight checks.

"Pretty sure, given the flight path so far, we're headed back to New York," she told us.

"Makes sense," I said. "Crohn never left the state after he escaped. He must have a hiding place. Not in the city, though. Not with the Bureau and the courts of hell hunting for him. By now his old bosses must have found what's left of Prospero."

Around four in the afternoon, our target landed at a tiny commuter airport downstate, about a hundred miles north of New York City. From there, the GPS ping slowed down. Moving at highway speed. We touched down two hours behind them and ran to the rental kiosk. Twenty minutes later the four of us were on the move again, Aselia behind the wheel of an ice-white Ford Expedition.

Winding roads cut through tall, rolling hills dressed in the colors of autumn. We curved around the feet of snowcapped mountains as the Ford's windshield wipers slapped out a slow and steady tempo, driving back droplets of icy rain. Jessie sat impassive, shielded behind her dark glasses, but one hand squeezed her armrest in a death grip. I didn't say anything. There wasn't anything to say.

"The Catskills," Aselia murmured. "Makes sense for a hideout. Remote, secluded. There used to be hundreds of vacation resorts out here. Used to be. A handful of them, once they closed doors, never got torn down. You could hole up there forever if you had someone running food and supplies out to you."

"Signal stopped moving," Kevin said.

Jessie sat bolt upright. "What do we have?"

He leaned forward and tapped Aselia on the shoulder. "Take a left up here. And what we have . . . yeah, exactly right. Check this out."

He rattled the keyboard and called up a Google Earth scan. An overhead view of what looked like a ski lodge, though the slopes were deserted, and the patchwork, crumbling roof looked like a meteorite had hit it.

"Levine's Grand," Kevin said. "Shuttered in 1968, and the place has been sitting vacant ever since. The property's passed from developer to developer since then, but nobody's ever managed to tear the old construction down, let alone build anything new."

I studied the map. One two-story lodge, plenty of approaches, minimal cover. A few outbuildings still dotted the property, but most had rotted to the foundations over the decades, leaving behind nothing but wooden skeletons and concrete pits. The original lodge wouldn't have had much of a security system, and I doubted Panic Cell had time to lay down any electronic countermeasures since their arrival. Human sentries would be our biggest risk: one shout, one stray gunshot, and those hostages were as good as dead.

"They had to refuel as often as we did," I said to Aselia. "Meaning they were in a plane like ours, not Panic Cell's C-130. If the rest of Crohn's men have been rounding up captives and loading them onto that cargo plane . . . is there any chance they could avoid big airports altogether and just land it near the resort? It'd be safer for them, less chance of anyone spotting the hostages."

"Pass the laptop up—lemme see."

I held the screen up.

She glanced away from the road just long enough to catch a glimpse, then nodded. "Oh, sure. That big, long patch of open ground just east of the resort? That's plenty."

"That isn't a landing strip," I said.

Aselia grinned. "There's a reason the military's been relying on the Hercules since the late '50s. You can bring those birds down on beaches, in forest clearings, tundra—you name it. A C-130 lands where it *wants* to land."

"If we had to evacuate those hostages—fast—could you fly it out of there?"

"Standard crew is *two* pilots, plus a navigator and a flight engineer." She tilted her head, thinking. "But can I get her up in the air, then land her safe, someplace out of the line of fire? That I can do."

The sliver of the moon, a stark icy crescent, rose over the Catskills. Nearly full dark, no street lamps, no city lights to guide us. Just the Ford's high beams cutting through the gloom and the steady slap of the windshield wipers, a metronome beat in time with my heart. Aselia killed the lights a half mile from the abandoned resort, guiding us down a narrow, broken road by instinct and touch. A quarter of a mile out, we stopped. She shut off the engine. Its growl faded to silence, replaced by the faint patter of raindrops.

I could barely make out the main building: just a bulky and broken shadow, squatting in the thin moonlight. The bones of a dinosaur left to rot in the freezing rain. Then there was light, shining from a ground-floor window, and distant silhouettes in motion. Kevin's tracker had worked. This was the place, and April—along with Mikki, Benjamin Crohn, and his demon-worshipping henchmen—was inside.

I reached to my magic. A gnawing emptiness answered me. The burst of power I'd stolen from Romeo's lips in Atlantic City was long gone now, my advantage spent, and all I had left was the hunger. Soon I would have to decide: stay clean, and face the agony of withdrawal, or make a return trip to Romeo and feast.

Tonight, though, I didn't have a choice. I had to fight through the emptiness, fight through the hunger, and dig as deep as I could to survive and win. April was counting on me. They all were.

Jessie popped her pistol's magazine, checked her ammunition, then slammed it back into place. She locked eyes with me.

"No warning shots, Harmony. No prisoners tonight."

"No prisoners," I said.

FORTY-THREE

The frigid mountain wind numbed my cheeks and my toes and turned my breath to wisps of white vapor. Droplets of night rain felt like needles of ice. They prickled my face and hands, soaking through my blazer. We told Kevin to stay in the car. Jessie, Aselia, and I set out across the open badlands, single file and hunched low, moving fast for cover. Ruined outbuildings dotted the mountain valley, nothing left but collapsed wooden frames or twisted tangles of metal pipe. As I was about to break from the shadows, scurrying toward the next patch of safe ground, Aselia grabbed my arm and pulled me back.

"Hold on," she hissed, one hand cupped to her ear. "Hear that?"

I looked up. A faint droning cascaded through the air, like the rising trill of cicadas.

"Plane engine?" I asked.

"C-130, circling for a landing. Figure it's about five minutes off."

"You can tell by the sound?" I asked.

"It's what I do." Aselia looked to Jessie. "Your call. Storm the place now, or wait for them to bring the other hostages in?"

Jessie frowned. "Have to wait. If they get any kind of a warning out, the plane won't land, and they'll probably just kill everybody right on the spot. Let's roll with it."

Strobe lights emerged from the sky, shadowed wings and mighty propellers boiling from the darkness. The fat cargo plane bounced down on frozen wet grass, wheels thumping, engines screaming, as the C-130 lurched hard on the brakes. It wobbled, unsteady, then jolted to a stop.

The propellers wound down. The cargo door at the back of the plane began its slow hydraulic descent, inner lights washing out across the field. We circled around the long way, using the resort for cover, getting closer.

Four men, rifles slung over their shoulders, marched the hostages out. I counted six in all. They had their hands shackled behind their backs, heads bowed, and most sporting fresh bruises or black eyes. Linder was the first one in line.

"Let 'em pass," Jessie breathed, crouched beside me.

They left one soldier behind to guard the plane. He stood at the foot of the ramp, his rifle cradled and ready.

Jessie holstered her gun and drew her knife instead.

She gestured for us to hold back. She moved in alone, a panther in the night, her footsteps silent on the wet grass. He didn't see her coming. All he saw was the flash of serrated steel. Then he was on his knees, clutching at his throat and choking, sliced arteries spraying the last few seconds of his life across the steel ramp. Jessie kicked him in the small of the back, knocking him flat, and stepped over him as he died. She marched up the ramp, flicking scarlet droplets from the edge of her blade. A moment later she reappeared and waved us over.

We jogged up the ramp to join her. The belly of the C-130 was empty. I could see where Vigilant's funding had really been going all this time: an electronics suite took up one side of the cargo deck, with a hundred-inch screen flanked by a grid of smaller monitors, all dark now. They had an armory under lock and key, a small holding cell for prisoners. While I marveled at the engineering job they'd done to fit everything on board, Aselia headed up to the cockpit.

"What do you think?" Jessie asked her.

She nestled into the olive canvas pilot's seat and ran her fingertips over the console. "I think I'm right at home. Give me twenty minutes. I'll be ready to fly when you are."

Jessie turned without another word, leading me back into the dark. We skirted the field, eyes on the yellow glow behind the resort's broken and sagging windows.

"Must have brought in a portable generator, set up their own lights," Jessie whispered. "So we've got Crohn and Mikki in there, plus at least five guys from Panic Cell."

"Probably just the five," I whispered back. "We've already dropped a few of them."

"Yeah, so, two against seven. I'll take those odds. We need shock and awe: hit 'em fast, take everybody out before they even know what's happening. Let's get closer."

Around the back of the resort, a second-floor patio—outdoor seating for a restaurant, if I had to guess—drooped on broken and sagging timbers. Jessie pointed. I cupped my hands, crouching, and boosted her foot. She grabbed the railing's edge—my stomach clenching as the wood groaned, old nails slowly ripping from their planks—then scrambled over the top.

I jumped up. Jessie snagged my wrists and pulled me to her. We didn't take any time to catch our breath. Through a shattered patio door, ringed with remnants of old and jagged glass, and across an abandoned café choked in dust, we closed in on the sound of voices.

A balcony looked down onto the resort's indoor swimming pool. The wide hall was lit by harsh standing lights, fat yellow cords snaking across the ruptured concrete to a humming gas generator in one corner of the room. Urban explorers had left their mark here over the decades: graffiti tags festooned the basin of the empty pool and the rotten wooden walls, layer upon layer of garish paint. Water leaked from sagging timbers overhead, and dirty rain collected in brackish, dark puddles. We dropped low, hiding behind a chunk of collapsed drywall, looking down on the scene.

Crohn stood triumphant at the lip of the pool with April silent at his side. She played at being sullen, defeated, but I recognized the steely look in her eyes. She was calculating every angle. Mikki and one of the Panic Cell troops herded the other hostages into the pool, sitting them down on the concrete. Another soldier angled the lights, while a third set up a digital camcorder on a tripod.

"You won't get away with this," April said. Her voice, defiant, echoed through the cavernous chamber. So did Crohn's condescending chuckle.

"Of course I will. Weeks from now I'll have a new name, a new face, a new *life*. You didn't beat me, April. You never could. The best you could manage was mild inconvenience."

He stared at her. "What?" she said.

"You're still beautiful when you're angry. I remember why I fell for you." He took a deep breath, letting it out as a sigh. "Then you had to go and ruin everything. God, we could have been perfect."

"You had to go and spit on your oath of duty. You falsified evidence, Ben. Your career was never about justice or the law—it was about *you*. You and your damn spotlight."

"You don't understand the pressure I was under," he snapped. "I was a Bureau superstar. The best profiler in the *world*. You can't imagine the expectations that put on my shoulders. I couldn't fail, not even once. So yeah, sure, I put my thumb on the scales once or twice."

"And after that? You willingly joined the forces of hell, Ben. What's your excuse for that? You were the director of the FBI. What more could you possibly want?"

"How do you think I became the director in the first place? They gave me the job." He glared at her, eyes narrowed. "You still don't get it, do you? Hell *won*, April. The war is over. They rule this planet. And humanity? Humanity is a lost cause. So, yes, I joined the winning side. And now I'm going to do it again. Mikki? You ready?"

Mikki stood on the far side of the pool, hands on her hips. "Looks like we're ready to make some home movies. Want me to toss her in with the others?"

"No," Crohn said. "I want her to watch this."

Mikki snapped her fingers. One of the gunmen walked up to the pool's edge with a big red plastic can. He upended it, splashing the contents over the bound hostages below as they struggled against their cuffs and choked for breath. The fumes rose up, sharp and pungent. Gasoline.

The trooper behind the video camera gave Crohn a thumbs-up. A light on the camera strobed green.

"I'm afraid you've all outlived your usefulness," Crohn told the hostages. "Vigilant Lock, in its many incarnations, has been shut down from time to time. Normally, that means scrubbing our wayward operatives and starting over. This time? Well, sad to say . . . everything must go."

He snapped his fingers, as if remembering something.

"Oh! There is just one other thing."

I froze, feeling the muzzle of a rifle press against the back of my head. Beside me, Jessie slowly raised her hands, another trooper plucking the pistol from her grip. Crohn grinned up at our hiding place.

"We've got room for at least two more corpses. Bring 'em on down, gentlemen."

# # #

They took our weapons and marched us downstairs, standing us beside April. A moment later, another trooper came in from the rain, his buzz cut glistening and fatigues soaked dark. He jerked his thumb over his shoulder.

"I found their vehicle about half a klick out," he said to Crohn. "Empty, no passengers. I disabled the engine just to be safe."

Kevin hadn't stayed in the car. I'd never been so relieved at somebody *not* following orders. Hopefully he'd run to the plane to hole up and wait with Aselia.

Mikki shot a look at Crohn. "You said I could have Kevin."

Crohn waved an open hand. "How far do you think he can get on his own, on foot? We're in the middle of nowhere. Patience."

At my side, April squirmed in her wheelchair. I saw her hand slip down, curling around a sheaf of papers she'd been sitting on. Torn-out pages from a crossword puzzle magazine. She hid them against her hip as Crohn turned our way.

"You see, April? Now I win. Oh, you thought you'd trick me. Harmony placed a call on a compromised line, feeding your location to Linder, and set you up as a target." He pressed the back of his hand to his forehead, dramatic. "Oh, *clearly* my obsession with you would blind me to the obvious ploy! And I had *no idea* that you knew Linder was my prisoner, so I'd be sure to fall for your ruse. I certainly wouldn't imagine that you'd put a GPS transmitter in your wheelchair so your friends could follow you here."

He dropped his hand and shook his head at her, snickering.

"Your little Trojan horse play was as desperate as it was pathetic. This is the best you can do? Really? I knew where your team was and what you were planning, every step of the way. All I had to do was leave the doors wide-open and let the three of you walk right into my trap. I have to admit, April, I'm disappointed. You used to *almost* be my equal. I thought you could give me a better battle of wits. Apparently I aged a little more gracefully than you did."

"Are you sure about that?" April asked him. Her hand slid backward, under her armrest, pushing the rolled-up sheaf of crossword pages toward me. "Maybe that was my plan all along—I *knew* you'd know—and I was doing something else entirely."

I stepped close, as if I were being protective of her, one hand on the back of her chair. Her fingers fed the rolled pages toward me a half inch at a time. As soon as Crohn's gaze was fixed on her, captivated, I grabbed the papers and slipped them behind my back.

"Oh, really?" His eyes twinkled as he grinned at her. "Please, enlighten me."

I did the honors, guessing April's game.

"We know you killed Prospero," I said, "and we know you stole the contracts for the demons he paid you with. They're the source of your strength, bound inside your body. But that's the thing about infernal contracts: light them on fire, and the demon goes free. That'd be real bad for you."

I held up the rolled pages. Puzzle side in and mostly shielded by my arm, so they'd just look like a flood of tight, small-font print.

"Once you took the contracts from Prospero's safe, zero chance you'd go anywhere without them. Your life literally depends on it. So while April was keeping you distracted, Jessie and I were hunting them down. Now, I don't do a lot with elemental flame, but using my magic to ignite a few pieces of paper isn't much of a chore for me. Surrender. Now."

Crohn barked out an incredulous laugh.

"Are . . . are you kidding me?" He laughed again, shaking his head. "No, really, are you kidding me right now? That's your ruse? Your final move? Your life-or-death gambit? A stupid *bluff*?"

He reached into the breast pocket of his suit jacket, turning his jackal smile on April.

"Your student is right. Those contracts are irreplaceable, which is why I would never let them out of my sight."

Behind us, a pair of troopers moved closer. Their rifles, aimed and ready, cast long shadows across the concrete under the standing lights.

Crohn slid a glossy black envelope from his inside pocket and showed it to us.

"I keep them right here. Always. I have no idea what those papers are, Agent Black, but they're nothing to do with me."

I was close enough to hear April breathe two words—"*Thank you*"—as a faint, defiant smile rose to her lips.

She rested her thin hands in her lap and cracked her knuckles.

FORTY-FOUR

"We done?" Mikki asked, standing across the concrete lip of the pool. "Do I get to have some fun now, or what? Who dies first?"

Before Crohn could respond, April spoke up.

"Before you kill me, Mikki, one question. Just to satisfy my curiosity. What *was* your exit strategy? I mean, you know Ben is planning to murder you, right? You'd have to know that."

She blinked. "What?"

Crohn rolled his eyes. "Ignore her, Mikki. It's a desperate and facile attempt to throw a wedge between us. In fact, I was going to save April for last, but I'm finding her voice increasingly *shrill*. Burn her."

"Given that you're still here," April said, "and the men of Panic Cell are still aiming their guns at us instead of him, that tells me that you really don't know whose side you're on. You know he's defecting from the eastern coalition, but to where? Did he tell you he'd been taken in by the western courts of hell? That they'd offered him—and all of you—safe harbor? Because that's a lie."

"The Court of Jade Tears is opening their arms to us," Crohn said.

"That's funny," Jessie said. "We had a sit-down with their hound, and she said different. Hey, Mikki, know who's really coming to the rescue? Bobby Diehl."

Mikki's gaze shifted between Jessie and Crohn, uncertain.

"That's right," I said. "Your old employer. You know, the man who abandoned you after the Red Knight incident? After you and Roman Steranko risked your lives doing his dirty work? The man who never made a single rescue attempt after we took you into custody? He never bothered. Did he even *pay* you?"

"No," she snarled. She turned her full attention on Crohn. "They had *better* be fucking lying. Bobby Diehl left me twisting in the wind and stiffed me on my fee. I don't give second chances."

April pointed at the hostages in the pool. Their heads bowed, still coughing, spitting as the spilled gasoline stained the concrete beneath them.

"Why would the western courts want video proof of Vigilant's entire directorate being murdered? Why would they care? With Ben out of the picture and his old authority broken, the eastern coalition has no control over Vigilant Lock. When it comes to the cold war between the courts, Vigilant is no longer a viable weapon."

"Revenge," Crohn snapped.

"For what? Most of these people didn't even know until today that they worked for the courts of hell. They aren't the ones who perpetrated this fraud. They aren't the ones who used human operatives as a deniable front for cold-war rivalry."

April turned to Crohn.

"*You* did," she said. "So we're meant to believe that your new employer wants these people dead, but they're welcoming you, the man who really committed the offense, with open arms? No. Makes no sense. The only person nursing a grudge against Vigilant—the one who knows he's being targeted, square in our sights—is Bobby Diehl."

"Sir?" One of the soldiers behind us spoke up. "Is this true, sir?"

"No, it is—it is *not* true." Crohn gritted his teeth, backpedaling. "Kill her, damn it! Kill them all."

April cupped one hand to her ear, serene. I heard what she heard: the distant flutter of a helicopter's rotors.

"I can prove it," April said. "The Concierge, a covert transport specialist, has been sent with an exfiltration vehicle. There to take you all to safe harbor, your reward for a job well done."

"Sure," Mikki said, squinting at her. "That's the plan."

"Mikki, dear, I can't see the eastern windows from here, but you're closer. Would you take a look, please?"

Mikki strode to the line of shattered windows. She flung out a hand, pointing at us.

"Cover them," she said. "*All* of them. Crohn, you stay right where you are until I figure this out."

"Mikki—" he said.

"No. Shut up. I'm trying to think." She leaned out the window and into the dark, looking out across the icy grass and broken concrete.

"I'm not an aviation expert," April said, still holding her hand to her ear, "but that's definitely a helicopter. Doesn't sound like a big one, though. Not a troop transport, not a roomy executive model, either. Mikki, let me know if my guess is correct, if you'd be so kind. Is that . . . a *two*-seater?"

The sound of rotors died as the helicopter touched down on the lawn. Mikki turned from the window, toward us again. Her pale, rain-spattered face was a mask of frozen fury.

"Yes," she growled. "Yes, it is."

April blinked, feigning surprise. "Goodness me. So, a seat for the pilot, a seat for Ben . . . what about you and these other gentlemen? Looks like you weren't invited, after all. Which means, after you did his killing for him and cleaned up all his messes, the next item on his agenda would be silencing *you*."

Mikki didn't respond with words. She responded with fireflies. Pinpricks of magical light danced in a swirl around the black envelope in Crohn's hand. He yelped, turning his back and jamming the envelope into his pocket, desperate to break her line of sight. He drew his pistol with his other hand. His coattails flared as he whirled around again and shot at her. Mikki threw herself flat to the concrete. The bullets whined over her head, blowing out chunks of rotten plywood.

The two men behind us had gotten too close and too distracted. Jessie spun, grabbed one rifle by the barrel and ripped it from the gunman's grip. She flipped it around and fired two short bursts. One trooper dropped, then the other, writhing on the lip of the pool with bullet-riddled chests. Another gunman, over by the generator, toggled his rifle to full auto and opened fire on us. I flung out my hand, calling to my magic, and the hail of gunfire sank into a wall of hardened air. A flick of my fingers and the bullets veered left, turning in midair like a derailed train.

Crohn was on the run. Frantic, hands over his head, he barreled through a pair of double doors and out into the rainy night. Jessie squeezed her trigger, and the third gunman's skull collapsed, his lifeless corpse slamming against the generator and leaving a slug trail of blood on his way to the floor. She spent the rest of her rounds aiming for Crohn's back, shots going wild as he vanished into the dark.

"I'm going after him," she growled. "Get Mikki."

She broke into a loping, feral run. April spun her wheels and rolled the other way around the pool. I only had eyes for Mikki. I hadn't fed the gnawing hunger at the pit of my stomach, the curse Nadine had left me, since Atlantic City. Coasting on fumes now, and just pulling the power to block those bullets, left my stomach in knotted cramps.

No choice. If I failed, none of us would make it home alive.

Another Panic Cell gunman emerged on the balcony. I turned just in time to see him sighting me down the barrel, his aim perfect—then a single bullet drilled through his forehead and out the back of his skull, painting the wall scarlet behind him.

April, with a fallen gun snatched up and held high at her shoulder, gave me a grim nod from the other side of the pool. She laid the rifle across her lap and kept rolling.

I stood in Mikki's path. She came to a dead stop, five feet between us. Both of us standing on the lip of a concrete pit, the air thick with gasoline fumes, and the bound hostages below one heartbeat from death by inferno.

Her lips twisted into an eager smile.

"Look at this," she said, her voice a singsong taunt. "No sprinklers to short-circuit my powers this time around. We're inside, so no convenient thunderstorm to call down. What now, huh? Come on, let's *do* this shit! Show me what you got."

A line of raw power surged along my spine as I thrust out my arm. It snapped along my elbow, curved and kept going, hardened air rippling and streaming from my clenched fist. The torrent smashed Mikki square in the face. Her lip split, blood drooling down her cheek, and she spat a broken tooth as she fell to the concrete.

She grabbed her face and shrieked, "You fucking *bitch*!" from behind her clasped hands.

I grabbed a weapon. A fallen chunk of wood, three feet long with a wicked, splintered edge, and I came at her like I was swinging for a home run. She scrambled back on her bloody hands, getting her focus back, and I felt her power home in on me like a sniper's scope. The sudden torrent of heat stole my momentum and pushed me back a step, stumbling, as I struggled to hold her off. Fireflies danced around my body, a sheen of sweat glistening on my skin as the room became a sauna.

I had a mixed bag of tricks, and I was reasonably good at a bunch of them. Mikki only had one—and when it came to pyrokinetics, she was the best in the world. She was a living cannon with one big nuclear-tipped shell, and it took everything I had to force it back down the barrel. My muscles clenched, pulse jackhammering in my ears, my flow of power like a fast-dying river feeding into the rage of a sun.

My improvised weapon ignited. I threw it, away from the pool, trying to keep the hostages clear of the fight. It clattered across the concrete and hit the broken wall. The rotten wood erupted, smoke billowing in the corner of my vision as the flames spread wild and fast.

"Old places like this are firetraps," Mikki crowed. She put one hand to her temple, a vein at the side of her skull bulging as she slowly overwhelmed me. I couldn't move, my muscles locked in place. I felt like I was trapped in a suit of steel armor, fire heating the metal red-hot. I didn't give up. Couldn't give up. If not for me, then for everyone who was counting on me. I pushed forward, inch by inch, standing in the path of the inferno.

Then the torrent broke as a figure threw itself on Mikki's back, clasping desperate hands over her eyes and breaking her line of sight. She screamed, raging, flailing around as the attacker clung to her like a rider on a rodeo bull.

"Hey, Mikki," Kevin shouted in her ear as he grappled with her, "heard you were looking for me!"

She threw an elbow into his ribs, knocking the wind out of him, and flipped him over her shoulder. He landed on his back hard, grabbing his hip as he writhed in breathless pain. He'd bought me two seconds. I used one to sprint toward her, cocking my fist back, and the next to throw every last bit of my remaining strength into a roundhouse punch.

Mikki sprawled as she thudded to the deck, out cold. I grabbed Kevin by the hand and helped him sit up.

"Figured you could use some help," he said, then winced, clutching his chest. "Sorry I didn't stay in the—*ow*."

"You okay?"

"I'm *so* not okay. I can move, though."

I pointed at Mikki. "Cuff her and find something to blindfold her with."

I patted down one of the dead troopers, then another, until I found a pair of handcuff keys. I jumped down into the pool bed and landed hard in a crouch. Flames raced along the walls now, roiling, devouring the old, dead wood like a horde of burning termites. A haze of black smoke flooded the hall, tickling my lungs.

I got Linder's cuffs off and handed him the key. "Get everybody out, *now*. Run 'em to the C-130. Aselia's getting ready to fly. If we're not there in ten minutes, tell her to take off without us."

The hostages looked like drowned rats and stank of kerosene. Linder herded them out into the rain, away from the hungry fire, while I helped Kevin with Mikki. He'd torn off a dead man's sleeve and tied it over her eyes. I used Linder's cuffs to bind her wrists and threw her over my shoulder in a fireman's carry. We were the last ones out the double doors as the resort burned at our backs.

Jessie and Crohn were squaring off in a patch of icy grass. From their torn clothes, the smears of dirt on their hands and faces, they'd already been going at it tooth and nail.

Her eyes flared like beacons of light as she growled under her breath. She and Crohn circled each other, shoulders hunched, and he beckoned. She leaped. Bounding in, her fists twin blurs as she unleashed a series of jackhammer-strong punches to his chest. I heard Crohn's ribs snap like peanut brittle under her knuckles. He staggered back, stunned, and she dropped into a spinning kick that knocked his legs out from under him. He landed flat on his back in the icy grass.

Then he smiled.

As he pushed himself up, his crushed chest crackled and flexed under his dress shirt. His bones were knitting themselves back together. "My turn," he told her.

This time he was ready for her, turning her fists with his, blocking every swing. The two of them moved like dancers on a film set to fast-forward, a deadly tango of stone-shattering punches and bloody knuckles kissing the air as they dodged and wove around each other. Then Jessie misjudged her timing, off by a fraction of a second, and Crohn's fist plowed into her gut. He pressed in, outmatching her supernatural speed and taking advantage of the moment, treating her like a boxer working a speed bag.

Jessie hit the ground. She rolled, groaning, just as his foot slammed down where her face had been a heartbeat ago. She scrambled to her feet, bleeding, battered, looking like she could barely stay standing.

Crohn wasn't going to give her a choice in the matter. He moved in for the kill.

FORTY-FIVE

I dropped Mikki to the grass. "Watch her," I told Kevin and shoved my sleeves up.

Jessie looked my way. Wavering, she shook her head. Then she spat a gobbet of blood onto the dirt.

"Stay back," she said, her voice a broken rasp. "He's too strong."

Crohn chuckled and glanced my way. "Oh, the more, the merrier. Your friend here isn't even making me break a sweat. I'd be happy to—"

She took advantage of the distraction. Jessie lunged in, throwing a punch that could splinter wood straight into Crohn's chin. He grunted, staggering back, and grabbed her by the shoulders. He spun her around, and she latched on to one lapel of his coat, trying to wrench his arm back. The thud of his fist against her face sounded like a boxer punching a slab of beef.

April was off to my right, sighting them down the rifle, but she didn't take the shot. Too much risk of friendly fire, and besides, we'd seen Nyx throw Crohn halfway into a marble wall. Bullets probably weren't going to help here. I called to my magic. My stomach knotted, and Halloween-orange sparks guttered from my fingertips. I didn't have anything left.

Nothing but me, anyway. I took a deep breath, feeling a raw twinge in my side, and charged. I threw myself at him. I hit Crohn's leg in a running tackle, wrapping my arms around him and trying to buckle his knee. He stumbled. Jessie pressed the advantage, still wrestling with his jacket, tugging it partway down one shoulder and tangling his arm up. He shrugged the jacket off, tossing it to the grass behind him, and batted her away with his freed arm. His other hand locked around my throat.

Crohn hoisted me up off my feet. His fingers squeezed tight, choking the air from my lungs and turning the world hazy gray. Then he tossed me aside. I hit the wet turf hard on my shoulder, rolling, thumping to a stop with my back against a pile of jagged concrete rubble. Jessie made her move, darting in from his left, but even her ferocious speed just wasn't enough: he caught her wrist, yanked it down, and drove two sledgehammer punches into her stomach. She doubled over, and he backhanded her hard enough to send her sprawling at his feet.

He stood over us. The flames of the resort rose up at his back, a bonfire to light the midnight sky.

"Disappointment after disappointment," he told Jessie. He punctuated his words with a vicious kick, slamming his heel against her rib cage. She grabbed her chest and groaned, rolling to one side, scrambling to get away from him. He followed. Slow, relentless, toying with his prey.

"I thought you wolf-bloods were supposed to be *tough*," he said. "Was that the best you could manage? You really thought you could beat me?"

Jessie looked up at him. Even with her face battered, blood trickling down a cracked lip, she smiled.

"Nope," she said.

"Ah. That old indomitable human spirit. You had to give it your all in the face of certain doom, and go boldly to your death with your chin held high, is that it?"

"Nah," Jessie said, still catching her breath. She nodded my way. "Optimism is my partner's thing. I'm all about the dirty tricks. See, I didn't have to beat you. I just had to get your jacket off, then distract you for about thirty seconds."

Crohn stopped. He stared at her. Then he looked behind him.

April sat behind him, at the edge of the bonfire. His discarded jacket lay draped across her lap. And the glossy black envelope, holding his infernal contracts, held firmly in her upraised hand.

"Teamwork," I breathed, forcing myself to sit up.

Jessie looked my way. She raised a shaky hand. "Long-distance fist bump."

Crohn blinked. He took a step toward April. She moved her hand closer to the crackling flames. He was fast, but he wasn't that fast. Black smoke billowed from the ruin, forming a rippling shroud at April's back.

"April," he said, stretching out his fingers like a man reaching for a life preserver.

"Pride goeth," she replied. Her eyes were steel, unblinking. Pitiless.

"April, don't do this. We can work something out. C-come with me, you'll be rewarded—"

"Come where?" April nodded to the patch of lawn where the helicopter had touched down. Nothing but windswept grass and rubble now. "Your ride left when the fire broke out. Bobby Diehl was your last refuge, the only bridge you hadn't burned, and even he abandoned you. It's over, Benjamin."

"April . . ." He shook his head, forcing a desperate smile. "Come on, it's me. We were *partners*. We shared our lives—we shared everything. We had some good times, didn't we?"

"We did. I was very much in love with you, once."

"So don't do this. Give me the envelope, and we can—"

"Once," April said, cutting him off. "Before you betrayed your oaths, your duty. Before you decided nothing in the world was more important than looking out for yourself. You sold out the human race, Ben. You sold us out, and for what? Power? A fat bank account? Was it worth it?"

"*Idealist,*" he sneered, the word a curse on his lips. "You're fighting a war you can't win."

"That indomitable human spirit, I suppose," she said drily. He inched toward her, like he was about to make a move. The envelope inched closer to the flames. He'd never make it in time to snatch it away from her, before she cast it into the fire, and they both knew it.

"I wanted what was mine," he said, "so I went and I *got* mine. They offered me money, power, the world on a silver plate, and I took it. Anyone else in my position would have done the same. I'm just one piece in hell's plan, April. You can stop me, but what happens the next time? And the time after that?"

He spun, looking back at Jessie and me, then at April, shaking his head.

"This war will take everything you have and everything you are," he said. "It'll grind you down until there's nothing left, and hell will still win in the end. It always does. Don't you understand why?"

"Enlighten us," April said.

"Because there are more men like *me* than there are women like *you*," he said. "There always have been, and there always will be. And while you're wringing your hands about righteousness and duty, we'll take what we want and do as we please. It's the way of the world."

I rose to my feet. I walked over, held out my hand, and Jessie clasped it. I hauled her up. She wiped blood from her lip with the back of her hand and leaned against me.

"You're wrong," I told him.

He turned my way.

"There's more of us out there," Jessie said. "A lot more. You just weren't listening until now."

Crohn looked back to April. He spread his hands at his sides.

"April," he said, his voice softer now. "Don't do this."

April contemplated the black envelope. She turned it in her hand, the glossy material glowing in the light of the hungry flames barely an inch away.

"I know a little witchcraft myself," she said. "It's only one tiny thing. A magic word. Tiny, but so very powerful against people like you."

"Don't do this—"

"The word is no, Benjamin."

"April, *please*!"

She flung back her hand. She opened her fingers. The black envelope spun, fluttering, landing in the fire.

"No," she said.

I felt a gust of raw magic on the frozen wind. A swirling tempest, rising with the sound of shattered steel links and keys turning in ancient locks. Crohn stood between us, frozen and trembling like he'd stepped on an electrified rail.

His skin began to bulge. Under his dress shirt, his chest and back bubbled and rippled, tumors the size of softballs swelling up. Then, one by one, the tumors burst. He fell to his knees, screaming, blood guttering down and staining the ivory cotton. Tiny hands, like infants with claws, pressed out against the inside of his neck, his forehead, tearing at his body from the inside.

He flung out his arms. More clawed hands burst through. His skin shredded as grasping, flame-charred fingers dug at his flesh and yanked ragged fistfuls back inside him. Crohn's scream became a choking gurgle as a tiny scaled arm burst from his mouth, scratching at his nose, latching hold of one eye and wrenching it from his skull. The greedy hand dragged the eye back down his throat.

He was disappearing. Imploding, one bloody piece at a time.

He thrashed on the wet grass. One pant leg lay flat now, the stump of his left leg receding by the moment. One shoulder a bony, exposed ruin, and the opposite arm gone, the clawed hands tearing at him in a piranha frenzy. He looked to me with half a face, his remaining eye wide with abject terror. Then they took that one, too.

The last wet chunk of Benjamin Crohn's body turned itself inside out, squirming in the dark, and vanished. The demons bound inside him had stolen every last piece, leaving nothing behind but a pile of shredded, sodden clothes.

April grabbed hold of her wheels and pushed herself forward, rolling across the uneven grass. She passed Crohn's remains without a second glance.

"Let's get to the plane," she said. "We still have work to do."

# # #

On the C-130, as Aselia prepared for takeoff and Jessie tossed Mikki in the holding cell, I looked over the freed hostages. They were wet, scared, shaking, strapped into jump seats and trying to process what they'd been through. They reeked of gasoline and fear sweat. I knew a few of their faces from the news. By the time we landed, I'd know them all by name. Them, their role in Vigilant Lock, what they'd done, and what they could do for us going forward.

Jessie came back, and Linder waved her over. They murmured back and forth, hands passing close together. She passed him something, but I couldn't get a good look before he slipped it under his jacket. Then he turned to one of the hostages, an older man seated at the end of the row.

"Senator McGillis? Could I speak to you for a moment before we take off? Privately."

He mirrored Linder's genial smile as he rose from his seat, walking alongside him as they strolled to the back of the plane.

"It's funny," Linder said as they walked past me. "When we were abducted, I was actually on my way to see you about some pressing business."

Linder shot him in the back of the head.

The senator's corpse crumpled to the floor. Linder put the heel of his Italian loafer on the dead man's shoulder, gave him a shove, and sent him rolling down the loading ramp to fall in a twisted heap in the grass. Rain pattered down on his wide-eyed face.

Linder handed Jessie's pistol back to her, nodded his thanks, and turned to face the others.

"The esteemed gentleman from Kentucky," he said, "was a loyalist to the infernal courts. We're taking a new direction. Severing old ties. As of today, Vigilant Lock is exactly what it was always meant to be: America's first and only line of defense against the forces of hell. We will rebuild, we will regroup, and we will pursue our nation's enemies without hesitation or mercy."

Jessie moved to stand beside me. She holstered her gun.

"Good," she said. "Now tell them what I told you."

Linder's gaze swept across their shocked faces. "Benjamin Crohn is dead. You all work for me now."

He pointed at Jessie and me.

"And I work for them," he said. "Remember the chain of command, and we won't have any more problems."

FORTY-SIX

We landed at the Chautauqua County airport, dawn's light gleaming off the C-130's mighty wings. A convoy of limousines waited at the airstrip. We'd been in constant motion since takeoff: deciding how to massage the news, to spin the abduction story, to simmer everything down. By the time we landed, three networks were already running with the tale of how the kidnapped officials had been taken by a terrorist cell and freed in a daring early-morning raid. That'd keep the media cycle distracted for a week at least.

The second news story, competing for attention and clicks, was the sad tale of how Benjamin Crohn was found dead in his holding cell. Disgraced and facing prison time, he'd hanged himself with his bedsheets.

Two days later the sunrise found us at another airport, another cold morning. I walked across the tarmac with a cardboard box in my hands, six cups of steaming coffee nestled inside. The loading ramp echoed under my footsteps as I strolled into the belly of the plane.

"This surveillance suite is pretty decent," Kevin was telling April, both of them ensconced by the bank of screens. "But honestly, the software they were running is a little out-of-date, and I've spotted some redundancies. Think I'm gonna start by beefing up the satellite uplink."

I leaned in, holding out my carton like a waiter, and they both reached for coffee. "Here. Brain fuel."

April lifted her cup to me. "Much obliged."

Jessie swooped in like a vulture, snatching a cup for herself. "Aw, *yes*. Coffee. You are my favorite person. Did you bring me a Danish?"

"Only have two hands," I told her.

"Your favorite-person status is now dangerously precarious."

Up in the cockpit, Aselia's overalls were coated in black grease. So were her hands and her face. Beside her, Marco was elbows-deep in the open console. We hadn't seen him since our escape from the bayou, but he'd shown up like magic yesterday morning with a rucksack on his shoulder and a battered toolbox in each hand.

"*No*, Marco," Aselia said, "no tinkering. No experimental parts. We're doing everything by the manual, okay?"

The frog-mouthed mechanic looked back over his shoulder and waved a placating hand. "Okay, it's okay. Just fiddlin'."

"*No fiddling.*" She took two cups, passed him one, and went right back to looming over his shoulder.

We had an unexpected guest.

Linder stood at the foot of the loading ramp. "Permission to come aboard?" he called up.

"Grudgingly granted," Jessie told him. As he strolled up to meet us, she spread her hands wide. "Oh, and just in case there's any question about this whatsoever, let me be perfectly clear: we're keeping this plane."

"I had no doubts," he replied. "You're going to need it. The directorate has just authorized your full access to Vigilant Lock's archives as well as increased funding. What I can't offer you, unfortunately, is a vacation."

He held out a black USB stick.

"Your next mission," he said.

Jessie took the stick and passed it over to Kevin. A moment later the bank of screens blossomed with maps, data, surveillance photographs.

"Urgent priority," Linder said. "And there's another waiting as soon as you're finished. Oh, by the way, Mikki's been safely returned to her old cell at Site Burgundy. I won't repeat what she said upon arrival, but it was . . . quite colorful. So. I'll leave you to it. Good luck, Agents."

As his limousine pulled away, my phone chimed. I strolled down the ramp, out into the crisp breeze, as Fontaine's syrupy drawl filled my ear.

"You sure know how to open a can o' worms, don't you, darlin'?"

"It's what we're good at," I said. "Did you get the bounty for taking out Crohn?"

"Mmm, you should have heard my tale of derring-do and bravery. I engaged him mano a mano, mortal combat in the wilds of Vermont—"

"It was New York," I said.

"You have your version of the truth, I have mine. And mine pays better. Anyway, I just wanted to call and give you a friendly warning. You know that no-kill order the western courts had on you and your lady friend? It's officially been rescinded. You're anybody's game now."

"Apparently we served our purpose."

"You did. Though I don't think they're gonna come after you just yet. Caitlin doesn't break a playing piece she might be able to use later down the line. Same can't be said for the eastern coalition. They're hoppin' mad that you yanked their own hustle out from under 'em. Sounds like they're looking for payback, and price is no object. Heck, they might even hire *me* to hunt you down."

"Would you take that bounty?" I asked.

"I would," he said, his tone lightly teasing, "but I'm just too darn busy at the moment. We'll see how it goes. My old compatriot Nyx, on the other hand . . . well, you've got another handful of enemies in DC.

Nadine and family have hooked their horses to Senator Roth's wagon, and you put a heck of a scare into the man."

I walked back up the ramp, taking a last look back at the sunrise.

"He'd better be scared," I said. "He's on our list."

"Tread carefully. Lots of people—humans *and* demonkind—have a vested interest in Roth's ascendancy to the White House. Lots of people with fingers in lots of pies. And then there's Bobby Diehl—"

"In hiding, about to be under indictment, and his corporate empire is crumbling piece by piece as we speak. The IRS is having a field day."

"You know better than that, darlin'. A man like Bobby Diehl doesn't hide. He lurks. And plots. What I'm saying is, you've got a whole bunch of people gunning for your head now, and they're gonna come after you with everything they've got. You ready for that kind of heat?"

I gazed across the belly of the plane. To Jessie, to April, to Kevin. Since the day I joined this team, each of us had been through the crucible. One by one we'd faced the ghosts of our pasts, stared them in the eye, and laid them to rest. Nothing to hold us back now.

We had a job to do.

"I've got a message for all of them," I told Fontaine. "For the courts of hell, for Bobby Diehl and the Network. For anyone and anything who threatens the people we've sworn to protect. You can pass it on, if you like."

"I might be so inclined. What's the message?"

I looked to my team, my family, and smiled.

"Three words," I said. "Bring it on."

EPILOGUE

Roman Steranko hated meeting new clients in person. Meatspace was risky. Nobody could slap handcuffs on his wrists when he was in his element, safe behind a keyboard. Still, ten thousand dollars with no strings attached was a hell of an incentive. He wandered through an empty warehouse in the badlands of East Los Angeles, twirling a business card between his fingertips. Light filtered in from high, dusty windows, casting pale shafts across the bare concrete floor.

Almost bare. At the heart of the room stood a wheeled metal cart, and on the cart, a thick circle of stone about five feet across. The face of the smooth stone bore a graven pentacle, the five-pointed star surrounded by runes that made Roman's vision blur. A power cable jutted from the side of the rock and ran to a portable generator.

He reached out to touch the stone, then paused as a voice called out from the shadows.

"I wouldn't do that if I were you."

Roman turned to face her. She was a tall, lean woman in designer clothes, her jet-black hair worn in elegant braids—and the left half of her face concealed behind white porcelain. Scarred, twisted burn tissue peeked out around the edges of her mask.

"It's some kind of summoning matrix," she said, her voice casual. "Golden Dawn seal, modified Enochian warding glyphs, and I couldn't begin to guess what the electrical generator is for."

"Peachy," Roman said. "You the client?"

She held up a business card with crisp black type, identical to his own, in a hand concealed by a long white surgical glove.

"Afraid not. I'm Dr. Victoria Carnes, and I suspect I'm as puzzled as you are. Charmed to meet you."

"Roman. But if we're both—"

The side door opened with a metallic clang. Sunlight streamed in around the silhouette of a new arrival. Tall, broad-shouldered, the woman with dreadlocks filled the doorway with her body—and consumed the entire room with the sudden force of her presence. She strode in like a conqueror, her turquoise eyes glowing in the shadows as the door swung shut at her back. She held up a business card.

"Which one of you invited me?" asked Althea Temple-Sinclair.

Roman and Victoria showed her their own cards in response.

"I'm Dr. Carnes," the masked woman said, "and this is Roman. We were just comparing our befuddlement. I thought we might be competing for the same job, but something tells me the three of us don't share the same skill sets."

Roman half smiled, pointing at her and then himself. "Doctorate, doctorate . . . well, an education—that's something two of us have in common."

Althea loomed over him. Roman's smile vanished. She leaned in close, and he swallowed, hard.

"Now why would you assume I'm not educated?" she asked, her voice deadly cool. "Is it because I'm big or because I'm black? Please, *elucidate*. Satisfy my intellectual curiosity."

"I—I didn't mean anything by it." He took a shuffling step back. "Just making conversation."

"Stick to what you're good at."

The generator turned itself on. It kicked to life, crackling, the cables beginning to hum. The ritual stone made a sound like a movie projector, celluloid slapping the reels as the rock glowed faint azure.

"I would step back," Victoria said. "Maybe two or three steps."

Motes of light swirled above the stone, and a new sound came with it—faint, as if heard from the far end of a tunnel. Screaming. A raw shriek of agony that went on and on, without breath or relief.

"Maybe five or six steps," Victoria said.

"This is not cool," Roman murmured, edging toward the door.

The sound grew, and the light churned, a cyclone now—then, with a crescendo and a flash, it stopped.

A man hung in the circle of stone. He dangled from a crude rack of splintered wood, suspended by rusted hooks driven through his arms, his shoulder blades, the bottom of his chin. He'd been skinned, his own flesh drooping and crudely sewn back on his body, rents dangling loose here and there. His face was melted wax, with one eyelid stretched and dangling like a curtain of meat. His scream gave out. He stared with one mad and awestruck eye at the gathering before him.

He wasn't entirely flesh, wasn't entirely spirit. Translucent, he faded in and out as the glowing stone pulsed under his feet.

"How long was I in hell?" Benjamin Crohn panted, his voice a cracked-leather whisper. "What . . . what year is it?"

Roman threw his hands in the air and headed for the door.

"That's it," he said. "This shit just got *way* too weird. I'm out."

A second generator, concealed in the dark, hummed awake. A projector mounted in the rafters flickered on, and projected a shaft of hot light across the cinder-block wall. The window of light became a television screen. And on the screen, a grinning face waved to the room.

"Hey, folks," he said, "Bobby Diehl here. Don't touch that dial! Or that doorknob, at least—not if you want to get rich."

Roman turned toward the screen. "Bobby? You still owe me money from the Red Knight job. And from what I hear, your company isn't doing so good these days."

Victoria glanced his way. "You two know each other?"

"Temporary setbacks." Bobby waved his hand. "Water under the bridge. I've got a new and exciting proposition, and I guarantee you're all going to want to get in on the ground floor."

Althea raised her chin, staring up at Bobby's image. "Sounds like an infomercial. You've got my attention for the next ninety seconds. Then I walk."

"I won't even need half. See, you folks may be strangers, but you all have something very special in common. Each and every one of you has had an unfortunate run-in with some mutual enemies."

New windows popped up around Bobby's face. Photographs, surveillance stills, a few moving frames from a security-camera feed. Victoria bared her teeth and let out a feral hiss at the screen, her burned face twitching. Althea's eyes smoldered in the shadows.

"Harmony Black," Bobby said, "Jessie Temple, Kevin Finn, and *Dr.* April Cassidy. To say they've caused a little trouble for all of us is an understatement."

"I want Harmony's *face*," Victoria said with a snarl.

"Kevin," Roman muttered. "I owe that little twerp some payback. Hard-core payback."

"Do whatever you want to the rest," Althea said, "but Jessie? Jessie is mine."

Roman looked between her and the screen. "You've got the same eyes."

"She's my kid," Althea said. "My blood. She just needs reminding of that fact."

Gleeful, Bobby twirled his hand. The photographs whirled across the screen, lining up on his left. He sat behind his desk and gestured to them one at a time like a newscaster giving a weather report.

"Let's see what they've got. Quite a mixed bag of talents! There's the witch, the wolf, the hacker, and the profiler. Now what do we have here, in this fine assembly of upstanding citizens?" Bobby put his hand to his mouth, as if just realizing something. "Well, would you look at that. The witch, the wolf, the hacker, and the profiler."

Roman put his hands on his hips. "Where are you going with this, Bobby?"

"I'm just struck by the fact that the four of you can do everything the four of *them* can, but unhindered by pesky little things like morality or ethics." Bobby grinned. "Let me lay it on the line for you: I'm starting a team of my own. And you four are my first-round draft picks. My MVPs."

"And what's in it for us?" Roman asked.

"For you? Money, revenge, and access to tech you can't even dream of. Diehl Innovations has next-*next*-generation electronics, and I'll equip you with the best of the best. For Dr. Carnes, money, revenge, and access to a cutting-edge surgical facility, pun fully intended. Your own staff, your own supply of body parts. Please don't harvest the staff *for* body parts—it's hard to find good help these days. For the lovely Ms. Temple-Sinclair—"

She slammed her fist into her open palm. "Money, revenge, and my kid. That's the deal. Nonnegotiable."

"Wouldn't dream of haggling. There's a private island where the two of you can spend some valuable mother-daughter bonding time. It's equipped with a spacious estate, a gourmet kitchen, and a *very* sturdy cage. Now, as for former director Crohn . . ."

Bobby held up a remote control, smirking.

"Sorry, pal. You cost me a lot of money and caused a lot of headaches, so for you it's more of a 'Do what I tell you, when I tell you, until I decide you've paid your debt to me' kind of situation. Oh, and if I hit this button, the containment pentacle goes off-line, and your little playmates drag you back to hell for all eternity. Which would be *hilarious* for me, but really suck for you."

Crohn's glimmering shade stared up at the screen with his one good eye, silent.

"We'll need resources," Althea said. "Reliable transport, air and ground—"

"The Concierge will see to your needs on that end," Bobby said. "Think of him—or her, not really sure, to be honest—as the fifth member of the team."

He spread his hands wide. "So. For the three of you who actually have a choice, what do you say? Are you in?"

"In," Victoria hissed, her gaze riveted on the image of Harmony's face.

Roman shrugged. "Sure, why not? Sounds like fun."

"It's almost unanimous," Bobby said, putting his hand to his ear. "So, what say you? What's the final verdict?"

Althea stepped forward. Front and center, squaring her shoulders as she stared up at the screen. The projector light flickered in her predator's eyes. Behind her, Roman, Victoria, and Crohn looked on.

"I'm in," Althea told him. "We're all in. Let's get to work."

AFTERWORD

For Jessie and her team, a new day is about to begin. And a new chapter in a very old war. Vigilant may have won its independence, but with everyone from the courts of hell to Bobby's new team lining up to take a shot at them, the good guys are going to have their hands full.

But they have a plane now. That might help a little.

In any case, the adventure will continue—and thank you so much for joining us! Couldn't do what I do without you. I also couldn't do it without Andrea Hurst, my developmental editor; Sara Brady, my copyeditor; and Adrienne Procaccini at 47North. Thanks also go out to Christina Traister, our audiobook narrator, and to Susannah Jones for lending a hand with my location research in NYC. As always, any good stuff is because of my team; any mistakes are entirely mine.

Want a heads-up when new books are coming out? Head over to www.craigschaeferbooks.com/mailing-list/. Once-a-month newsletters, no spam. You can also find me at www.facebook.com/CraigSchaeferBooks, as @craig_schaefer on Twitter, or just drop me an e-mail at craig@craigschaeferbooks.com.